PROPHECY

"How?" cried Lord Miresnare, lifting his empty hands toward's Naul's flying robe tails as the master mumbler fled towards the low archway and worn threshold stones that led to the mumblers' cells.

Naul paused and turned, and pointed at the freshly oiled iron rings set around the edge of the hall. "You have but one night, my Lord, to change this hall to your advantage and arm against losing everything that you have worked for. But even that may fail."

Naul laughed and swung his pine-oil lamp and spread his arms up towards the tall crystal windows. "The one who will claim your throne will be led forward by a stranger from a land beyond Rainbow's End and the shifting fogbanks. From a place that you have never even dreamed of."

"There are no lands beyond the fogs!" shouted Lord Miresnare. "Nor shall a wanderer take my throne!"

Naul laughed, his voice echoing as he fled the hall. "He will come, my Lord, two men in one shadow with a single tread of footprints . . . ."

D0038574

Also by Mike Jefferies

LOREMASTERS OF ELUNDIUM:

1. The Road to Underfall
2. Palace of Kings
3. Shadowlight

Published by
HarperPaperbacks

GLITTERSPIKE HALL

HALL MIKE JEFFERIES

BOOK ONE OF THE HEIRS
TO GNARLSMYRE

HarperPaperbacks
A Division of HarperCollins*Publishers*

This is a work of fiction. The characters, incidents, and dialogues are products of the author's imagination and are not to be construed as real. Any resemblance to actual events or persons, living or dead, is entirely coincidental.

HarperPaperbacks   *A Division of* HarperCollins*Publishers*
10 East 53rd Street, New York, N.Y. 10022

Copyright © 1989 by Mike Jefferies
Illustration copyright © 1989 by Mike Jefferies
All rights reserved. No part of this book may be used or reproduced in any manner whatsoever without written permission of the publisher, except in the case of brief quotations embodied in critical articles and reviews. For information address HarperCollins*Publishers,*
10 East 53rd Street, New York, N.Y. 10022.

A trade paperback edition of this book was published in 1989 in Great Britain by William Collins Sons & Co. Ltd.

Cover art by Geoff Taylor

First HarperPaperbacks printing: June 1991

Printed in the United States of America

HarperPaperbacks and colophon are trademarks of HarperCollins*Publishers*

10 9 8 7 6 5 4 3 2 1

To all the daughters

GLITTERSPIKE HALL

1

In the Shadow of the Glitterspike

*Y*ALOOR, first champion beast of the Glitterspike, had slept undisturbed for four seasons of
the sun, securely shackled by heavy iron chains
to the base of the tall column of shimmering crystal
that rose as the heartstone of Lord Miresnare's castle
and held power over the people of the city of Glor and
the wild marshlords who roamed the quickmarshes of
Gnarlsmyre. It stood where nature had erupted it, the
highest pinnacle of the roachback of rocks that rose
above the marshlands. It towered less than a double
hand touch from the broad dais of Lord Miresnare's
throne, set in the centre of Glitterspike Hall. It over-
shadowed the mudbeast's deep-worn chain grooves
and stood sheer and beautiful, twisted and turned,
vanishing from sight in wide indigo archspans
amongst the smoke-blackened rafters high overhead.
The Glitterspike was ice-cold to the touch, its precious
gemstones and veins of molten silver ghosting secret
patterns of liquid moving fire beneath the dawn-dark
featherings of hoar frost that clung around it as so
many glistening skirts in the great empty echoing hall.
But now the huge mudbeast was waking fitfully,

grumbling and grunting, turning to scratch at unseen mites and borer biters that had burrowed beneath his age-scarred armoured hide. Snarling he shook his ragged head, and lifting his curved and broken horns he blinked his leathery eyelids and slowly turned his head from side to side, listening, catching the whispers of faraway sounds that the dawn was bringing to him. Dawn dark noises of armoured boots and untrimmed wild claws on the frozen ground beyond the locked doors of Glitterspike Hall were coming in on the morning breeze. The sounds came from below the crowded narrow streets of Glor that clung in silent rows in the steep shadows of the hall. They came from far beyond the last mud-slapped hovel of the city and the high wall of rock that shut out the wilderness of the still-frozen quickmarshes waiting for the warming sunlight to melt their treacherous crust.

Yaloor wrinkled his nose and caught the rancid smell of the marshlords. They were closer now, climbing onto firmer ground above the shifting quickmire, and they were driving savage mudbeasts before them. Yaloor rose, flexing his claws, knowing by the stench of the marshlords that it was again the season of the joust when he would fight against the mudbeasts to decide the fate of the daughters of the Glitterspike. Crawling forward he crushed the gnawed bone ends of the last magic mumbler Lord Miresnare had thrown to him four seasons ago in the closing moments of the mumblers' dance on the eve of the joust, waiting as they swirled around him, the pine-oil smoke of foresight billowing out of their swinging lamps and rising in a fog of phantoms to show him,

Yaloor, triumphant in victory. Greedily he had
snatched up the helpless mumbler and feasted on his
carcass before throwing the dry bones aside to shatter
on the ground.

Link by link Yaloor's oiled chain slipped and clattered, tightening around the thick base of the towering finger of crystal, and as he paced restlessly around
he woke and scattered the long-spined hunting dogs
chained beside him.

Bellowing he lowered his head as he caught the
sweet scent and heard the light footsteps of Marrimian, Lord Miresnare's eldest daughter, whose life
and honour he had been snared and shackled to defend
from the marshlords. Marrimian slowed her step,
shivering, as she passed beneath the low archway that
led from the warren of chambers of the daughtery she
shared with her sisters into the cold echoing vastness
of Glitterspike Hall. Something had troubled her
dreams, nagging and worrying her awake, making her
rise and leave the warmth of her tiny sleeping chamber to seek out her guardian beast. Her breath
wreathed in frost-white streams of vapour in the frozen dawn draughts that swirled and eddied through
the hall, stirring the secret pleats and folds of her embroidered cloak with probing ice fingers.

"Yaloor," she whispered against the emptiness as
her eyes widened, searching the gloom. Her gaze followed the guttering glow of the dying reed lamps in
each iron basket of fire-dark embers that hung from
the tall fluted-stone columns. They grew smaller and
shrank into pinpoints of fire as they stretched away
into the distance on either side of the hall.

"Yaloor," she called again, catching the sound in her throat as she saw the great mudbeast rush forward, straining at the chain that bound it to the column of crystal in the centre of the hall. Its clawed feet kicked up bone splinters and puffs of stone dust, its huge shadow leapt out at her across the polished floorstones in the flickering reed lamplight. Stifling a cry Marrimian shrank back beneath the archway, doubting that her courage was strong enough to face his dripping jaws and rending claws. The great beast ground to a halt, sensing her fear. He lifted his ancient head and roared at the streaks of daylight beginning to pale the tall crystal windows.

Marrimian followed Yaloor's gaze towards the windows that looked out over the endless quickmarshes and stretched towards Rainbows' End. She listened and caught the faintest whispers of distant voices beyond the crackling sound of the rime ice melting on the windows. She frowned and listened to the dawn-dark silences and heard the dreaded noise of cruel, far-off shouts and muffled shrieks of pitiless laughter mingling with the crunch of mudbeasts' claws across the ice and the whistling crack of the iron-tailed whips that drove them relentlessly forward. And then she knew that the nightmares that had pulled her so roughly from her bed were not hollow glimpses of un-named terrors but that the breaking dawn would herald the eve of the Allbeast Feast. Once more the seasons had turned and the marshlords with their waders and their hunters were converging on the city. She shuddered at the thought of them steering their captives through the streets, cursing and shouting and loosing their wild mudbeasts on anyone they caught wandering in the narrow lanes and steep alleyways. She knew that with their journey's end they would rampage through the hall, demanding their right by her father's lore to joust for her hand and for all the lands of Gnarlsmyre as her dowry, and they would set their mudbeasts in single combat against her champion beast, Yaloor.

"Protect me, Yaloor," she cried, forgetting her fear of the mudbeast and clenching her hands in panic as the distant sounds of the wild marshlords grew louder.

Quickening her steps she fled across the hall, through the lattice black shadows of the slender, fluted columns, without an upward glance to the darkened galleries that crowded overhead or a sideways look to the rows of empty door arches where the maze of winding passageways and silent courtyards, sprawling in every direction around the steep sides of the great hall echoed her rushing footsteps. Breathlessly she pressed herself into Yaloor's warm side and was glad of his hot rancid breath upon her cheek as he nuzzled her gently, and the familiar feel of the coarse hair. She reached up to stroke him and comb her fingers through the tangled lanks that sprouted from his armoured hide and which pressed prickle-sharp against her skin. But this safe moment passed in the guttering hiss of a reed lamp, and hot tears of hapless frustration welled up in its place. Somewhere deep inside her a voice cried out for those innocent childhood seasons before her father had cursed her womanhood, when she had played between Yaloor's claws in blind ignorance of why the marshlords and all their wild men marauded through her father's hall.

Marrimian blinked and stared up at the feathered patterns of ice melting on the tall windows. She knew that nothing could change her fate and allowed a sigh of bitterness to escape between her lips. She remembered so clearly the first time her father had cursed her for being born a woman, a mere helpless prettier, too weak to rule even the meanest hovel or keep it against those who would take it from her. She remembered how she was cursed for being the eldest of more daughters than he cared to recall, and how she had to carry the pain of his failed dreams of fathering a son and heir to continue the ancient line of Miresnare and its rule over Gnarlsmyre beyond his time and into the future.

Marrimian swallowed and blinked the sour tears from her eyes, her jaw set firmly against the breaking dawn. No matter how much her father's injustices rubbed her raw she was his first-born and must fulfil the duties he had charged to her keeping: to overwatch the preparations for the joust and make sure that the glitter and splendour of the hall overawed the marshlords and kept them in their place before the joust began. She must also make sure that her sisters were safely locked up and out of sight, well before the first marshmen burst through the doors of the hall, for they were dangerous and wild, with ugly unpredictable tempers. They might try to snatch a daughter and hold her for ransom; using her to steal a quickmarsh or an island of marsh oaks before his mudbeast clashed with Yaloor.

Marrimian shuddered as she remembered how those filthy marshmen who called themselves lords had swarmed through the hall in their reeking beastskin cloaks at the last joust and screamed and shouted in delight as they set their savage beasts on the servers, and climbed over the eating boards, smashing the crystal goblets and treading the trenchards into ruin as they fought for the best places at table. She felt the bile rise in her throat as she recollected the rending screams and howls of pain as Yaloor clawed down mudbeast after mudbeast, his feet sticky from the wash of their blood that was spilt because of her womanhood and that of her sisters.

She dropped her head into her hands and cried out against the brightening sky for one scrap of magic to fall from the mumblers' lips in the dance of foresight that they would tread around the Glitterspike before the sun reached the noonday hour; one word or billowing phantom in their lamp smoke that would make her father stop the joust. But in her heart she knew that there was no hope of that.

Marrimian had listened to the whispered hall talk about how the magic mumbling men had foretold her birth in their ritual dance and the snaring of the mudbeast Yaloor to protect her until a male heir was born, and how that foreknowledge had been enough magic to swell her father's pride and cover the despair he felt at siring his first daughter. He swept down through the city to find the marshlords and their gatherings of hunters who always came into the lower circles at the fourth season's end to barter mudbeast flesh for iron crafts, woven work and sweetmeats. Legends told of how he goaded and prodded them into risking the flesh of their beasts by putting them one by one in combat against his champion, Yaloor, and how he promised the victor of the joust the hand of his first-born daughter and all the lands of Gnarlsmyre when she came of age.

Marrimian shivered with fear and drew herself closer to Yaloor for the seasons had swiftly passed and she had grown of age, and the marshlords had become more pressing and wild to take her or, indeed, any of her sisters, with each new joust that echoed through her father's hall.

Yaloor felt her tremble with fear and he roared, echoing his voice through the maze of dark alleyways, courtyards and corridors that encircled the great hall, waking with a start all those who served the Glitterspike.

"Defend my honour and keep me from the hands of the marshlords," Marrimian whispered, reaching out to touch his armoured claws. He snarled, scenting her, and lowered his head, brushing his broken horns against the weave of her smooth-spun gown, remembering how from her cradle days he had defended her, the first-born of Glitterspike Hall.

Doors were thrown open, running footsteps echoed through the gloomy corridors, voices called for light. The lampwicks brought fresh glowing tapers, reeds harvested from the edges of the frozen marsh that burned with the smell of sap. Scullions bustled and clattered in the low-arched kitchens, coughing and spluttering in the fog of ember smoke as they kindled the dying fires, fanning bright flames with their apron tails. Dressers and servers moved quickly through the great hall setting neat lines of tables for the Allbeast Feast and pegging and hammering long grease-scraped eating boards onto the stout wooden trestles.

Ragmen glided silently all about them, polishing the stone-flagged floor with their ragbound feet. Benchers knelt their way carefully along the deep beastskin couches that lined the hall, brushing the coarse black-spined fur into star-shaped patterns with their twists of tightly-bound twigs.

"The marshscum are crowding at my doors—I have seen them!" cried Lord Miresnare starting awake from a nightmare with a gasp of terror. He lay back in the warm darkness of his sleeping rugs, feeling cold sweat trickle wetly over the deep furrows of his forehead. He blinked and swallowed a shallow breath, and in that moment between sleeping and waking he cursed his pride for goading the marshlords into jousting for Marrimian's hand while she still lay wet in her snuggling clothes. And he cursed his foolishness for tempting them up through the city into his hall where he had blinded them with the riches trapped in the heart of the Glitterspike, and had mocked them and treated them as simple marshhunters before stealing the flesh of their beasts in the joust.

Lord Miresnare shivered and drew the rugs up over his head, waiting for the leering wild faces of his nightmare to fade, knowing deep down that he alone had brought those marshscum into his hall, so sure had he been of the magic in the mumblers' dance that foretold that none who challenged could defeat his champion, Yaloor. He was confident that today, when the mumblers danced again, they would foretell the birth of an heir who would sweep aside all other claims to his throne.

Slowly the dreams faded and the voices that taunted him with the knowledge that his first-born had come of age melted away, leaving him only with the hollow, empty fear that those marshlords he had cheated so easily and blinded with his splendour had seen, with the passing of the seasons, the weakness of his seed as he spawned only daughters. Reaching a hand out of the rugs he clutched at the heavy drapes that hung around his bed and shook them fiercely, making the layer of rime ice that had gathered in their thick folds crackle, though it burned the tips of his fingers. Faintly he heard Yaloor's bellowing shout echo through the darkened passageways, winding its way up the steep twisting stairways to the door of his sleeping chamber, and he shrank back in the jumble of sleeping rugs knowing that his champion beast had scented the marshlords closing in on the city and had woken to challenge them to a new joust.

"Daughters!" he muttered, soothing his fears with anger and cursing their weakness as he shouted for his dressers to bring robes and gowns and ordered the waiting heralds to summon all the daughters of the hall to await his displeasure.

Fretfully he descended the winding staircases and strode impatiently through the echoing passageways until he stood with a tight-knuckled hand clasped upon the smooth stone balustrade at the entrance to the great hall. "Daughters," he hissed through tight lips, freezing the noise and bustle of the hall with one long piercing stare, beckoning them to come before him as he slowly and stiffly descended the polished doorstone.

Marrimian had heard the heralds' shouts and the rough creaking of her father's boots pause beneath the entrance to the hall, and she felt his withering gaze sweep over her. She rose silently from within Yaloor's shadow, her eyes drawn towards the high-arched entrance to the daughtery, listening for the soft hurried footfalls of her sisters. Quick shapes passed beneath the archway and she counted anxious faces, hoping that none of them would overstay the summons.

"Pinvey!" she gasped, putting her hand to her mouth in horror as her sister, younger by six seasons, swept towards her across the hall with a rustle of scarlet silks, her full pouting lips blazing with brightly painted colours. "Where is your hall gown and what have you done to your face? Father will froth with rage to see you so gaudily dressed," she hissed as Pinvey swept past her in a haze of crushed anise scent, her bright lips curling back into a sneer.

"The marshlords are coming and I am ready to welcome them," Pinvey answered, spitting the words at Marrimian as she took her place amongst the crowding sisters, jostling and pushing those on either side as they crushed against her gown, snarling at their anxious faces as they waited for their father to speak.

Marrimian turned her head and stared after Pinvey, the rustling of her gown breaking the startled silence, her lips trembling noiselessly. The words of rebuke she as the eldest should have spoken were snatched away by the heady scent and the bright smears of colour on Pinvey's face. She frowned and quickly followed her, casting her mind back for a beginning to this brazen lust for the marshlords' company and her open defiance of the customs of the hall. Pinvey had always been different and had kept herself distant from the other sisters, vanishing for days on end in the maze of corridors and courtyards, but there had been no hint of this change in her. Marrimian would have thought longer but she saw Pinvey elbow Treyster, the youngest, making her trip headlong across the floorstones. She sprang forward and caught Treyster's arm and steadied her just as Lord Miresnare's voice rose impatiently from the wide entrance steps and called for their names.

"Be brave—answer clearly," she whispered, squeezing Treyster's hand and guiding her gently into her rightful place before their father.

Lord Miresnare stood above them on the first stone raiser, counting their heads and muttering their names, his piercing eyes clouded with anger. "Recite yourselves!" he ordered, losing count as they fidgeted, and he gathered up the hem of his cloak to twist it between his uncut fingernails.

Marrimian called her name first as the eldest, Syrenea and Aloune quickly followed. Cetrinea whispered hers, but Pinvey the beautiful flashed her eyes and laughed and sang hers boldly. Anslery and Alea answered with one voice but Treyster stuttered and stumbled and tried to hide behind the others.

"Come forward, you hopeless child, you wearisome

burden. Speak your name, girl, and be quick. There are marshlords at the edge of the city."

Marrimian took Treyster's hand and gently brought her forward, whispering her into a curtsey, but her father had already forgotten her lapse of manners and had turned away, his mind upon the joust. Blind to her hurt he muttered and pointed a finger towards the strengthening daylight. "If just *one* of you had been born a son who could have inherited my throne those mirescum who call themselves marshlords would not have grown so powerful as they watched my seed fail. If I had an heir the joust would be a thing of the past, a moment of rashness forgotten, and these dry lands with the city of Glor that rises above the quickmarshes would be safe."

"You cannot blame us! We did not choose to be daughters!" cried Marrimian, forgetting her place and speaking too loudly and out of turn.

Her father turned on her savagely, his finger stabbing at the empty morning air. "Nor did Yaloor choose to be chained to the Glitterspike to fight for your honour. The mumblers foretold his fate on the day of your beginnings, that if I had seeded a daughter she must be laid between the claws of the most fearsome savage beast here in the centre of Glitterspike Hall and through his strength and power I could rule until a male heir was born. If, if just *one* of you had been a son there would be no joust nor desperate dowry to settle. There would be no brawling marshlords and their hunters wetting the stones of this hall with the blood of the mudbeasts they snare in the marshes."

Marrimian stepped back hastily, away from her father's anger, feeling the bite of his hurtful words. "We would fight as bravely as sons to keep the marshlords from Glitterspike Hall. Give us arms, give us daggers, swords and long spears."

Lord Miresnare laughed bitterly, dismissing her words with a wave of his hand. These were women, they could not fight against the marshlords; they were his prettiers whose tasks were set out by lore. Women could not rule. There was no place in Gnarlsmyre where the people ever obeyed a woman—except perhaps in the healing houses. Only men were strong enough to rule.

"Go now," he ordered quietly, lifting his hands to clap for his Master of Archers and Spear Captain to come forward. "You have idled away enough time with this chatter. The marshlords will be at our doors before nightfall and there is much to prepare."

Pointing at Marrimian he ordered her to see that every server and lampwick had a dagger near at hand, reminding her that the marshlords were dangerous wild men and that she must hide all the daughters long before they arrived. Clapping his hands again he called for the mumblers and commanded them to dance around the Glitterspike and give him foreknowledge before the joust began.

Mertzork smelt the wind and listened to the rime ice rattling on the marsh scrub. He smiled secretly, scratching at the tingling layer of frozen quickslime that smeared his face after the long dark journey across Gnarlsmyre. Before him, black against the brightening dawn, towered the great ridge of rock crowded with the steep frost-glittering roofs of the City of Glor, its spires and countless crystal houses that clung in the shadows of Glitterspike Hall looking just as they had four full seasons before. The jumble of twisted and wind-cracked cliffs below the city, towering above the quickmire, still made him catch his breath and hesitate, for in the darkness they seemed to shimmer beneath the icy mist and take on the shape of two giant mudbeasts, their horns driven together in everlasting battle. Mertzork swallowed his fears and sneered, laughing at the legends he had heard in the marsheries of how the spine of rocks had risen up out of the quickmarshes in plumes of steam and fire, and drew the rancid salt-cured strip of beastskin he wore as a cloak more tightly about his shoulders.

"Mumblers' tales," he muttered to himself as he stared up at the tall spires and crowded black roofs of the city. "All of this shall be mine when the sandbeast Gallengab has torn Yaloor to pieces. The first-born daughter of the hall shall be mine, the city shall be mine, everything." He glanced over his shoulder past his marshwaders and the twelve rough-coated hunting dogs that drove the small miserable mudbeast they had snared three days ago towards the higher ground. He cast quick eyes back across the frozen quickmire to where he had planted the spear leaf rampon cuttings to waymark a secret path for his father's strongest marshhunters to follow with the sandbeast chained between them.

Mertzork licked his lips and laughed, letting the

sound chuckle out between his teeth, and kneeling on the ice he shattered a small round hole with his iron spike and pushed the last rampon root, white and fibrously thick, down into the soft quickmire. He rose quickly, rubbing his marsh-caked hands together and brushing them on his heavy woven tunic, and watched the marshlords emerging through the dawnlight all around him, driving their mudbeasts up towards the beasting pits and the iron cages that ringed the outer edges of the city.

Smiling, Mertzork raised the handle of his iron spike and shouted to the other marshmen. Pointing up towards Glitterspike Hall he called out Marrimian's name and made a foul gesture with the spike and then slowly licked each finger in turn. Many of the marshmen laughed and shouted back, cracking their iron-tailed whips at their marshwaders' feet, urging them up on to the firmer ground with a string of curses.

Mertzork hunched his shoulders and turned away, pushing the iron spike through his belt, and shouting his marshwaders forward. He had grown up amongst the violence of the marsheries where every footstep of firm ground that you could possess gave you power and wealth and a safe place to weather the wet seasons when the quickmires flooded. Every marshman's eyes were set on seizing Glitterspike Hall and more solid ground than any one of them could ever dream of. Mertzork laughed quickly to himself, knowing that he had snared a beast to match Yaloor, a beast that would win him the joust and all Gnarlsmyre, but he also knew that he must keep the beast he had named Gallengab a secret, for he was not yet of an age to snare beasts of challenge for the joust. He dared not trust anyone, even Andzey, his half-brother from beyond the low rocks of Fenmire Marsh, or Faxiol, his father's most loyal marshhunter who thought it was on Mertzork's father's orders that he drove Gallengab secretly across the frozen quickmire to arrive after the joust had begun. To trust was a dangerous weakness in those who sought power and a clever man kept all his secrets safely silent.

Mertzork knew the truth in those words and smiled grimly. His father had found Gallengab's lair beyond the rainbows and the thundering waterfalls on the edges of the quickmire, beneath the ever-shifting fogbanks, and had grown careless with his words, planning to share his knowledge of Gallengab's savage power amongst all the marshlords. He had believed that Gallengab could destroy the beast, Yaloor, and together the marshlords could topple Lord Miresnare and rule in his place. Those had been foolish words heated by marsh spirits, full of talk of trust and love and of working together for power. Foolish words that had driven Mertzork to silence him forever. He had awaited the moment, drawing his father out, making him show him the secret ways and wild places, following each footprint, memorizing each hidden step until he had stolen all his father's knowledge. Then, as the new sun rose clear of the ice crust, he had dropped a sharpwire over his father's head and brutally closed the loop. Afterwards he had eased his father's lifeless body off the path smoothing away all trace of his footprints in the mud as the quickmire closed over his head.

Mertzork smiled, curled his tongue across his teeth. The murder had given him his first taste of real power, which he would use with true cunning to snatch the title of Lord of all Gnarlsmyre in the moment of Gallengab's victory. He would keep all his father's rights to hunt the quickmarshes beyond Fenmire, only bequeathing them to Faxiol if he proved loyal when helping him unleash Gallengab in Glitterspike Hall.

Mertzork had nightdreamed too long. The sun was rising and the ground beneath his feet softened. The ice crystals in the marsh crust were shattering and spraying up between his broad, well-wrapped toes. He started forward, cracking his iron-thonged whip, but his marshwaders had already climbed above the marshes, hurrying through the lines of cages that led into the beasting pits, searching out the strongest cage as Mertzork had commanded.

The mudbeast chained between them roared and bellowed, its back arched in a curve of rippling spines. It threw its bulky weight at the caged beasts on either side and clawed at their bars, digging up the thawing mud and pebbles in a blinding spray. It ground its teeth and snapped as the marshwaders pulled at the chains and prodded it forward with iron spikes. The ground was firmer in the second line of cages but Mertzork was not satisfied. He struck the mudbeast squarely across its rump with his whip and drove it up to the next line of cages, pushing and thrusting his way through the crowds of marshhunters and waders who had safely caged their beasts and were now shedding their ropes and chains. He drove the animal so fast that his marshwaders had to run to keep taut their binding chains that shackled them to the beast. The ground before them rose into a wall of stone; deep pits had been hewn into the sheer rock, black holes that had the reek of evil between their empty bars.

The leading marshwader hesitated but Mertzork drove him forward. "The second pit, the one that is already open," he shouted above the roaring and bellowing mudbeasts caged below the ridge and pointed with the handle of his whip.

The marshwader reached the entrance then half turned and stumbled backwards, screaming in terror and clutching at something attached to his face. His chain fell slack and he let the mudbeast surge forward to overrun him. Mertzork let out a cry of anger. His marshwaders were retreating, fighting each other to break the shackles, scattering in panic. Dark shapes were swarming out of the pit, their brittle leather wings clacking, their armoured bodies rattling as they swooped on the marshwaders.

"Pindafalls!" Mertzork hissed, standing his ground and lashing out with the whip, curling the iron thong around a carrion bird that had hooked its talons into his leader's face. With one tug it broke free, pulling away the marshwader's eye and cheekbone. The marshwader screamed again. Mertzork threw the whip aside and snatched the iron spike from his belt. Falling onto his knees he hunched his shoulders, and pressing his head into his chest, he thrust the spike upwards, driving it into the armoured underbody of a swooping pindafall. Twisting the spike he flung the carrion bird against the rock face, hearing the sharp snap of its backbone as it hit the rock. All around him he could hear shouts and screams of terror from his marshwaders as he knelt there stabbing up at the carrion birds. They had panicked and tried to run to the safety of the lower cages but the crowds of marshmen drove them back laughing and calling for more sport.

"Kneel, you fools!" shouted Mertzork. "Even the mudbeast has the sense not to try and run. Look how he waits until the carrion birds have hooked on to his armoured hide and then rolls on them, crushing them to death. Kneel and use your spikes."

The pindafalls' attack lessened, their shrieks and clacking rattles grew fainter and fainter as they were drawn spiralling upward on the rising warm draughts of air above the beasting pits. Mertzork breathed deeply, pushed his iron spike into his belt and began slowly to rise.

One of his marshwaders turned towards him crying out a warning. A pindafall's talons hooked into Mertzork's back, its razor-edged teeth closing against his neck. Mertzork reached back beneath his collar, his fingers closing on the sharpwire he had kept well hidden. The pindafall's breath was on his face making him choke and gasp; it was opening its mouth, drawing back ready to strike. Mertzork looped the sharpwire over the bird's beak and with one desperate pull cut into the lower jaw, slicing through the beak and shattering the serrated rows of razor teeth in a shower of yellow bone splinters. The stricken bird clacked its brittle leather wings against his cloak, its webbed talons caught in the coarse-spined fur. Mertzork unclipped the cloak and let it slip from his shoulders.

In one quick upward movement he brought his iron spike above his head for the killing stroke.

The marshwaders had fallen silent, stepping backwards, and their pressing circle widened as they watched him through narrowed eyes. They caught their first glimpse of his ruthless, pitiless power. They saw the beginning of what they would grow to fear. Mertzork paused, his iron spike held quivering in the air. He watched their retreat and sensed their horror. Laughing he lowered the spike and tossed the carrion bird high into the air above their heads. "A gift from the marsheries of Mertz with my father's blessing. He is behind me in the marshes but he sends you greetings and this carrion bird as a feast to begin the joust!"

Stepping away from the surging crowd he watched the marshmen struggle and fight to catch the shrieking pindafall. They had forgotten him quicker than blinking in their greed to possess the carrion bird and tear it into a thousand pieces. Mertzork tucked the spike back into his belt and whistled to his hunting dogs to bite at the wounded mudbeast's heels. They drove it into the dark foul-smelling pit and he slammed the iron door shut. Turning he dug his toes fiercely into the two marshwaders who lay beside the cage, feeling their dead weight against his boot.

"Go and guard the mudbeast!" he shouted to the other marshwaders who had escaped with only cuts and bruises from the carrion birds' attack, and he ordered them to set the hunting dogs in a broad half-circle around the pit and await his return.

Mertzork stared up through the haze of morning smoke that hung over Glor and knew that he must

find a road up through the city, through a place of
strangers that he only knew from fireside tales and
wild rumours, and that he must find this road before
the start of the joust. He had been too young at the
last joust and he had not been allowed to venture beyond the beasting pits but he had heard whispers
about the people who lived in the City of Glor and he
feared their strangeness, their power to make all manner of wonderful things, even the magic that they
must have to build so many stone houses, all piled on
top of one another; but most of all he feared being lost,
for it was said that if a marshlord or any of his hunters
missed the path which was waymarked through the
city their mudbeast would be stolen from them and
they would wander on false trails until they starved
to death. Mertzork shivered, remembering another
handful of rumours that told of the crowded twisting
cobbled lanes, so dark and airless and with not a single
mark or footprint to show the way. Yet another part
of him was eager to see the scented passageways over-
hung with sweet vines and the tall crystal houses
where all the wonders of the world were grown from
tiny seeds. He must find the way himself and know
it step by step, just as he had learned all his father's
paths through the quickmarsh. He laughed quietly,
shaking his head and remembering his father's tales
of the crystal houses that were never touched by the
velvet fingers of rime ice that covered everything else
when the night wind blew. He remembered the stories of the scullions busy in their kitchens where the
flagstones were so hot they burned the soles of their
feet if they stood still.

Bending down he gathered his leading marshwader up in his arms and wiped at the edges of the ragged hole in his cheek. "You shall be my liftlatch that will let me through the gates. The hurlers must let us pass to find the healing women to tend your face," he whispered, whistling two of his hunting dogs to his heels as he tried to remember all his father had told him of the women who used venomous spiders to weave healing webs of the finest silk across an open wound. His father had once said that if a man so much as blinked or twitched the spider would open his jaws and . . . Mertzork shivered and, linking his hands to support the marshwader's weight, began the steep climb up towards the Hurlers' Gate, shouldering his way between lampwicks carrying heavy bundles of marshreeds for their lamps and harvesters with baskets of aspelgather balanced precariously on their heads. Stinking marsh water dripped through the open weave of their baskets leaving a slippery trail on the smooth stones of the road.

A voice shouted Mertzork's name, calling him back, warning him that he could not enter the city before the joust began, and for a moment he hesitated. Half turning he looked down across the crowded alleyways of thawing mud, smelt the rancid beasts and saw the throng of dirty close-shaven heads, their long plaited tails of hair and crested plumes that rose above the jostling crowd and then he shook his head. He was never going back to being the younger son who scrabbled for scraps in the mud. No, he was going up into the city to take the Glitterspike as his own and twist it to his own purposes. He was going to fill the great hall with his hunting dogs and have the marshlords, their hunters and their waders, bow and kneel down before him. He would claim the finest mudbeasts and chain them along the walls of the hall and there would be women of all shapes and sizes all around him for his pleasure. He laughed and hugged the injured marsh-wader to his chest. He had turned his back on the life of the beasting pits forever.

2

The Mumblers Foretell The Joust

"*I HAVE* seen the marshlords and would welcome them," whispered Pinvey, drawing her sisters through the low door arch into the kitchens and gathering them into a tight huddle around her. She had to raise her voice above the bustle and clatter of the scullions as she told her sisters what she had secretly seen four seasons before when the marshlords had crowded the hall for the joust.

"They were proud men that I glimpsed through the high tower window that overshadows the hall; violent men who fought for the best trenchards at the long eating boards. They cursed each other and set their mudbeasts loose amidst roars of laughter to spread havoc in the outer halls. Benchers were trodden underfoot, ragmen fled for their lives, there was such excitement, such . . . such . . ." Her voice caught in her throat, her eyes glittered and her lips trembled, moist and swollen with anticipation.

"But we are forbidden to look upon the marshmen. I have heard their voices, they are savages," cried Treyster, her face drawn and white with terror at what Pinvey had told them.

Pinvey laughed quietly, shaking loose her knots and bundles of black hair. "I have seen them and I tell you they are real men. Rough wild marshmen, savage, yes, but they are more alive and more exciting than any of the parchment-dry, powdered gentles that our father allows into Glitterspike Hall. These marshlords have the smell of freedom in their cloaks, and the sound of the world outside this stifling prison cries out in their voices. I would offer to go willingly, without that stinking beast Yaloor needing to spread the mudbeasts' blood on the stones of the hall trying to defend Marrimian's honour. I would go now, without a dowry, rather than grow old and shrunken waiting for the mumblers to chant an end to the joust."

Marrimian who had been overwatching the underscullions lighting the roasting fires caught a snatch of Pinvey's lustful boasting and crossed the wide kitchens in a dozen strides to hiss her into silence. Fiercely brushing her firegold hair out of her eyes she said, "You know nothing, fool, and you waste ignorant whispers on a moment's stolen glance. The marshlords are proud, you say, as they strut and swagger and scratch at the plagues of marshfleas, with blackened unwashed hands. The smell of freedom that you yearn to savour is the reek of ill-cured beastskins that hang rotting from their shoulders. It shows how much you have missed with your lust-blind eyes that you see nothing of the terrible power they hold in Gnarlsmyre for our father to let them set their beasts on the servants of the hall and allow them to fight and barge with daggers drawn for places at our table. Have you no sense, Pinvey, not to realize that you, nor any of us, are nothing without the strength of Glitterspike Hall? It is the chance to steal Father's throne and all the dry lands that they joust for. Once they have that they would use you for their pleasure here on your father's table and then laugh as they tossed you aside to bleed on the cold hard stones. Mark my words, Pinvey, there is no dowry for you. You are less than these scullions that busy themselves about us preparing for the jousting feast. They are at least skilled enough to cook and serve their masters once they have given pleasure."

Pinvey backed away, her hands clenched tightly in anger. "You thwart my every step and tread on all my plans. You stifle us all with every turn of your eyes. What do you know of the order of things in Gnarlsmyre or how much the shadow of the marshlords' power stretches across this place? You speak as if you were the heir of Glitterspike, just because you are the first-born, the favourite that Yaloor protects. But you are only a woman, a prettier to grace Father's table like the rest of us, and you are only safe while Yaloor lives. I know what is beyond the locked doors of this hall and below the crystal windows and I curse you, Marrimian, for the way you chain us to your skirt tails—with orders to do this or commands to do that. I shall have my revenge when Yaloor bellows his last hidebound breath. Then, when we are truly equal, I will throw you to the marshlords and make them spit on your face!"

Marrimian uttered a cry of fear at Pinvey's blind hatred and reached out to take her hand, but Pinvey jumped backwards and slipped through her fingers.

She caught at Alea's sleeve and together they fled, their quick footfalls and shrieks of sneering laughter muffling into silence in the maze of passageways and courtyards that led away from the kitchens. Marrimian took a step to follow, hesitated and then turned back towards the low archway where the others had crowded forward at Pinvey's outburst.

"Do *you* believe in this madness?" she asked, white-faced and dizzy, her heart pounding as she searched their faces and looked deeply into each one of them in turn. "Do you see me as more than I really am? I am but Marrimian, first-born of the daughters of this hall."

Syrenea smiled and slowly shook her head, blinking her long pale eyelashes. "You are the eldest by the first mother and you overwatch our lives and the keeping of the hall. The mumblers foretold the snaring of Yaloor to protect you and it was your birth, not your choice, that caused Father to bring the marshlords into the hall to joust for your hand. None of us would have chosen to be daughters."

"But there was so much hatred in Pinvey's voice. What have I done to make her turn so savagely and curse me?"

"I have seen benchers and lampwicks creeping into her chambers in the frozen hours of darkness. She has secretly been taking flesh with them," answered Treyster in a frightened whisper.

"Taking flesh?" hissed Marrimian turning sharply on the youngest.

Treyster would have answered, telling the others of the shouts of laughter and the screams of delight that she had heard through the heavy oak door, but the rattle of windbells and the scrape of mumblers' feet from the outer courtyards froze her with terror. She knew that she must run and hide her face lest the mumblers ill-fate her on seeing her or hearing her name. Marrimian too heard the mumblers' footsteps drawing closer, their high, chanting voices growing louder with each step. She looked up and saw the fear spreading amongst her sisters, quicker than a flame in dry crackling reed grass.

"Go!" she cried, pushing them with trembling hands and hurrying them out from beneath the kitchen archway, urging them to run with all speed to the safety of the daughtery.

"None of us must show our faces," she whispered to herself knowing that it would ill-fate the dance of foresight if they saw a woman's face. She stepped quickly back out of the passageway, catching only the briefest glimpse of the advancing mumblers, their swinging lanterns weaving a lace trail of scented pine-oil smoke towards her. Their eyes shone brightly with the blind gaze of foresight, their hollow cheekbones and chanting lips were masked in a web of shadows as they danced and swayed between the twisting ribbons of windbells that flowed out from their saffron robes.

Marrimian caught her breath and swallowed a cry of fright as she covered her eyes with her hands and pressed her fingertips against her eyelids lest they look beneath the archway and see her womanhood. The wind of their passing tugged at her hair and the silk weave of their robes pulled at her arms. Windbells were entwined about their fingers and their shrill rattle clattered in her ears; and then they were gone, their chant growing fainter and the scented smoke of their lanterns melting into nothing.

Taking a deep breath of relief Marrimian stepped backwards, not yet daring to open her eyes, and felt her way across the warm polished stone floor of the kitchens. She blinked and felt the sharp sting of marsh-oak smoke that was curling out from beneath the bread ovens to fog the low-vaulted kitchen. She was safe. The mumblers had not paused before the kitchen archway nor broken their rhythmic dancing steps. They had danced their way to the doors of the hall and she could faintly hear them calling and chanting the words of the joust. Gathering her wits she rattled a heavy chopping blade on the long grease-scraped table and called her scullions to assemble before her.

Frowning she bit her lip as they hurried forward. She remembered Pinvey's outburst and worried her fingers around the long bone handle of the knife, the blade cutting fine lines into the black-grained ebony wood of the table. There had been a look of stolen knowledge in Pinvey's eyes, a dangerous hint of half-truths of the world beyond Glitterspike Hall; pictures and images that the benchers and the ragmen must have fed her to get into her bed. False knowledge, but if Pinvey was planning to use it in some way to break the joust it could upset the balance their father strove to keep between the people of Gnarlsmyre and the marshmen who lived in the wilderness. Sighing she let the heavy knife fall from her hand. There would be a moment before the joust; somehow she would make the time to face Pinvey and talk the lies out of her, but now she must overwatch the final preparations for the Allbeast Feast. Nothing must be left to chance, or fate might turn against them.

Nothing in the daily hall work had been forgotten, from the oiling of the huge iron rings set a dozen paces apart along the length of Glitterspike Hall where the challenging mudbeasts were chained before they fought, to the laying with a three-haired brush of the final whisper of gold leaf upon the roasted pindafalls' wings. Every scrap of ceremony, laid down to over-awe the marshlords, must be ready before the first mudbeast reached the outer door. It would be a feast of kings, set to dazzle these ill-bred marshmen's eyes. Only the purest wheatcorns harvested from the high terraces of the great ridge of Gnarlsmyre would be used for the pandemain trenchards. Fresh marshfish had already been netted in the lower moats and were ready for baking, sprinkled with windflower seeds and crushed almond flakes and then glazed with primrose oils. Pink-shelled crawlers lay cleft beside the cauldrons of amber wine, ready for boiling, and trays of neatly buttered apselgathers that the harvesters had cut that very morning lay ready for the flame. Six pindafall birds, arrow-gathered as they circled the towers of the hall, would be turned on a spit fire of smoke-wood and basted in their own black juices.

Marrimian looked around her. The underscullians, fish cooks and the bake women bustled as they prepared roast sourwings and marshgeese, scrub wallow-ers and ravine sheep, each overscullian shouting her orders, some calling for dishes of blue cabbage or wild sand-leeks, some cursing the rounds of plaited garlic that would not sit correctly in the centrepiece of the feast—two peacocks roasted and refeathered with all the pluckers' skill that would be brought into the hall with music and tumbling dancers to her father's table.

Marrimian laughed then clapped her hands and dispersed the scullions who milled around her, sending them about their business. Each one had her task: to gather windflowers and curdled green creams from the crystal houses that clung to the lower walls of the hall; to catch extra fish from the moats and trenches; or to fetch from the drying herb rooms borage flowers and galingale grains to sweeten the feast. Marrimian called Galest, an overscullion, to her side and sent her down into the city to ask the gilders to bring sheets of the finest gold and silver to gild the pindafalls' wings and brighten this desperate joust.

"What of the marshhunters that drive the mud-beasts into the hall, my lady?" asked overscullion Ansel curtseying before her mistress and crushing her apron tails in her huge hands. "How shall we feed them?"

Marrimian looked up at the vast kitchen woman who stood before her and almost smiled at the way she wrung her endless spread of apron between her huge hands. She hovered awkwardly, her thickset legs and flat feet placed wide apart as she awaited her mistress's answer, her heavy jowls pulled back into a nervous smile that creased deep dimples into her fat red oven-scarred cheeks. Marrimian opened her mouth to answer when she caught sight of two scrawny underscullions hiding behind Ansel's broad girth, rolling their eyes and wringing their apron tails whispering sly comments, mockingly.

"Go to the gutting slab and draw out the pindafall offal," she snapped, dismissing the two girls with a crack of her fingers. Taking a deep breath to dispel the moment's anger she saw the hurt in Ansel's eyes at the cruel taunts the girls threw over their shoulders as they vanished into the gutting room.

"Bear no mind to it, mistress," Ansel muttered bravely. "It is the feast we must be thinking of."

Marrimian frowned, remembering the bellowing roars of the mudbeasts that she had heard from the safety of the daughtery and their stench that seemed to linger long after the joust was over and the blood had been scrubbed from the stones of the hall. "Yes, the marshhunters. Feed them hedgehogs baked in clay from the white mud geysers, marshroots, pottage of sandhare and smallwood flowers jugged in the hares' blood. Bake them trenchards from husk corn and mire oak corns but spread platters of blue cabbage and hard cheese rounds made from the black ravine sheep's milk on each of the lower tables."

Marrimian quickly forgot Ansel's hurt as she busied herself overseeing the milling scullions. She hurried through each of the huge kitchens that served Glitterspike Hall, leaving no preparation unchecked until she was satisfied that nothing had been left to chance. Now she must overwatch the ragmen and check all the heavy iron rings. She ducked through the low archway and vanished in a flurry of cloak tails, her scent of cedar oil slowly blending and vanishing in the acrid smoke of the smallwood that had been lit in the roasting hearth.

Ansel, pleased that her mistress had chided the underscullions, was also glad about the coming Allbeast Feast for a special reason of her own. She smiled to herself and hoped that she might catch a glimpse of the marshmen as she helped to carry the food to the doorway of the great hall. She as a woman was forbidden to enter Glitterspike Hall during the joust but in those moments as she handed the platters to the servers she could steal a look. She bent to her task of jugging the hares in their tall earthenware pots ready for baking, kissing their long ears, and singing a bedding song full of secret magic that would draw a marshhunter to her. Erek, the healing woman who lived in one of the narrow alleyways of the Shambles of the city, had sold her the song in exchange for a small tucket of galingale grains and crushed turnstole leaves. She hoped the magic would soon work, but just for luck she sang the song again as she gutted and rolled the prickly hedgehogs in their thick layer of sticky white mud. Straightening her back she wiped her large red scalded hands on a coarse muslin rag that hung from her apron strings and looked across the baking kitchens to where the tall ovens stood open, hot and ready for the trenchards. Bake women were running to and from the long stone slabs, their long shovels piled high with unbaked dough. Beyond the baking ovens Ansel saw the neat rows of fish kettles standing ready on the wet marble slabs of the fish hall. The marshfish and pink-shelled crawlers were struggling and flapping as they waited for the swift gutting knives. Turning back she caught the acrid smell of the smallwood fires in the roasting hearth and shuddered as she looked at the six pindafall birds hung ready on the spit, their black juices slowly dripping into the white stone basting jugs that stood upon the hearth. She hurriedly looked away, her fear of the birds rising in her throat. Even when they were roasted and their leathery wings were spread and trimmed with gold and silver, they still held menace and stank of death. She could not imagine how the marshlords could eat them, let alone fight amongst themselves to pick the carcasses clean. Ansel called her helpers to the long black ebony tables and told them to transfer the tall earthenware jugging pots to the tops of the ovens, while she arranged the clay-rolled hedgehogs on the lower shelves, leaving a finger's space between each one. She tested the oven's heat by spitting on the hot stone shelves and watching how long it took for the spittle to hiss and bubble. Turning she shouted for the scuttles, calling for more peat turfs, cuffing the soot-engrained collars of the apprentice girls wheeling their heavy barrows of turfs towards the oven fires, cursing them for spoiling her jugged hares.

"Call yourselves scuttles!" she shouted impatiently. "You will never become scullians if you ruin my clay-bake, and I will serve you up roasted alive at the All-beast Feast. Hurry yourselves and bank up the hearth fires. Clean the clinker crust from these iron grids or the pottage cauldrons will never boil."

Muttering and cursing she returned to the long tables and began to soften the rounds of hard cheese, but secretly she smiled, with an ear turned towards the high crystal windows as she listened for the bellowing roars of the mudbeasts in their beasting pits beyond the city walls.

"Give me foreknowledge!' demanded Lord Miresnare leaning forward in his high throne and beckoning the mumblers who hovered at the threshold stone of the great hall.

"Dance! Dance for me in an unbroken circle of magic around the Glitterspike. Dance close to the jaws of Yaloor the champion beast and foretell of his victories in the joust. Foretell if I will spawn an heir. Draw forth the name of the mother who can restore my tainted seed."

Naul, the master mumbler by the strength of his magic, swung his guttering lamp slowly from side to side, tasting the moment, seeing his fate in Yaloor's eyes as the smoke tail that escaped from the lamp swirled and clung to the hem of his saffron robes. Hesitantly he crossed the threshold and with cautious whispering treads, the toes of his sandals curled upwards, he shuffled over the smooth polished stone floor, leading the procession of mumblers into a silent circle around the Glitterspike.

"Would you draw out our foreknowledge and use it wisely?" he chanted as the mumblers locked hands and began to move, swaying to the left and right.

"You are the eye of the future," answered Lord Miresnare, impatient for the ritual to be spoken and the dance to begin.

"By our foresight the power of the Glitterspike shall flourish."

"Through your magic I will keep the marshlords at bay. Now, dance, dance, before they hammer on my door," he cried, sinking back fretfully with his hands clenched.

Slowly and with measured dancing treads the mumblers began to chant. Faster and faster they wove their magic circle, foretelling in their movements the beginnings of each new leaf and branch, each clinging root and seedling plant that would grow across the length and breadth of Gnarlsmyre. Now they were leaping high into the air, their windbells wildly clattering and the lamps swinging, blazing white-hot against their woven cloaks. Naul cried them on; the magic was flowing from him, burning its way through his fingertips out into the unending circle, searing their skin and making their knuckles burn. Bright flashes of foresight glowed in their glazed eyes. Strange voices shouted through their lips and a bitter wind blew through the doors extinguishing the rows of tall reed lamps and plunging the great hall into shadowy darkness. Only the Glitterspike glowed and sparkled as its heartstone reflected the mumblers' blazing lamps. Lord Miresnare cried out with terror as the daylight failed. Yaloor bellowed and leapt forward, clawing at the dancing mumblers, while the long-fanged hunting dogs chained beside him howled and snarled at the sudden darkness.

Backwards and forwards the mumblers danced, their blazing lamps causing long shadows to flicker in the rafters of the hall. Lord Miresnare shrank back in his throne and Yaloor cowered against the Glitterspike casting his shadow over the veins of molten silver that were etched through the tall finger of crystal. Terrible shapes loomed up within the hall crowding forward and reaching out between the dancers' flying robes. Marshlords laughed and screamed, their shadowy hands closing on the throne; voices mocked in the half-light amidst the sound of hurrying feet and the clash of steel. Lord Miresnare shouted and seemed to rise within the closing crush of bodies, trying to push them back with his frail hands, but having to retreat step by step from the ghostly hoards. The images dissolved and changed to phantoms of mudbeasts that broke out of the circle of dancing mumblers and bellowed and charged, ploughing their blood-soaked horns across the hall only to shrink back around the Glitterspike and vanish into a jumble of shadows. One hideous shape, close-chained beside Yaloor, rose up above the swarming beasts and seemed to turn its claws and almost topple the throne. As it melted back it tore at the Glitterspike, smashing its outer edges of crystal and sending huge cracks through the heartstone, breaking open the veins of molten silver so that precious liquid splashed out across the floor. With a grinding crash the tall column of crystal broke free from its foundations and snapped in two. Rafters began to splinter, walls to crack and crumble and the hall was showered with broken stonework. Dust billowed up in choking clouds.

"What? What does this mean?" cried Lord Miresnare through trembling lips as new phantoms of the mumblers' foresight reached the steps of his throne and threatened to engulf him.

Naul stopped the dancing circle and the mumblers

froze into silence, their glazed eyes turned up towards the throne.

"Mean?" whispered Naul as the daylight began to return and sparkle in shimmering patterns on the crystal windows and the phantoms faded into nothing. "It is a glimpse of tomorrow, my Lord. It is what might come to pass without the magic of the mumblers."

Lord Miresnare shook his head. "No, those nightmare shapes cannot be the future. Each time you have danced before the joust you have shown clear pictures of whom Yaloor whould defeat and once in better days you cried out the name of the woman with whom I had to lie to spawn an heir. I never found her," he ended bitterly.

Naul wrung his hands in anguish, the windbells clattering on the hem of his robes. "We cannot predict what our magic will foretell. We are but a mirror held up against the darkness of tomorrow."

Lord Miresnare hesitated, half rising from the throne, and stared down at the mumblers. "Dance again," he hissed. "Show me some victory, show me that there is still a spark of hope that I might beget a son. Or I'll throw you all to Yaloor."

Naul took a slow tread and stopped. "If we dance again, my Lord, the foresight may show you even greater tragedy."

"What greater tragedy can I have than the burden of the joust and a string of daughters at my heels! Now dance! Dance!" shouted Lord Miresnare, his voice filled with rage. "Search with your magic and give me a clear sight of victory. Dance again before the marsh-lords reach my doors."

Naul averted his eyes from his master's anger and whispered the mumblers forward, guiding the circle to sway and spin around the Glitterspike. Lifting his head he shouted for foresight above the shrill clatter of the windbells and the screams of new phantoms that leapt up in their dancing circle.

"There must be no joust!" shouted Naul. "Listen, Lord, it is in the voices that cry within our circle. That is what the magic foretells. Ruin and disaster, black despair and the end of all you have strived to keep. All will be lost and Yaloor will be defeated if the joust begins."

Lord Miresnare rose from the throne, clutching his head in his hands. "Ruin? The beast Yaloor defeated? The end of the Glitterspike! But what sight of the woman who will sire me an heir? All I see are dark monstrous shapes spilling out of your dancing circle and clamouring for my throne and yet the noise of those phantoms is no more than the rattle of your windbells and the bitter morning wind blowing amongst the towers of this hall. Where do you hear such tales to frighten your master on the eve of the Allbeast Feast?"

"Do you doubt our magic eye of the future, my Lord? Was your own sight blind to the monstrous beast that rose up within our circle to tear the Glitterspike from its foundations and snap the thick column of crystal as easily as you would break a stalk of summer-dried marsh grass? Were you deaf to the shouts and the clamour for your throne and the hoards of mudbeasts that shrank against the Glitterspike lowering their horns to defend it?" cried Naul, his glazed eyes blazing with the light of foresight.

"Phantoms! Twists of magic!" shouted Lord Miresnare, his voice full of doubts as he pointed a quivering finger at the strong column of shimmering crystal that still stood as it had before the mumblers had danced, rising up to vanish amongst the rafters. "You have spun strange magic in your circle, magic that reeks of treachery. Who has whispered to you to foretell of ruin and dark times that will weaken me on this eve of the Allbeast Feast?"

Naul cried out in fear and the circle shrank away from their master. "Lord, we can only foretell what might come to pass. We have no power to change what shows within our circle. It is for you to take our knowledge and with it make the future. The monster beast that rose so threateningly amongst us is more than a phantom or a legend, it is wild and dangerous and more than a match for your champion, and I fear that the marshlords have discovered its lair somewhere on the very edges of Gnarlsmyre. Did you see how easily it destroyed all your labours to rule the Glitterspike? Did you see the splintering timbers and the collapsing walls that vanished in clouds of choking stone dust? The magic forewarns you, Lord, that Yaloor will be destroyed, the city sacked and plunged into ruin if you proclaim the joust."

"But how can I stop it?" cried Lord Miresnare falling onto his knees. "The marshlords know that I have no heir and they will scent treachery if I bar them from the hall. They will rise up and take the throne, the city, everything. With each joust they have grown impatient to snatch these dry lands that the city stands upon. It has only been the joust and each marshlord's greed to win it all that has kept them divided."

Naul paused, bringing the dancing circle to an abrupt halt and twisting his head as if listening, straining his ears against the sudden stillness. Lord Miresnare lifted his head to listen too, but heard only the soft hiss and splutter of the mumblers' swinging lamps. Slowly he rose from his knees and retreated step by step from the dancing circle till he stood at the crystal windows that framed the morning sun. "Magic has forewarned that the marshlords have snared a beast to match Yaloor that will bring an end to everything I have strived for, but surely there is something I can do? Dance—dance again!"

Naul moved the mumblers to dance again, crying out for more magic as Lord Miresnare pressed his forehead despairingly against the crystal smoothness of the glass and stared out at the crowded city below. He knew he dared not close the city or wall it up against the marshlords. The people would starve to death in the wet seasons without the cured and smoked flesh of the marshmen's beasts to feed them. There would never be enough sweetmeats grown in the crystal houses even if he had four seasons' warning to prepare for siege.

Naul's chanting voice rose shrilly above the clatter of the windbells. "The marshlords must be welcomed to the Allbeast Feast, confident that you are ignorant of the beast that they have snared."

"But why? Surely there must be something I can

do?" cried Lord Miresnare helplessly, watching the savage pindafalls rising up on the warm morning draughts of air. They spiralled effortlessly between the slender spires on outstretched leathery wings that hummed and rattled as they searched the weather-cracked roofs and tight dark alleyways for easy meat. He stabbed an angry finger at the pindafalls and shouted, "The marshlords gather just like those carrion birds, to strip the city bare and snatch all Gnarlsmyre for their own.

"All my efforts to divide the marshmen through their greed shall be as hollow as the ritual of the joust for Marrimian my first-born. I know they have watched me with hunters' eyes, measuring the spring in my step, the straightness of my spine, waiting for me to hold up the heir to the throne. They have measured my weakness and waited for me to grow old and my seed to fail and wither away, but they come too quickly, thrusting too impatiently for my throne. I will not give in without a fight!"

Naul gave a great cry and brought the dancing circle to a halt again in a dense cloud of lamp smoke. "And fight you shall, Lord," he cried. "By using your power as master of all Gnarlsmyre and lord of this hall to change the joust. Yes, that is what the phantoms of the dance foretell. You shall by trickery strip the marshlords of their beasts and chain them with Yaloor around the base of the Glitterspike where the marshlords, nay, any one, must fight them all. And the prize shall be—yes, the throne itself."

Lord Miresnare strode across the hall in a blind fury.

"Do you take me for a fool to risk such a game—to offer my throne to all the marshmen of Gnarlsmyre?" he snarled, reaching for Naul with savage fingers. "I could never separate the marshlords from their mudbeasts nor chain them with Yaloor around the Glitterspike. The hunters stay shackled to their beasts until they are secured to the iron rings along the outer edges of this hall. The marshscum would scent any changes that I make and if the merest whisper of my defeat echoed in their ears we would all be trampled in the first wild rush for my throne."

Naul turned to flee but slipped on the polished stones of the hall and as he fell he felt his master's hand close about his throat and pull him roughly to his feet.

"Which of the marshscum will take my throne? Which of them did you see in the lamp smoke?" Miresnare shouted above the shrill clatter of the mumblers' windbells.

Naul shook his head, clawing wildly at Lord Miresnare's fingers. "There was none clear to see. The one closest to the throne was neither city man nor marshlord," he choked, falling on to his knees as Lord Miresnare released his grip.

"Who then will steal my throne?"

Naul stumbled forward, shaking his head and gasping for breath, and pointed at Yaloor as the beast bellowed and clawed at the floorstones sending up a shower of bone splinters. "Yaloor was in the midst of our foreknowledge and we saw the mudbeasts chained around him to defend the Glitterspike."

Lord Miresnare hesitated, not knowing which way to turn. The dancing circle was broken by his own impatient rage and he could ask for nothing more from the mumblers. "How?" he cried, lifting his empty hands towards Naul's flying robe tails as the master mumbler fled towards the low archway and worn threshold stones that led to the mumblers' cells.

Naul paused and turned, and pointed at the freshly oiled iron rings set around the edge of the hall. "You have but one night, my Lord, to change this hall to your advantage and arm against losing everything that you have worked for. But even that may fail."

Naul laughed and swung his pine-oil lamp and spread his arms up towards the tall crystal windows. "The one who will claim your throne will be led forward by a stranger from a land beyond Rainbows' End and the shifting fogbanks. From a place that you have never even dreamed of."

"There are no lands beyond the fogs!" shouted Lord Miresnare. "Nor shall a wanderer take my throne!"

Naul laughed, his voice echoing as he fled the hall. "He will come, my Lord, two men in one shadow with a single tread of footprints."

Lord Miresnare stared at Yaloor, deaf to the slow crunch of his jaws and the grinding scrape of his claws. What if Naul had foreseen the truth? He could not let the joust proceed. He must change the game. Turning towards the high-arched entrance he snapped his fingers and shouted for stone setters, iron forgers, ragmen, and for an extra guard of archers. There was work to do.

3

Treacheries on the Eve of The Allbeast Feast

MERTZORK gathered the injured marshwader more securely in his arms and squeezed through the throng of early morning travellers converging on the city from the marsheries that were less than a night's journey across the frozen wastes. Quickly he searched for a way to hide from the hurlers. He looked among the iron-ore carriers with their squat baskets of broken rock, the harvesters and the reed gatherers with the heavy bundles of fresh reed they had gathered from the quickmire's edge. There were kitchen swillers with their bundles of rags, twig gatherers with burdens of marsh-oak twigs, travelling acrobats and tumblers, all swelling the bustling throng, all pushing and shoving for their place, glad to have their feet on firm ground and eager for their journey's end. But none of these could help him, he thought. He needed to mask the smell of the beasting pits and disguise his dress.

He turned his head and caught the strong scent of the sap in the reedcutter's freshly cut reeds and ducking beneath a heavy bundle he stole a handful of the sweet-smelling brittle stalks. "Say nothing of the mudbeasts or of our battle with the pindafalls in the beasting pits," he hissed, shaking the delirious marshwader awake and forcing the handful of reeds firmly between his bloody fingers. "You are a reedcutter now and the carrion birds attacked you on the marsh edge while we were gathering reeds."

Cursing the marshwader's delirium Mertzork stole another handful of reeds, crumpled the brittle stalks and spread them across his shoulders and down the front of his rough hemp jerkin, letting the sweet-scented sap mask his odour. He smiled to himself and let the crowd carry him steadily forward into the shadows of the Hurlers' Gate.

The progress of the travellers was slowing, and they pressed together as they filed through the narrow archway, shouting and jostling for more space, those on the outside snagging their sleeves and cloak tails on the wrought iron studs of the first great gates. Mertzork caught a glimpse of the hurlers at the second gates. They were perched on high seats set onto the smooth stone walls, yet even from twenty paces he could feel their piercing stares as they slowly swept their gazes across the crowd. They would stop a traveller here and there with their long curved silver-headed canes, or cry out for someone's purpose in the city with voices loud enough to splinter wood or shatter stone. Holding his breath Mertzork shrank down as low as he could amongst the reedcutters and shuffled forward, his scalp prickling as he waited for a hurler's silver cane to hook around his throat. Something bumped against his leg as he drew level with the archway. He looked down and saw several of his hunting dogs pressed in on either side. "Scatter!" he hissed and kicked at them. A reedcutter shouted and stumbled just behind him, tripping as a dog pushed between his legs, sending the heavy bundle of reed stalks toppling from his shoulders and showering the crowd with the razor-sharp reeds.

"Wait your turn," cried one ore carrier, tottering forward beneath the weight of his basket of rocks. The crowd behind pushed against him forcing him through the mess of broken reeds. Angry voices echoed his cry and cursed the clumsy reedcutter.

The crowd began to sway, forcing a passage around the luckless reed carrier scrabbling for his reeds and, carrying Mertzork and the injured marshwader with them, swept through the first gate arch. Harvesters shouted for order as they slipped and stumbled on the smooth cobblestones, losing their balance and scattering baskets of apselgathers across the narrow entrance. The ore carriers tripped up in the sudden surge and fell, showering dangerous lumps of rock over the heads of the crowd. There were cries of pain, fists were raised and fighting broke out. Impatient tumblers sprang up and ran nimbly across the shoulders of the crowd, shouting mockeries behind them.

"Order! Order!" shouted the hurlers above the rising panic. Releasing the locklatches on the inner gates they gestured a company of bowmen to clear the road. "Be still, by the order of Lord Miresnare, be still or we will seal the city and send you back into the marshes!"

Mertzork saw the bowmen load their short bows and heard the heavy wooden gates begin to grind across the cobbles; they were slowly closing, pushing the reedcutters on either side of him back beneath the archway. It might be hours before they were opened again. He knew he must act quickly or see all his plans come to nothing. He sprang forward and using the wounded marshman as a battering ram knocked the reedcutter blocking his path onto his knees. With merciless feet he trampled over the struggling man then twisted and slipped between the closing doors. Behind him the doors slammed shut, muffling the screams of the injured reedcutter and dulling the shouts of the angry crowd.

The bowmen closed around him with their barbed steel arrow blades aimed at his heart. "Purpose? Purpose?" chanted the hurlers, leaning forward in their high seats and hooking two silver canes around his throat as they pulled him through the circle of bowmen to stand before them.

"We were gathering reeds when a carrion bird attacked. I just had to get in before the gates closed," Mertzork stuttered, feeling his scalp prickle and not daring to look up and meet the hurler's searching gaze. "We must find a healing house quickly." He pointed a trembling finger at the ugly wound in the marshwader's face.

"Be still!" commanded one of the hurlers loosening his pull on the silver cane and turning his attention back to the angry voices beyond the gates. There was a great shout and black reedsmoke billowed above the archway. Fists and pieces of iron ore were hammered on the heavily studded doors, the bowmen cursed and, retreating a dozen paces between Mertzork and the city, knelt and took aim, loosing their arrows over the walls and into the crowd.

"Let these reedcutters past and be quick. They spoil our aim," called one of the archers impatiently. The hurlers turned their heads and stared at Mertzork, frowning as they saw the rag bindings between his toes and the smears of melting marsh mud on his breeches.

"Your robes are the dress of marshlords and marsh-scum are not permitted into the city until the dawn of the Allbeast Feast—until tomorrow," one hissed, pulling Mertzork closer.

Mertzork stabbed a finger at the marshwader's bloody face and begged the hurler to let him past. The hurler bent forward, looked down at the marsh-wader's face and hesitated. Easing his pull on the cane he gripped Mertzork's chin and gazed searchingly into his eyes for the truth.

"Send the cursed reedcutters to Erek the healing woman, her spiders will cure them both," sneered one of the archers, pushing the long cane aside and point-ing urgently at the billowing smoke. "We have more important things to deal with." The crackling roar of the reed flames was growing louder and louder, smoke trails of choking fumes were seeping under the doors and finding ways through all the thundershakes and weather cracks of the heavy wooden gate.

"Clear the road and open the gates. We will drive that rabble back," shouted another archer, pressing the trigger spring on his short bow to send a steel-tipped bolt spinning past Mertzork's shaven head to strike the door in a shower of splinters.

"Will you take your friend to this woman Erek?" asked the hurler, smiling at some secret thought. He pushed Mertzork through the line of archers with the long cane, making him stumble awkwardly beneath the weight of the marshwader in his arms.

"As long as my legs will carry both of us, but which road shall we take?" he called over his shoulder as he stared at the maze of steep alleyways and narrow lanes that had their beginnings twenty paces beyond the hurlers' chairs.

"Up that alley there," the hurler indicated vaguely. "The forty-fourth twist of the Shambles will lead you to her door." For a moment he followed Mertzork with his piercing eyes, puzzled that a reedcutter should not know of Erek's venomous spiders and her hatred of all men. He turned back to the fray, frowning, quickly forgetting Mertzork in his concern to restore order. The bulging gates were opening, the crowds were surging forward, only to confront a steadfast line of grim-faced archers.

Mertzork, hardly believing his luck, hurried forward into the nearest dark alleyway and lowered the marshwader's body onto the ground, out of the way of the crowd. He flexed his burning muscles, then looked up the gloomy alleyway. Was this the one the hurler had indicated? He thought so but there seemed nothing to choose between one lane and another— they all appeared to go in the same direction, spiralling upwards, through layer upon layer of narrow roofs and blank, empty windows. As long as eventually it led to Glitterspike Hall . . .

Hazy smoke drifted, eddying and twisting through

the lanes as it was caught up in the warm draughts
of air wafting across the city. Impatiently he waited
for his arms to stop tingling and his eyes to grow accustomed to the darkness before lifting the marshwader and cautiously making his way up the road,
cursing as he snagged his toes on the sharp, uneven
stones and skinned his shins on the countless winding
steps. The climb became steeper, sucking the breath
out of him and knotting his muscles with the effort
of each new step that he took. His heart banged in his
chest and the blood throbbed in his head. As he
climbed higher the crowd grew less until he was walking on deserted paths. The cold, blank, mud-slapped
walls with their blind windows crowded ever closer,
seeming to edge in on either side of him, and he dared
not blink or look away. He felt as if the air was growing thicker beneath the overhanging balconies that
were almost touching above his head; they seemed to
bear down on him, blocking out the morning sunlight.

The rising alleyway had narrowed until now both
his elbows brushed the rough mud-plastered walls as
he passed. He could not easily go forward while he
carried the marshwader so he stopped and allowed the
limp body to drop heavily to the ground. He turned
and stared down the steep lane that fell away below
him. It looked unfamiliar, the houses were different
from the ones he remembered passing and he knelt
down and felt for his footprints just as he would have
done in the quickmarsh. Then he cursed his own foolishness as he remembered the tales of those who lost
their way in this city and he wished he had waymarked each twist in the path just as his father had

taught him in the wild lands beyond the quickmarsh when they crossed firm ground. He retraced a dozen steps and realized that he was completely lost, for what looked to be one narrow alleyway was in fact a whole maze of paths that sprouted new branches at each twist and turn, many of them becoming dead ends.

Mertzork reached up on tiptoe to the small rough crystal windows set into deep alcoves in the damp mud walls and banged his knuckles on the dirty opaque glass, shouting for help. Sinking back he crouched against the wall, suddenly noticing the silence that pressed in all around him. He rose and went back to where he had left the marshwader and shook him, trying to waken him. Mertzork's palms were damp with sweat and his scalp tingled as he huddled in the gloom, and for the first time he felt real terror as he thought of being swallowed by the city's stifling darkness.

Mertzork shivered as he rose to his feet and tried to look between the rows of houses and guess which one of the blind alleyways would lead him upwards or back to the Hurlers' Gate. Cursing he spat and wondered what had happened to the crowds that had slowly filed through the gates beneath the hurlers' watchful eyes. To where had they so magically vanished? He spat again and cursed his impatience to escape the gate watchers' eyes and then he held his breath, twisting and turning his head, listening for the sounds of the city. In the distance, muffled and faint, he could just about make out the rumble of iron-bound wheels, the thunderous hiss of the ironmasters' furnaces and the quick rattle of the coopers' hammers mixed with the vendors shouting out their wares.

Looking up at a narrow strip of hazy smoke-filled sky between the overhanging balconies he could see the faraway shapes of pindafalls' wings and heard the sharp clack of their wings and their screeching cry as they soared in ever-widening hunting circles away beyond his sight around the steep-gabled roofs and sheer spires of Glitterspike Hall.

Two shadowy figures trundling unshod wooden wheels suddenly appeared to his left and squeezed past him, hurrying on their way before he had time to clutch at their flying cloak tails.

"Wait! Stop!" he shouted, jumping to his feet and calling after them. He reached down and bundled the heavy marshwader over his shoulder as he followed the vanishing figures, running as fast as the steep uneven steps would allow, tripping and stumbling under the weight of his burden.

"Wait!" he cried in despair, reaching a new twist in the warren of gloomy lanes only to find that the figures had disappeared. A door slammed shut in an alley to his right and a heavy latch lock rattled and then silence settled in the half-light.

Mertzork took a deep breath and once more slid the marshwader off his shoulder. He clenched his fists, trying to control his anger and fear amongst the tall overhanging buildings that pressed in all around him. It had seemed so easy out there in the endless stretches of quickmire with the sunlight and the fresh wind on his face as he planned his victory, scheming and plotting, idly dreaming while he waited for the right wind to freeze the ground. It had appeared such a simple task to find a secret way through the city to the doors of Glitterspike Hall but now he realized why the other marshlords kept so carefully to the path waymarked for them. The city was a dangerous place that would swallow him alive if he did not act quickly.

"I will not give in to you!" he hissed striking the nearest wall, numbing his hand with the force of his anger. He picked up the marshwader again and step by step began to feel his way forward into the lane where he had heard the door close. His fingers found the doorpost and his toe snagged against a shallow threshold stone. He felt across the pitted grain of the door and found the twisted iron ring of the latch. He closed his hand around it and loosening the iron spike in his belt he turned the ring and pushed hard against the door. It creaked open a crack and then swung easily inwards. Mertzork blinked in the sudden shaft of bright sunlight and stumbled forward over the threshold. He found himself in a small courtyard.

He blinked again and rubbed his eyes as he sat back on his haunches and gazed spellbound at the scene before him. In the centre of the courtyard a huge circular forge set low into the flagstones blazed and crackled sending smoketails and dancing sparks twisting up into the sunlight. Three tall figures, stripped to the waist and clad in spark-blackened leather aprons, laughed and shouted to one another as they wrestled to hold a hoop of sparkling fire-red iron steady in the flames with their long-handled forging tongs. Beside them a wheelwright bent over a raised flat stone clamping his unshod wheel into position. With a shout

he straightened his back and stepped quickly aside as
the ironmasters in one movement lifted the white-hot
hoop out of the fire and placed it over the wheel.
White smoke billowed up as the hot iron touched the
wooden felloes of the wheel and strikers crowded forward swinging in rhythm as their long-handled hammers drove the iron hoop down. Quenchers filled the
spaces between each striker pouring buckets of marsh-
chilled water, quenching the hot iron and sending up
clouds of hissing steam as the hoop shrank onto the
wheel.

Mertzork stared at the ironmasters as they laboured
in the smoke and clouds of hissing steam but as it
drifted clear of the courtyard he saw them all staring
openmouthed at him. "I have lost my way," he blurted
out and indicated the marshwader on the ground beside him. "I am looking for Erek the healing woman,
with the spiders that will heal his face."

One of the wheelwrights stepped off the tyring
stone, crossed the courtyard in six strides and
slammed the door, bolting the liftlatch to bar Mertzork's retreat. Turning he spread his hands broadly
on his hips and held Mertzork's eye. "Marshmen and
their like are not allowed to wander freely in this city
before the Allbeast Feast, and even those who fetch
and carry for the hall must not stray from the road
marked out for them. That is Lord Miresnare's law
and it must be obeyed."

"We are reedcutters," cried Mertzork, "not marshmen, and we were going about our business when a
pindafall bird stooped and tore away my brother's
face. Look! Look at it!"

"You may or may not be reedcutters," the wheel-wright said in disbelief, reaching into a satchel that hung from his belt. "If you *are* a reedcutter sit this reed-stalk taper in my lamp, and if it sits true I will give you the way up into the Shambles where the healers weave their healing webs."

Mertzork took the reed and slowly turned it over and over in his hands, trying to remember what a trimmed reed looked like. He had watched reedcutters scythe down whole banks of reeds and trim them with swift slashes of their curved knives, and had never given them a second thought. Lamps were for cities, marshmen used roughly bound torches and threw them aside when they were burned down. The iron-masters, strikers and quenchers had gathered around him in silent suspicion and were watching his every movement.

"You had better trim that reed to fit snugly in my lamp and burn without a single wisp of smoke or we will burn the truth out of you as to why you wander unattended in the city before Allbeast Feast," called a voice from the circle.

Mertzork looked up and tried to smile as he fingered the brittle reed and hoped that it would fit the lamp that the wheelwright was thrusting towards him. Swallowing and nervous he pulled the burnt reed stump out of the lamp and forced his new trimmed reed into the opening. The wheelwright gave a hard triumphant smile as the reed stalk crumpled between Mertzork's clumsy fingers, and he took the lamp away from him. "You are no more a reedcutter than I am Lord Miresnare," he hissed, leaning forward and gathering the loose ends of Mertzork's collar in his strong hands. "Truth by word or by fire?" he whispered, lifting Mertzork off the ground.

Mertzork choked and gasped for breath, his feet kicking wildly as the wheelwright lifted him higher and higher.

"Word or fire?" he asked, suddenly releasing his stranglehold on Mertzork's neck and letting him fall into a heap on the smooth flagstones of the courtyard.

Mertzork coughed and gingerly rubbed at the black bruise lines on his neck. He looked up fearfully at the grim-faced circle that stood over him and saw that there was no escape from these hard city people.

"Word," he whispered trying to clear his throat. "It is true that we are not reedcutters and that we broke the Lore by entering the city but if I had told the hurlers that the carrion bird had attacked while we were driving our mudbeast into the beasting pits they would have barred us from the city and sent us back to the healers in the marsheries. The marshwader would have bled to death on the journey across the quickmarsh."

The wheelwright could see a glimmer of truth in his story but he knew that the marshlords had their own healers and had always thought that they travelled with them to the joust and he narrowed his eyes. This stranger had taken the hurlers for fools if he thought that they could not see through his poor disguise, but it was a sly trick for them to direct him to seek out Erek. Surely even the marshmen knew that she hated men and had turned her healing gifts into dark magic, whispering the spiders to weave webs of death?

Slapping his thigh the wheelwright suddenly laughed and extended his hand to help Mertzork to his feet. The hurlers must have had their reasons and he would carry on with their plan.

He shrugged and put his hand upon the latch lock. "I will show you the road up into the Shambles. Quickly, gather up your marshwader and follow me."

Mertzork smiled with relief and reached for the marshwader; he would much rather have just allowed him to die on the courtyard but the ironmasters and their strikers were watching him, whispering amongst themselves; clearly they were not at ease with his story. He secretly stole a small square of chalk from the pile that lay scattered on the ground hoping that no one would notice one piece was missing, and as he looked up he saw that the wheelwright was holding the door open. They helped him lift the marshwader back on his shoulder. Curling his lips in a triumphant sneer Mertzork followed the wheelwright and this time secretly marked each house with chalk. He was determined that he would not be so easily lost again.

"How did you know straightaway that I was not a reedcutter?" he asked, catching up and falling into step with the wheelwright.

The wheelwright laughed. "Every craft has its secrets and each serves the other and so keeps the balance of our lives. You could no more trim a reed to fit a lamp nor carve the felloes of a wheel or dowel them together than I could snare a mudbeast and drive

it into the beasting pits. You have no reedcutter's
apron and your fingernails are not long and grown
over for hooking the reeds. Your feet are marshbound
for hunting on the frozen quickmire, not wrapped for
weaving sledges and working at the mire's edge."

"But did you doubt me and grow suspicious because
I had lost the road to the Shambles and could not find
my way to Erek the healing woman's doorstone?"
asked Mertzork.

The wheelwright smiled, his eyes sparkling with
cunning, and he pointed with a half-carved felloe stave
that he had taken from his apron pocket up into a dark,
foul-smelling alleyway that brooded in silence a pace
before them. "No, the city is a warren of crowded
lanes and unknown alleyways that have been hewn
out of the steep slopes below Glitterspike Hall, and
each twist and turn of the countless steps would trip
and trap even the most seasoned traveller. However,
ask any wheelwright and he will give you the quickest
path into the Shambles. It is our craft to know the
way. Look, this is your entrance. Just follow the
thicker strands of sticky web for one hundred paces
climbing to the left. But beware, touch nothing but
the latch lock on Erek's doorpost."

Mertzork took a hesitant step into the dark silent
entrance to the alleyway and felt the loops and tails
of fine gossamer threads that crisscrossed the narrow
land above his head as they brushed against his face.
"How shall I know which doorpost? Will you lead me
to Erek's door?" he cried, stepping back from beneath
the canopy of dense webs and turning his head to
where the wheelwright had been standing only to

hear shrieks of laughter and quick footsteps vanishing into the maze of lanes below the Shambles.

Mertzork bared his teeth and snarled at the wheelwright's treachery. He closed his fingers around his hidden sharpwire and shouted after the fading laughter, "I will find you, felloe maker, and I will squeeze the breath out of your throat for abandoning us."

Muttering and cursing he pulled the marshwader against his chest and stared into the entrance. He gathered his courage as he watched the silken webs tremble and sway as if shaken by a hidden wind or tugged by unseen hands. "Spiders!" He tried to laugh his fears away and hugged the marshwader tighter to him, wishing that he had not squashed spiders for sport while he waited for the night wind to freeze the quickmarsh. "I will carry you to Erek's doorstone and leave you to the spiders' healing webs while I go on. I must search out a path through this miserable warren of lanes and alleyways to the very doors of Glitterspike Hall. And back to the Hurlers' Gate."

Holding his jerkin collar as tightly together as he could in fear of the spiders and drawing a shallow breath he trod cautiously into the Shambles, ducking his head beneath the low trailing threads. Silence closed about him. Even his footsteps were muffled to nothing. It was dark and airless. He tripped on the first uneven step and cursed, throwing out his hand to keep his balance, almost losing his grip on the marshwader. His fingers touched the webs, tearing through their revolting stickiness and sending swarms of black spiders scuttling up into the dense canopy of webs above his head. He cried out in terror and shrank

away, covering his face with his hands. The webs were
alive with spiders that glowed in the dark: red ones,
silver-black ones, ghostly-white ones and yellow ones,
of every shape and size. They crowded closer, making
the canopy sag beneath their weight. Dropping the
marshwader he snatched his iron spike from his belt
and struck out for the entrance, cursing and shouting
in the airless silence as he scythed through the threads
that hung across his path.

The dense canopy suddenly broke, spilling a thick
swarm of spiders onto his head. He screamed as they
ran across his face and cried out in terror as the broken
web ends of the canopy snagged his arms and tangled
between his legs. They seemed to be alive, clinging on,
wrapping around him, and slowing his headlong rush.
They stopped his fleeing footsteps and smothered him
with their cold stickiness. He was being pulled deeper
and deeper into the Shambles. Large furry spiders
were swarming all over him, binding him in a tight
cocoon of strong, ice-cold threads. He struggled, fighting to free his hands. He fell and crushed countless
spiders as he rolled helplessly across the smooth dry
stones of Erek's doorway.

A voice shrieked with wild laughter and two bright
eyes burned with white fire in the gloomy hovel. He
kicked out just once as the figure bent over him and
bit into his neck. His fingers burned and tingled with
an icy numbness, empty blackness spread through
him and he felt as if he was tumbling and falling into
a cold, bottomless quickmire.

Erek mumbled and muttered to herself. She scuttled
out to drag in the unconscious marshwader and darted

quick glances up and down the narrow alleyway to check that none of the other healing women had seen her spiders snatch the wanderers. Swarms of spiders scratched at the sack of dry wrinkled skin that hung beneath her chin. Slamming the door behind her she moved towards the fireplace and spat into the glowing embers of her fire, then threw a thick woven thread that she had sewn into Mertzork's ankle bindings over the low mantel beam and slowly, hand over hand, hauled him up to dangle upside down and ripen above her firestone.

Cackling with delight she rubbed her gnarled fingers together, clicking their swollen knuckles, and prodded the marshwader's ugly wound with her blackened fingernails. "By scullion's spit and mumblers' spines," she hissed snatching her hand away from the wound and sucking her fingertips. He had the raw taste of marshman's flesh and there was the smell of the wild quickmarsh on him, not the stale taste of city people that she had expected. Frowning she leaned forward and searched the marshwader's face and hands, sniffing him from head to foot and scattering the bundle of broken reed stems that he still clutched between his fingers.

"These are not reedcutters, these are wilder men," she muttered clearing a space around the marshwader by brushing away the swarms of spiders that had scuttled forwards, sending them back into the shadows. She felt the rough weave of the marshwader's clothes and scented the beasting pits on the rag bindings on his feet. Pinching at the crusting edges of the wound on his face she tried to squeeze out a little blood but it was all dried up. She sat back on her haunches and whispered to the white healer spiders from the darkest crevices of her hovel to weave their magic webs across the ugly wound on his face and nourish him for a later feast.

Slowly she turned back towards the firestone and watched Mertzork turning in the draught from the chimney and frowned. She had never trapped a marshman in her snares. They were always careful to keep within the waymarks that led them up to the doors of Glitterspike Hall for the joust and even in the seasons before the joust began they had never ventured very far into the city. Smiling she wet her lips and whispered to the black death spiders, calling them one by one along the low mantel beam towards Mertzork's dangling thread. But then she hesitated, hissing them into stillness. He would taste better if she knew his secrets, and she could grow wiser and stronger knowing what lay beyond the gates of Glor. Muttering she reached out with her crooked fingernails, pulled him away from the firestone and stared into his venom-glazed eyes. She lifted his eyelids and searched out all his hidden secrets. Cackling to herself she began to feast on all his darkest plots. She shivered and leaned closer, brushing away the black spiders that had crowded on the dangling thread, and she frowned, wrinkling her high-domed forehead as she scented the drifting, ice-cold fogbanks that billowed on the furthest edges of Gnarlsmyre. Mertzork's shallow breaths ghosted her searching mirror and she saw a monstrous beast rise up amongst the tiny beads of moisture.

Erek turned her head and listened at his ear. She heard the distant rattle of Gallengab's chains and heard his savage roar. Far-off shouts and cursing voices made her press closer to Mertzork's ear to catch the sounds of the marshhunters who drove the beast by secret roads across the frozen quickmire. She laughed and put her dribbling lips to his ear and asked in hurried whispers for the beast's purpose. Trembling, her age-stained skin whitening with surprise, she listened to Mertzork's answer and quickly pushed the searching glass back beneath his lips to test his truth. She cackled as she discovered that he had murdered his father for knowledge of the beast Gallengab and that he had snared him to destroy Yaloor and to take the Glitterspike as his own and put an end to the rule of the Miresnares.

Erek sucked in her cheeks and swallowed a ball of venomous spittle. Her breaths were coming in short gasps; she hunched her shoulders and stared fearfully into the darkest corners of her hovel and gathered her hate of Lord Miresnare to her. She remembered all that he had done, how he had sacked the Shambles for healing potions to sire a male heir and had killed those healers who had failed him. She remembered how he had snatched her only child and cursed her out of the city as an evil hag. After all those seasons of bitter hatred her healing powers had festered into dark magic, and now she had stumbled on the means for sweet revenge. Reaching forward she spread her dusty skirt hems over Mertzork's head as if to hide what she had found and hastily wiped her magic searching mirror with a cloth of the finest gossamer. Crushing the cloth between her fingers she threw it onto the fire and watched it shrivel to nothing in the flames. She gloated at the power she had snared in her web, and searched beneath the folds of her skirt for a phial of clear liquid that would keep the marshman safe from the black spider's lethal bite.

As she found it she closed her fingers about the smooth crystal neck and bent closer to lick the skin behind Mertzork's ear. "This drop of spider's spittle will thicken your blood against their poison," she whispered, plunging the phial's tapered needle point deep into his neck and snapping it in two.

"It will keep you safe to do my bidding and spread the full measure of my revenge against Lord Mire-snare, and . . ." She paused, hunching her back against possible prying eyes and listening ears as she sealed the bleeding wound on his neck with a sharp pinch and twist of her fingernails. "And when your beast has trampled the champion Yaloor and Glitterspike Hall lies in ruins, Miresnare and his daughters shall stand before me begging for mercy. And that shall be the full payment for sparing your life, marshman."

From the depths of unconsciousness, Mertzork felt the sharp prick of the needle and the hot liquid burn through the numbness of his bones. It tingled in his veins and raced with a rich hotness into his fingertips. Far away he could hear the healing woman calling to him. She was whispering her secrets and urging him to be still. He blinked and opened his eyes then cried in terror as he saw the ground swaying beneath him and felt sticky threads of the cocoon that held him dangling from the low mantel beam. The horror of his capture flooded his mind. He twisted his head and screamed in panic, struggling frantically, but there was no escape from the black spiders that were scuttling down the cocoon towards his face.

"Be still and let the spiders scent and taste you," hissed Erek impatiently, stuffing a sticky tangle of webs into his mouth to stifle his screams.

Mertzork shuddered as he felt the soft coldness of their claws on his neck and he screwed his eyes tightly shut as they scuttled behind his ears, into his nose and across his eyelids down onto his shaven scalp. They were hurrying everywhere, their fangs needling his skin with a thousand tingling bites.

The healing woman whispered something over him and the spiders vanished as silently as they had come. Now he was revolving slowly, Erek was rhyming and singing, then spinning him faster and faster above the firestone. Mertzork tried to shake his head, he was dizzy and desperate for breath. He opened his eyes and struggled to spit out the choking tangle of web from his mouth.

Erek saw his eyes open, shouted her laughter in the flickering firelight and tore the webs away from his face, quickly pinching his lips into a silent line. Rocking backwards and forwards she teased the sticky threads away from the cocoon and called to the marshman, "Be still or the threads will snag." Muttering to herself, she attached the loose ends of the cocoon around the prickly spines of a live hedgehog that lay squealing in her hands. Twisting the thread she deftly wound it about the hedgehog's body, drawing it tight as if it were a spindle.

Mertzork tried to shut his eyes against the dizziness as he felt the threads loosen and unravel from around his heels. Kicking out he fell heavily beside the fire-stone and sprawled forwards. He pulled himself shakily to his knees, and crouching back pressed himself against the warm chimney wall, his blood pounding in his ears, and sat fearfully watching the healing woman tie off the last strand of sticky thread around the ears of the hedgehog.

Looking up, Erek smiled at him, her lips drawn back across a row of wet empty gums, and she thrust the hedgehog firmly into his hands whispering, "Go back to the Hurlers' Gate. There set the hedgehog on the ground and it will find you the quickest secret road to the doors of Glitterspike Hall. But follow it quickly before the warmth of the sun melts away the gossamer thread."

Mertzork hesitated, afraid to close his fingers on the sharp hedgehog spines and shrank away from the healing woman. "What do you know of my search for a secret path to the doors of Glitterspike Hall?" he asked, his eyes narrowing at what she might have stolen from his mind while he hung helplessly trapped in her cocoon.

Erek threw her head back and shrieked with laughter. "I know everything!" she hissed, hooking a fingernail beneath his jerkin collar and roughly pulling him out of the chimney stack. "Everything from the sharp-wire that tightened treacherously around your father's throat to your first foolish footstep into the webs that hid my doorstone. I have listened at your ear and drawn out all your darkest whisperings."

— *69* —

"Why do you not kill me then and use what I have found to win the joust yourself?" he cried in confusion, knowing that every marshlord in the beasting pits beyond the city would have cut his throat to call Gallengab his own.

Erek smiled, shaking her head, and pushed him towards a low footstool beside the firestone and motioned him to sit. "I could no more set the beast loose in Glitterspike Hall than you could cast spells or weave webs, especially as I am a woman. Selfish greed is the greatest weakness amongst you marshmen and that is what feeds the power that Lord Miresnare has over you. No, for us both to succeed we must use each other's strength."

"But why?" whispered Mertzork. "Why should you help me to win the joust?"

Erek leaned forward and hunched her shoulders, listening to the empty silence beyond her doorstone. She remembered that long-forgotten rush of footsteps, the shouts and screams and the clash of steel as Lord Miresnare and his murderous guards swept down through the healing houses in the Shambles searching at sword point for magic to spawn an heir. She shivered as she saw again the splintering doorpost and the monstrous shape of his anger spilling its black shadow of fear across her threshold. He had snatched her beloved baby boy from his cradle webs and had carried him aloft demanding to know his name, mocking her weakness and her feeble magic. He had laughed as he told her that since she could not help him he would keep the child to dance within his circle of mumbling men.

Boiling with rage she told the marshman how Mire-snare had driven all the healing women out of the city to perish in the melting quickmire and had ordered the hurlers at the gates to keep them out. Mertzork gasped and leant closer to the magic woman hanging onto every word that fell from her lips. He asked her how they had managed to re-enter the city.

Erek laughed quietly, her eyes flickering in the fire-light. "We watched and waited, strengthening our healing arts, and then one by one, in secret, we passed through the Hurlers' Gate. Some disguised them-selves, as you did, some wove silken webs across the hurlers' eyes, and some . . ." Erek paused and chuck-led, swallowing back her secrets. "It is enough to have tasted my hatred, Mertzork, and the shadows have grown long while you feasted on it. Now, follow the setting sun out through the Hurlers' Gate and hurry Gallengab to the Allbeast Feast but beware—you must not arrive too late."

Mertzork rose to his feet, the hedgehog held care-fully between his fingertips. "Is there magic in this hedgehog spindle?" he asked and then looked down at the thick silken web that almost hid the marsh-wader's face. "What of him?"

"We must eat," Erek cackled, pushing him over the doorstone and showing him the way down through the Shumbles, whispering to him to follow the wheel-wright's groove on the left-hand side of each lane until he reached the city gates. And then she whispered, "There will be strong magic in all we do to topple Lord Miresnare."

The mumblers' chants and the shrill rattle of their windbells had faded into the evening silence. The leaping shadow phantoms of their dance had long dimmed with the passing hours, even the lingering pine-oil scent of their foresight had faded.

Marrimian, wearied of her overwatching, paused beneath the servers' low door arch and turned her head away from the clatter of the kitchens. She heard a new and unfamiliar noise and frowned. The ring of iron hammers and the sharp tap of masons' chisels echoed from the far end of the great hall. She hurried out, darting past ragmen who still slid backwards and forward across the hall, and stared open-mouthed up at the gilded columns and the huddle of stone setters who were moving the huge iron rings that held the mudbeasts securely along the outer wall before the joust. The rings were being moved into a tight circle around her champion beast, Yaloor.

What was happening? If there were changes Lord Miresnare's first-born was always the last to know. Biting her lip in hurt and anger Marrimian turned to the ragmen, but they had vanished, gliding noiselessly past her into the maze of dimly lit corridors on their polish-soaked rags.

Marrimian muttered impatiently to herself as she hurried through the great hall, only to stop abruptly, her lips moving noiselessly as she stared at the empty polished stones where the long eating boards had previously been hammered into place, ready for laying. They had all been moved.

"By Yaloor's claws! Who has dared to tamper with my overwatching?" she cried, her fingers clenching and unclenching helplessly at all the changes that had been taking place while she had been guiding the scullions. The ragmen had reappeared to glide around the gilders' rickety thong-bound ladders, without an upward glance at the long-fingered craftsmen brushing fine leaves of crackling gold and silver onto the fluted stone columns.

Gathering speed Marrimian ran forward, her skirt hem billowing out behind her, scattering the servers with their piles of freshly baked trenchards and pushing her way through the patterns of gliding ragmen until she halted breathlessly before the Glitterspike.

"Who ordered this chaos?" she shouted, making a startled stone setter drop his chisel. He bowed to her.

"Lord Miresnare, your father, my lady. He showed us where to reset the iron rings."

"But why, tell me?" she asked through tight lips.

"We know not, my lady, our task is but to serve the master of all Gnarlsmyre," answered another of the dusty masons pointing with the handle of his blunt iron hammer respectfully past the beast, Yaloor, to the stooping figure of Lord Miresnare who was pacing backwards and forwards, pausing only to peer anxiously out of the windows.

"By your father's orders we are to reset the iron rings, before the dawn of the Allbeast Feast . . ."

"Father," she cried, cutting short the mason's explanation and turning. Yaloor roared and bellowed softly to her as she ran towards him. Frowning she slowed and watched the beast sink down onto his haunches with a rattle of his armoured hide. She took a cautious step between the iron rings, whispering and soothing the beast with reminders of secrets they had shared, and Yaloor lowered his head and scented her hand. "Well, at least someone here is true to me," she sighed, scratching her fingers through the coarse tangle of his hide. Looking up she stared at her father, her mind full of confusion, her eyes blinded with helpless tears.

Lord Miresnare sensed her near him and looked at her with blank eyes, a half-smile touching the corners of his mouth as if he would speak to her. But he turned away and continued his endless pacing in the window recess muttering to himself in a long-forgotten chant.

"Father! It is I, Marrimian, your first-born," she hissed, running to him and shaking his sleeve to make him stop and listen to her. He paused mid-stride, blinked and turned towards her.

"There is no time for idle chatter, daughter, no time at all," he said irritably, recognizing her and raising a gnarled hand to brush her aside. "No time now to waste on the daughters of Glitterspike Hall."

"Father!" she cried again, stepping in front of him and firmly gripping on to both of his sleeves to stop him pacing around her. "What was it in the mumblers' dance of foresight that has made you move the rings? What awful thing have they foretold that has turned you against me?"

Lord Miresnare laughed harshly, fidgeting to be free of her. "You have done nothing but be born a woman. Now be gone and leave me what little time I have before the new sun brings the marshlords cla-

mouring at my doors," he snapped, trying to turn away.

Marrimian paled, her lips thinning into a determined line, and hung on grimly to his sleeves. "What did the mumblers foretell that has made you change all my preparations?"

Lord Miresnare sighed at the pleading in her voice and felt himself shrink a little, wearied by the weight of the mumblers' foresight. He leaned forward letting his chin rest for a moment on the top of her neatly plaited firegold hair and whispered, "Yaloor will be defeated, girl, that is what the mumblers foretold. The days of the joust for your hand are over. They foretold that my throne and all that I rule now stands as if set upon the frozen quickmire waiting for tomorrow's hot sun of change to melt its treacherous crust. I cannot stop the marshlords from demanding the joust but to try to survive their onslaught without a male heir the joust must be changed into a game, a direct quest for my throne."

Marrimian trembled at her father's words and made to answer, when she felt him stiffen and pull away from her as if ashamed of sharing with her his secrets, his fears. Looking up she saw his eyes harden and turn to look down towards the beasting pits.

"I will carry your secrets as well as any man, and I will help you to defend the throne," she whispered, searching out his hand and squeezing it tightly. "Tell me what I must do and I will fight as bravely as any son."

"No!" snapped Lord Miresnare. The moment of sharing had passed as quickly as a cloud covering the sun. There had been no place in the mumblers' foresight for his daughters, not one word had touched on their fates. They were of no consequence. He stared at Marrimian again and flexed his hands to push her away, but then hesitated, his face softening, his mouth wrinkling into a smile as the seeds of an idea grew in his mind. Perhaps he could use this daughter to help him change the joust. Drawing her close he bent forward and brushed his lips against her ear.

"Tomorrow's feast must dazzle the marshlords. They must not see the changes in his hall nor guess that I know that they have snared a beast to match Yaloor until I have all their mudbeasts securely chained around the base of the Glitterspike. Now if they were to see you robed in your finest gown you could lead them forward through the hall. You could dance, or do anything to distract them, but make them bring their mudbeasts to these iron rings."

"What would you have me do?" she gasped. "Parade my womanhood in front of these men? I am your firstborn. I have my honour to consider."

Lord Miresnare laughed cruelly and pinched her wrist as he pivoted her to face the high throne. "First- or second-born makes no difference, girl, one of you must bait the trap. You are only a daughter—not an heir. If you will not do it I will use one of my other useless daughters."

Marrimian felt his words cut into her heart and she nodded, unable to speak for fear of crying. She backed against the window arch, her legs buckling beneath her with hurt and terror, her knuckles white-clenched on the fretted stonework to keep from falling as her father's cruelty echoed in her head. She tried to swallow her anger and fight back the urge to tell him how she had always loved him, no matter what he said or did, that she would rather stand and die beside him defending the hall than be used as a lure, but instead the vision came to her of the marshlords swarming through the hall, screaming and lustfully shouting for her, and she swallowed her words. She turned her eyes and asked in a trembling voice for how long she must lure the marshlords, before the mudbeasts were chained to the iron rings and she could flee to the safety of the daughtery. But her father had moved on, immediately forgetting her as he strode away with his cloak tails billowing out behind him. He snapped his fingers and called the lampwicks about him, telling them to fill the lower hall with blazing light that would reflect all the beauty of the gilders' craft but to leave the high galleries of the great hall, where he would place six companies of archers, in shadowy darkness.

* * *

Pinvey, trailing Alea behind her, spent most of the daylight hours cursing Marrimian and muttering that they would all become dried-up old hags before real men were allowed anywhere near them. No matter where they wandered through the echoing halls or sunlit courtyards, or which twist or turn they took in the endless gloomy corridors, they could not escape from the preparations for the joust, and it rankled and fed Pinvey's hatred to see all this bustling activity squandered on her elder sister. Alea became worse

than a sore that she would not scratch with her constant gigglings and whisperings of what she would let
the marshmen do to her, and Pinvey, tired of her vir-
ginal boasting, lured her into a little-used courtyard
overgrown with bramble weeds and creepers of
twistleaf and tricked her into peering into a darkened
windowless storeroom where, she whispered, the hoemasters slept naked on piles of old hemp sacks. While
Alea craned on tiptoe at the doorstone Pinvey tripped
her up and thrust her through the doorway, bolting
the heavy liftlatch. Turning her back on the screams
she ran without stopping to the secret chamber that
the benchers and flesh gutters had shown her.

Pinvey paused for breath after her long climb to the
top of the darkened spiral steps and felt with her fingernails for the narrow doorslit. Scratching at the
grainy wood she prised it open, ducked her shoulders,
and squeezed into the dark secret cubbyhole. A secret
place that still held the dizzy scent of those dangerous
wild nights when she had eaten the roasted flesh of
pindafalls and drunk strong wine and rolled on the
soft couches with man after man, stealing the knowledge of the world beyond the doors of Glitterspike
Hall as they lay with her. It was a place of whisperings
and secrets high above the darkened galleries. Kneeling, she pulled the door shut behind her and listened,
tilting her head from side to side and letting the noises
of the hall below soak into her. She held her breath
and craned her neck. There were voices drifting up
from the window recess; she could hear hurried whispers every time the stone setters rested their hammers.

"Marrimian!" she hissed, baring her teeth in hatred

as she caught the sound of her sister's voice whispering, pleading, trying to coax something out of their father.

Creeping silently forward she stumbled over the sharp bones of a discarded pindafall carcass that she had once gorged with the benchers and spat out a curse beneath her breath as she rubbed the ragged cut on her knee. She felt forwards, pushing aside the loose trinkets and sparkles that she had stolen at every unguarded opportunity until she touched the stone wall and found the narrow opening that served her as a spy hole to watch the hall below. Settling on her heels she pressed her ear against the window and listened.

"No more joust?" she muttered, frowning as she caught snatches of her father's voice and the soft rustle of Marrimian's skirts as the sounds drifted up to her. Turning her head she listened and heard him tell Marrimian that she must help him trick the marshlords.

Squatting back and resting her elbows on the prickly strips of mudbeast hide that littered the low couches lining the cubbyhole Pinvey stared down into the great hall and thought of the snatches of words that she had heard, realizing with despair that if there were to be no more jousts then the marshlords would never see her nor claim her as their own. Miserably she tried to listen to her sister's voice and hated her all the more for her whispering closeness with their father, remembering all too clearly how he had shunned them all, pushing them aside as weak prettier—in favour of Marrimian, she believed, Marrimian the first-born, Marrimian the beautiful, the clever, the . . . Pinvey clenched her fists and bit on her whitened knuckles, tasting her own hot salty blood as the hateful anger boiled through her.

"Parade my womanhood?" rose Marrimian's cry from the hall below, cutting through Pinvey's hatred and making her sit forward in the darkness of the cubbyhole and strain to catch every word and whisper that could be twisted to her advantage.

She started to laugh, thinking of Marrimian almost naked before the marshlords, her knees locked together in terror, her hands across her breasts in fear of what they might do to her, and almost gave herself away, but caught the sound on her lips, strangling it back into her throat. Their father looked angry, his eyebrows drawn together. He kept rubbing his hands then, wringing the hem of his cloak between his fingers as if trying to wash away something that displeased him, he hurried away across the hall.

Pinvey licked at the drying blood on her lips and tried to thread together all that she had overheard. Frowning she drew her lips back across her teeth in a mirthless smile, remembering how Marrimian had always hated the joust and had called the marshlords and all those who filled the hall at the Allbeast Feast by the foulest names. And now she was being commanded by their father to parade in revealing clothes before them. But why?

Of course. It was obvious. The first-born was to have the choice of the marshlords, perhaps the only choice there would be now that her father was stopping the joust. "Marrimian the clever," she snarled, her mouth pinched into a mean wrinkle of hatred, but she hesitated. There must be a way of using the secrets that she had overheard.

Rising silently she felt for the pindafall carcass and unknotted the long thin greasy cords that had held the bird on the roasting spit. They were charred and stiffened with the bird's juices and crackled between her fingers as she looped and hid them beneath her skirts. Ducking through the doorslit she hurried down the spiral steps and began to plan how she could snatch Marrimian's place and strut before the marshlords herself. She reached the bottom step and halted, her ear pressed against the heavy tapestry that hung across the entrance to the secret stairway. She listened to the sound of the ragmen's gliding feet and the heavy bumping of the lampwicks' reed baskets as they moved from lamp to lamp calling out the night-time hours as they trimmed the wicks and set the marshdamp, slow-burning reeds to light the frozen hours.

Pinvey pushed the tapestry a finger's span away from the hidden stairway, looked out and then slipped silently out along the gloomy corridor, passing through a little-used archway into the great hall. Pausing, she gathered her brightly coloured skirts into a bunch and hid them beneath a dark night-spun cloak that hung about her shoulders. She smiled and her teeth flashed in the lamplight as she moved into the darkness below the overhanging galleries where her cloak hid her from prying eyes, and she watched Marrimian, shadowing her every move. She waited, counting out the night-time hours as her sister overwatched the final preparations for the Allbeast Feast, setting the long eating boards, smoothing the gilders' final brushstrokes and rearranging everything to suit their father's schemes.

Pinvey knew she must be patient, but she was sure that she would trap Marrimian alone before the new sun thawed the frozen quickmire heralding the morning of the Allbeast Feast. Then fading footsteps and tired laughter made her start awake and shrink back into the shadows beneath the galleries. Muttering she cursed herself for dreaming when she should have kept her eyes open. She searched the hall, only to see Marrimian despatching her kitchen scum through the archway to the kitchens. She hurried across the empty hall on quick tiptoes, loosening the loops of cord beneath her skirt.

Marrimian yawned and stretched her arms, flexing her fingers and bending her aching back. The sound of the scullions' voices grew fainter. Alone at last she could turn her tired footsteps towards the daughtery and sleep what remained of the frozen hours in her soft feather bed. All the preparations for the Allbeast Feast were just as her father had commanded, but she would never have needed to overwatch so many preparations if she had had the help of her sisters. She sighed, wishing that Pinvey and Alea had offered their help as she turned towards her chamber, and heard the rattle of the night wind against the tall casement window arches as it spread new layers of rime ice in brittle feather-edged patterns across the crystal.

Marrimian shivered and drew her cloak collar tightly about her shoulders, casting uneasy eyes back into the gloomy emptiness of the great hall. Something had nagged at her throughout these last few hours, as though a shadow was dogging her footsteps. Often she had turned or looked over her shoulder but amongst the bustle she had dismissed her uneasiness, thinking that it was nothing more than the fear of what tomorrow might unfold. But now that she was alone, every creak and whisper of the wind, every grumble of the settling stones of Glitterspike Hall seemed to be shouting a warning, picking at her nerve strings. Marrimian stopped midstride and turned her ears to the silence, and there it was again, as persistent as a leaking gutter dripping onto mossy stones, a half-heard echo of hidden footfalls that always tailed off into silence moments after she stopped.

Marrimian spun around, her eyes narrowed, half in fear and half in anger, but the corridor was empty, nothing moved in the flickering lamplight, nothing save the trembling fabric of an old heavy tapestry that swayed where it hung from the rough stone wall, tugged by icy night draughts.

"Who follows in my footsteps?" Marrimian called, retracing a dozen strides towards the hall, stopping beside the tapestry and putting her hand out to feel the texture of the ancient threads.

The tapestry moved at her touch, suddenly billowing out as if it had arms, and engulfed her. She staggered backwards with a cry of terror as something forced the thick tapestry threads across her mouth, stifling her cry. Stinging cords were looped with burning tightness around her hands and she was bundled forward into a dark hole. A voice hissed at her ear to be silent as a passing lampwick called out the hour. Sharp nails scratched across her face, prising her mouth open, and spiteful fingers forced a knotted scarf between her teeth.

"Pinvey!" Marrimian choked through the scarf in surprise as she recognized her sister's voice in the darkness.

"Be quiet and climb those steps!" Pinvey hissed, prodding her towards the narrow spiral stairway. "Climb or I will slit your throat and leave you to rot here behind the tapestry."

Marrimian felt the sharp prick of a knife between her shoulder blades and scrambled forward, stumbling blindly on the steep stone spiral, skinning her knees and tearing the hem of her skirts before she reached the narrow doorslit and fell headlong, sprawling amongst the discarded bones.

Pinvey squatted down beside her, sneering, her face flushed and blotched with the ease of her triumph, and clawed roughly at Marrimian's hair as she pulled her up onto the low couch beneath the window hole and tied her ankles. "I know all your secrets," she hissed, drawing her lips back across her teeth and pointing with her blade down into the shadows of the great hall to where Yaloor growled and grumbled in the flickering lamplight that danced within the circle of new-set iron rings. "Yes, I know it all, the pleading and the wheedling to lure the marshlords with your womanhood, forcing our father to let you be the only one that they see." Pinvey laughed and rocked back on her heels. "But I am more cunning than you ever dreamed, sister. I have shadowed you, listened, watched, waited for the chance, and now my moment has come with the dawning of this new joust. It will be me, Marrimian, not you, who will parade and strut, showing the marshmen the delights of my body. It will be me who has the pick of these wonderful marsh-lords!"

Pinvey clapped her hands, gave a squeal of delight and thrust her face into Marrimian's. "Yes, sister, you will sit and look on helplessly from this secret chamber amongst the gnawed bones of my plotting as I steal your hopes and dreams."

Marrimian shook her head, her eyes wide and frantic as she tried to shout through the scarf and tell her sister the truth of what their father had asked her to do, but Pinvey laughed and pushed Marrimian's face against the window hole. Then she rose nimbly to her feet and skipped down the spiral stairway in shrieks of laughter. She must select her most revealing gown and trim it back for her wild dancing.

Mertzork knelt and waited, crouching in the shadow of the Hurlers' Gate just as the healing woman had forewarned. He must wait for the daylight to fade and the sun's hot searching eye to sink out of sight into the quickmire. Shutting out the noises of the city he turned his ear towards the gates and listened for the telltale sound of the crackling rime ice spreading its fingers across the treacherous marsh crust below the beasting pits. Faintly he could hear the frozen wind rattling in the reed grass and he knew that it would now be safe to slip out of the city into the gathering darkness.

He rose and passed silently between the watchers'

high chairs but foolishly he paused and turned to stare up at the hurlers and became trapped by their magic watching spell. They forced him to gaze at their shadow-wrapped forms. They were hunched forward as if they would topple from their chairs to smother him. Something moved near the gatehouse, a door opened spilling lamplight across the cobbles. The hurlers turned their nightblind eyes towards the light and the spell was broken. Mertzork blinked and ran as fast as he could towards the closing gates.

Angry voices called out behind him as archer guards crowded through the lighted doorway, arrows hissed and shrieked past his head. He ducked, squeezed through the gates and vanished into the growing darkness.

Moving from shadow to shadow, the sound of pursuit fading fast, he found his way down into the beasting pits. He followed the rising noise of the marshmen and the bellowing roars of the mudbeasts and breathed a sigh of relief as he blended in easily amongst the jostling crowds that thronged the narrow pathways between the beasting pits and lost himself in the groups of brawling marshhunters who were gambling on tomorrow's joust, throwing rough dice cut from pindafall bones. He coughed on the harsh smoke of the countless cooking fires as he made his way to the beginning of the quickmarsh, steering well clear of the marshhunters who had driven his miserable little mudbeast into its iron cage earlier that day.

He hurried downwards without a backward glance, careful to keep the healing woman's hedgehog spindle well hidden beneath his jerkin. He passed the last beast pit and now stood at the edges of the quick-marsh, shivering, wishing that he had planted the last rampon leaf closer to the edge of the quickmarsh. He loosened the iron spike from his belt and tested the depth and strength of the thickening ice. He knew that he dared not wait there until the crust had properly frozen. Time was his enemy; he had to trust to luck and try to run across the ice if he was to reach the trail of plants that he had used to waymark the path for the hunters driving Gallengab towards the city.

Taking a deep breath he sprang forward and raced across the thin ice, feeling it craze and fracture into spreading star patterns with each light tread. Ahead, black-etched against the night sky, rose a clump of marsh oaks, the trees groaning and creaking as the rime ice ground against their trunks, squeezing the rough bark into smooth growth rings above the marsh crust.

Mertzork began to flounder. He cursed his earlier haste and wished that he had remembered to weave the thick marshbindings between his toes, splaying them out to run across thin ice, but now it was too late for that. The sticky cold mud was oozing, bubbling up and clinging onto his feet; he was sinking deeper and deeper, his strides were slowing. Desperately he reached up and snatched at the overhanging branches, feeling his fingers slide against the brittle, finger-fine, ice-covered twigs, only to hear them snap and feel a shower of stinging icicles scatter over his closely shaven head. He was sinking, helplessly, lost and alone in the frozen darkness.

"No! You will not take me!" he shouted at the bubbling mud, striking out with his hands at the unbroken ice that stretched out all about him. "No!" he cried desperately as the edges of the ice snapped off at his touch and the thick cold mud began to suck him down.

The hedgehog squealed and wriggled beneath his jerkin, scratching at his skin, making him remember the healing woman. "Find me a way over the ice!" he urged, unclipping the animal and reaching forward in the oozing mud to push the tiny creature as far as he could out onto the unbroken ice. Just in time he remembered to clutch the end of the gossamer thread.

The hedgehog sniffed the darkness and scuttled in a small circle before it ran out away from the clump of marsh oaks towards a single tree that grew in the centre of the marsh.

"That way is madness. There is nothing but half-frozen mud and liquid pools of quicksand that will never freeze hard enough to hold my weight," he shouted after the vanishing hedgehog.

But in desperation he waded forward, following the gossamer thread that shone in the darkness and sinking deeper with each slow floundering step. The mud was up above his waist, freezing him with its heavy coldness. He wanted to scream, to shout, to cry out for help, to call on the healing woman to pull him out of the quickmire, but he swallowed his panic and struck out though he sank faster with each movement. Just as the quickmarsh reached his chest he felt something solid beneath his toes. Hope leaping in his heart, he forced his other foot to follow and hung on desperately to the thread as he felt his way up onto the tangle of marshoak roots that had grown out beneath the quickmire on a ledge of honeycombed rocks submerged in the frozen marsh.

Slowly and with heavy dragging feet he edged along the roots and felt the pull of the cold mud lessen. The surface of the ice around the tree became strong enough to take his weight and he hauled himself onto it. Laughing with relief he knelt on the ice. He called the hedgehog back to him and did his best to rewind the spider's thread around its prickly body, hiding the animal once more beneath his jerkin. He patted the spine-sharp bundle whispering, "What strong magic I have!" before he bent to the task of reweaving the marshrags between his toes.

This done he climbed to his feet, flexing his toes and brushing the stinking marshmire off his clothes. Fortunately the tight-sewn beastskins kept out the wet and the cold. He stepped cautiously onto the thickening ice, leaving the safety of the marsh oak and its tangled trail of roots behind him. The fourth season's moon had risen clear of the forest of tall broken reed stems and cast its shimmering silver light across the frozen mire. He turned and saw the bright lights of Glitterspike Hall and the endless ribbons of lights of the city woven between the steep weatherbeaten rocks that crowded below it, and he swore that he would soon take all of it for his own. Then he hunched his shoulders and hurried forward, searching for the last slender spearleaf rampon cutting he had secretly planted. He found it easily enough, ghost-white in the moonlight, spreading its black shadow across the frost-glittering ice.

From rampon leaf to rampon leaf, for hour after hour, he traced the twisting path that he had way-marked far out across the quickmire.

Then, far beyond his sight, still masked in deepest shadows he thought he could hear the scraping of Gallengab's claws and the thunderous roar of his voice and his footsteps quickened. He called out against the silence, urging his father's marshhunters who drove the beast to hurry, for marsh mist was rising and morning would overtake them before they reached the rocky outcrops below the beasting pits, and all would be lost.

Eventually, hideously huge against the starlight, its claws grinding the ice to powder, loomed Gallengab. Bellowing and straining against the iron chains that bound each leg he snarled and lunged forward at Mertzork, opening his reeking and cavernous mouth where strips of half-eaten rotting vegetation hung between his crowded razor fangs. He shook his hide, making the coarse ice-covered hair clatter like the sound of windbells, and lunged again.

Mertzork cursed and staggered backwards, out of the reach of those murderous claws as they scythed through the air above his head. He had forgotten how quickly the beast moved and how many marshhunters had fallen beneath his claws before they had snared him and shackled him with the thick bands of iron on each leg.

"My father, Mertz, curses your idleness and threatens to feed you all to Gallengab if you arrive too late and he misses the joust. Now move the beast faster!"

Mertzork shouted, angry that he had been so easily caught off-balance and made to look the fool.

Skirting the beast he lashed at the marshhunters' backs with his iron-tipped flail and drove them on as fast as they could run across the quickmarsh, cutting raw weals into their skin as the flail tore through their cloaks and underjerkins.

One of the marshhunters cried out as the flail stung his back and he stumbled, tripping over the chain that bound him to the beast. Gallengab felt the chain slacken and lunged at the falling hunter, hooking him up before his hands had touched the ice and crushing him between his claws.

"Faster! Faster! Or we will arrive too late," snarled Mertzork, pushing the nearest unfettered marshhunter forward to snatch up the loose snaking chain where it danced in a shower of frozen sparks across the ice. "Faster or I will feed you all to the beast and finish the journey on my own!"

Pulling and straining against the beast's chains they ran through the night hours, into thickening mists which covered their path. Deep reed banks loomed on either side, appearing suddenly out of the white blanket of fog. They were wandering blindly across the thawing quickmarsh, the ice softening, cracking and splintering in showers of fine icicles beneath Gallengab's weight.

"Faster, faster!" urged Mertzork, wielding the iron-tipped flail until the marshhunters' backs ran with blood.

He shrieked promise after promise in his father's name as their reward for bringing the beast safely to

Glitterspike Hall. His flail arm grew tired and his legs grew numb in their desperate race to reach higher ground before the hot new sun showed its burning rim above the horizon. Cursing he drove them relentlessly forward knowing that the great ridge of rocks, the crowded maze of city streets and the sheer walls of Glitterspike Hall must lie somewhere just ahead.

Suddenly the ice beneath them began to crumble, rough boulders of every shape and size slipped and twisted, loosened by their feet in the melting mud. They were amongst sparse clumps of marsh scrub and low bushes that dripped with beads of glistening mist. The ground was firmer, rising sharply into shifting banks of broken scree that slipped beneath their marshbound toes and made them stumble. Dense groves of marsh oaks loomed before them, their silent tangled branches arching high above their heads. Mertzork frowned and looked back towards the quickmarsh, searching the thickening blanket of grey swirling mist. This was not the way he had taken from the marsh's edge into the beasting pits; he had followed a broad, well-trodden, muddy road between high banks of petrified rock. The leading hunters were slowing the pace. They fanned out to left and right keeping the binding chains tightly apart to hold Gallengab safely between them as the beast snarled and tried to turn and claw at its captors.

Suddenly a sheer wall of rock reared up in front of them.

"Which way now?" shouted Faxiol, the master hunter, who had to step backwards quickly and crack a three-tailed whip at the beast as it reared up and scythed at the overhanging branches with its claws. He shouted at the unfettered hunters to throw their weight onto the chains to hold the beast steady, then pointed to Mertzork and said, "The way before us is blocked. Where are your father's waymarks?"

Mertork cursed beneath his breath, realizing that they were truly lost. He knew that he dared not show the marshhunters his indecision. They still thought that he was leading them to his father along a path he had marked. He could not retrace their footsteps across the mire because the ice crust was thawing. He must choose and seem sure of his purpose. He must choose the right direction or all his murderous schemes would come to nothing.

"Help me, healing woman, help me," he whispered, stepping back out of sight into the swirling mist and setting the hedgehog down onto the wet ground. Crouching, he watched which way it chose to scuttle and twice turned it to check before he rose.

"Follow the rock wall to the left. The waymarks must have withered, but that is the way to the beasting pits, I remember it clearly, and the wide road leads up to the Hurlers' Gate." He smiled secretly, gloating that he had such strong magic at his fingertips.

Bending he scooped up the prickly hedgehog and scratched its small pink ears and then quickly re-wound the sticky spider's thread that had become un-ravelled as the hedgehog searched out the path. Frowning, Mertzork tried to pull the untidy thread tighter but the hedgehog squeaked and scrambled in his clumsy hands and he hastily hid it beneath his jerkin and cracked his flail at the waiting marshhunters, urging them forward.

Skirting around the beast Mertzork ran ahead, half doubting the hedgehog's magic. He followed the sheer rock wall, keeping the fingertips of his right hand on the damp cold stone. The groves of trees were thinning and growing further from the path to leave narrow verges of short razor-sharp grass that cut through the cloth into the hard skin on his heels. Broken drystone walls lay across his path and sudden roaring waterspouts boiled arching out of the rock above his head to cascade in glistening icy showers onto the steep fields. Ravine sheep, startled by his coming, scattered through the broken walls, their bleating cries swallowed in the mist. Hill goats scrambled away as he approached, climbing magically up the sheer rock wall, the clattering of their brass bells vanishing in hollow echoes before he could blink the cold mist off his eyelashes. The ground became muddy with the dark heavy earth humped up into steep ridges and he felt as if he was treading across frozen waves as he climbed over them, trampling through neat rows of thick-leafed plants and strange shrub-like growths that seemed to sprout along the top of each ridge.

The dry-stone walls seemed to crowd closer. There were rickety branch-woven shelters hung with drying plants, handcarts, rough hemp sacks and tall baskets lying as if abandoned on the edges of the fields. Mertzork frowned and paused. He had never crossed so much firm ground before nor seen so many strange-leafed plants growing together. It was so different from the tumble of rocks and thin scrape of earth that

made up his father's marsheries. He watched the carts
and ran his fingers along the spokes of the wheels and
the weave of the baskets and he pulled the crinkly
purple-leafed roots out of the ground and bit into
them. Cursing he spat at the bitter taste and wondered
what sort of place he had stumbled upon. Behind him
he could hear the marshhunters driving Gallengab
over the stone walls and he hurried to keep before
them. The mist was thinning and swirling faster as
it dissolved beneath the heat of the morning sun; for
long moments now he could see the shimmering
spires of Glitterspike Hall and the steep-gabled roofs
of the city. The black pindafalls were soaring on the
warm currents of air and the rock wall was curving
away from him and descending through dense scrubland. Once the mist boiled apart and he caught a
glimpse of sparkling sunlight on water, slow meandering curves of water that wound between tall marsh
oaks, black ebony and pink bark trees. The mist began
to swirl but just before it closed about him again he
saw in the distance the high arches of the Hurlers'
Gate and the low choking haze of blue-grey cooking
smoke that hung above the beasting pits.

Mertzork laughed with relief and whistled through
his teeth. Now he could see the road to the Hurlers'
Gate he realized how dangerously far they had wandered from the path after they had passed the last rampon leaf in the dense marsh mist. "You have great
magic to have scented out our path," he whispered to
the hedgehog as he patted the sharp spines beneath his
jerkin, and began the steep ascent, following the rock

wall down through the scrubland to where he had glimpsed the water.

Now there was a clear, well-trodden path through thorn bushes that rose on either side to the height of his shoulders. He slowed as the scrubland gave way to tall black ebony trees and he stretched out his hands as he passed between them, and then gasped and snatched his hands back to his sides as they vanished into the velvety black shadows. Looking fearfully from side to side and afraid that the trees were spun with magic he ran out from beneath their low trailing branches. He jumped the deep-cut draining dykes as he skirted the bright pink barks that grew along the river and began to search amongst the more familiar marsh oaks for a bridge or a shallow place for them to cross. But the river looked deep and far too dangerous for the marshhunters to drive the beast across.

Muttering under his breath Mertzork scrambled down the steep bank, his feet sinking into the soft earth, and stared at the river. He frowned as he scratched at his dirty close-shaven head and watched the water swirling around a line of tall polished poles that rose at regularly spaced intervals across the width of the river. Searching in every corner of his mind he tried to guess their purpose.

Gallengab bellowed behind him and made him jump as a shower of loose earth from the bank above his head came crumbling down to splash into the river, sending widening ripples swirling away with the current. Faxiol cursed from somewhere amongst the trees and shouted at the marshhunters to keep to the firmer ground away from the steep banks until they reached the ford and then to follow the line of poles across the river. Mertzork laughed quietly to himself as he caught Faxiol's warning shout and ran splashing through the shallow water beside the bank to the beginnings of the ford, eager to hide his ignorance and make his father's hunters think that he knew the way. He still wanted them to believe that he was merely the messenger, the guide that was leading them by a secret road to the beasting pits. He forged his way across the river and almost fell headlong, stumbling forward in the ankle-deep water as he snagged his marshbound toes on the rough surfaces of the huge stone slabs that had been laid as a wide road just beneath the icy water. Spitting out a string of oaths he half limped, half ran with giant splashing strides, spraying the water up into plumes of icy droplets. He scrambled up the further bank and turned and shouted to the marshhunters, telling them how shallow the water was and urging them to hurry.

"Time runs away from us and we will arrive too late for the joust," he cried, glancing up anxiously at the sun that stood almost overhead. Gallengab lost his balance on the steep bank and slid into the water, bellowing and fighting against his captors, sending up fountains of white spray as he churned his way across the ford.

Mertzork cursed the hunters' slowness and passed on ahead of them through the grove of black ebonies that crowned the bank. He looked towards the Hurlers' Gate. The gateway still seemed so far away and the two watchers on the high inner walls looked no more than tiny specks, perched unmoving in their seats with the harsh sunlight reflecting two dazzling narrow lines from the silver-headed canes that lay across their knees. Searching the road between the gates his gaze fell on the long black shadows that darkened the ground beneath the hurlers' chairs. Cautiously he slipped out from the grove of ebonies and measured his own shadow in the sunlight and he cried out at the progress of the sun, fearing that darkness would have descended and the freezing night wind begun to turn and blow across the desolate quick-marshes, bringing with it the rancid smell of the beasting pits, long before they reached the Hurlers' Gate. Cursing and muttering to himself for losing the path in the mist he hurried forward, keeping close to the rockway as the sun dipped towards evening. Breathlessly he reached the gloomy shadows of the gates and turned his head to listen. The beasting pits were empty just as he had expected. All the mudbeasts had been driven up through the city to Glitterspike Hall. Even the narrow muddy pathways between the deep-set pits and the smaller cages were deserted. Children ran shouting somewhere down on the marsh edge and there were the sounds of the campfollowers and underhunters in the rough rock shelters but the sight of them was masked by the dense choking haze of cooking smoke.

Suddenly a mudbeast roared in the upper cages, echoing through the empty pits as it scraped and rattled its fetters on the bars. Marshhunters shouted at it and hammered with their iron spikes against its cage and Mertzork cursed his carelessness, remembering that they were still guarding the beast for him and were awaiting his return.

He crouched back into the shadows of the gate. They must not see him or cast suspicion on him by meeting the hunters who were driving Gallengab towards the gates for they were bound to ask for news of his father. Faxiol and the hunters must not doubt him, at least, not until they had passed through the gates and into the city. Gallengab bellowed and surged in zigzag leaps down the last steep slope beside the rock wall into the shadows of the Hurlers' Gate. Mertzork waited, his breath held in one stifled gulp behind tight lips until the beast loomed above him, shutting out the gloomy half-light, before he sprang out onto the road and turned the startled hunters with cutting strokes of his iron-tipped flail, driving them beneath the first high arches of the gates.

"Hurry!" he shouted. "My father will curse your slowness and is probably fretting, waiting before the doors of Glitterspike Hall."

The gate watchers were startled by Gallengab's roaring voice and they sprang to life in their high seats and tried to block his forward rush, crossing their long-handled silver canes across the entrance and calling to the marshhunters in piercing voices for the beast's name and why he had come so late into the city on Allbeast Feast, for it was their right and custom to know and count each beast that challenged Yaloor and it was necessary to enter their names in the book of jousts.

Faxiol frowned at the hurlers' cries and turned, blocking Mertzork's path with his feet planted firmly apart. "Your father would not have gone before us without so much as a whisper to the gate watchers or a name for them to scribe into the jousting book. How do you know that he waits before the doors of Glitterspike Hall?"

Running footsteps and voices calling Mertzork's name echoed closer in the upper levels of the beasting pits. He heard them and half turned, seeing all his plots and cunning lies begin to crumble to nothing. He ducked beneath Faxiol's hands and lashed out at the nearest marshhunter, catching him behind the knees with the sharp edges of the flail, sending him stumbling forward, tightening the chain that bound him to Gallengab. The other hunters jumped, straining on their own chains, and Gallengab began to lumber, roaring and snarling, beneath the second archway. Rearing up he clawed one of the hurlers from his chair, snapping his long-handled cane, and then dropped him screaming and crushed him into silence on the hard cobbles of the road within the city.

"Whose orders?" sneered Mertzork, taking Faxiol by surprise as he loosened the hidden sharpwire from his jerkin collar. He dropped it with a practised sweep over the master hunter's head and tightened it around his throat.

"*Mine* were the only orders," he snarled, dragging the helpless hunter backwards through the gateway, drawing the sharpwire tighter with each stride as he hauled him up towards the maze of lanes and alleyways before them.

"Which road shall we take?" cried a dozen frightened voices from around Gallengab as the marshhunters fought to hold him steady.

Mertzork stopped and spun round, letting the sharpwire loosen, and Faxiol fell forgotten onto the cobbles as Mertzork searched for the waymarkings that should show clearly which road led up to the doors of Glitterspike Hall. But there was no time to waste. Gallengab was surging forward, the hunters and the waders were crowding through the gate, though for the moment they hung back in fear of the beast. Mertzork cursed himself for not remembering what the waymark put out for the marshmen looked like. Then he remembered the hedgehog and unhooked it from beneath his jerkin. With quick fumbling fingers he set it carefully down on the ground in front of Gallengab.

"Go before us and find the fastest road to the doors of Glitterspike Hall," he whispered, giving the hedgehog a firm push and watching the small awkward bundle of gossamer thread scuttle and hop its way into the largest entrance leaving a clear trail of thread unravelling across the cobbles behind it.

"Follow the thread," Mertzork ordered turning to the marshhunters, but they hesitated, looking uneasily at the vanishing hedgehog and, whispering against the magic, began to edge backwards, pulling Gallengab across the cobblestones towards the gates.

Mertzork shouted at them and snatching the key to their shackles from Faxiol's belt he moved between them and the gates. Narrowing his eyes with murderous hate he loosened the iron spike and let the key dangle from his fingers. "You are bound by those chains to my beast and I hold the key to your freedom. Obey me and deliver Gallengab into Glitterspike Hall and you shall live. Turn against me and I will trip each one of you to fall beneath the beast's claws."

"Your father will skin you alive for this," choked Faxiol struggling to his knees.

Mertzork laughed and kicked at the stricken hunter. "My father is dead, and I claim his marsheries, this savage beast and all that was his."

Faxiol again tried to rise, whispering through his bruised throat, "Andzey is the oldest by two seasons. You are stealing his rights."

"Andzey is nothing!" hissed Mertzork, and cracking his flail at the marshhunters' heels gestured to them to follow the trail of gossamer up into the city.

Pausing, he crouched beside Faxiol and would have slit his throat but changed his mind. Sneering he leapt to his feet. "I shall spare your life, master hunter, so that you can search out my half-brother and tell him that I have snatched it all for myself—the throne, all the dry lands of Gnarlsmyre, this City of Glor and even the daughters of Glitterspike Hall shall all be mine while he wanders somewhere in the stinking quickmarsh, searching for a mudbeast fit for the joust."

Mertzork took one last fleeting look at the gates and the crowd of hunters and waders spilling through them, then turned on his heels and raced after Gallengab. "You will all kneel before me!" he shouted behind him as the darkness swallowed him up.

4

The Beasts are Snared Around The Glitterspike

*L*ORD Miresnare fretted and picked at the silver scrolls fine-laced with golden threads that decorated the hem of his jousting gown and paced anxiously back and forth across the smooth-polished stones of the great hall. Ragmen silently followed his every step, buffing away the scuffs and scrapes left by his iron-shod boots, careful not to impede their lord as they glided backwards, bowing their way out of his path each time he turned.

"What if they sense that I know of the beast that can defeat Yaloor?" Miresnare muttered, clutching at the collar of one clumsy ragman who had failed to move quickly enough, and towing him backwards across the hall. "What if these marshlords hesitate as they rush into the hall and look for the places where they chained their beasts four seasons ago?"

"Lord," the ragman cried, his feet slipping as he overbalanced, his thin collar tearing through Lord Miresnare's fingers as he fell sprawling onto the floor.

"Silence, you fool!" shouted Lord Miresnare, angry at the interruption and pushing him roughly aside and trampling on him. He swept his doubting gaze across all his preparations, looking for a fault or something he might have overlooked in the hurry of the night before. And realized for the first time the extent of the pomp and splendour that surrounded him.

He had to shade his eyes against the dazzle from the gold and silver reflecting in the sunlight. Yes, an excellent job, enough to disorientate the rough and ready marshmen. He had rewarded the gilders with sweetmeats to please their prettiers and two leather pouches of sparkles for each of them. He smiled, and turned his attention to the polished floorstones, touching them with the tip of his boot, for they had the look of frozen water and shimmered in the sunlight streaming through the crystal windows, reflecting pools of gold and silver from the dazzling columns. The long eating boards were laid ready for the feast, set with the most beautiful crystal goblets and brimming jugs of potent sweet liquor to tempt a thousand thirsty marshmen.

There was nothing, nothing he had overlooked or forgotten. Laughing, he turned towards the Glitterspike and cast his eyes over the shimmering richness of its heartstone and the shadowy veins of liquid silver. He looked past the champion beast, Yaloor, and to the throne itself. But the dais before the throne was empty, there was no clash of bright colour, no alluring centrepiece to his dazzling show. There should be whispered music and a soft gliding form with painted lips to lure the marshmen forward. Marrimian had deserted him at this one moment when her womanhood had any worth at all.

Suddenly, before he had any time to call her name

in anger, he heard violent shouts and the hammering of iron spikes on the doors. Mudbeasts roared, causing a pandemonium of frightened cries and barking dogs. Lord Miresnare cursed Marrimian beneath his breath and stole a final glance towards the empty dais as he raised his hand to signal his doorwardens to fling open the doors and allow the Allbeast Feast to begin. Then, out of the corner of his eye he saw a lithe, shimmering figure run to the throne.

"Pinvey?" he half whispered in surprise as he saw her, her face a mask of vivid colour, her body only half clad in a translucent golden gown that clung in liquid ripples to every voluptuous curve as she swayed in a hypnotizing, sensuous dance across the dais. The mouth of every serving man was hanging open in lust and amazement. Lord Miresnare laughed with relief and let his raised hand fall. A rush of marshlords spilled through the higharched entrance into the hall in a thunder of shouting voices. They had been shouting and cursing amongst themselves, squabbling to gain the best iron rings to chain up their beasts. But now they fell silent in wonder, gazing at the splendour around.

At a sign from her father Pinvey began to sing, magic songs of lust her lovers had taught her, and danced her sinuous dance. Every marshman's eye was on her, mudbeasts and joust forgotten. Her heavy scent filled the air, dulling their minds with desire.

Lord Miresnare laughed again, his fears dissolving as he hastily stepped back from the rush of oncoming beasts lumbering across the hall. He whispered

harshly to his hallwardens, who tore their eyes away
from Pinvey and rushed after the beasts.

Holding a silk corner of his gown stuffed with
sweet-smelling primrose leaves to his nose against the
choking stench of the mudbeasts and unwashed
marshmen, he watched, nodding with satisfaction
each time a hallwarden caught a mudbeast and drove
the twisted locking pins down through the heavy
marsh-rusted chains it wore to the new circle of iron
rings around Yaloor. He had cast his eyes quickly over
the beasts, assessing their strength, but there was none
chained within the circle that could defeat Yaloor.
From the huge scaly wallowers whose armour rose in
prickly spines and who balanced on twelve-toed,
curved-clawed feet to the small savage grey-striped,
razor-spined clactors that hissed and spat boiling
venom across the polished stones—there was none
that matched the phantom of the mumblers' foresight.
Stepping back from the milling throng Lord Miresnare signalled to Pinvey with a twist of his hands to
dance faster. She must keep the marshscum's rapt attention until this beast from the mumblers' magic had
entered the hall and been safely chained within the
circle.

Pinvey spun fast and faster, swinging her hips,
wriggling her stomach, stroking her full breasts, making the hoard of marshmen cluster towards her. She
laughed triumphantly, the sound echoing above the
mooing of the tamed beasts, and she stretched out her
arms as if beckoning the marshlords to her. She began
to ease her gown to slip voluptuously from her shoulders and shivered with delight as she heard them gasp

at the soft white swell of her breasts. Possessed by lust and licking her lips she urged the marshmen to draw closer.

Suddenly the silence was broken as the marshmen swayed and moved as one towards the dais, their voices rising lustfully.

Lord Miresnare watched them surge forward and shouted a warning as the edges of the crowd pressed too close to Yaloor. Yaloor roared and charged at them, his heavy chain snaking tight behind him as he snatched at the nearest marshman and crushed his chest beneath his claws, then hurled the screaming man against the wall of the great hall.

Pinvey's spell was broken and Lord Miresnare seized her roughly and pulled her to safety. The shackled beasts bellowed across the circle and collided with one another as they rushed the full length of their chains, clawing at their former masters who hastily retreated in horror.

Gathering together as they had never done before, their faces grim with startled anger, the marshlords began to advance step by step towards the Glitterspike, but they were hesitant and they muttered in uncertain whispers. Their eyes searched everywhere at once, blinking at the gilded splendour. They craned their necks to peer into every shadow for fear of new traps that Lord Miresnare might have set against them. He had never in all the jousts tried to lure them into Yaloor's claws with a daughter's beauty, nor changed the position of the rings. In that moment of uneasiness they saw they were defenceless—their host had stolen their beasts.

With rising anger they advanced on the dais where Lord Miresnare stood, sharpwires and daggers ready beneath their beastskin cloaks.

"Not one more step!" thundered Lord Miresnare seeing their ugly hatred, and pointing an urgent finger up into the darkness of the high galleries he shouted to the lampwicks. A string of lamps appeared aloft revealing a guard of bowmen. The flickering light threw their long shadows across the hall reflecting on two hundred steel arrow blades ready trained on the marshmen below.

"They are master archers, every one of them, and they can reload their bows before you can blink an eyelid. I could kill you all if that was my purpose, and leave your carcasses on the high roofs of this hall for the pindafalls to strip clean. None would mourn you here."

Lord Miresnare paused. His eyes fell on Pinvey who, furious that the stampeding mudbeasts had distracted and scattered the marshlords, was shedding her gown of gold. Quickly he beckoned a hallwarden to cast his cloak over her nakedness and remove her from the hall. He sent another to fetch Naul with all speed. Turning back to the marshlords he smiled, but his eyes were hard and without humour. "If any one amongst you so much as moves or blinks an eye my bowmen will kill you."

Looking up he gave a secret signal and his master bowman loosed an arrow sending up a shower of stone chippings as it buried its blade a finger deep in the stone floor at the feet of one of the marshhunters. In the terrified silence they all watched as the hallwarden bundled a struggling Pinvey towards a low archway beneath the galleries. Her voice was raised in shrieks of anger as they disappeared.

"Women are a curse," Miresnare muttered as he turned back towards the marshlords. "No more will my first-born be for barter with the blood of your beasts." Then with a set face he began to tell them of the new game for his throne. "Nor will the land of Gnarlsmyre be her dowry," he cried as he passed through the crowd of stunned marshlords with a measured step and he smiled as he saw them part and shrink away from him as he spoke. "Now there is a different game—" and he took his place at the head of the long eating boards, where his servers had now filled the cups.

He lifted his crystal toasting goblet in his right hand and paused, turning impatient eyes towards the low archstone that led directly from the mumblers' cell. He breathed a sigh of relief as Naul appeared, the sharp scent of his pine oil lamp fogging the archway and wafting into the hall. The sound of the windbells on the hems of his saffron robes clattered in the uneasy silence as he ran across the hall and bowed before his master.

"Where is the phantom beast of your foresight?" Miresnare hissed in the mumbler's ear. "I cannot hold the truth of this new joust for my throne for much longer. I must start the feast."

Naul pulled away from his master. Whispering a magical chant he ran lightly on his toes amongst the still marshlords, scenting at their rancid robes and listening at their ears for word or rumour of the beast.

Passing back through the marshmen his pine-oil lamp swinging in a smoky blaze of flame, he danced out beneath the high archway and ran two dozen leaping strides down the echoing passageway that led by twists and turns to the open doors and the fading sunlight. There he listened to the sounds of the rime ice crackling as it began to form across the quickmire far beyond the noise of the city. He nodded, satisfied. Then he returned to the hall.

"Well? What do they know of the beast?" hissed Lord Miresnare catching hold of Naul's wrists as he danced his way to his master's feet.

Naul laughed and threw his head back, letting the smoke of his lamp envelop them both in a swirling blanket of secrecy. "Nothing, my Lord, these marshmen know nothing of the phantom beast that reared up in the dancing circle. They are ignorant of its snaring and came at this full season's end only to joust for your first-born's hand."

"Then it is you who have woven false magic with your phantom beasts and hideous shapes within the dancing circle. You who have tricked me for some secret purpose into making these changes!" hissed Lord Miresnare, his hands tightening about the master mumbler's throat.

"Lord, Lord, I can take no advantage of what the dance foretells, my task is only to show you what will come to pass. There *is* a beast. I heard its roar out there beyond the city's edge. It is getting closer with every grain of sand that trickles through the hourglass."

Lord Miresnare eased his grip on Naul's throat and rubbed his watering eyes, waving away the thick pine-oil smoke. "Could it flounder and be lost in the quick-mire? Could it lose its way up through the city?" he asked in a hurried whisper, shaking the mumbler.

Naul shrugged his narrow shoulders helplessly. "My power can only foretell what will come to pass, but you have moved the iron rings and claimed the marshlords' mudbeasts. It will not lose its way nor flounder. What has begun cannot be changed. It is the future now."

Lord Miresnare let the mumbler slip from his grasp and stepped backwards out of the swirling smoke. His gaze swept across the throng of uneasy marshlords and hunters who were growing impatient and seemed to have forgotten the archers in the galleries as they edged towards him. Each one of them felt swelling anger to have been tricked of his mudbeast without a chance to pit its strength against Yaloor.

"Take up your cups!" Lord Miresnare cried, signalling to the bowmen in the galleries to ease the bolts on their bows. Stepping aside he beckoned the marshlords to gather round the tables and when every grumble and muttered curse had melted into silence he pointed with a gnarled finger towards the empty throne.

"I have grown weary of watching you match your beasts against my champion for the hand of my first-born because it tests nothing of your worthiness, your wits or courage to rule in my place but shows only the strength of the beasts you have snared and driven into my hall."

Lord Miresnare paused for breath and swept his quivering fingers back over the bellowing circle of mudbeasts that fretted and paced in the shadow of the Glitterspike until they pointed directly at the throng of waiting marshmen. "It is you, and you alone, who think yourselves worthy of taking my place, whom I shall test. Yes, your own strength and courage will be tested against the beasts that you have brought into the hall."

A low angry murmur rose amongst the marshlords but Lord Miresnare stifled it with a sharp snap of his fingers and called out that any who drank from his feasting cup would have the right to test themselves in single combat against the mudbeasts chained around the Glitterspike. The one who could pass unharmed between the beasts and touch the Glitterspike could claim the throne and all Gnarlsmyre.

"The throne?" shouted an awed voice.

"All the dry lands around the city of Glor!" exclaimed another, above the babble of excited chatter that broke out as Lord Miresnare's words sank in.

"What weapons can we use to fight the mudbeasts?" cried a deep voice from the marshlords' midst.

"They have nothing but tooth and claw," Lord Miresnare smiled grimly, casting his hand in the direction of Yaloor and the restless circle of mudbeasts. "So for it to be a true test of your courage and worthiness to take my throne you must go amongst them empty-handed. When you have all drunk I shall sit upon my throne in patient judgment just as I have overwatched each joust. I shall await the one amongst you who can tread unharmed through the circle of mudbeasts and touch the Glitterspike."

"How many days can we joust? When can we start?" shouted an impatient voice.

Lord Miresnare frowned. The old joust had lasted until Yaloor had killed all the mudbeasts; sometimes it was over in days, sometimes it had taken weeks of slaughter. He threw up his hands helplessly as he searched for the answer.

"How long? How long?" shouted another voice and a roar of laughter followed as they saw Lord Miresnare's confusion.

High above the great hall in Pinvey's secret cubbyhole Marrimian shuddered with horror. She had overheard almost every word. She feared for her father, seeing now why he had changed the iron rings and gilded the hall so brightly, knowing that the marshmen would never have given their beasts willingly nor at that point agreed to such a challenge. Helplessly she watched them surge forward and heard their laughter as they mocked her father and shouted at him to run and warm the frost on the seat of his throne or they would touch the Glitterspike and claim it first.

Their own goblets were tossed aside or thrown high into the air, only to fall and shatter into countless pieces and be trodden into a sharp gritty powder beneath their careless feet as, scrambling and fighting amongst themselves, they overran the eating boards, knocking the servers aside, and snatched for the jousting cup. More of the sweet nectar was spilt than swallowed in the mad rush to wet their lips and be the first to reach that sheer finger of shimmering crystal.

They swarmed across the hall into the circle of waiting mudbeasts, shoving one another in their greed. But their laughter turned to curses and shouts of triumph into screams of pain as one by one from the first wild onslaught they were crushed or torn apart by the mudbeasts' claws.

Marrimian tried without success to turn her head away from the window hole, the bile rising in her throat at the sight of the blood and torn flesh strewn around the circle of iron rings.

Concealed in one of the passageways Pinvey heard the marshlords' eager shout for the precious heartstone of the Glitterspike and the dry lands that they had always dreamed of and she knew that they had forgotten all other desires, especially for the daughters of the hall, and she cursed her father for not letting her continue her dance. Turning, she sidled into the hall and crouched in the shadows of a low archway, watching the marshmen, licking her lips hungrily and choosing champion after champion from amongst those who made the first wild rush only to see them torn and crushed to die screaming between the mudbeasts' claws in their foolish haste.

Scullion Ansel had been run off her feet, breaking open the hedgehog bakes and finishing the jugged hares, basting the roasts and piling with dishes the heavy black ebony trays that the underscullions presented to her in a never-ending chain. She heard the echoing great shout of the marshmen's first rush to touch the Glitterspike. Then the kitchens filled with

— 115 —

ragmen babbling excitedly of the chaos. Forgetting the food, she gathered up her skirts and fled the kitchen. She ran as fast as her bulky weight would allow down the twisting passageways to one of the low servers' archways that led into the hall.

"Give me room," she cried, pushing and shoving and trying to force a passage through the crowd of servers and scullions craning their necks to see what was going on. But the crush was too great.

"Give me passage," she cried again, hearing the screams of the marshmen as they fought amongst the mudbeasts. She *must* see a marshhunter or even a wader, and make him cast his gaze upon her, if the healing woman's spell was to work. Cursing, and fearing that she would be too late, she bunched up her apron tails beneath her arm and turning to the warren of passageways that crisscrossed behind her she followed an old almost forgotten route that she had used to fetch marshfish from the lower moats when she was an underscullion.

Twisting and turning, the noises of the great hall fading far behind her, she passed through the maze of well-gardened courtyards, blinking at the bright sunlight that reflected in shimmering patterns on the crystal houses. She felt her way along damp leaky alleyways, slipping on the mossy cobblestones until, with her face still blotched from the heat of the oven fires, she ran out into the high passageway that led from the outer doors into the great hall. Pausing for breath she pressed herself back against the rough stone wall and crept step by step along the corridor towards the great hall. Her apron tails were damp and crushed in her sweating hands, her heart pounded in her huge chest, her eyes were wide with expectation and fear. What if Lord Miresnare was to see her or the doorwardens or hallwardens were to stumble on her? She had thought of nothing but seeing the marshmen, nothing of what would happen to her if she was caught beyond her place in the kitchens or the narrow servers' corridors. The shouts of the marshmen and the bellowing roars of their mudbeasts grew louder as she crept towards the door.

Lord Miresnare leaned forward in the high throne and watched the beginnings of the new joust but his face drained of colour as he saw the terrible bloodshed.

"What drives them on?" he shouted to Naul above the shrieks and bellows of the beasts. Reaching over the armrest of the throne he tugged at the master mumbler's sleeve, making him crouch closer.

"Surely they will reach the Glitterspike and claim my throne by suffocating the mudbeasts and even overwhelming Yaloor beneath the heaps of their own reckless dead? You foretold that greed would keep them apart yet they fight together."

"They will not reach the Glitterspike. You have my life against it, Lord," answered Naul pointing down into the circle. "Greed or treachery will overmaster them all."

Miresnare frowned, doubting the mumbler's words, but moments later his eyes narrowed in anger as he watched a band of marshscum trample across their own dead and attack a small razor-spined clactor beast, toppling it beneath their combined weight and stabbing secretly at its soft undergroves with daggers they had kept well hidden beneath their cloaks.

"You have disobeyed my rules," he shouted leaping to his feet. He cried to his bowmen to arrowstrike any treacherous marshlord who carried the glint of steel in his hands. The marshmen scattered away from the stricken clactor at Lord Miresnare's shout but most of them fell, arrowstruck, before they could hide their murderous blades or run a dozen paces. Only two of them escaped, by shedding their cloaks and trying to run in through the circle, ducking underneath Yaloor's outstretched claws and throwing themselves at the Glitterspike. Stumbling forward they collided with one another. Lord Miresnare cried out with his eyes tightly shut as he waited for one of them to claim his throne. Naul laughed and touched his arm, making him open his eyes. He stared down at the two tangled bodies, their arms locked together, their daggers plunged through each other's hearts.

"Greed," whispered Naul in the strengthening silence as the great rush of marshmen hesitated then halted and slowly began to retreat from the mudbeasts, dropping their daggers and discarding sharpwires as the bowmen's short bows followed their every step.

"Greed will set them apart and treachery is their weakness, my Lord," laughed the mumbler. "Because they strive to win the greatest prize they will kill each other for it."

Lord Miresnare laughed and rubbed his hands together in relief, delighted with the new game. As the dead were carried away he shouted to the lampwicks

to light the reeds against the lengthening shadows that
were cast across the hall then signalled to the surviving
marshmen to take up new cups and refresh themselves
at the long eating boards. He called for the
servers to bring in the food. "Eat, eat, break the
trenchard bread and strip the pindafall roasts to the
bone. Celebrate this, the first real joust for my throne
and all that I possess with the greatest Allbeast Feast
ever to be set upon the tables of Glitterspike Hall,"
he cried to the despondent marshmen.

He ordered his servers to carve the meats. He raised
his cup to the rabble of marshscum, glad now of the
mumblers' foresight and confident that these marshmen
would never have the wit nor the strength to pass
between the mudbeasts to try another treacherous
rush to touch the Glitterspike beneath his archers'
watchful eyes.

"What does set the time of the game? How long by
your rules will the joust last?" asked one of the marshmen
as he reached for a trenchard, yet hesitating to
break the bread or touch the meat, watching the archers
in the high galleries with suspicious eyes.

"Be cautious, Lord," hissed Naul, crouching beside
the chair, touching Lord Miresnare's sleeve and making
him frown. He bent down until the mumbler's
lips were almost brushing against his ear.

"I foresaw no end to the game, my Lord, not until
the hand of the one who will claim the throne has
touched the Glitterspike. Beware of being too eager
to close the hall against these marshmen; it will only
make them believe there is a weakness, a secret flaw
in the circle of iron rings or that the beasts can be

tamed. Remember, rumours will grow and draw all men in a black tide of greed against you."

"There can be no end to the game—I will never give my throne to these marshscum. So how shall I answer them?" whispered Lord Miresnare.

Naul shook his head. "You must entangle them in the rules of the game. Remember, my Lord, the strength of this challenge is in their hopelessness—it confronts them each daylight with something they cannot overcome; and they must face it alone and without friends."

Lord Miresnare frowned, letting the mumbler's words sink in and take shape. Slowly he lifted his eyes and gazed up and down the lines of men at the eating boards, hearing their angry mutters and rasping breaths and the soft scraping of the borer biters that infested their robes, searching through the rotting mudbeast-skin cloaks they wore as they waited on his answer.

Slowly, he raised his cup, his face bleak and empty as he spoke the lore of the new game. "This hall will stand open to you from every sunrise to every sunset, open to every challenger. But with the setting of each sun you must stand or kneel or lie wherever the hours of frozen darkness overtake you. At the end of this feast my guards will escort you all to the Hurlers' Gate and from tomorrow's dawn the way to my door will no longer be marked. It will be set with snares and hidden traps."

The marshlords crowded forward, their voices raised in hurried whispering at the Lore of the Joust they had not wanted to hear before, and they reached for their trenchards only to freeze as Lord Miresnare's voice continued. "Remember, you cannot take one step either backward or forward after the sun has set, but all those who serve the Glitterspike can use each span of frozen darkness to thwart your road into the hall. You cannot bear arms against my champion Yaloor nor any of the mudbeasts that I have claimed and chained around the Glitterspike, nor can you gather together to share the final triumph. One hand only will touch the Glitterspike and be rewarded with my throne and all Gnarlsmyre."

Naul screamed.

"The beast! The phantom beast that we saw rising up within the dancing circle!" he cried, cowering back against Lord Miresnare's chair and pointing with a trembling finger across the hall towards the high-arched corridor that led by so many twists and turns to the outer doors.

The mudbeasts bellowed, scrambling and straining against their iron rings, the marshmen turned from the tables frowning suspiciously at the mumbler's shout and the noisy crowds of servers, ragmen and the lesser peoples of the hall who had thronged to its outer edges all fell silent, following the direction of the mumbler's pointing finger.

Tiny feet pattered on the polished stones, two small eyes appeared out of the darkness, reflecting in the lamplight. Lord Miresnare arose, his chair toppling behind him, his face darkening with anger as a small hedgehog scuttled into the hall. It seemed to hop and waddle, sniffing in every direction as it ran forward, searching for the Glitterspike, and as it moved, a fine silver gossamer thread unwound from beneath its body trailing out into the darkness of the corridor.

"Is this the beast that I have risked my throne and all Gnarlsmyre for?" thundered Lord Miresnare, closing his fingers about the mumbler's throat and lifting him off the ground.

Naul pointed desperately across the hall. Lord Miresnare looked up and cried out in terror, letting the mumbler slip forgotten through his fingers as he saw the shadow of Gallengab loom out of the corridor, his huge bulk filling the high archway, his shadow threatening to swallow up the hall.

Scullion Ansel frowned. She had heard the strange scratching, scuttling sound above the noise of the joust in the great hall and she moved a step away from the ancient tapestry that hung against the wall and stared open-mouthed at the small hedgehog that hopped and scuttled past her, unravelling its fine gossamer thread. Biting her knuckles in puzzlement she thought that the hedgehog must have escaped from its roll of mud before yesterday's baking for the feast. Fearing that she would be punished if it entered the hall she bent down and whispered coaxing words to the prickly creature, stretching out her huge hands to scoop it up in her apron. But she shrank back in terror, pressing herself against the tapestry as a black shadow filled the corridor and the air rang with Gallengab's roaring voice and the clank of chains. There was a sudden rush of claws and marshhunters' feet as they drove the beast towards the hall. Somebody barged into her, knocking her against the wall, whip tails stung her cheeks and flail heads cut into her arms. She tried to scream, gagging on the beast's stench, and just as she tumbled backwards, falling through the tapestry into darkness, she saw a tall strong figure with a close-shaven head looming over her, his hands stretching out to grab her.

Mertzork had seen the fat woman crouching against the wall and after Gallengab had rushed past he reached out for her, planning to squeeze directions out of her, but she vanished as if by magic through the wall of heavy woven cloth. Spitting at the tapestry he dismissed her and hurried after Gallengab. He ran around a sharp twist in the corridor to halt abruptly beneath the high-arched entrance on the threshold stone of the great hall.

His eyes were immediately drawn to the splendour of the Glitterspike and he gasped at the richness of the heartstone that shimmered in the column of sheer crystal, admiring the ghosting veins of molten silver that seemed to whisper, to lure him forward. Dazzled by the bright colours and endless glittering reflections created by the gilders' skill he had to blink several times to break the spell. He swept his wide-eyed gaze across the familiar crowds of marshlords and was met by a host of silent faces, all turned towards Gallengab in stunned amazement.

The mudbeasts chained around the Glitterspike roared and bellowed. As he looked at them and took in the magnificence of his foe, Yaloor, he frowned. Surely in all his father's stories of the joust the beasts had been shackled to iron rings along the outer edges of the hall, not around Yaloor. His thoughts were broken when Gallengab suddenly strained forward against his binding chains and dragged the hunters skidding and sliding across the polished floorstones of the hall.

A figure moved in the shadows of the entrance beside him, a hand touched his arm making him jump and quickly turn his head. Breathlessly he stared into Pinvey's face and saw all her beauty. She laughed, whispering her name, and pressed herself back into a shallow alcove, the tip of her moist tongue showing between her white teeth as she smiled at him.

Mertzork blinked and stared for a moment. Her gown of beaten gold shimmered in the gloom of the alcove, tracing the swell of her breasts and clinging in rippling folds between her thighs. He shook his head and tore his eyes from her, turning away, anxious to follow Gallengab into the hall. The marshhunters chained to the beast were shouting desperately for the key to their shackles and Mertzork laughed and ran into the hall and hurled the key between them. He threw back his head and shouted out that he would challenge Yaloor or any beast within the hall for the hand of Lord Miresnare's first-born daughter.

Laughter and shouts of ridicule broke out amongst the marshmen crowding the long eating boards and Mertzork spun around towards them, his face darkening with anger, his eyebrows creased with confusion. "The joust! I have come to claim the right to joust!" he shouted angrily just as the last of Gallengab's shackles was broken open.

The beast roared and bellowed behind him, then

reared and plunged its way across the hall towards the Glitterspike. The strong binding chain spiked and bolted by an iron hoop to its front leg snaked out behind it and sent sparks dancing high into the air as the beast rushed forward. A shout of laughter rose along the eating boards and a dozen voices sneered at Mertzork, taunting him and laughingly telling him how Lord Miresnare was about to steal his beast and chain it with theirs to guard the Glitterspike.

Mertzork spun round and leapt after Gallengab shouting, "No—none shall steal my beast!"

He threw himself forward and tried to grasp the twisting iron chain and hang on to it but his marshbound feet skidded and slipped on the polished stones of the hall and he was swept helplessly towards the long eating boards, tumbling over and over as the chain burned through his fingers. Gallengab snarled and clawed at the swarm of hallwardens that surrounded him but they were quick to hook up the end of the long chain and slip it through the one remaining iron ring and hammer home the locking bolt before he could attack them. Then with terror in their eyes they dropped their hammers and scattered. Miresnare smiled, his lips thinning triumphantly as he watched them, for now he had the two most savage beasts in all Gnarlsmyre, side by side to defend his throne, just as the mumblers had foretold.

He looked down at Mertzork who was climbing to his feet and looking suspiciously around him, then laughed and rubbed his hands together. He lifted up the brimming crystal cup and offered it to Mertzork saying, "Drink of my lore, marshlord, and celebrate the beginning of the new joust for my throne, the joust in which I test your strength and courage to pass alone and unarmed between the mudbeasts and touch the Glitterspike, for you have completed the circle of beasts by bringing the champion of legends into my hall to defend my throne!"

Mertzork stared up, speechless, into Lord Miresnare's eyes, the bleak reality of his words and his triumphant laughter echoing through his head. Slowly he took the cup and numbly he brought it to his lips.

Ansel slowly came to her senses and clambered to her feet, skinning her shins on what felt like the first stone raiser of a spiral stairway in the cramped darkness behind the tapestry. Turning, she felt for the coarse ribbed weave of the back of the tapestry, half afraid to push the heavy cloth aside and go back into the corridor, but the other half of her was in turmoil, her heart beating wildly. The healing woman's spell had worked. The first marshlord or hunter or whatever he was that she had set her eyes upon had reached out to take her. Hesitantly she grasped the cord-bound edges of the tapestry and began to pull it aside when she heard a strangled cry and a thump as if someone was kicking something in the darkness above her head. Slowly she let the tapestry fall back into place and turned to the stairway, putting a cautious foot on the first step and feeling her way inch by inch up the winding stairs until she reached a narrow door. Gingerly she turned the lift-latch and the door creaked open against her knuckles.

Screwing her eyes against the gloom she looked into the tiny room and saw her mistress upon a mouldy bone-littered couch, trussed so tightly with thin greasy pindafall cords that her hands and fingers had swollen and turned black beneath the cruel knots.

"Mistress, mistress, who would have done this? Who could have left you to die in this black hole?" Ansel tried to soothe her as she edged and squeezed her bulk through the narrow doorway and pushed her way across the room to her side. She unsheathed a saw-toothed skinning blade from beneath her crumpled apron and in quick skilled strokes cut through the binding cords and the tight double knot in the scarf that gagged her.

Marrimian cried out and fell forwards across the couch, tears streaming down her face as the blood rushed into her tingling hands and numb feet making them burn and sting with waves of pain.

"Pinvey, it was Pinvey," she stuttered, trying to form the words in her bruised mouth, forcing the sound out between chattering teeth as she sobbed, her shoulders heaving uncontrollably.

Ansel took her and comforted her in her strong scullion's arms but Marrimian fought against her and cried out, "I must get into the hall. Pinvey took my place and Father has . . ."

Lord Miresnare's voice rose in peals of triumphant laughter from the hall below, cutting through Marrimian's voice and making both women rush to the small window. Marrimian gasped and pointed at the huge beast now chained amongst the mudbeasts in the circle around the base of the Glitterspike. She asked Ansel in a hushed whisper, "Who and what is that?"

"I do not know, mistress," she answered shaking her head. "But that marshlord getting to his feet near the long eating boards, the one the other marshlords are laughing at, he was the one who brought it into the hall. Look, your father is offering the crystal jousting cup to him—and, mistress, he will be mine!" she finished hotly, pointing down at Mertzork and telling Marrimian how the magic spell had made him reach out for her just before she had toppled backwards against the tapestry and stumbled on the secret stairway.

Marrimian hushed the scullion into silence and pressed her ear to the window slit, trying to catch her father's words as he lifted up the master mumbler and set him upon the table, calling him the jousting master and shouting something about the quest for his throne. She was sure that he clearly said that it would be open to all who drank from the cup.

"I am the first-born—I will drink from that jousting cup," she cried, turning and rushing for the doorway only to fall headlong amongst the discarded pindafall bones as her cramped legs buckled under her. "And you must help me," she urged, clutching at Ansel's hand and pulling her roughly through the narrow doorway.

Skirts and apron tails flying Marrimian dragged Ansel downstairs and through the high entrance to the hall. Using her bravest voice she demanded the right to joust as they crossed the hall. "Here, give me the cup. Let me drink," she called to her father.

"You?" cried Lord Miresnare springing forward to meet her, his face blotched and darkening with anger. Marrimian slipped past him, snatched the crystal cup from Mertzork's hands and drained it dry.

The marshlords stared at her in dumb astonishment. Their quick eyes followed her and their mouths hung open at her boldness.

"I am your first-born and of all those present I have more right to try and touch the Glitterspike than any of them. You have offered your throne and all Gnarlsmyre to any who drank from the cup. Ask your mumbler if I have the right," she shouted fiercely, smashing the cup in pieces at her feet. All her life she had loved and tried to serve him but now her eyes were blazing with defiance at how he had used her. Her bruised chin thrust out angrily as she remembered all the hurts she had swallowed in silence.

Lord Miresnare blinked and stared at her as Naul gravely nodded his head. "By your lore she has the right, my Lord. You said that all who drank from this cup . . ." His fearful whisper failed as he saw his master's face.

Lord Miresnare's eyes narrowed and his hands clenched with anger as he took a giant step to tower over her. "No! You cannot take part in the joust. You are but a woman, a nothing here. You even abandoned your duty and allowed your sister to take your place and welcome the marshlords to my hall. I disown you as my first-born. You are now less than that fat scullion behind you."

Marrimian opened her mouth to answer, to shout against the harshness of his judgement, to tell him of the secret cubbyhole and Pinvey's treachery, but he had turned away, calling for the servers to bring on the roast peacocks. Then, without meeting her eyes, he snapped and gave clear orders that she and Ansel be driven out of Glitterspike Hall. As punishment for daring to challenge him they were to spend a night beneath the freezing stars.

Later, long after the feast, when the guards had cleared the hall, Lord Miresnare sat heavily on his throne, wrapped in silence, and thought over his judgement on Marrimian. He nodded to himself: he had been right to banish her. No woman should ever challenge a man, her place was to obey and to serve, to sire heirs, to . . . Sighing, Lord Miresnare stared at the beast Gallengab and wished that just one of the women he had been with had given him a son, then none of these jousts would have been necessary. He could have slept easily, knowing that the line of Miresnare would go on for ever and ever. He yawned and made to rise but something in the mumblers' foresight nagged at the back of his mind and made him uneasy. He rose from the throne, and paced to the tall crystal windows where he stared out into the frozen darkness and shook his head. There could be no travellers or wanderers from far lands to touch the Glitterspike. He had sent out many of the cleverest hunters to search, just as his father had done before him; there was nothing beyond the boiling white waterfalls of Rainbows' End nor the sheer overhanging rock cliffs where the sun rode into the darkness. Nothing existed beyond the shifting fogbanks save swirling darkness. This he knew.

5

The Shadowtreading

*F*AR beyond the frozen quickmires and the bleak
secret untrodden edges of Gnarlsmyre lay the
land of Elundium. It had remained hidden from
Lord Miresnare's adventurers, masked by the thick divide of billowing fogbanks that forever drifted across
the shifting quicksands. There had been nothing, not
even a whisper of its people nor of the proud warhorses and savage battle owls that roamed and stooped
across its windswept hills and wild grasslands that had
suggested the existence of any world beyond Gnarlsmyre. There had been nothing to disturb the house
of Lord Miresnare nor threaten the throne he so jealously guarded, not so much as a passing shadow. In
Elundium deep winter's snow had begun to melt and
the spring sap to rise in the hoary oaks and tangletrees
that grew in clumps along the greenways. The warhorses were crossing the quiet snowy landscape in
slow-moving crescents towards the Rising. Border
Runners trotted at their heels, their quick shadows
ghosting on the frost-white snow, while all about the
Granite City owls gathered in silent stoops and waited
for the dawn to break.

Thanehand, the King of Elundium, woke at the owls' dawn screech in the warmth of his swansdown bed and stifled a yawn. He turned his head and smiled at Elionbel, his Queen, who slept beside him, and gently brushed a lock of sleep-tangled hair across her forehead before he slipped quietly from the bed. Shivering, he drew a heavy fur-lined cloak about his shoulders against the chill dawn air and tiptoed lightly across to the high windows that overlooked the steep frost-crusted walls of the lower circles of the city. He could see lamplight and movement in the stable yards beyond the great wall. There was the faint rattle of blacksmiths' hammers and bright sparks lit the darkness as they danced across the anvils and drifted up to mingle with the haze of forging smoke. He could hear the clatter of hooves on the freshly swept cobbles. A proud stag crossed the stable yard with its great crown of antlers glittering in the shadows of the grey hours before the dawn. It scraped at the snow and roared out; two horses answered with a neighing shout.

Elionbel turned, calling out against her dreams, and Thane turned to her, whispering her back into sleep. "Tanglecrown the Lord of Stags grows impatient for the road. Esteron and Stumble fret for their bridles for when the sun breasts World's Edge it will be the beginning of the seventeenth Shadowtreading and we must travel to the Rising."

He smiled down at her, his eyes softening as he remembered that other frozen morning full seventeen suns ago when defeat had towered over them and they had bravely stepped into the last ray of sunlight to face

Kruel, the son of Krulshards, Master of Darkness, who had swallowed all Elundium in his shadowlight. Thane laughed quietly as Mulcade the Lord of Owls stooped silently from the king post beam and settled on his shoulder.

"Each one of you played your part to win the sunlight and rid Elundium of Krulshards, and Kruel's foul shadowlight," he whispered, caressing the aged owl's chest feathers as he remembered those last desperate moments when all seemed lost to the darkness. He recalled how when the last ray of sunlight streamed across the snow a wild stumbling thrust with his broken sword caused him to fall at Kruel's feet and accidentally give him a shadow, a shadow made from the fragments of the malice from Krulshards's cloak which destroyed his power and reduced him to an innocent helpless infant. He had wanted to destroy the child but Elionbel had stayed his arm.

"You showed me the way to true kingship," he whispered looking down at her. He knew what strength she had and realized how she had made him see the power of forgiveness in victory and how mercy should temper his judgement. Thane smiled and slowly nodded; that was the real beginning, when they had picked up the baby between them and named him Krann, rescuing him in memory of his courageous mother, and they had pledged to bring him up in the sunlight to know nothing of his nightmare beginnings . . .

Cryers were moving through the lower circles of the city, the great gates swung open, rumbling across the cobbles. The first daylight of the new Shadowtreading had begun. Thane reached forward and gently shook Elionbel's shoulder, whispering her awake.

Elionbel started up and cried, "Shadowtreading has dawned."

She gathered her clothes in her arms and called for her dressers, knowing that she must hurry. Noise and laughter filled the corridors of the granite towers, there was a rush of armoured boots and shouts for warm winter cloaks against the weather. Horseshoes clattered in the courtyard below the tower windows and Kyotorm, the Keeper of the Wayhouse Tower on Stumble Hill, and Eventine, his wife and Lady of Clatterford, called up for their king to lead them to the Rising. Thane laughed and waved a greeting to his friends and shouted for hot food to warm them and a blazing fire to be stoked up in the hall to melt the snow from their boots. He stamped his own feet into long riding boots as Elionbel scolded her dressers for being clumsy as they pinched her neck between her collar ties.

"Why must we always leave in such haste?" she laughed, catching the spirit of the early morning journey as she flung her cloak about her shoulders, her fingers trembling as she closed the catch.

"Because a journey soon started is quickly over," said Thane.

He turned to pick up his armoured gloves and frowned at his thoughts. He had always been against this Shadowtreading ceremony to mark his victory over the shadowlight. He had wanted to forget the darkness and put Krulshards and all those nightmare daylights behind him and build a better world, but the people demanded it and gradually the ceremony had come to mark the ending of the old sun and the beginning of the new one. Sighing he pulled on his gloves, flexing each finger in turn to loosen the stiffened metal joints.

They had taken Krann to the first Shadowtreading but he had grown fitful and had screamed in terror as the mummers danced out their story on the new snow and the people had drawn away from him with fear in their eyes.

Elionbel raised the heavy fur-lined collar of her cloak and took Thane's arm, whispering that there would just be time to share hot cakes and mulled cinnamon wine with Kyot and Eventine before the horses were brought to the doors.

Thane smiled at her and pointed out beyond the city to where the first finger of sunlight showed above World's Edge and cast long shadows across the snow. "Just time enough to be easy with one's friends by the fireside. How different from our first journey to the Rising. No time then to break bread or raise a cup. One moment we were safe inside Candlebane Hall surrounded by the deep waters of Swanwater and the next we were riding down through the city on a roaring torrent, out through the gates and into the eye of a snowstorm to escape from the shadowrats!"

Elionbel laughed. "But today we will first have hot cakes and stand by a warming fire before we journey to Willow Leaf and his people at the Rising." Then as they reached the door she held back, asking, "What of Krann? Must he stay here again today? Surely we must take him with us soon; we cannot hide his beginnings from him forever."

Thane frowned and shook his head sadly. "The time is not yet right, it is too soon. Better he lives in ignorance of his beginnings until he is full grown, lest it throws a shadow across his path. Perhaps at the turn of the next sun."

Elionbel sighed quietly to herself and let Thane lead her down the broad steps into the hall where Kyot and Eventine were warming themselves by the fireside after their long journey across Elundium. Their daughter Fairlight had been with them but had disappeared, probably to find Krann.

"Well met, dear friends. Let us break fast before our journey," Thane laughed as they embraced.

The clatter of horses' hooves on the road beyond the door of the hall made Thane hurry. He swallowed the last of the mulled wine and leapt down the steps two at a time, pulling on his gloves as he tried to catch his flying cloak tails and fasten the silver buckle at his throat. Almost as an afterthought he called back to the others to follow him.

In his room overhead Krann had awoken to Fairlight's urgent knock, to the noise of the horses and the ring of the blacksmith's hammer as the Gallopers milled in the courtyard. He pulled on his clothes and let her in.

"Are you coming today? What did Elionbel say?" Fairlight whispered excitedly.

"She said no, I was too young, but I must ask Thane," he answered gruffly.

He followed her flying figure headlong down the spiral stairs and burst breathlessly into the yard where the company were now mounted and eager to start. He gripped Thane's stirrup in his hands and implored him to allow him to attend the Shadowtreading.

Thane pirouetted Esteron, the lord of horses, casting dancing sparks across the cobbles, and reined him to a halt. He looked down into Krann's pale blue eyes and smiled tenderly at the way he brushed aside his white-blond hair with long delicate fingers.

"Who would guard the city if you rode with us?" he asked gently, his eyes softening, trying to blunt Krann's disappointment. "Who will keep Elundium safe for our return?"

"There are guards enough—and my half-brother Rubel who stalks my every step like a shadow. Why can't he guard the city? I have never seen a Shadow-treading ceremony and you will tell me little about it."

"You came once when you were very small and it frightened you, my love," interrupted Elionbel riding Stumble up beside Esteron. "When you have full grown then you may ask again."

"But I have waited eighteen suns while all the others of my age, even Fairlight who is younger by one sun, are riding with you. I am no longer a child with childish fears."

Thane frowned, his mouth setting into a firm line. "And you are my brother by marriage to Elionbel and better suited to the task of guarding the city than Rubel who broods on his own dark thoughts. You are tall, strong and quick-witted. I command you to guard the Granite City in my absence with your life. Now go to it with good grace and let us have an end to this argument."

Krann stepped back in defeated silence, his face empty with disappointment. Avoiding even Fairlight's sympathetic eyes he turned and walked away, tears threatening to blur his azure eyes.

When the clatter of hooves had faded beyond the gates of the city and the travellers had become mere dots on the snow-white landscape towards the distant horizon line Krann turned with heavy feet to climb the steps of the tower. He felt utterly alone. He had always felt alone, different, always distanced by a wall of polite whispers, half-truths or downright falsehoods that seemed with the passing suns to have been built between him and the people of the city. No one seemed to want to share his friendship and he had grown up an isolated figure within the Granite City, always on the edge of the colourful, laughing crowds that flocked around Thane and Elionbel. At first he had thought people were wary of him because they were in awe of Thane, but as he grew older he realized this couldn't be true. He began to catch brief glimpses of what others thought and sensed the suspicions they would never put into words. This strange gift of perception merely increased his misery. He knew without doubt there was something about him people were frightened of; that there was some terrible shadow that Thane, Elionbel and everyone strove to hide. There was obviously a secret surrounding his birth and those early suns beyond his memory no one would discuss.

People often spoke with affection of gentle, brave Martbel, the mother he had never known, but nobody would tell him who his father was nor anything about his beginnings. If he pressed for an answer people would say, embarrassed and impatient, "Oh, he was a powerful man" or "a foreigner, not one of us" and hasten to change the subject. Even Thane and Elionbel were dismissive, though always affectionate.

Only Rubel, his half-brother, muttered dark hurtful comments such as "how could such a fair face hide such a black heart." He always felt uneasy in Rubel's company—as, it seemed, did others. Rubel would often sit alone and watch him for long silent hours without blinking, and if Krann turned away and then spun quickly back he would sometimes catch Rubel bending forwards as if to touch Krann's shadow, almost as if . . .

A noise beyond the archway, a clattering of hooves on the cobbles, broke his thoughts and made him turn. His misery and self-pity forgotten he laughed and clapped his hands as Fairlight cantered into the courtyard. She sprang lightly from the saddle and ran to embrace him, laughing. Her cheeks were hot-flushed from the icy wind and her tangle of fire-bronzed hair streamed out across the hood of her cloak.

"No one knows I have ridden back," she whispered, her eyes sparkling as she took his hands and let him lift her up off the cobbles in his strong arms.

Krann laughed with her, delighted that she, his one true friend, had stolen a few moments to be with him.

"You must not stay too long," he answered setting her gently back onto the ground. "The road to the Rising goes through wild country and there may be wolves, or . . ."

Fairlight laughed and hushed him into silence, her eyes glowing with mischief. "I still think King Thane should have let you come with us," she whispered, looking quickly round the courtyard for prying eyes before she thrust a bundle of clothes and a long bow into his hands.

Krann stepped back in surprise. "You came back for *me?*" he exclaimed, searching her eyes and finding the only person in all Elundium who did not fear him or try to hide anything from him. Her mind was clear of dark secrets. Whatever she knew she would always gladly share with him, even the knowledge of where she had hidden her mother's spine-matched arrow blades that she had borrowed without asking from the armoury to hunt the grassland hares.

"But the King has pledged me to guard the Granite City, you must have heard . . ."

Fairlight flashed her eyes and pressed him into silence with a firm finger on his lips. "It is not fair to leave you here. It is like filling two cups with wine and me drinking them both if I go and you are left here in the city. Neither of us has ever seen the Shadowtreading ceremony and Mother and Father would not even talk about it to me. So here I am. I have borrowed an archer's cloak and helm and I left ready a spare relay horse with a full quiver of arrows clipped onto the saddle for you while Mother and Father were having breakfast."

Fairlight drew closer and put her lips to his ear. "No one will recognize you dressed as an archer. You can follow the King's procession at a safe distance. The horses' hooves have trampled a clear path in the snow."

Krann frowned and shrank back clutching the cloak and helm; the long bow caught in the rough surface of the cobbles. "But if Thane finds out, if Rubel sees me leaving the city . . . you know he watches my every move."

Fairlight shook her head and pulled him close to her. "Rubel will be too busy looking for *you* to notice an archer leaving the city, and it will take him a dozen daylights of searching before he finds you have gone. My father and the King are like brothers and I am sure Thane will not be any more angry or punish you more than my father punishes me. Think of the adventure. Remember how we used to play seek-the-shadow in the armoury when we were younger, upsetting the rows of arrow stands and sending the forests of neatly stacked spear shafts spilling into the walkways and how that archer who guards the armoury used to chase us out. What about when that old horseman, Breakmaster, hauled us both by the scruff of our necks before the King for setting the relay horses free from the stable yards, and when we blocked the great gates of the city with broken carts and pretended we were getting ready for a siege. Well, did he beat you for all that?"

Krann laughed, remembering all those wonderful times he had shared with Fairlight on her infrequent visits. Yes, Thane had always punished him with his

hand or the flat of his sword but there had always been
an edge of laughter in his voice and he had thanked
the long-dead magician named Nevian for the great
distance that lay between the city and Stumble Hill
fearing that if Fairlight visited more frequently the
city would soon be reduced to a state of chaos! Slowly
Krann nodded, his face breaking into a smile; perhaps
if he followed at a distance and watched the Shadowtreading in secret, perhaps . . .

"I will find you a place to watch from," Fairlight
urged, breaking into his thoughts. "And you can gallop home long before we leave the Rising," she cried,
springing back up into her saddle and spurring her
horse towards the archway. "I must catch the others
at the first resting place!"

Turning, she called over her shoulder where she
had hidden the horse in the lower circles of the city
and then she vanished in a shower of bright dancing
sparks down the broad winding road out of the city.

Krann sighed, uncertain about the adventure that
beckoned him, then gathered the bundle of clothes
under his arm and began slowly to mount the broad
steps. The very name of the Rising always brought
dark images into his mind and the voices that cried out
to him in those moments between sleeping and waking nudged and prickled him. Suddenly he stopped
midstride. He must see the Shadowtreading, he must
take advantage of Fairlight's help. Unknowingly she
had offered him the chance to see his past and he must
take it, now, without a moment's hesitation. He
breathed deeply to build his courage then turned and
descended the steps.

*　　*　　*

For the six long frozen daylights of their journey to

the Rising Fairlight hung back whenever she could and rode in the vanguard of the King's company, watching for Krann as they forged their slow path through the deep snowdrifts, between ancient copses of tall trees that stood etched in winter colours way-marking their road. She would leave hidden bundles of food for Krann among these trees and mark them with a bright arrow feather whenever she could, but she fretted and worried for him in the long nights of frozen darkness, knowing that he dared not light a fire. Journey's end brought her little comfort for the Rising rose bleakly above the snowy landscape and there were few places that she could hide Krann from curious eyes save beneath the clumps of tangletrees that grew beside the greenway's edge.

"There is nowhere else to watch the Shadowtreading. I have asked and they say that it is always danced on top of the Rising in front of Lord Willow's long hall," Fairlight hissed above the frozen chattering of Krann's teeth as they huddled together beneath a clump of low, snow-covered tangletrees on the edge of the crossroads in the shadow of the Rising.

"Then I have travelled in your footprints through the ice and snow for nothing," he muttered miserably, trying to rub some warmth and a little life back into his numb fingers. "I must have been mad to have broken my pledge and come on this . . . this . . ." Words failed him as he pulled his cloak collar up over his head. With every footstep the feeling of dread had seemed to weigh heavier and heavier on his shoulders;

it was as if the landscape, each dip and hollow, each brittle-fingered branch was holding its breath with dark foreboding.

"There! It should be there!" he cried hoarsely, pointing suddenly towards the centre of the crossroads, his eyes unfocused.

Fairlight caught hold of his frozen hands and rubbed them in her own, whispering and soothing him and pulling his cloak more tightly against the bitter evening winds. "What should be where?" she asked, brushing the settling frost out of his fringe.

But Krann only shook his head and shrugged his shoulders, answering that it was nothing, just a shadow crossing the snow.

"I will come for you after supper," she whispered. "And I will lead you up to the Rising under the cover of darkness. No one will notice you in that archer's cloak and helm and you must hide in the place I have found. It is less than a dozen paces from where the mummers dance the Shadowtreading."

"No!" answered Krann firmly. "That would be madness. What if Thane finds me or Willow's people stumble on my hiding place? No, let me return to the Granite City while there is still time. Suppose I discover or see something terrible that King Thane and my half-sister Elionbel have tried so hard to keep from me."

Fairlight gripped his arms and shook him firmly, a frown creasing her forehead. "What would they try to hide from you? What disturbs you apart from the cold that gnaws at your bones? First you see things

that are not here and now the King and your sister
are hiding things. What is wrong?"

Krann blinked and shook his head and muttered
fearfully, "It is as if I have been here before, as if I
know what happened and yet it is beyond my grasp.
I cannot see it, nor describe it, but I just have this feeling of dread."

"Nonsense!" laughed Fairlight rising. "It is only the
frost or too many dark nights without hot food and
a bed. Neither of us has ever been here before and we
could never have found the way without the hoofprints of Esteron to follow. Now, keep warm and wait
patiently, I will return after the sun has set."

Krann nodded miserably, knowing in his heart that
no matter what Fairlight said he could have found
without assistance the road through the trackless
leagues of deep drifted snow, following the solitary
copses of trees. Even the footprints he had followed
had somehow seemed familiar. Despairing, he sank
down beneath the tangletrees and watched the evening shadows lengthen across the snow. He wished
he had never cast that archer's cloak across his shoulders nor put his foot into the stirrup. The Rising
loomed so large and sinister against the landscape, it
threatened to engulf him with the secrets that it held.
He would have slipped away into the darkness and
forever turned his back upon the Shadowtreading but
he was trapped. Fairlight had taken the horse he had
ridden from the Granite City and hidden it amongst
the other archers' horses in the stable yard on top of
the Rising.

Fairlight returned soon after the first lamps had

been set upon the high rim of the Rising and she laughed and whispered quick instructions as she led him out across the trampled snow. "Hold the bow properly and stop peering around so much. Try to look like one of my father's archers," she urged as they crossed the narrow causeway and began the steep climb up the ramp to the top of the Rising.

"Look at those tiny white flowers that are opening on either side as we pass. Their heady scent is making my head spin," Krann gasped, staggering against her.

Fairlight smelt the sweet heavy scent and laughed, softly catching Krann's arm as he stumbled dizzily against her, and she led him through the last of the flowers up onto the top of the Rising.

"This place is so magical," she sighed. "These must be nightflowers sown around the Rising against enemies. Mother once told me that the nightflowers defended King Thane when he fought against the darkness. They open when danger threatens, and will not let the enemy pass."

Krann laughed for the first time since he had left the Granite City. "Well at least I don't think I am the enemy!"

"Why should you be an enemy?" asked Fairlight, leading him towards the long hall that stood on the far side of the Rising beyond an area of untrampled snow that a group of Willow's people were carefully raking smooth with long-handled birch bundles.

Krann shivered and moved closer to Fairlight as they skirted the raked snow. "Willow's people always send a tingle down my spine whenever they visit the Granite City. I think it is their shell-shaped ears and the way their eyes bulge," he whispered as they reached the door arch on the side of the long hall.

"It is because they used to live in the dark. They were slaves to it," Fairlight answered, her lips brushing against his ear as she pushed him through the doorway into the low empty hall. "They were born in the darkness of the City of Night and Willow Leaf led them to their freedom. Has the King told you nothing of his battle against the darkness? Haven't you pressed Willow with a thousand questions when he has visited the Granite City?"

Krann shrugged his shoulders helplessly. He had always wanted to ask but somehow he had been steered away from such questions.

Keeping close to Fairlight's heels he followed her down the side of the long hall, looking furtively all around him as they hurried through the bright pools of light that reflected on the polished rafter beams from the flickering candle lamps set in silver brackets upon the walls. Fairlight slowed as she reached a dais set with six richly gilded chairs. Their armrests were carved in the shape of snarling Border Runners and their headrests were finely chiselled to represent Battle Owls stooping with their wings outspread, their talons unhooked and ready to strike.

Fairlight bent down and lifted a corner of the heavily embroidered blue- and gold-threaded cloth that had been spread across the dais, pulling up the folds that fell in neat pleats of twisted emblem thread to hang a hand's span above the floor. "This is the place to watch the Shadowtreading, beneath the King's feet, under the dais. No one will ever guess that you are hiding here," she laughed, her eyes sparkling with excitement as she pointed into a small space between the roughly pegged wooden joists that made up the frame of the platform.

Krann hung back. To be here at all was bad enough, but to sit beneath Thane's feet—he began to shake his head and open his mouth to answer, to tell her no, but a door latch clicked, he heard footsteps and familiar voices echoing through the empty hall.

"Do you want to be caught?" hissed Fairlight, thrusting him forward and pushing him headlong into the small dark space, settling the embroidered folds neatly back into place and stilling the moving cloth with her hand.

"But I will see nothing here of the Shadowtreading nor of anything else," he muttered, knocking his elbows and grazing his forehead as he struggled to turn around in the narrow space beneath the dais.

"The wall of the long hall is folded away just before the new sun rises. Wait patiently and be quiet. Mother and Elionbel are walking towards us," Fairlight whispered hurriedly and ran to greet them. Laughing she linked her arms with theirs and with eager talk of the Shadowtreading turned them back towards the door arch saying how she was so excited she couldn't sleep, begging them to tell her tales of how the King had won the sunlight.

The women's voices had receded, the door latch clicked, its echo filling the silence, Krann was alone in the very heart of the Rising, sheltered from the biting wind that had found a way through every fold and buttonhole on his long journey through the snow.

Warm and dry at last in the cramped darkness beneath the dais he curled up in his cloak and slipped into a fretful sleep crowded with shadowy images that swarmed across the snow. He heard nothing of Thane, and Willow's troubled voices as they stood on the rim of the Rising wondering at the bank of brilliant night-flowers that had bloomed along the outer edges of the Rising.

An icy draught of wind woke Krann as the floor-boards above his head creaked. Wood splinters and dust showered down onto his face, making him sit up with a start, and he had to stifle a cry in the cramped darkness as he hit his head on the stout crossbeams. He could see a strip of grey dawn light and white un-trampled snow between the edge of the throne cloth and the floor. Armoured boots were crossing the wooden platform, familiar voices murmured above his head in excited whispers, voices rose all about him. Rows and rows of feet were crowding in on either side. As far as he could fathom they were shuffling, standing on tiptoes, edging forwards, and then the last section of the wooden wall of the long hall was carried away out of sight. The whispers died away into a sudden silence and every breath was held along the length of the hall. The sky was brightening and morning colours spread across the snow. Krann strained his ears against the silence and heard a distant creaking sound, a rustle as though a thousand branches were bending in the wind, but there was no dawn wind, not even the slightest draught to swirl the glittering frost crystals that hung in the air above the Rising. The sounds were closer now, voices began to whisper and feet shuffled anxiously around him. There was something on the edge of the Rising. Krann could see tree shapes with bent and twisted branches, they were approaching in a slow-moving semi-circle, as if by magic. Krann frowned. He had not known what to expect, but the trees seemed familiar. Armoured mummers in pale masks danced between the trees, clapping wooden swords above their heads; but one figure in a kingly mask walked majestically amongst the dancers. He was unarmed and wore a crown of gold.

Mummers dressed as horses cantered in bounding strides around the King; they reared and plunged, their flowing manes streaming out behind them.

"Border Runners!" whispered Krann, watching mummers dressed as savage dogs pass between the trees and join the swelling circle dancing around the King, their jaws snapping open and shut.

Krann held his breath as the whirling dancers reached a climax, leaping high in the air then standing rock still. Slowly the tree shapes closed in around the armoured mummers and turned their lower spear-shaped branches out towards the rising sun. Dark, hideous shapes silently breasted the Rising. Krann shrank back under the dais whispering, "No!"

He bit on his knuckles as the nightmare warriors began to glide noiselessly forward. Something deep down in his mind seemed almost to know why they wore cloaks woven from night-dark cloth that billowed and flowed out behind them. Strange voices chanted in his head, cruel laughter shrieked all around him as the hideous mummers crossed the snow and swallowed up the dawn. He half rose, cracking his head on the cross joists of the dais, and made to stumble forward to stop the dance, to stop whatever dreadful act was to follow, but he froze and shrank back into the darkness as a tall figure climbed over the rim of the Rising and burst between the hideously masked mummers. His frost-white hair flowed out from the top of the mask as he leapt high out into the centre of the smooth untrampled snow and danced in strutting mocking steps, beckoning the besieged King to leave the safety of his armoured warriors and the shelter of the trees.

The King held up his empty hands and pointed to the rising sun as if waiting. A mummer wearing a mask carved in Willow Leaf's likeness and mounted on a pure white horse dappled with summer shadows cantered up onto the Rising. The rider carried a broken sword in his hand half wrapped in the tatters of a black shadowy cloth. The King clapped his hands and sprang over the armoured mummers' heads towards the galloping horse. The hideous figure with a mane of frost-white hair rose up to meet him and in slow, dancing steps turned to face the dais. Krann gasped, the blood draining from his face as he stared into the mirror image of himself; into the hideous mask, the pale blue eyes and sneering lips, that loomed towards him.

He screamed and toppled backwards as laughing voices clamoured inside his head. He bit savagely on his knuckles and felt his own hot salty blood wash across his tongue. Crying and shaking with terror he curled himself up into a tight ball in the darkness and pulled his cloak collar over his head. He blocked his ears with his fingers and wept tears of shame. He did not hear the thunder of stamping feet and the roaring cheers of the watchers that crowded all about him. Their shouts of joy masked the sounds of his despair as the mummer king in the golden crown took the broken sword from the galloping horseman and stabbed at the footprints of the hideously masked mummer with the frost-white hair and weakened him with each downward sweep of the blade. Soon the king sent him to his knees to roll helplessly in the snow as the first ray of the new sun spilled across the top of the Rising, drawing long shadows from the dancing mummers.

Willow Leaf had taken his seat of honour on the dais at King Thane's right hand but he did not cheer as loudly as the others seated with him nor stamp his feet so hard on the cloth spread across the dais. He frowned and leant forwards in his gilded chair as the great shout went up and he turned his shell-shaped ears from side to side, listening, just as he had listened in the darkness of the City of Night when the Night-beasts had hunted him, and he caught the whispered cries of Krann's torment from beneath his feet.

The Shadowtreading was reaching its climax. The armoured mummers leapt and spun, the trees burst apart and new armoured mummers appeared magically in the snow. The mummer king had spread the torn remnants of the black cloth that had been bound around the broken sword into the shape of a man's shadow at the feet of the fallen enemy. Kneeling upon it he held up a newborn baby. He held out the baby to King Thane.

"Let the shadow be trodden into a new beginning,"

cried Thane, rising to his feet as a great shout of triumph thundered through the long hall. He held up his hands for silence.

"New beginnings must herald old endings, thus we will drink to the new sun from the wayside cups and dance and feast until the daylight's shadows lengthen with the setting sun. Then by candlelight, as is my custom, I will sit and give my judgments to you, the people of Elundium."

Bowing to Queen Elionbel he took her hand and led her out across the snow to greet the Shadowtreaders and reward them with twisted threads of golden emblem thread. The watching crowds followed, laughing and singing as they spread across the snow. Servers brought forward cauldrons of steaming broth against the cold and nightboars were set to roast above the fire pits. Heavily laden trays of finger treats and brimming wayside cups were passed from hand to hand as the Shadowtreading feast began.

Willow Leaf put the strange sounds he had heard out of his mind, and he laughed and raised his cup and toasted the strengthening sunlight.

Krann shivered in the darkness beneath the dais and waited until the last of the crowd had left the hall before he made his escape. He pushed back the heavily embroidered folds, emerged into the hall and looked quickly up and down. He was trembling and tears were running down his face. He crouched for a moment as if gathering himself and then rose and fled through the doorway at the furthest end of the hall without a backward glance. The milling crowds feasting in the snow took no notice of him as he slipped noiselessly into the stables. He selected a grey-white stallion with dapples the colour of summer shadows and mounted it with despair in his heart. His cloak billowed and flapped behind him as he cantered out through the archway of the stable yard and swept in a cloud of stinging snowflakes over the rim of the Rising. He gathered speed as he galloped headlong down the steep snow-covered ramp over the frozen dyke below.

Willow spun round as the horse galloped past, and gave a cry as he saw Eyrus vanishing over the rim of the Rising. He shouted and loosed the dagger from his belt as the startled feasters turned towards him. Thane strode through the feasters and Kyot knocked an arrow onto his bow.

"It was Krann, I'd swear by Nevian's cloak, it was Krann on my horse," whispered Willow, watching the galloping figure disappearing into the distance from where they stood at the rim of the Rising.

Fairlight saw nothing of Krann's flight. Now she slipped away from the feast and hurried back into the empty hall through the archway.

"Wasn't it wonderful—all those trees bursting apart," she laughed, her voice bubbling with excitement as she crossed the hall in a dozen running strides and knelt down beside the dais. "Krann!" she called again, more urgently, into the empty silence. There was an edge of worry in her voice as she gathered the folds of the throne cloth in her hands. "Krann, you must hurry before King Thane mounts the dais again to sit in judgement. Krann?" she cried, throwing back the hanging folds to reveal the dark empty space.

"For whom do you search, my lady Fairlight?" asked Thane from the doorway, making Fairlight cry out in surprise. She rose quickly to her feet as the King followed by Willow and her parents advanced to where she stood.

Fairlight shrank back, her eyes wide with panic, but Willow held her wrist. "Whom? Whom, my Lord?" she stuttered, her mind racing, trying to cover up what she had done as his eyes met hers.

"Krann," Thane hissed in a voice shaking with anger. "The one person in all Elundium who was not ready yet to see the Shadowtreading. That, my Lady of Stumble Hill, is whom you were searching for. Well you won't find him here. He has fled the Rising on Lord Willow's horse!"

"Krann?" gasped Fairlight, feeling the blood rush to her cheeks and hearing it pounding in her ears. She tried to think of some excuse, some lie, but no words would come.

Willow nodded grimly and let go of her wrist. "He fled in terror just as the feast began because of what he saw in the Shadowtreading."

"It was a game," cried Fairlight. "He was the only one not allowed to come to the Shadowtreading and I made him follow. I hid him beneath your chairs. It was my fault that he was here."

"You fool! Did you not see the mummer with the wig of frost-white hair? Did you not know of how we won the sunlight?"

The hall was completely silent and all eyes were turned towards the King. Fairlight hung her head and

shook it miserably as Krann's name was passed in a
ripple of whispered fear through the length of the hall.

"What have you done, child? What tragedy have you
unravelled with your meddling?" Eventine whispered, stepping past King Thane and taking her
daughter's hand.

The crowd shifted uneasily and moved closer, craning their necks as they waited for her answer.

"I wanted Krann to share the Shadowtreading with
me. It was to be such an adventure," she answered
through trembling lips as she sank onto her knees, her
head in her hands, and wept tears of shame. "I did not
know, no one ever told me of the Shadowtreading or
what part Krann must not see. I still do not truly understand what drove him to flee . . ."

Eventine unclasped the silver buckle on her heavy
winter cloak and cast it across her daughter's shoulders. She looked up into the King's eyes. "It is I, my
Lord, who must shoulder the blame and carry Fairlight's treason, for I kept her in ignorance of Krann's
beginnings and pledged all those in the Tower on
Stumble Hill into silence."

"But why did you do that? Why was she so ignorant?" cried Thane gripping Eventine's arms.

She smiled, meeting his eyes, and brushed her firegold hair back across her shoulders. "In your moment
of triumph, my Lord, as you held the baby who had
once been Kruel up into the sunlight and renamed
him Krann you pledged us all to forgive him and to
forget the terror of the shadowlight. But they could
not, my Lord, I saw it in everyone's eyes, just as you
must hear it now as they whisper Krann's name

— 157 —

around the hall; the fear, the terror of that darkness is still with them, this they will never forget. But we, Kyot and I, made a pledge that if we were blessed with a child then it would know nothing of Krann's past or what he sprang from so that in time he would have at least one real friend in all Elundium who did not watch his shadow each time he moved."

Thane stood very still in the silence, his eyes growing wet as he held Eventine's gaze. "Krann was blessed to have one such friend just as I was blessed to have you both at my side in the darkness. It is I who have betrayed him by keeping his beginnings secret, for so many passing suns, and silencing his curiosity."

"Lord," cried one of Willow's people, squeezing through the listening crowd and pointing urgently out into the distance. "The escaping horseman has taken the wild road towards Underfall but he will perish if he doesn't turn back, there are blizzards sweeping across the grasslands."

Thane ran to the threshold and looked quickly at the dark heavy clouds that boiled along the horizon and cursed the weather. "Krann will be lost," he shouted, turning on Willow, but his words were already snatched away by the wind as the blizzard swallowed them up in its stinging swirling whiteness. Thane gave orders for the heavy doors to be closed against the storm.

"Sprint shall follow his footsteps," called Kyot, turning to gather his bow.

"No! There will be no search," cried Elionbel from the doorway, tears and fresh snowflakes melting on her cheeks. "It is enough to lose one loved one in such a blizzard, I would not risk another for all the wrong that has been done. No, let us hope that by magic that once flowed through Nevian's rainbow cloak that Krann comes unharmed through this daylight."

Thane slowly nodded, his face saddening as he listened to the rising wind shriek and wail around the long hall and he knew that Elionbel was right, it would be madness to risk venturing out until the storm had passed.

Krann felt a bitter wind tug at his cloak and he twisted in the saddle to see the white wall of the blizzard boiling along the greenway on his heels. Crying out he spurred the horse forward and ran before the storm, crouched low over the withers, blind and uncaring to where Eyrus took him, weeping in rhythm with muffled hoofbeats, "I am evil, evil, evil."

The blizzard overtook them and wrapped its stinging silent whiteness around them like a frozen blanket. It made Eyrus slow and flounder as he tried to forge a passage through the deepening drifts. Krann cried out against the swirling storm, shouting his angry despair at the blinding snowflakes. Hardly caring where he went he spurred Eyrus amongst the white wilderness of low tangletrees that grew along the greenway's edge and hoped for death, a white death that would purge the shadows.

Suddenly Eyrus whinnied and crouched down, bending his hocks and forelegs, giving Krann less than a moment to throw himself clear as the horse scrambled beneath the spreading branches of two ancient tangletrees. Their gnarled twigs and sinewy branches had grown together into an enormous thick-knotted canopy which time had made weatherproof against storms. Krann followed the horse through the narrow opening and for all his misery gazed in wonder at the loops and tails of ice than hung down in shimmering jagged crystals from the roof of closely woven branches.

"Fairlight would have loved this," he muttered, shaking the snowflakes from his cloak and falling onto his knees. The thought of her brought to mind the leaps and twisting steps of the mummers' Shadow-treading dance and he flinched and clutched at his cloak with numb fingers as the mummer with the mask of piercing blue eyes and the shock of frost-white hair seemed to loom before him.

"It is *me* they danced about—it is my beginning they tread in their dance," he sobbed, falling forward in a huddle of despair on the frozen ground.

Eyrus snorted and pawed at the earth beside Krann's head, breaking small twigs and strips of bark that time had scattered around the two age-cracked trunks. The scraping sound of the horse's iron-shod hoof made Krann look up, "Eyrus!" he whispered. He had been so lost in his own misery he had not seen which horse he had taken in his haste to flee from the Rising.

Carefully Krann rose until he was squatting on his haunches and then gingerly reached out to touch the horse, half expecting it to flinch or to lash out at the evil that he now knew was a part of him, that everyone in Elundium had known about except him. But Eyrus snorted and brushed his velvet-soft muzzle against his cheek, then turned away to forage on the frozen ground for grass stems that had survived the frosts. Krann frowned at the turmoil of doubts and questions that filled his mind. He rubbed his frozen hands together and began to collect up the broken twigs and strips of bark that the horse had loosened from the ground. When he had gathered a small heap he lit them with his spark and stared at the thin spiral of blue smoke that rose. He began to sift through all the half-forgotten fragments of memory from his childhood and searched for signs of the evil, knowing that they must be there somewhere no matter how well King Thane and his half-sister had smothered them. He sat hunched forward biting on his knuckles as he stared into the dancing flames, but the fire did little to warm him as he reached back and touched the threads of his past. Above his head some of the icicles began to melt.

He could find nothing. No dark warriors, no leaping hideous beasts, no moments that he could hold up as a mirror to reflect the Shadowtreading. A blanket of childhood innocence covered all. He sighed and began to close his eyes, weary of all the misery, when the first whisper broke upon him and he started awake. It hissed in his ear and filled the air about him with snatches of a story of a shadowy army and a black mantle that swallowed the daylight. It shrieked and laughed of a time and a place he had never seen nor heard of and he cried out, spilling question after question through his lips, but the voices melted away into the roaring darkness of the storm that raged about their tangletree shelter and he could not be sure what he had heard and what was in his mind.

Drawing closer to the fire he shivered, knowing that no matter how innocent his childhood had seemed there must be more to that mirror image in the evil mummer's mask and he realized that he would have to know the truth of it but he must search it out himself. The Shadowtreading had revealed that there was a monstrous beast in him, but fate had opened his cage in the Granite City and set him free to find the answers. He lifted his head and listened to the storm, knowing that once it lessened he must set out to seek these places of which the whispering voice had spoken.

6

A Night in the Shambles

*M*ARRIMIAN blinked back tears of anger as she walked proudly out beneath the high archway without a backward glance into the long passageway that led into the great hall, but her lips were drawn into a bitter line of silence as she turned and watched her father's bowmen bow respectfully and retreat, slamming the thick-beamed doors against her.

"He is a cruel man to treat you so," muttered scullion Ansel from where she stood beside her mistress. "Only a brutal and heartless father would turn out his own daughter to die in the frozen hours."

Marrimian silently nodded as she sank down in a huddle against the cold damp wall, shivering, then she looked up at the scullion. "I had every right to drink from that cup, it doesn't matter that I am only his daughter. The mumbler said that everyone has the right. And he should not have punished me by giving Pinvey my task of welcoming the marshlords."

"She stole your place!" hissed Ansel her face blotching with anger. "She left you trussed up in that dark hole above the hall. It is she and not you who should be shivering out here."

Marrimian laughed quietly and rose to face Ansel. "Perhaps one day I will make Pinvey pay for her crimes, but we'll freeze to death if we have to stay here all night. What are we going to do? Where can we go?"

Ansel shrugged her shoulders and pointed up to the night sky sewn with its carpet of glittering ice stars. "We won't stay here and freeze to death while those who have punished us lie warmly in their beds. I'll think of something!"

Marrimian frowned and thought for a moment, stamping her feet against the gnawing cold. "I would not have claimed my right to joust just to prove that I am as worthy as any man but he goaded me, and Pinvey's treachery made me rush forward. I had to do it, I had to . . ."

Marrimian's voice trailed away as she stared out into the darkness, looking beyond the strings of tiny lights that shone as brightly as ribbons of precious stones in the maze of steep cobbled streets below. "But how can I joust? My father forbade it and laughed at me when I snatched the jousting cup and drank from it; he cursed me and called me weak."

Ansel slapped her large hands together, trying to warm her numb fingers as she undid her apron and spread it across Marrimian's shoulders in the deepening darkness. "You are right, mistress. The mumbler did say that all who drank from the cup had the right to joust, I heard him clearly as you did."

Marrimian shrugged her shoulders and pulled the apron tighter against the biting night wind. "It is easier in the saying than the doing, no matter what the mumbler said. Lord Miresnare will not allow it and if we do somehow join the joust it will have to be in secret, hiding our womanhood until the moment when my fingertips touch that slender shimmering finger of crystal."

"We must find shelter or warm beastskins, mistress," urged Ansel, "or the doorwardens will find our frozen carcasses picked clean by the carrion birds in tomorrow's dawn. We must descend into the city and find shelter from this icy wind."

Marrimian nodded in shivering agreement and tried to smile but cried out in pain as the fine layer of hoar frost that had silently woven its brittle feather patterns across her face cracked into a thousand sharp-edged pieces.

"We must keep moving until I think of somewhere we can go," urged Ansel, seeing how quickly the cold had overtaken her mistress.

Clutching her sleeve she pulled Marrimian away from the doors of the hall causing her to trip as they hurried, following the broad road that led down into the dense shadows of the crowded houses that lined the lanes and alleyways just below the hall.

Ansel hesitated for a moment and then hurried into the frozen darkness between the rough stone walls that closed in on either side of them. Marrimian stumbled frequently, grazing herself on the uneven steps, scraping her knuckles on the walls. She shouted to the scullion in rising panic, "Where are you taking me?" She had never strayed beyond the doorways of the hall and she feared the unknown.

"To Erek, the healing woman. She will give us shelter from the frozen hours," answered Ansel, feeling her mistress's terror as her fingernails cut painfully into her arm. "She will protect us," she soothed, trying to give Marrimian some courage and calm her fears as she picked her way down through the darkened maze of alleyways and tried to remember a road that she had only taken in the daylight.

Suddenly voices were all about them, heavy bodies jostled and pushed past them, pressing them back against the wall. Doors opened and slammed shut and lamp light spilled out of noisy crowded taverns and briefly lit the narrow lanes. People hurried down the narrow streets.

"Who are they?" whispered Marrimian turning to Ansel as the crowd thinned and the sound of voices faded.

"They are the harvesters and the gatherers who live beyond the city. They must have been waiting for the quickmarshes to freeze so that they can return to their homes," replied Ansel hesitantly as she felt her way down a particularly narrow twist of steep uneven steps. "You see, mistress," she whispered, halting at a gap between two tall overhanging houses and pointing out into the darkness, "by daylight the quickmarshes are too dangerous to cross unless you know the secret paths that the marshlords use, but during the frozen hours the marsh crust freezes and is strong enough to take the weight of . . ." she paused, searching her mind for something heavy, and clapped her hands saying, "something the weight of a mudbeast."

Marrimian shivered and watched the lines of lights

grow dim as they moved away from the city. "What if they become lost and cannot find their way back into the marsheries before the new sun rises?" she asked, biting her lip anxiously.

"Then they must find a safe place, my lady, but that is a part of their craft, to know the marshes," muttered Ansel, brushing her mistress's question aside as she turned her attention to which of the six lanes that opened before them they should take.

"Have you ever ventured out into the quickmarsh?" Marrimian asked keeping a firm hold on the scullion's arm, afraid of being left behind in this maze of dark lanes.

"Yes, a little way," answered Ansel, nodding absently at her mistress's questions as she searched every entrance with her broad fingertips. "Every underscullion must travel far enough in the quickmarsh to reach the apselgather beds and learn to harvest . . ." She fell silent and took a large step into the fourth entrance and found what she was looking for—the soft touch of gossamer beneath her fingertips. She knew that they stood at the entrance of the Shambles.

Ansel drew a deep breath, took hold of both of Marrimian's hands and placed them firmly on her waist and told her in a hushed whisper to follow in her footsteps and to touch nothing, nor to cry out if anything brushed against her or ran across her face.

Marrimian pulled back against the scullion. "Look," she whispered. "There are eyes. I can see eyes watching us from just inside that narrow alleyway."

Ansel laughed quietly and called out against the darkness, whispering a chant that the healing woman had taught her, and row by row the luminous eyes blinked shut or turned away. "They are nothing to be afraid of, my lady, they are only the healing woman's spiders that guard the entrance to the Shambles."

"Spiders! I hate spiders!" cried Marrimian and shrank back in terror. She felt the scullion's strong hands grip her wrist and she knew that if she had been free she would have fled and lost herself in the darkness.

"Be still, my lady," Ansel whispered, keeping a firm grip on her wrist. "Be still and be safe. In the great hall you are mistress of everything and you know which passageway will lead to which courtyard and whom to meet upon the way but out here there is danger for you and you must stay close to me."

"But I fear spiders, and the cold clinging darkness," gasped Marrimian.

Ansel smiled. "These spiders are only like the healing spiders that were put upon your cuts when you were a child."

Marrimian shuddered as she remembered those horrible creatures with their soft white underbellies slowly crawling over her skin, spinning those itching silken webs that soaked up the poisons and knitted the ragged edges of her childhood wounds.

"Walk slowly and fear nothing," soothed Ansel breaking into her thoughts. Moving forward into the Shambles she pulled her reluctant mistress along behind her.

Marrimian tried to call out, to beg the scullion to choose another path, but her voice was swallowed up in the stifling silence. The sounds of the city had vanished and even their footsteps had become muffled to nothing beneath their shoes. She looked down, trying to see the cobbles as she sensed that they were walking on something that felt as soft as a carpet though it was sticky and clung a little at each step. She looked up, her eyes widening with panic as she saw the thick canopy of woven threads that shone in the starlight. She clung tighter to Ansel's waist and screwed her eyes shut against the nightmare they were shuffling through but she still felt the webs brush against her from the rough mud-slapped walls on either side of her where they hung in gossamer patterns. Something was moving behind them, she could sense it creeping closer and closer. She opened her eyes and twisted her head to look over her shoulder and felt her heartbeat freeze: the luminous eyes that had crowded the entrance of the Shambles were following them. Spiders were scuttling silently along the walls across the threads above their heads.

Marrimian hid her head in Ansel's ample breast, her breaths coming in short strangled gasps as the panic rose to choke her. She held hard to the scullion's waist and pushed her, almost making her trip and lose her balance. Just at that moment a low door arch loomed and Ansel reached out to touch the liftlatch. The latch turned as if moved by some unseen hand just as Ansel's fingers touched it. The door swung silently inwards upon a low-beamed shadowy room, a fire of twisting flames flickered in the hearthstone and two ill-trimmed reed lamps hanging beside the mantelshelf guttered and filled the room with a smoky haze. Crouching on a carved stool beside the firestone was the oldest woman that Marrimian had ever seen. She leered up at them and rocked backwards and forwards, beckoning to them with a gnarled swollen hand, whispering them over her doorstone.

Marrimian shivered and pushed against the scullion, the hairs on the nape of her neck tingling. Something heavy scuttled across the hem of her skirt and she glanced down quickly and screamed and felt her legs turn to jelly. A black tide of spiders had crawled a hand's span up on the hem of her gown. Crying out she crumpled against Ansel, and fell into dark nightmare dreams where cold hands touched her, smothered her and wrapped her in silence. Ansel caught her before she fell and saw nothing of the healing woman's pitiless searching eyes as she dragged her mistress over the doorstone and laid her down at Erek's feet.

"And what sweetmeat is this?" cackled Erek wiping at the fine threads of dribble that had escaped from her sunken gums and hung in glistening loops from the point of her chin.

She bent forwards and picked up the rich embroidery of Marrimian's feasting gown, brushing away the spiders hidden into its folds, cursing them and sending them out into the alleyway to guard the entrance to the Shambles and keep the other healing women from nosing into her affairs. She looked up at the scullion from beneath cunning hooded eyes and whispered, "What new spells do you seek to barter with this rich lady that you have stolen from Glitterspike Hall?"

Ansel frowned, her eyebrows drawing into a deep

furrow above her flushed cheeks, and shook her head, pointing down at Marrimian. "Be kind to her—this is Marrimian the first-born of Glitterspike Hall. I have not stolen her, I brought her here because her father Lord Miresnare banished us, giving us no time even to gather our cloaks, and threw us into the frozen hours. She is gentle born with soft and delicate skin and she will freeze to death without shelter and a coarser cloth than my apron tails against the cold."

Erek laughed shrilly, cracking her knuckles slowly one by one, the noise of each joint sounding harshly in the firelight as she looked down at Marrimian. "How I have plotted and dreamed my webs of hatred against your father," she hissed, bending over her, and whispered her black spiders to swarm across the floor.

"No!" cried Ansel moving between her mistress and the advancing spiders, "I brought Marrimian here to you because she has been banished. You are a healer and the wisest woman in all Gnarlsmyre and you can help her."

Erek cackled and halted the spiders with a snap of her fingers. "Everything holds a price, kitchen woman, and this one would command the highest price of all. What would you barter for my help? What have you got in your apron pockets that is worth a kingdom?"

Ansel looked shocked, the colour fading from her oven-scarred cheeks as she searched desperately for an answer. She had never seen this greed and hatred in the healing woman before; she had thought of her as a little odd with her mutterings and shrieks of cackling laughter but beneath that she believed her to be a kind old lady only too pleased to barter herbs and sweetmeats from the kitchens of Glitterspike Hall for songs and spells that she weaved with her spiders' webs to lure lovers.

"You owe me much," Ansel answered bravely, looking the healing woman in the eye and pointing to the rows of jars and magic potions that lined the far wall. "The magic words you bartered with me for a tucket of galingale grains and turnsole leaves did not do as you promised and win me a marshlord or a marshhunter to share my lonely life. No, the first man from beyond the Hurlers' Gate that I looked upon rejected me with curses spilling from his tongue and pushed me aside. So your spell failed." Her indignation made her an imposing figure as she stood her ground, her large hands planted firmly on her hips.

Erek hesitated and retreated to step towards the firestone muttering under her breath. She had never known spells to fail; clearly the scullion was lying to save this daughter of Miresnare's. Twisting her head she spat into the flames, sending bright vapours of steam hissing up the chimney hole. She turned back, reached out and snatched at Ansel's wrist, pulling her close to the fire. "Kneel, scullion!" she growled, revealing an edge of the hatred that had festered in her heart and blackened her healing arts since that terrible day when Lord Miresnare had sacked the Shambles in search for the potions that would spawn him an heir. "Kneel and let me listen at your ear. If you have spoken the truth you shall barter it against the first-born's life but if your lips have lied the spiders shall have her."

Ansel knelt very still, her neck tingling as the healing woman's hot breath touched her shoulder. She shivered and screwed up her courage tight as she felt the dry and crackled skin against her ear. Erek listened, her forehead wrinkling, her eyes narrowed. Suddenly she shrieked with anger and made Marrimian start awake and the scullion jump. "Mertzork the marshlord was never meant for you, kitchen girl. He was to drive the beast Gallengab into Glitterspike Hall and destroy Yaloor. He was to have ended Miresnare's rule and taken all Gnarlsmyre in payment for working my revenge."

Pushing Ansel aside the healing woman squatted beside Marrimian, gripped her neck with one gnarled hand and scratched at her eardrum with the long curved fingernail of the other. "Be still, be still," she hissed, pressing her ear against Marrimian's and learning all that had come to pass in Glitterspike Hall. Erek cursed and released Marrimian, sat back on her haunches and stared at her, her hatred for Lord Miresnare bubbling through her.

"Now you can see that I spoke the truth, you must help my mistress," pleaded Ansel, anxiously tugging at Erek's ragged sleeve only to dislodge a dozen spiders that were hidden in the folds and now ran silently up her arms. Ansel shook the spiders off in terror and shuddered as she whispered, "A promise is a promise, the marshlord should have been mine, so now you must help my mistress."

Erek turned on the scullion and hissed her into silence as she pointed with a curved fingernail to a rag bed that lay in the deep shadows of the hovel. "That marshwader shall be yours instead—go to him!"

Turning back she pulled her stool close to Marrimian and sat silently staring at her, trying to search out all the secrets of her life in the hall. "Why do you hate me so much?" asked Marrimian suddenly sitting up. "Why did you send that beast to destroy Glitterspike Hall and ruin all my father has tried to achieve?"

Erek scowled, then her mouth split into a black humourless grin. Leaning forward she scratched at the sack of dry wrinkled skin that hung in folds beneath her chin before she answered, "Your father, Lord Miresnare, banished all the healers, calling them weak, treacherous women. All of us were driven out through the gate of the city at arrow point to perish in the quickmarsh because we could not foretell or brew a magic potion that would give him a male heir to carry his rule into the future."

Marrimian gasped and put her hand to her mouth. She had heard whispered talk of how her father had raged through the city striking terror in every house but she had never believed that he was capable of such evil. "I thought it was all wild rumours. I never dreamed that he could be that harsh," she whispered.

Erek threw her head back and shrieked with laughter. "I have more to hate him for than that. The terror, the burning, the sacking of the Shambles were nothing to what he did to *me.*" For a moment Erek paused, her hooded eyes growing watery as she remembered. "He snatched my only child, my lovely one, to be chained to dance amongst his mumbling men and he threatened to throw him to the beast Yaloor if I so much as set one foot upon his doorstone or dared to think or ask about him until a male heir was born."

Marrimian shivered and stared at the healing woman and then slowly took hold of Erek's hands. "There is one of the mumblers who has your likeness," she whispered hesitantly. "He is the master mumbler and the one who foretold that the beast would enter the hall. He could be the child that my father stole from you."

Erek shrieked and almost toppled from her stool. She snatched her hand away from Marrimian's and frantically fumbled beneath her rags for the searching mirror that she kept hidden there.

"Breathe slowly," she cried, her fingers trembling as she held the mirror against Marrimian's lips. "Think of the mumblers dancing in their magic circle, think of the one who has a likeness to me as your breath ghosts the mirror with the mists of truth," she whispered, watching the picture of the leaping mumblers wrapped in their wreath tails of pine oil slowly form in tiny beads of moisture.

"Who is he? What is his name?" she moaned, rocking back and forth on her low stool and hugging the mirror against her sunken chest, smearing the picture away with hot teardrops that fell unchecked upon the glass as she wept.

"He is called Naul," Marrimian whispered gently. "He leads the dance of foresight. He foretold the destruction Gallengab would spread through Gnarlsmyre if he challenged Yaloor. He forewarned my father that the joust for my hand must change, that he was to trick the marshlords into chaining their

beasts around the base of the Glitterspike before pro-
claiming a new game that would give the throne and
all Gnarlsmyre to the one who would walk through
the circle of shackled beasts and touch the Glitters-
spike. Naul, your lost son, is the joustmaster of this
game and sets the rules to thwart each challenger."

Erek narrowed her eyes and pressed her lips into
a thin bloodless line. "I only have your word and a
misted image in the mirror. How do I know that he
is really my blood? Perhaps you are lying to save your
own life. No son of mine would ever help a Miresnare
to thwart my magic. If there was really blood between
us he would not help to stifle my revenge."

Erek shrank away from Marrimian and began whispering and muttering under her breath as she turned
over all she had learned and planned how to use it to
feed her revenge. Turning she glared at the scullion,
wishing that she had looked through her at the mumblers before, instead of bartering her magic to sweeten
her cooking pot. Erek's eyes narrowed and her sunken
lips scowled as she remembered that her barter with
the kitchen scullion was not complete and could prevent her from taking Marrimian as a hostage. Thinking quickly she smiled at the scullion and soothed her
with words and asked her if she would take the handsome marshwader who lay on the rag bed and thus set
the barter right between them. Marrimian saw a glimmer of mistrust and a feather-edge of hatred in the
healing woman and she opened her mouth to warn
Ansel to be careful with her answer but Erek hissed
her into silence and clamped her hand across her

mouth lest she spilled a word of how finely her fate was balanced upon her reply.

Ansel hesitated, sensing that something was wrong; she knew that the healing woman had no right to gag her or talk roughly to her mistress. She turned her head and looked carefully at the marshwader hoping that he would somehow help her but he had raised himself onto his elbows and only watched, his one good eye following her every movement, most of his face hidden beneath the healing web that covered the hideous gash that the pindafall's jaw had torn in his cheek. He would never, with that blemish on his face, be as handsome as the cruel marshlord who had pushed her through the curtain, but his eye was gentler, with a straight and honest look that made her heart beat faster and her breath escape in shallow gasps. She blinked and forced herself to look away, knowing that if she denied the barter and angered Erek she would never be able to ask for her help again and would always be alone, for who would cast their eyes on fat Ansel the scullion with her blotched and oven-scarred cheeks and clumsy spade-shaped hands?

Ansel swallowed and turned back to the healing woman and steadily held her eye. "My mistress must come before all things, even the marshwader. My barter must be taken up with you promising to help my lady Marrimian."

Erek's eyes hardened as she looked at Marrimian, knowing that by the Law of Barter she must help her. "What is it you would have me do?" she hissed, twisting her knuckles together as she waited for the answer.

Marrimian thought for a moment, casting her eyes over the jars of potions and the trembling webs of gossamer that hung in countless folds from the low ceiling. She glimpsed a power in the room that went far beyond healing and she said quietly, "I need your help to touch the Glitterspike and take from my father what is rightfully mine."

Erek was shocked into silence. Then she began to sneer and laugh and curl her dribbling lips back across her empty gums at Marrimian's foolish words and pointed at her gown. "But you are a woman—you cannot joust with men. Even if I had the magic to help you and you touched the Glitterspike you could not rule. Nobody would listen to you nor obey you. No, ask for something within my power."

But Marrimian brushed her hair angrily out of her eyes and insisted that it was time, time long overdue, to change this rule of men, that she was ashamed of what her father had done and she cursed the day the Shambles were sacked. She was helpless, as helpless as all women in Gnarlsmyre, but no matter how weak and vulnerable she was she must try to put things right for everyone.

"And you would change everything with a rush of skirts to touch the Glitterspike?" scoffed Erek sitting bolt upright on her stool and spitting into the fire to brighten the flames.

Marrimian hesitated and looked helplessly about her trying to pluck her half-formed ideas and nagging whispers from the shadowy room. Spreading her empty hands for help she turned towards the healing woman. "Yesterday these words were less than whispers in my head. Then I was Marrimian, the first-born, the Lady of Glitterspike Hall. Ragmen bowed and scullions knelt when I passed them by, my whims were quickly honoured in every way. But my father always cursed me and hated me for being born a woman and clearly I was a burden, an object to lure the marshlords to joust for my favours, because there was no male heir to continue the line of Miresnare. I am of his blood but to him I am nothing more than a prettier; my words and thoughts, no matter how much I laboured over them, were always brushed aside and dismissed as idle-headedness. Yet how I yearned to please him and to be as a son would be. But now I am banished and my heart has hardened against this so-called power that men hold over us and I see what a fool I have been to try and please. The new joust has barely begun before my father snaps his fingers and tells me that I no longer serve a purpose because I am a woman, a mere nothing, even though he proclaimed that all who drank from the jousting cup had the right to try."

"You would make us equal with men and give me the right to serve at the tables beside them in the great hall?" asked the scullion in an awed whisper.

Marrimian frowned and shrugged her shoulders. "I am not sure what I mean, it is all a muddle, but I would try to judge all people on their merits, their bravery and honest courage, their wit and their temper, and not hold them in low esteem because they were born women."

Erek turned away from Marrimian and stared into the fire. All this high talk of touching the Glitterspike and ruling Gnarlsmyre was ridiculous—the marsh-men and the guards, every man in the hall, would turn on her and would ridicule her and cast her out. No, it would be better to use Mertzork, she had some power over him. Let him do the touching and then he could bring this mumbler, Naul, to her and she would know for sure if he was of her blood. That was a much safer scheme. But for now she had to appear to help in order to complete the barter she owed the scullion. And perhaps at the same stroke she could rid herself of this troublesome pair.

"You cannot return to Glitterspike Hall to joust against the marshlords and all those who thrust for the throne unless you are disguised. You will only have the chance to prove you are an equal if your woman-hood is well hidden. Only in the moment of your tri-umph can you strip off the mask of your disguise."

"What should be my disguise? How shall I wear it?" asked Marrimian, hesitating in confusion.

Erek cackled quietly, rocking backwards and for-wards on her stool and twisting cunning words around her tongue before she answered. "Before you can thrust for the throne, my Lady of Glitterspike, you must disguise yourself as a marshman. You must learn their ways, their speech, their smells and learn to walk easily beneath the weight of a beastskin cloak."

Marrimian shrank back with a cry of horror on her lips as she remembered their foul stench, their en-grained layers of marsh filth and the swarms of insects that lived on their rancid cloaks and crawled unhin-dered on their dirty skin. "I could not," she whispered, shuddering and swallowing at the bile that was rising in her throat. Yet she saw the truth of it—she would never be allowed to take part in the joust unless she appeared to be a man.

"To succeed, you must! You must!" urged Erek, rubbing her hands together and narrowing her hooded eyes into cunning slits. "You must go to the marsheries and learn the marshmen's ways." She scuttled across her hovel and bent low over the marshwader. "This man shall be your guide." She bent and whispered in his ear, telling him to take them to Mertzork's marshery and keep them safe until she sent for them.

Then Erek rummaged in a black wooden chest beside the hearth-stone for a gossamer-woven cloak to cast across Marrimian's shoulders to warm her against the frozen hours. She pushed Ansel's hand into the marshwader's and hissed, "Now my barter is more than complete. This marshwader shall be forever bound to you, scullion, to guide your mistress in all the footsteps of her journey, and to fill all the seasons of your loneliness."

Marrimian reached out to the healing woman and tried to hold her hand in thanks but she quickly withdrew her arm as swarms of spiders ran silently towards her fingertips out of the folds of Erek's cloak. She asked in a frightened whisper, "How will we survive beyond the city? Surely the marsh people will see that we are of the city and tear the clothes from our backs and drown us in the mire?"

Erek shook her head as she began to herd them towards her doorstone. "You will be safe with the marshwader, he will overwatch you." And she urged them to hurry before the marsh crust melted in the heat of the new sun.

"How far beyond the city are the marsheries?" Marrimian called as the dark silence of the web-choked alleyway swallowed them up.

Erek answered in a chanting shout, "As far as they need to be!", her voice ending in shrieks of laughter. That and the sharp snap of her closing door latch were the last sounds they heard of her as they passed the furthest tangle of webs that guarded the Shambles to feel the cold night air brush against their faces and see the glittering canopy of ice stars shining above them in the night sky.

7

Vanishing Footsteps in the Quickmarsh

"*TREAD* warily," the marshwader tried to say as he spun round and snatched at Marrimian's wrist. She had trodden too closely to the marsh edge and her right foot had slipped off the path into the treacherous mire. As he pulled her back to safety he smiled, stretching the maze of healing webs that were still bound across her face.

He pointed down to his filthy ragbound feet. "Tread in my footprints," he gulped, the words escaping in a muffled whisper through the silken webs as he tried to make Marrimian step where he did.

Ansel understood and nodded, her eyes round and shining, her cheeks hot-flushed. She squeezed his hand and touched her mistress's sleeve. "Tread where he does, my lady," she whispered, "before the slimy mud seeps back into his footprints and blends them with the rest of this mire."

Marrimian nodded miserably, her skirts held in a tight bunch above the greenish slimy mud that had covered her shoes and was creeping up over her ankles. She looked to both sides of the narrow path they were following and tried without success to see through the reeking swirls of morning mist. She shivered and awkwardly pulled the thin gossamer cloak more tightly about her shoulders.

"Ask him how much further," she muttered without turning to Ansel. "Ask him if we will ever be free of this stinking mire."

The marshwader laughed, the noise gurgling in his mouth as he heard Marrimian's words, and he pointed towards the horizon's rim where there was a glimpse in the mist of a low jumble of rock and strange-looking buildings raised on tall stilts above the quickmarshes. Shrugging impatiently he put his hands to his mouth and tore a hole in the healing web and sucked in a mouthful of pure marsh air. Just then Marrimian staggered and slipped towards the edge of the path. She cried out as her foot sank into the soft mud and would have fallen further if the marshman had not clutched her flailing arms and pulled her to safety. He laughed and took deep breaths of the cold morning mists that were rising off the marshes all around them. "Watch where you tread and keep a sharp eye on the shadows of the pindafall birds as they cross the sun," he said. His words sounded clearer now through the tear in the spiders' webs.

He grinned, his teeth flashing with a yellow whiteness as he looked past Marrimian into the scullion's eyes.

"I am Ansel," she whispered nervously and blushed, clumsily fluttering her eyelashes, her large hands twisting her apron into a bunch of knots as the marshwader stared up at her.

His one eye softened, and he stabbed a finger at his

chest. "I am Vetchim. My lord and master was Zenork whose marshery straddles those rocks upon the horizon line."

"Zenork?" questioned Marrimian sharply, making Vetchim look up at her. "Did he play a part in snaring Gallengab? Is that how you earned the tear in your face?"

Vetchim laughed without a trace of humour in his eye and slowly nodded as he told her how Zenork was Mertzork's father but had been murdered by his own son. He recounted how Mertzork stole Gallengab and kept him a secret from the other marshlords, even using the ugly tear the pindafall had gouged in his face to gain an entrance to the city. "He is a dangerous marshlord and treacherous even to his own people."

Suddenly a shadow swooped low across the marsh. Vetchim opened his mouth and shouted a warning and threw himself against the women, flattening them into the sticky green mud. Marrimian cried out in terror as the swift-moving shadow crossed the sun and she shrank down into the oozing cold mud beneath the marshwader and shut her eyes. She turned her head away as razor-hooked talons tore through the thick cloak that Vetchim wore and shredded it into a mess of ragged ribbons. The pindafall shrieked, its jaws snapping shut empty, and wheeled away from the path to vanish in the thinning mist with its black leathery wings rattling in the warm currents of morning air.

"Beware! Everything is dangerous out here," hissed Vetchim, slowly rising and turning his head to follow the fading sound of the carrion bird.

Somewhere just beyond the path, hidden by the ghost-tails of mist, a voice screamed. It was a half-choked cry of terror that was abruptly silenced.

"What was that?" Marrimian whispered fearfully, turning towards the swirling mist, the sticky mud of the marsh forgotten as it dripped from her fingers.

The marshwader shrugged his shoulders and began to turn back onto the narrow path. "It is nothing, a voice from the dead, a ghost calling to us from the quickmarsh."

"That was a woman's voice," cried Marrimian catching hold of the marshwader's sleeve and stopping him. "That cry came from somewhere out there. We must try and rescue her."

Vetchim frowned and hurried forward, his eyes narrowed. He seemed uneasy and fine beads of sweat were damping the edges of the healing webs. "It is unlucky to listen to the voices. The quickmarsh is thawing and the marsh crust is melting. We dare not leave the path to look for ghosts. Quick, follow me. If anyone has lost their way in the mire that strangled cry would be the sound they made as the pindafall bit off their head."

Marrimian stared uncertainly at the marshwader's back. There was something in his manner she did not trust, something that made her doubt the healing woman's words of counsel, but she could not be sure. She could see the sense of leaving the city and learning a little of the ways of the marsh people before she demanded her right to try to touch the Glitterspike but it had all been too easy and she had agreed to it too quickly, without question. She was so used to obeying orders. But no longer. "I will go no further!" she suddenly cried, planting her feet firmly in the sticky mud. "I will go no further until I know a little more of this marshery you are taking us to and I wish to know more of your part in the snaring of Gallengab, and where your loyalties lie."

Vetchim blinked, spun around and looked at Marrimian. "It is not our custom to share the secrets of snaring mudbeasts with women, nor will I explain the ways of the marsheries. Erek said you were to follow me, so that is what you will do, and you will wait for Mertzork or Andzey to answer your questions."

Without another word on their fate he turned and ordered them to follow and to be quick before his footprints vanished in the softening mud. He had listened to all that had been said in the healing woman's hovel and he knew that Marrimian was a rich prize. He must get her safely to the marshery and give the message from Erek that these women must be safely chained up to use as ransom or, in desperation, in a haggle or a barter. Vetchim laughed silently as he splashed through the mud, sure in his mind that Mertzork would reward him well, perhaps even bestow on him the title of marshhunter or give him a quickmire of his own to hunt and a dwelling set high above the slippery mud for his pleasures with the scullion. She was no beauty but she was sweet-natured and modest. Better qualities in the marshes than good looks.

"No, I will not follow a man who will not give a straight answer," called out Marrimian, stamping obstinately and refusing to move. The marshwader had reached the end of his small store of patience.

"Push your mistress along, woman," he shouted angrily at Ansel. "Make her follow and be quick, before the pindafall birds steal your silly heads."

Ansel narrowed her eyes and frowned at the harsh hurtful tone of the marshwader's voice. "Why will you not follow?" she whispered, putting her lips close to her mistress's ear and hoping that somehow Marrimian could put her own nagging doubts about this man to rest, doubts that had been gnawing and slowly growing from the moment the healing woman had joined their hands together.

"These marsh people are different from us, they are savage and I fear to go amongst them," Marrimian whispered to the scullion. "And I fear that the healing woman has sent us on a fool's errand; it feels wrong following this marshwader towards some unknown marshery."

"Mistress!" hissed Ansel throwing up her hands in dismay. "What is it you foresee?"

Marrimian grimly shrugged and firmly set her jaw as she held the marshwader's eyes so boldly that it made him blink and look away as she demanded, "We will not move until you tell us more."

Ansel nodded and folded her huge arms as she felt her feet sink deep into the mud and touch the hard rock of the path that lay just below the surface of the quickmarsh. "Yes, we want some truth, Vetchim," she grumbled echoing her mistress's doubts.

"We are stronger together," whispered Marrimian. "Do not let his answers separate us."

Vetchim frowned and shook his head helplessly as if trying to shake out an answer that would hurry these women along. If they had been marshwomen he would have beaten them and dragged them to the council for punishment, but then marshwomen would never have answered him back nor demanded explanations, their place was to serve. The best of them were fleshers and hide cleaners, the simpler ones merely gatherers and carriers, beasts of burden who scavenged food when the quickmarsh was frozen.

"Truth! I will tell the truth of all I know of what lies before you, if you do not do as I say," he blurted out, spreading his empty hands towards them, feeling that his tongue was running away from him in his impatience to have the journey over and the two women safely in chains. "Within the marshery a woman is punished for speaking out of turn as you do, or for meddling in the affairs of men; she must gather and harvest, bear children, toil from the first glimmer of daylight until the marshes freeze and if she fails to serve her master's pleasures then she is punished and cast out to die. But if you are a good woman and answer a man's desires you will have the honour of fleshing the hides of the mudbeasts that he kills and none of the other marshery women will be allowed to soften those skins with their teeth; they will be yours alone to chew."

Ansel swallowed in disgust and spat into the melting marsh crust at her feet. "I would not chew on a beastskin, no, not even a hare or a hedgehog, not for you nor for any man in all Gnarlsmyre!" she replied hotly. There had been none of this foul talk in the kitchens of Glitterspike Hall, no mention of the horror of what these marshmen would make you do once they had taken you from the city. It had all been whispers and hot looks of bedding, of serving and easing their burdens and of sharing those lonely cold nighttime hours.

Marrimian laughed quietly, the sound ending in a hopeless whisper. "Would you go with him now!" she asked watching the marshwader's every move.

Ansel shook her head fiercely and puffed out her red oven-scarred cheeks and scowled. "No mistress, I would not!"

Vetchim sneered and threw up his hands. "Then you can stay here and perish for all I care. Without me to guide you to the safety of the marshery you will vanish beneath the marsh with the first false step!"

Laughing he turned his back on them and hurried forward for twenty paces and then stopped and turned, pointing down to where the soft mud had quickly filled his footprints, smoothing them into the stinking surface of the marsh. "Now try and make your own way if you dare!" he sneered, curling back his lips in helpless anger at the way that Marrimian and her questions had so easily thwarted his schemes.

He proceeded another dozen steps, carefully looking over his shoulder to check that neither woman had tried to move. Laughing grimly to himself he strode forward towards the marshery that lay in a jumble of low rocks on the horizon line, hoping that for all their bold talk the women had just enough sense between them to stay still and not flounder off the path. He would be back to fetch them when they had terrified themselves into submission.

"What now?" cried Ansel wringing her apron tails

between her fingers and mopping at the trails of hot sweat that trickled down her face in the heat of the noonday sun.

Marrimian sharply ordered her into silence and arched her hand against the harsh sunlight. She watched the marshwader vanish into a mere speck in the shimmering haze that hung above the bubbling marsh crust.

"We are lost and abandoned to perish," wailed Ansel, slapping at the countless stinging insects that hummed and droned in thick clouds around their head. "We are helpless, we are lost . . ."

"Quiet!" snapped Marrimian. "Give me a moment's rest from your incessant wailing. Let me try and think of a way out of this stinking mire. The marshwader is not a fool; he knows my worth amongst his people, that is what was making me uneasy. What did the healing woman whisper to him before she hurried us out of the door? I should have listened more closely and refused to leave the city and insisted on finding another way to enter the hall. I was so frightened and confused . . . No, he has not abandoned us, scullion, he knows that we dare not move and I'll lay ten of Yaloor's sharpest claws that he has gone to fetch a dozen other marshmen to drag us into those hovels that we saw on the horizon's edge, standing out above the marsh, before this heat haze distorted everything."

Ansel muttered to herself and stared down at the marsh crust that hissed and bubbled at her feet sending up foul vapours into the stifling air. It was all her fault that they were trapped in this nightmare place, if only she had not bartered galingale seeds and turnsole leaves. **What a fool** she had been to leave the kitchens in her lust **for a** marshman. Now she could clearly see that she belonged in the city amongst her own people.

Marrimian was shaking her arm, breaking into her thoughts, making her blink and look up. "There must be thousands of paths," she whispered fiercely. "The marshwader left us because he thought we would be too afraid to try and find a way out of this place, but . . ."

"No!" cried Ansel in terror, gripping at her mistress's sleeve. "We will flounder with the first false step. Look what happened when your foot slipped off the path. If the marshwader had not caught you . . ."

"That is why men think of us as weak fools, because we stifle adventure with too much caution. Now, Ansel, down on your hands and knees and help me find the beginnings of the road back to the City of Glor."

"But, mistress!" cried Ansel as Marrimian pulled her firmly down.

"Do as I do!" Marrimian said through clenched teeth as she plunged her hands into the slimy stinking mud and felt for the hard rock of the hidden path.

Ansel shuddered and pushed her hands through the warm squelching mud beside her mistress, wrinkling her nose at the foul stench that rose to engulf them. Marrimian laughed bitterly, trying to toss a fallen lock of hair out of her eyes, and looked at the endless expanse of quickmarsh that heaved and bubbled all around them. She frowned, sat back on her haunches and stilled the scullion. "Look around you, Ansel, and tell me what you see."

Ansel wrung and squeezed the mud from between her fat fingers as she swept her gaze across the quickmarsh. "Bubbling mud, reeds and bulrush stems, half sunken rotting marsh trees and low lumps of scrub-covered mounds, mistress," she answered, blinking at the trickles of sweat that were stinging her eyes.

"No, there is more in the marsh than that. Think back to the maze of alleyways and corridors that sprawl around Glitterspike Hall and tell me how you found your way through them."

Ansel puffed out her cheeks and thought hard, trying to remember. She shrugged her shoulders, held up her large mud-caked fingers and began to recall. "There were rough stone corridors where the servers walked, brick floors for the scullions to use and passageways that sloped downwards and always ended just above the moats where we gathered marshfish, or, by branching to the right, led to the crystal house where we harvested fresh vegetables. Beyond the walls of Glitterspike Hall there were walkways for the harvesters to leave us the apselgathers fresh-picked before the sun rose, slippery floors where the ragmen greased their ragbound feet, and . . ." Ansel sighed, throwing up her hands and giving up the count. "There were a thousand signs, my lady—the smell of the herb larders, the warmth of the bake ovens, sometimes you could just close your eyes and follow your nose. But we'll never see it all again, I know it," she ended, wailing.

"So, look around you again, and this time use your

eyes," hissed Marrimian impatiently, pointing out into the marsh. "Watch where the bubbles rise and how the marsh grasses grow across those lumps. There must be a thousand ways to cross this mire if only we could read the signs in the treacherous mud."

"Trees must have roots, mistress, and roots must cling on to something," cried Ansel catching at the threads of what Marrimian was searching for.

Marrimian laughed and nodded. "I watched the marshwader picking his way across the marsh and for a while I despaired, thinking we were lost. But there was no magic in what he did, he was merely following a clear path over the mud because he could read the signs. Cast him loose in Glitterspike Hall and he would be as lost in that maze of alleyways and corridors that is so familiar to us as we are here. I know he would not sink from sight as we could beneath this marsh if we do not tread with caution, but to him the danger would seem as great and just as terrifying."

Ansel crouched forwards dubiously prodding at the soft mud and asked, "What signs must we search for and which way should we look for them?"

Marrimian frowned and shrugged her shoulders. "We dare not follow the path that the marshwader took; that would be too dangerous and would only lead us towards the marshery. We must try to retrace our footsteps." She hesitated, remembering the terrible scream that they had heard in the mist. "Or we could search for a way out towards those low, odd-looking, scrub-covered mounds beyond the leaning marsh oaks—I am sure that was a real voice and not a ghost that we heard."

Ansel shivered, her arms sinking elbow-deep into the mud as she felt for the hard rock of the path. Something wriggled between her fingers, its sharp slippery scales cutting into her. "Mistress, mistress," she cried, leaping back and nearly losing her balance.

Marrimian caught hold of her apron bows and hauled her back to safety, laughing as she saw the mud-covered marshfish wriggling and flapping in the scullion's terrified grip. "Well at least we will not starve!" she cried, turning her head away and shielding her face from the fine spray of sticky mud that the slapping fish was showering over them. Ansel gave a grunt of surprise as she saw what she had accidentally caught beneath the mud and quickly killed the fish with one twist of her strong fingers. She scraped the worst of the sticky slime from between its black-spined fins and thrust it into the deepest pocket of her apron.

"Everything is different here," she muttered darkly, cleaning her hands as best she could on the corners of her apron. "The people live by savage laws and even their fish fight against you with their razor-sharp scales. It looks just like the marshfish we catch in the clear waters of the moats at Glitterspike Hall, but it isn't, it's . . ," Ansel fell silent, searching for the words to express her fears.

Marrimian smiled at her. The thick marsh mud smearing Ansel's cheeks had cracked and crumbled in the hot sticky heat. "You have touched on the truth, Ansel. This is a new and very dangerous world for us," she answered, beginning to laugh at the scullion's strange appearance. "Even we are changing as we try to move through it. No one would recognize us now in Glitterspike Hall, they would scream in terror and call for the guard to remove the two fierce marsh warriors that had invaded them!"

Ansel grinned back at her mistress, her teeth sparkling out of her mud-smeared face. As they began to feel their way along the narrow path, Marrimian noticed something moving in the distance to one side of the path. She sat up and stared into the shimmering heat haze. "Quick!" she cried. "That's the marshwader and a whole crowd of his people. I think they've seen us."

"The bubbles must be from the fish!" Ansel called triumphantly. "They must mark the edge of the path. There are so many of them. Look, I have caught another!"

Marrimian stepped over the scullion as she tossed the tiny fish back into the marsh and moved forward, following the calm line that zigzagged between the bubbles as quickly as she dared. But the marshwader was getting closer, he was waving his arms and shouting, gaining on them in giant strides.

"Why don't we follow that line of bubbles that leads off amongst those marsh oak. Look, towards that low reed-covered mound; that is where the cry came from," cried Ansel pointing across the marsh and splashing closely on her mistress's heels.

Marrimian followed the scullion's pointing finger and glancing quickly over her shoulder at the advancing marshmen saw that they must do something now or be overrun. Taking a deep breath she turned and set off. She slipped and gave a cry of panic as she sank up to her waist in the thick clinging mud, "Ansel help me," she shouted, trying to turn, but first one foot and then the other touched something solid and she waded forward, calling out to Ansel to follow and holding her hands above her head. She heard the scullion jump off the path and splash through the marsh behind her.

"They have stopped following us," Ansel called between laboured breaths. Indeed, the marshmen had halted and were pointing at the marsh ahead of the women, shouting. But they were too far away to hear now.

Marrimian hesitated and almost stopped, fearing what might lie ahead and sensing panic in the warning shouts of those behind her. The path was much narrower than the one the marshwader had led them along and seemed to wander in large loops as it rose and dipped below the surface of the mud sometimes a hand's span deep and sometimes sinking them up to their armpits in heavy treacherous mud. Ansel was close behind her, wading as fast as she could. Suddenly she cried out and slapped at the surface of the mire with the flat of her hands as if trying to drive something away. Marrimian felt the mud swirl around her feet. Something was sliding up over her toes and winding itself in tightening coils around her ankles. It tugged and made her flounder. She reached out towards the marsh-oak branches that hung and swayed in the hot stifling air above her head.

Vetchim was splashing backwards and forwards on the main path, shouting and pointing at something beside them. Suddenly a green-scaled tentacle broke through the marsh crust and sent slow heavy ripples across the surface as it snaked towards Ansel. Vetchim leaned back and hurled his spear. The marshmen gathered on either side of him and sent their spears spinning high into the hot air above the mire to sink with dull splashes all around the two women. The tentacle beneath the surface was pulling at Marrimian's ankle, burning a raw weal in her skin as it unwound. Suddenly the marsh crust boiled up around them and writhing tentacles, some as thick as tree trunks, broke through the surface, sending up fountains of stinking slime as they reached between the marsh oaks for Marrimian and the scullion, tearing up the smaller trees and throwing them into the heaving surface of the mire.

"The mound! We must reach the mound!" shouted Marrimian, wading forward between the last two oaks and feeling the path rise with each quickening step. To her right the marsh crust was rippling, sending waves of mud and green slime washing towards them. Something was rising up out of the mire; bulbous eyes stared at her out of a hideously misshapen head. The marshbeast's dozen tentacles were thrashing, boiling up the heavy mud, curling and winding around the marshmen's spear shafts and trying to pluck them out from between its slippery scales.

Ansel cried in terror as she saw into its open mouth, a reeking black cavern of darkness, and she reached in her pocket for the marshfish, cast it into the yawning hole and waded as fast as she could away along the narrow path. Marrimian had reached the low reed-covered mound and she turned and reached out her hand, catching hold of Ansel's wrist and pulling her up out of the mire. Together they scrambled up on top of the mound and watched the scaly shimmering marshbeast vanish in a froth of bursting bubbles as it sank back beneath the surface of the marsh crust. The widening ripples grew sluggish and became still. Here and there along the edges of the sunken path a bubble of gas rose to burst, sending a fine shower of mud pattering across the marsh.

"What kind of beast was that?" asked Marrimian scraping away the thick crust of mud from her ankles, grimly touching the rawness, shuddering as she remembered the cold clinging feel of the creature.

"I'll never ever set foot in that stinking slimy mud again," cried Ansel. "That thing was grabbing at my apron and I'm sure one of its horrible waving arms was trying to pull the marshfish out of my pocket. That's why I threw the fish at him."

Marrimian laughed at the scullion's defiance and it was a relief to laugh now they were safe above the mud. Turning she watched Vetchim shouting and waving at them from the main path. "Your marshwader is still angry with us for slipping through his fingers," she observed, nudging Ansel's arm and making her look round.

Ansel frowned and brushed back her untidy wisps of hair and puffed out her cheeks. "He's not *my* marshwader," she muttered crossly, shaking her fist at him, but she wasn't quite sure how she really felt about him, not deep down inside. She had yearned for someone to share her life and desperation had driven her to beg the healing woman's help, but nothing would ever tempt her, no amount of loneliness, to live in these nightmare marshes, to chew on rotting mud-beast hides and wade through this stinking mud. She shivered and stole another look at the marshwader. If only he had been a ragman or a lampwick, or even a humble duster instead of a marshman, she would have done all his bidding and carried out all his desires, following in every footprint . . . She sighed and angrily slapped at the swarms of insects that had risen out of the rough grasses of the mound to bite and sting her arms and legs.

"These creepy crawlies are just like the borer biters that infest the marshmen's cloaks," she muttered, turning towards her mistress, but Marrimian had moved up over the top of the mound and was searching for something in the rough reed grass.

Marrimian was frowning and biting her lip. There was something strange about the mound and the reed grass that grew on it; the grass wouldn't break no matter how hard she pulled and it had a pungent, almost familiar smell about it. She moved over the crest of the mound between a row of lumps and stopped. "Ansel! Ansel!" she hissed, beckoning to the scullion and pointing urgently down at the marsh.

Ansel struggled to her feet with difficulty. Thick layers of mud had dried between her skirts and petticoat, forming them into a tangled knot that snagged and rubbed her legs as she strode over the mound.

"What is it, mistress?" she began but the words died on her lips as she reached Marrimian's side. They stared down at a row of corpses chained out below them in the mud. "Who were they?" Ansel whispered in horror, sinking down on her knees and crumpling her mud-stiffened apron tails between her fingers. She shuddered and looked away, feeling choking bile begin to rise in her throat. Her mistress pointed down among the mud-smeared bodies. "That one moves," she hissed. "That one over there must still be alive. Quickly, help me fetch it up onto the mound."

Ansel forced herself to look down at the row of half-submerged bodies that were staked across the path and saw the small shivering shape that her mistress had indicated. Marrimian had bunched her ruined mud-smeared gown in her arms and was picking her way through the litter of rotting bodies. Swarms of insects rose in stinging clouds from the bloated corpses, maggot wormed and wriggled beneath their half-eaten skin, making them seem to move as her shadow crossed over them. Marrimian hesitated. The stench of the corpses was making her choke, she raised her sleeve and pressed it to her nose. What if something was eating the figure from beneath the mud, perhaps the poor wretch was dead after all, like the others. Engulfed by fear, Marrimian half turned and lifted her foot to retrace her steps but the figure cried out and strained against the stakes that bound it across the path. Marrimian turned back and swallowed her fear. Gathering her courage she forced herself to find a path between the rotting bodies. Her heart was pounding, making the blood thunder in her ears; she was dizzy and light headed from the stifling odour. The marsh crust bubbled and rippled. Something seemed to be following each squelching step she took.

Crouching, half kneeling, her fingers fumbling with the wet slippery rawhide knots, Marrimian wrenched the bindings apart and pulled the trembling body up out of the mire. It blinked white staring eyes at Marrimian and shivered in her arms, its broken teeth rattling and chattering as it tried to speak. Marrimian bent closer to listen. Something crawled out of the dripping folds of the figure's ragged smock and slithered across Marrimian's hands; she shuddered and cried out, shaking her hands and clumsily dropping the body back into the mud.

"Ansel, Ansel," she hissed, tearing at a fat black slippery leech that clung on to the back of her hand.

Ansel took a huge gulp of fetid air and hurried through the rotting corpses, picking her way with giant strides to where her mistress stood. "Leeches!" she whispered, letting the air out of her lungs in a rush and taking another deep breath. "There are only three ways, mistress, to take off a leech. By fire to its tail, a twist of salt, or . . ." The scullion paled taking Marrimian's hand firmly between her fingers.

"What is the third way?" Marrimian whispered, their eyes meeting.

"I must bite its tail," Ansel answered, swallowing and forcing her mouth open as she brought Marrimian's hand up to her face.

Marrimian stopped her, pulling her hand away. "I would ask nothing of you, Ansel, that I would not do myself."

Without a glance or a second blink of the eye she bit savagely on the tail of the leech and spat its wriggling blood-bloated body into the mud at their feet.

"Mistress!" Ansel cried as Marrimian staggered and she caught and steadied her in her strong arms, whispering and soothing her as she wept, her shoulders trembling uncontrollably.

Marrimian grew still and straightened her back, she steadied herself and smiled at the scullion and shivered in the cooling air. The sun was drooping, the afternoon had quietly worn away while they had floundered in the marsh. "I have done it, Ansel," she whispered, reaching down for the captive that had sunk back into the mud. "I have found my courage in our first day out here in the quickmire just as the healing woman foretold. By biting the tail off that leech I have taken my first real step back towards the Glitterspike. Come, help me drag this poor half-eaten wretch out of the mud."

"Beware, mistress, it must be covered in leeches," cried Ansel, wrapping her apron tails around the narrow shoulders before lifting the frail body.

"Leeches hold no fear, but let us see whom we have rescued," Marrimian laughed, brushing the slime and the mud from the half-conscious figure and crying out in surprise as she saw a young girl's face. Grimly they both lifted her out of the mud and dragged her up onto the mound.

Marrimian knelt beside her and gently shook her, calling, and asking her name. She blinked and slowly opened her eyes, gave a cry and sat bolt upright and stared at the mound. Cautiously she reached out and touched the coarse reed grass, ran her fingers through it, and then snatched her hand away as if the grasses were on fire.

"Bea . . . be . . . Beast," she stuttered trying to rise,

struggling against Ansel's strong hands on her bone-thin shoulders.

"Mm . . . m . . . mudbeast," she whispered, the words stumbling from her as she pointed down at the mound.

Marrimian frowned and looked from the girl down at the mound. The sunbaked earth beneath their feet had not lost the warmth of the sun although the day had turned towards evening. Clearly the girl was terrified of something but surely they were safer up here above the marsh and there were no mudbeasts that she could see, there was nothing but marsh oaks and these reed-covered mounds. Surely . . .

The mound trembled, it moved as faintly beneath her feet as grasses bend and sway when touched by a gentle summer wind. The marshgirl cried out, stabbing her fingers at the mound, and curled herself into a tight shivering ball, whispering and chanting. Marrimian spun around looking everywhere at once. Her eyes settled on the marshwader across the mud and she frowned as she watched him and the whole company of marshmen kneel, their arms and hands spread out in grotesque horn shapes above their heads. That was how she had seen them salute mudbeasts when they had awakened them from their slumbers to attack Yaloor. But there were no mudbeasts in sight . . .

"There is something wrong with this mound," she began, her voice sounding shrill in the sudden silence as she turned to the scullion.

The mound trembled again and rocked backwards and forwards then began to rise up out of the marsh. Ansel cried out and lost her balance, falling heavily to her knees and clutching at the rough grasses as the mound shook more violently.

"We are upon a mudbeast's back!" shouted Marrimian. She threw herself down beside the marshgirl, catching hold of her wrist as she began to slide down towards the mud.

"I knew there was something strange about the mound. It has the smell and the feel of Yaloor; I sensed it the moment I set foot upon it, but the hair is different," she cried, knotting the fibres that she thought were reed grasses around the marshgirl's wrist and calling to Ansel to do the same before she slipped and fell back into the mud. Hand over hand Marrimian scaled the sides of the huge beast and tied herself between the first two humps of its crest. The beast had risen high above the marsh bellowing and ploughing up waves of black slimy mud with its wide curve of horns. Marsh mud dropped from the weed tangles that clung in loops and twists about its legs. It sent up fountains of mud with each lumbering step that it took.

Tilting its head it stared up over its shoulder at Marrimian and roared, snapping its jaws and making her choke in the hot foul draught of its breath. She swung dizzily and clung onto the high perch between its humps and cried out, searching her mind for all the beast-calming chants the mumblers had once taught to her in her girlhood days—powerful rhymes of magic that as she spoke them brought back the smell of the mumblers' pine-oil lamps and the sound of the windbells on their robes; strong magic that had once calmed the beast Yaloor so that he let her sit between his claws or ride upon his shoulders.

"*Lonog belo, bet Belowen; Lonog belo, bett Belowen,*" she shouted, her voice faltering into silence. She could not remember more than a handful of the magic words, seasons had clouded her memory; Yaloor had grown old and used to the scent of her and needed no chants to keep him in check. The beast grunted, arching its back and rippling the muscles just beneath his hide to shake off his unwelcome burden.

Ansel and the marshgirl were tossed and shaken, bumped and bruised until their teeth had almost rattled loose in their heads. Marrimian tried desperately to shout her few remembered words of magic, her untied right hand flailing helplessly through the air as the mudbeast gathered speed and surged out into the stinking mire following some hidden path that lay deep below the mud.

"Hold on to its fur," she cried, not daring to turn to Ansel as the beast rose up out of the marsh onto the main path in a wave of boiling slime and shook its hide from end to end, dislodging the lumps of slime and tangled weed from beneath its dripping underbelly.

Vetchim and the company of marshmen cowered backwards, scattering and trampling on each other as the huge beast bellowed and lowered its horns; it lumbered amongst them, crushing the slower marshmen beneath its claws.

"She rides upon the mudbeast!" cried one of the marshmen, his eyes bulging with fear as he tugged at Vetchim's sleeve and pointed up through the shower of hot slippery mud at Marrimian perched between the highest humps of the beast as it blundered past them and turned towards the distant jumble of rocks and huts on the low horizon line.

Vetchim sank to his knees and wrung his hands together and cried out, "Marrimian shall be the Queen of Beasts!"

Marrimian turned her head at the marshwader's shout and, raising her right hand, laughed to mask her terror. She clenched her fist against the setting sun and made as if to urge the mudbeast on out into the endless quickmarsh.

8

A Sacred Guardian Soars Above the Throne

*T*HE marshlords and their hunters paced impatiently through the empty beast pits waiting for the Hurlers' Gate to open, anxious for the chance to find a safe road to the doors of Glitterspike Hall and the shimmering finger of crystal. But dawn had yet to fade the frozen starlight above the City of Glor or give the merest whisper of the new morning in the endless frozen quickmarsh. Far above, in his mumbling cell, Naul yawned and stretched, shaking off the weariness of a long night of setting hidden traps and laying false and treacherous trails through the maze of streets and alleyways below the hall. He had done all his master had asked and removed or changed the names of every street in the lower circles of the city. He laughed quietly to himself as he left his cell, and slipped into the great hall, careful not to wake the slumbering beasts chained around the base of the Glitterspike, and sank back into the high chair that Lord Miresnare had set for him beside the throne. Tilting his head to one side he began the morning ritual of numbering: he counted the seasons, the mudbeasts chained in the circle below him around the Glitterspike, all the feasting days that he could remember, and whatever else came into his mind.

"Today! Yes, today," he whispered, finishing the count on the number for good omens. "Today we will dance again for our master and our voices will be heavy with magic." Naul grinned, narrowing his hooded eyes as he peered at the lightening sky. He was well pleased that his magic had thwarted Mertzork, and he rubbed his hands together as he remembered the way the other marshmen had driven him far out into the marsh cursing him for murdering his father and threatening to cut his throat if he ever showed his face in their marsheries again. Reaching out he spun the pine-oil lamp that hung beside him and watched the thin spiral of smoke rise up to vanish amongst the blackened rafters. Knotting his fingers together he stared out across the empty hall waiting, listening for the beginnings of the new morning. He wrinkled his nose, trying to catch the first scent of the bake ovens and hear the first clamour of the scullions, and to detect sounds of the hall coming to life. Nothing.

Naul glanced across the circle of sleeping beasts and caught his breath in a shallow gasp. There was something moving high up on Gallengab's shoulders, something small and white. He blinked, scratching at the rough stubble on his shaven skull, and climbed up onto the seat of his chair to steal a better look. Gallengab grumbled in his sleep and flexed his claws, sending ripples of irritation through his coarse, heavy coat. Naul steadied the spinning lamp and blinked again, his eyes watering in the pine-oil smoke that curled up to envelop him. As he watched the beast's shoulders a small white shape, no larger than his fist, appeared, rising up out of Gallengab's matted fur, and turned towards him.

A door slammed, breaking the night silence. A voice echoed in a corridor, then another, and hurrying footsteps clattered beyond the low archways making Naul look up and frown, his lips shaping a curse as lampwicks spilled into the hall chasing the night shadows before them with their flickering torches. He looked back to the beast's shoulders but the white shape had vanished.

Before long, servers appeared, cleaning the long eating boards, polishing the goblets and crystal cups, setting places in readiness for the new day. Ragmen glided silently through the low archways, their ragbound feet wet with ebony sap polish to buff away the scuffs of yesterday. The mudbeasts chained in the circle were beginning to stir. Yaloor bellowed and Gallengab roared with hunger, straining against the chains that bound him. They snarled as they snatched at the bloody carcasses of hill sheep that the early servers were throwing into the circle.

Naul muttered under his breath and sank back fretfully into his high chair, turning his head from the revolting sight of the gorging beasts. He would find out later what secret Gallengab carried on his shoulders.

"The stench is worse than the beasting pits below the city," grumbled Lord Miresnare, appearing suddenly beside him, wrinkling his nose in disgust as the beasts in the circle tore at the bloody carcasses, noisily crunching the bones to fine powder.

Naul jumped hastily to his feet to greet him, but was brushed aside as his master sat down heavily in his throne. His furrowed face looked drawn, his eyes bloodshot as if he, too, had passed a sleepless night. "And what terrors does this new day hold?" He fixed his master mumbler with a piercing glare.

"Lord, the mumblers will form a dancing circle," Naul cried, signalling to a hallwarden to summon them all.

"Can your dancing circle tell me where my treacherous first-born daughter is hiding?" he demanded, holding Naul in his unblinking gaze. "There is no sign of her, nor that ugly scullion who follows her every footstep."

Naul fidgeted uneasily, moving from foot to foot, setting the windbells on the hems of his robes clattering with shrill music. "I have counted the numbers and they add up to good omens, my lord, but I cannot foretell what the omens are or what the dancing circle will unfold."

Lord Miresnare waved the mumbler irritably into his chair and beckoned the hovering servers to attend them. He tilted his head back to swallow huge mouthfuls of morning pottage and then cursed the servers as they started mopping the stray spilt dribbles from his chin with torn crusts of white trenchard bread. "On another morning I would toss you to the beasts for your clumsiness," he growled, dismissing them and lifting his large crystal cup with both hands. "How stands the new game for my throne? Have any of the marshmen found a way up through the first circle of the city?" He gazed round, searching each dark entrance to the hall. In a moment the sun would rise and cast its first rays across the floor, and the joust would begin again . . . But where was his first-born? She could not have died of cold, no bodies had been found. Perhaps her sisters knew?

"Daughters, daughters, stand before me and tell me where you have hidden Marrimian," he bellowed, clapping his hands above the clamour of the hall. Servers, doorwardens and counsellors all turned anxious eyes towards the entrance of the daughtery, waiting for them to rush and do his bidding, but there was no response.

To soften his master's anger, Naul half rose in his chair and silently beckoned his mumblers into a circle around the mudbeasts, bidding them sway with the slightest twist of his hand. They moved in a dreamlike dance until the blue spirals of smoke from their lamps fogged the morning sunlight of the hall, cloying the senses, and all other activity ceased.

Just then Treyster ran into the hall, tears of distress running down her cheeks. She was followed by Aloune. Of Pinvey and the others there was no sign.

"Where are your sisters?" shouted Lord Miresnare, annoyed now at the interruption. "Where is Pinvey? Where are you hiding Marrimian? Come now, speak."

"We don't know where they are, Father," trembled Aloune. "We awoke this morning and they were gone."

"Gone? How can they have gone? Have they all turned against their father, worthless prettiers? What new treachery is this?" His mind worked quickly, remembering Pinvey in her transparent gown, the way she had lured the marshmen forward. He had sensed a wildness in her, a dark danger. But where could they have gone? Still, they were no use now, now that the game had changed.

He heard a great rattle of windbells and looked up, his daughters forgotten, as the mumblers began to chant.

Naul clasped his hands around his knees, his fingers tightly laced as he watched the quickening dance, but with each swirling step his eyes were drawn towards Gallengab, who snarled and stalked and shook his crested mane, dislodging flakes of something white as he moved between the mudbeasts chained around the base of the Glitterspike.

The air was darkening, hazed with the heavy scented smoke. The hall was silent now, each man and woman shrinking back beneath the low stone door arches, frozen with fear as the magic crackled between the dancing mumblers' fingertips. Then shouts and ghostly cries seemed to echo from the edges of the hall and phantom shapes dressed in beastskin robes sprang up in the swirling half-light to drift between the dancing mumblers, mirroring their swaying steps and weaving in and out of the mudbeast circle.

Yaluu bellowed and leapt at the phantoms, tearing at the smooth polished stone and driving them out of the circle. Gallengab roared and crouched down beside the Glitterspike, his back arched in shivering ripples. He growled, shaking himself as if trying to dislodge something from between his matted shoulder blades. Naul leaned forward in his high chair, his fingers trembling as he reached out to touch Lord Mire-snare's arm.

He froze as the mumblers gave a great shout and stopped the dancing circle mid-stride. Their wind-bells clattered wildly as their circle split apart and a single phantom figure cloaked in beastskin rags strode through them in amongst the bellowing mudbeasts, calming them with its voice and touching them with its ghostly hands. It sang with a voice that filled the hall with a sound like polished silver.

Lord Miresnare shrank back into the throne in ter-ror as the shadowy phantom turned and strode across the hall, growing larger with each step it took until it darkened the hazy sunlight as it reached out to touch the Glitterspike. "Is this your good omen? Look! This shows me my destruction!" he cried.

"The beast!" gasped Naul, mastering his fear and snatching at Lord Miresnare's sleeve, making him look beyond the towering phantom at Gallengab's twitching shoulder blades.

Lord Miresnare followed the master mumbler's trembling hand and cried out, gripping the carved armrests of the throne. There, in the coarse tangle of Gallengab's hair, was the rarest and most sacred of creatures, a white pindafall of Gnarlsmyre. It turned its pitiless glittering eyes towards the throne then strutted forward, freeing itself from the matted hair, and balanced on unsteady nestling legs, its talons hooked into Gallengab's crest. Slowly it spread its damp leathery wings and snapped open its cruel beak to shriek the phantoms into silence. Twice it cried out and flapped its drying wings before stretching its slender neck and rising up, gliding in a spiral around the throne.

Naul shrank down, covering his face as the white-winged pindafall soared over his chair, its wings clattering and humming. It turned and swooped down on the silver-voiced phantom, its talons clawing through the empty air as the figure, shedding its beastskin robe, dissolved, in a flash of bright light. Flapping its wings the white pindafall dived between the mud-beasts and rose in silent soaring loops to vanish amongst the smoke-dark rafters of the hall.

Lord Miresnare let his breath escape between his teeth in a shrill whistle and slowly turned to the master mumbler. "You have greater power than any other mumbler who has ever trodden in the dancing circle. You can even summon up the ghostly phantom of the white pindafall bird to defend my throne," he whispered, slapping a hand on the mumbler's wrist and pulling him to his feet.

Naul smiled and laughed nervously, spreading his empty hands and pointing up to the dark rafters. "The bird is real, my Lord. I merely foretold that today was a day of good omens. The beast, Gallengab, brought the bird into Glitterspike Hall as an egg in his thick heavy coat."

"Real? The bird is real?" frowned Lord Miresnare, hunching his shoulders and fearfully searching the dark roof of the hall with his piercing eyes. "Then you did not use your magic to summon it?"

"Lord," answered the master mumbler pointing to the crumble of white shell pieces scattered around the base of the Glitterspike. "He was hatched here beside

the Glitterspike as the mumblers danced. He arose in the heat and the sweet scent of our magic lamps and he silenced the phantoms' shouts, then . . ." Naul fell silent. There had been something about the silver-voiced phantom that brought shivers to his spine, something familiar about that singing voice, and yet he could not be sure if the sacred bird had destroyed the phantom or if the phantom had merely cast its cloak aside and vanished because the magic of the dancing circle was broken.

"And?" pressed Lord Miresnare, making the master mumbler blink and think quickly to hide his doubts.

"Clearly, Lord, the bird is a good omen. He is the rarest of winged beasts in all Gnarlsmyre and drove the phantom out of the circle before it could touch the Glitterspike. Surely . . ."

The white pindafall shrieked and swooped out of the darkness. The clattering rattle of its wings drove everyone in the hall for cover save Treyster who left the safety of the low archway and fled across the room to her father's throne. "Why is the white bird so special, Father?" she asked in a frightened whisper as she huddled beside him.

Lord Miresnare muttered under his breath at his daughter's stupid ignorance and turned harshly on her. "Because long ages ago they were a great delicacy and we ate them all until there were none left, you fool. Because, because . . ." He waved his arm, irritably, brushing her question aside, and craned his neck to see where the bird had alighted.

"It is safe, my Lord," whispered Naul. "The bird has settled on Gallengab's shoulders."

Lord Miresnare watched it carefully, his eyebrows crinkled in a frown. "None of us will be safe," he muttered to Naul. "These carrion birds attack without a sound save from the clatter of their brittle feathers, gliding on the warm draughts of air. I will have to set watchers around the throne."

Naul laughed quietly and shook his head. "It will be a great power and strike fear into all who enter the hall, but you, my Lord, and all who serve you will be safe, if you are well hatted in helms of hammered steel. For I foretell that this white pindafall shall become the emblem crest upon this high throne and it will protect you and feed upon the flesh of those who try to touch the Glitterspike."

Lord Miresnare thought for a moment and then slowly nodded his head at the mumbler's words of wisdom. He snapped his fingers, calling for the armourers to bring metal helms for all the people of the hall, and while the armourers ran backwards and forwards with their measuring strings, winding them around heads, he leaned forward in his throne and watched the rare white bird glide silently down between the mudbeasts and tear a strip of hill sheep carcass from beneath Yaloor's claws then rise again in widening loops to vanish amongst the rafters.

Naul laughed, rattled his windbells and called for silence, stilling the rising clamour for the metal helms with one billowing twist of his pine-oil lamp. But before he could speak or warn the people of the hall not to enter bare-headed a dozen marshlords burst through the low archways, slipping the leashes from savage hunting dogs and shouting to them to attack the mudbeasts.

Lord Miresnare leapt angrily to his feet, cursing all the master mumbler's failed efforts to prevent the marshmen from finding a way to his door. Raising his fist, accidentally knocking off his metal helm, he almost motioned his archers in the gallery to arrow-strike the dogs, then remembered it was against the rules.

Naul crept to his side. "I swear there was no way through the maze," he stammered. "They must have tortured a wheelwright to give directions, or used some foul magic."

"Watch," Lord Miresnare whispered as a silent shadow crossed the sunlight and the humming clatter of the white pindafall's wings grew louder. It stooped on the marauding dogs, shearing through their skulls with its razor-sharp teeth and raking its talons through their coarse brindle coats, tumbling them over the smooth-polished floor.

Yelping and howling the surviving dogs scattered, leaving a trail of bloody paw prints as they rushed for the low archways and the dark hiding places beneath the long eating boards. The advancing marshmen hesitated, their shouts of triumph dying on their lips. Stumbling and barging into each other they turned in panic as the white carrion bird wheeled around the Glitterspike and soared across the hall towards them. One marshlord tripped and fell, struggled to rise and screamed in terror as the pindafall hooked its talons into his beastskin cloak and turned him over to gouge out his eyes with an upward flick of its talons. Flapping its leathery wings it slowly circled the hall and rose up into the darkness of the rafters where it perched to watch the empty polished stones below.

"We will find a way to cross the hall," shouted an angry voice from beneath one of the low archways where the marshlords had fled for safety.

"We found a path through the mazes you set to trap us in the city," sneered another voice. "That was easy. Your city folk were all too eager to save their miserable hides by giving us knowledge."

Coarse voices laughed and whispered in the darkness of the archways. An unwary ragman crouching near them suddenly cried out as strong hands seized him. He was lifted up and held aloft by two of the marshmen, a shield against the white pindafall's talons as they tried again to reach the Glitterspike.

"These marshscum are breaking the laws of my joust," thundered Lord Miresnare, rising angrily from the throne and thrusting aside the armourer who had retrieved his metal helm.

"No, my Lord," answered Naul breathlessly, fumbling in his sleeve for the heavy parchment scroll on which he had carefully scribbled all the words of his master's new joust before the echo of the words had faded at the beginning of the Allbeast Feast. "They can use any means to reach the Glitterspike so long as they do not bear arms against the mudbeasts chained within the circle. From the first shaft of sunlight . . ."

"Yes, yes," snapped Lord Miresnare impatiently, stabbing a finger at the advancing marshmen and their hunting dogs pressed close beneath the struggling body of the ragman. "But I did not give them leave to destroy the people of Glitterspike Hall in their greed."

"Lord, there is nothing written. The law does not forbid . . ."

"You fool!" growled Lord Miresnare. "You allowed me to speak too hastily at the feast. You let me think that these marshscum would be easily thwarted, that they would weaken and give up this hopeless quest, that my throne would be safe."

Naul shrank down beneath his master's anger, then jumped with fright as the silent shadow of the pinda-fall smoothed its way across the throne, blocking out the morning sunlight. Lord Miresnare turned to watch the carrion bird glide between the bellowing mudbeasts towards the helpless ragman.

The bird shrieked, its cry freezing the hall into silence as it climbed steeply and hung over the ragman's body. Flapping its wings once, its talons twisted away the thick rag binding on the man's feet, spinning him over, then tore him from the marshmen's grip and hurled him crashing to his death on the hard stone floor. Slowly the pindafall circled the Glitterspike then wheeled, snapping its beak open and shut, swooping down on the fleeing marshmen, driving them back into the safety of a low archway.

Lord Miresnare laughed uneasily, then as the pinda-fall turned again, flying towards the throne, his grip tightened on the master mumbler.

"Sit still, sit perfectly still and show no fear," Naul whispered hoarsely, his lips trembling as he fought to steady himself on his high chair.

The bird was getting closer, the edges of its leathery wings fluttering in the warm up-draughts of air above the throne. They felt a hot dry wind against their necks and heard the clatter of brittle feathers behind them, then a soft click as the bird alighted on the throne. The high, carved headrest creaked beneath the bird's weight, the black ebony wood splintering as its talons cut into the grainy surface.

Lord Miresnare held his breath and felt the sweat begin to trickle out from beneath his metal helm to escape in tiny rivulets over the wrinkles of his ancient skin. The bird shrieked and its hot fetid breath made Miresnare choke and reel, then with wings outspread it glided down across the mudbeasts, twisting its slender neck from side to side as if searching. With a clatter of brittle feathers it alighted on Gallengab's shoulders and began to scratch around for borer biters, raking its talons through the beast's tangled coat, shuffling in awkward backward steps.

Naul laughed with relief. A moment later he grabbed his master's sleeve in concern. One by one the marshmen, looking furtively behind them, were slipping out of the hall.

"What, are they leaving already?" asked Miresnare.

"I expect, my Lord, they are searching for a way through the corridors and alleyways of Glitterspike Hall, to those archways closest to the Glitterspike," pondered Naul.

Lord Miresnare spun round in his seat, an anxious cry escaping his lips. He stared at the rows of empty shadow-dark archways and the dread of what those marshscum would do to snatch the advantage and find ways to touch the Glitterspike made his blood freeze. "They will force my servers, my scullions and all my ragmen to tell which path to take. No one will be safe from them. This game that you foretold has become a waking nightmare and I was a fool to listen to your magic."

Naul slowly shook his head. "You had no choice, my Lord. But have no fear. My thoughts run ahead of theirs. Last night I began to lay false mazes in all the passageways to that side of the hall and only I and the stone setters who labour with me know which of the passages still lead to the hall. We will spread these false endings with each night of frozen darkness until not even the oldest of the scullions nor the most sure-footed ragman can find their way without a glance at my maze slate."

"Maze slate?" echoed Lord Miresnare leaning closer to the mumbler. Naul swept his hand under his chair, taking out a rough, heavy square of slate covered in strange markings. Lord Miresnare frowned. "But who will serve me if none knows the way? Who will find me—my servers, dressers, guards?"

"That is easily solved, Lord," hurried the mumbler without pausing for breath. "Only those who serve you shall be allowed to read my slate and they shall be escorted by your chosen guards."

Lord Miresnare smiled, his lips turning into a thin line at his mumbler's cleverness.

"What of your daughters, my Lord? Are they to know the way through the mazes?" asked Naul.

"My daughters?" muttered Lord Miresnare angrily. "When we find them, lock them up. Confine them to the daughtery. They will be better out of sight. Nothing but trouble."

Pinvey crouched forwards in her cramped hole high above the hall and clenched her fingers in hatred of her father as his words drifted up to her. She had sensed a change in him when he had cast Marrimian out of the hall; his eyes had grown cold and hard, and clearly she and all her sisters had outlived whatever scrap of usefulness he had once seen in them. She had acted quickly under cover of night. Waking those of her sisters whom she hated least and swearing them into silence she had taken them by her secret stairway up to her hidden room. There she would watch and listen and make plans.

"What is he saying?" asked a fearful whispering voice behind her, making her turn sharply.

"Be quiet!" she hissed, glaring at Alea and Syrenea in the half-light of the small room. Seeing them cowering in the doorway made her doubt the wisdom of bringing them with her. But everything was in confusion and she was sure of nothing any more. Even the scattering of sparkles and trinkets that she had stolen over the seasons looked dull and worthless where they lay amongst the discarded pindafall bones on the couches. Everything was changing.

"That mumbler is blocking the corridors and passageways; he is turning them into a maze to prevent the marshlords from reaching the great hall and our father has just condemned us to be prisoners in the daughtery," she snapped, turning her back on her sisters and staring down into the hall, searching her mind for what she should do.

"We will be safe in the daughtery," whispered Syrenea.

"Safe? *Safe?*" mocked Pinvey, turning her head and spitting the words across the room. "We will be crumbling bones before we are remembered. Father is going mad. No, we must stay here at the very heart of things and as close to the marshlords as possible."

"But how can we get close to them if they cannot find a way through the mumblers' mazes?" wailed Alea hopelessly.

"And what good would it do us if we were with them?" added Syrenea miserably, wishing that she had stayed with Aloune, Treyster and her other sisters and had not followed Pinvey into this gloomy hole.

Pinvey hissed them both into silence and licked her lips as the germ of an idea sprang from her sisters' mutterings. "We will go to them," she said drawing her sisters to her. "Yes, we will steal the mumbler's slate and by following the corridors scratched into the surface we will find that marshlord who brought Gallengab into the hall, and to spite our father we will help him to touch the Glitterspike." Pinvey shivered with desire as she thought of Mertzork and she felt her breasts swell and her nipples harden beneath the weave of her gown. "He will be mine," she whispered rocking backwards and forwards.

"What about us? Where will we find marshlords for ourselves if you steal the best?" Alea muttered jealously, breaking into Pinvey's thoughts.

Pinvey laughed throatily as she held her sister's

gaze. "There will be more than enough to satisfy you, sister, especially if we have knowledge of the way through the maze to barter with."

As the day moved on darkness made the hall gloomy and swathes of shadows danced and twisted in the low archways as they fled before the lamplighters. Pinvey crept forward, tiptoeing lightly on the polished floor-stones and motioning Alea and Syrenea to fan out a dozen paces away on either side of her. She hoped that their fingers were not trembling too much and they would not drop the stolen sparkles they carried.

There had been no further sign of the marshlords and the throne was empty. The mudbeasts growled and bellowed softly as they settled around the base of the Glitterspike and Naul, weary of the long day of scheming, dozed in his high chair whispering and muttering of voices and wild leaping phantoms long forgotten.

Pinvey crouched down beside the mumbler's chair and curled her fingers around the rough slab of slate. She began to rise, the weight of the heavy slate knotting the muscles in her arms. The high chair creaked, the mumbler was waking, grumbling and yawning as he stretched his arms. The first lampwicks with their guards were spilling through the low archways, pools of flickering lamplight flooded across the hall and an archer in the gallery glimpsed the three sisters on the dais of the throne and cried out. Naul started awake and reached down to protect the slate.

"Now! Throw the sparkles now!" commanded Pinvey, snatching up the slate and toppling backwards beneath its weight.

All around her sparkles and bright trinkets danced and clattered onto the hard floorstones. The mud-beasts roared, the guards fanned out shouting as they drew their swords. The slate slipped through Pinvey's fingers and splintered into dozens of pieces as it struck the floor with a terrible crash.

"Quickly, gather up as many pieces as you can," cried Pinvey, falling onto her knees and scooping up her skirt full of shards before she rose and fled for the nearest darkened archway.

Syrenea and Alea ran at her heels, their hands full of jagged pieces, not daring to look back at the milling crowd of guards and lampwicks. A few were in pursuit but the majority were scrabbling on the floor to pocket the sparkles or collect what remained of the broken slate. Pinvey gasped for breath and slipped behind the heavy tapestry that hid her secret stairway and waited for the other two to catch up with her. She laughed, baring her teeth in a savage smile as she heard the master mumbler's voice rising angrily in the great hall. She realized then that she had stolen enough of his secrets to find the marshlord, to help him win the throne and to claim him as her own.

9

The Crones Search The City

*M*ERTZORK gingerly rubbed at the bruises on his neck and shoulders and gently touched the raw bumps on the top of his dirty shaven head. As he huddled up waiting for the darkness to hide him and the cold night wind to freeze the marsh crust, he remembered grimly how he had fled from the other marshmen several days ago. They had cursed him for murdering his father and had turned on him the moment Lord Miresnare's archers had herded them out through the Hurlers' Gate into the thickening darkness after the end of the feast. They had stoned him and set their savage hunting dogs on him; they had chased him down through the beasting pits and far out across the frozen quickmarsh, calling a curse on the day his mother had birthed him, for he was born with nothing but black treachery in his heart to have brought the beast Gallengab into Glitterspike Hall and cause the joust to be changed so that it played against them. The marshlords realized just how close they had come to destroying Yaloor if they had acted together and they promised to skin him alive and leave his raw body staked out in the marshes for the mudbeasts to devour if he ever dared to show his face in their marsheries again or set his ragbound feet within the beasting pits.

Mertzork's face burned with shame at the memory and to shut it out he thought about the woman in the dress of molten gold he had glimpsed as he drove Gallengab into the hall. She had whispered quick, lustful words in the darkness and the hot look in her eyes still burned in his head; he knew that she would help him in his quest. He had, whether the marshmen liked it or not, the right to try to touch the Glitterspike; he had drunk from the jousting cup at Lord Miresnare's table. He smiled, hugging his knees close to his chest; his lips split into a laugh as he imagined reaching out and touching the shimmering crystal and feeling the veins of molten silver hot beneath its sparkling icy crust. He had to go back and try again. He knew that with the healing woman's help, and perhaps the aid of Pinvey, he could snatch everything and bring all those who had cursed him to their knees.

Carefully he tested the frozen quickmarsh and finding it firm began to retrace his steps. He moved as silently as a shadow in the silver moonlight and slipped unseen and unheard until finally he reached the rocky outcrops below the beasting pits. With cautious steps he worked his way up towards the high archway of the Hurlers' Gate that seemed to cast a black shadow across the frozen stars. There was noise and movement in the upper lanes between the empty pits. Cooking fires fogged the cold night air, voices sang and shouted. Mertzork stopped, his nose twitching as he caught the sweet scent of oiled meats roasting in the crackling flames. He licked his lips, the gnawing hunger of his days of hiding in the marsh tearing at his belly. Slowly he turned, pulled forwards by the heady scent towards the huddle of rough shelters. Figures were moving around the fire and cast long shadows. A dog growled and rose to its feet, its hackles ridged along its back, forcing Mertzork to sink back into the dark entrance of one of the pits. The voices had changed, the laughter and the singing had stopped, he heard his name mentioned as the figures around the fire hurried out to where the hunting dogs were growling and snarling and pulling on their chains at the edge of the camp.

Mertzork caught the sound of harsh whispering and the faint rattle of chains and he knew that the marshmen were unleashing their hounds. Quickly he trod in the sticky evil-smelling mudbeast dung that littered the floor of the empty pit, forcing the cold slime up between his toes. It would mask his scent and the dogs would only be able to hunt him if they could see him. Returning to the entrance of the pit he looked cautiously to left and right. The dogs were closer, he could hear the soft patter of their paws and the clink of the iron links set into their strong spiked collars. They were growling and running in circles, searching the narrow lane for his scent. There was no way out of the pit; the dogs were moments from the entrance.

Mertzork turned and ran to the back of the pit and looked up at the rough rock wall. There was a black hole just above his head. He crouched and sprang, hooking his fingers in a shallow ledge. Behind him a dog snarled and leapt at his feet. He felt rows of canine fangs close on his ankle and kicked out. The dog's jaws slipped on the mudbeast dung and it fell heavily and yelped as it hit the floor. Mertzork pulled himself up onto the ledge and crawled into the entrance of what seemed to be a cave. Something rattled near his head and brushed against his arm; he shivered, blinking his eyes, and waited until they grew accustomed to this blacker darkness before he moved forward.

He looked down. Below, the floor of the empty pit was boiling with angry hunting dogs, their fangs and the whites of their eyes glowing in the moonlight that spilled through the entrance. The dogs were barking and leaping up to the ledge and marshhunters were calling and running towards the entrance. Mertzork took a deep breath and scrambled into the cave. He stopped abruptly.

"Pindafalls!" he hissed. He stepped back as he saw the low roof of the cave crowded with their long sinister hanging shapes.

Mertzork recalled the spine-chilling tales that he had heard of the pindafall roosts in the caves above the beasting pits, stories of these carrion birds that had made the hairs on the back of his neck prickle, and he feared to move.

The marshhunters had crowded through the entrance to the pit and Mertzork could hear them climbing up onto the ledge. If they caught him they would skin him alive and he dared not hesitate for another moment. Swallowing his fear he crept forward into the labyrinth of echoing caves and picked a way through the heaps of gleaming bones, squeezing between the first row of swaying sleeping carrion birds.

Their brittle folded wings clattered as he brushed against them, their leathery feathers bristling out into sharp spines that scratched his arms. He caught his breath and pressed his arms against his sides and felt them tingle and itch at the touch of the birds. The birds began to twist and turn their heads sleepily towards him, fluttering their bald eyelids. Their long beaks snapped lazily at his knees and ankles.

Mertzork shuddered and fought to smother the giddy panic that was rising in his throat at the cold dry touch of the birds' scaly skin. The hairs on the nape of his neck prickled and he forced himself to weave between the birds, ducking and crawling between their hanging bodies. He followed the steepest path that he could find up through the honeycomb of tunnels and caves.

The noise of the hunting hounds and the marshmen had faded into silence behind him and all he could hear was the faint rattle of the pindafalls' wings and the hot dry rasp of their steady breath. The air became heavier as he went higher and stank of decay, and the hard rock floor gradually became warm and soft, feeling almost spongy beneath his feet. Frowning he bent down and dug his fingernails into it but gasped in horror, snatching his hand away, and forced a scream of terror back down his throat. The soft floor covering had crumbled into a thousand wriggling borer biters and tiny insects that nipped and stung him as they ran across his hands and fell silently back into the seething floor, vanishing as they burrowed their way back into the soft spongy surface of the floor. Mertzork held himself rigid against panic as the floor began to boil up all around him and living ripples of insects moved towards him.

The pindafalls began to stir at the disturbance. Their wings were unfolding and rattling as they stretched their necks and turned their heads to burrow into the mass of writhing insects and catch them up on their serrated sticky tongues. A long scream of terror escaped from Mertzork's chattering teeth, he slapped and scraped at the swarms of stinging creatures that were running up his legs and yelped in agony as their long curved stings pierced his skin. He shouted as he leapt forward between the crowded rows of roosting birds and forced a way through them towards the patch of starlight that marked another opening in the caves. The pindafalls shrieked and flapped their wide leathery wings, filling the caves with a deafening clatter as they turned their razor-sharp beaks towards him, but he ran fast through the last low-vaulted chamber and out into the clear night air. Stamping his feet and tearing at the clinging insects, crushing them between his shaking fingers, he shuddered as he searched the folds of his cloak for any that he had missed. He turned back towards the black entrance of the cave, his iron spike in his hands, ready to use against the carrion birds who might swoop out and attack him at any moment, but the clattering din in the caves gradually faded into an eerie silence. The pindafalls had settled again, their talons locked onto the low roof of the caves as they waited for the first light of dawn. Mertzork breathed a sigh of relief and gingerly pulled his beastskin cloak tightly about his shoulders, half expecting to feel a crawler wriggle beneath his fingertips. The cloak shut out the icy wind and he climbed up through the empty frozen lanes above the beasting pits and crept into the safety of the black shadows of the Hurlers' Gate. There he began scratching at the grainy age-splintered wood of each of the great doors, feeling for a hand or a toe hold. Looking up he measured with his eyes the narrow spiked opening between the top of the doors and the bottom of the archway, searching for a way to enter the city secretly before the sun rose. Mertzork cared nothing for Lord Miresnare's laws forbidding those who had drunk from the jousting cup from entering the city or finding a way to his doors during the hours of frozen darkness. He liked the dark and he felt safer hidden in its smothering shadows.

At last his fingers found a long diagonal crack in the wood of the right-hand gate and, hand over hand, toe over toe, he began to scale the massive door. Sudden voices and the scrape of armoured boots on the other side made him freeze and press his ear to the crack. There were guards patrolling between the hurlers' high chairs. They were laughing and talking, weaving the rumours and gossip of the new joust into night-time tales to help them wear away the frozen hours. Mertzork pricked his ears as he heard one of the guards tell of a rare white-winged pindafall bird who guarded the throne.

"Yes, it defeated that rabble of marshscum and their hunting dogs that somehow found their way up through the master mumbler's secret mazes. It swooped down on them as they rushed the hall and scattered their dogs," laughed one of the guards as he stopped between the hurlers.

"I heard that the white bird tore their eyes out and hung them on the headrest of the throne as sweetmeats for our Lord and Master, Lord Miresnare," burst in another excitedly.

"The doorwardens of the hall told my brother, the lampwick there, that the beast Gallengab is so tall that his shoulders brush against the rafters," whispered the first guard, stopping before the gates.

"Now that *is* wild gossip!" laughed the archer standing on the threshold stone of the guard house. "I was here stringing my bow when that marshscum drove the beast through the gates and upset the hurlers—he was cracking an iron-tailed whip at its heels as it lumbered into the city—and I say that it was only half that size."

The hurler tutted, nodding his head backwards and forwards and pointing at the iron spikes set into the archway. "The beast bent those spikes with its shoulder blades as it squeezed beneath the archway. But do you know the strangest thing, the marshmen who had gathered for the joust stoned the one who brought the beast into the city. I saw them hurling rocks at him on the edges of the quickmarsh and they cursed him for changing the joust."

"But why did they do that?" asked the archer. "When because of him the throne lies open to the first to touch the Glitterspike. Surely that is better than jousting for any daughter of the hall!"

The hurler laughed and threw back his head. "No one welcomes change, especially the marshmen. Their lives are steeped in ritual as they follow the seasons and hunt the mudbeasts across the endless marshes, and, mark my words, there was some wisdom in their anger, for with this new joust everything must change in the city."

"There will be plenty of trouble!" muttered one of the guards darkly. "By Lord Miresnare's law we cannot hamper these marshscum in their quest for a path to the doors of Glitterspike Hall, but they can, it seems, torture and murder, plunder and steal as much as they like to find the swiftest road!"

"They call it a game, a joust for the throne, but I call it barbarity!" cried the archer angrily. "And I can't see why Lord Miresnare doesn't give us the power to put a stop to it!"

Mertzork smiled in the darkness, his mouth splitting into a wide grin as he thought of the trouble he had caused. He frowned as the voices faded and eased his tingling toes out of the narrow crack in the door. Letting go with his fingers, he jumped lightly to the ground. Clearly he must find another way into the city; the hurlers and a strong guard were watching the gates.

Moving silently he followed the wall and felt for a fault in its smooth cold surface, but no matter where he searched the wall rose up in an unbroken curtain of solid stone that marched away on either side of him into the darkness. Cursing himself for not thinking more carefully about getting back into the city he squatted down behind a loose jumble of rocks in the centre of the well-trodden path that skirted the wall and stared out across the frozen quickmarsh. Dawn

was greying the frozen marshes and the mire crust
was melting and sending up ghost-tails of mist to swirl
amongst the clumps of leaning marsh oaks.

The light was strengthening. Soon the early marsh
gatherers and any of the marshlords who had yet to
find a way up through the city would be crowding
through the gates. Mertzork looked about him and
searched for a place to hide. He whispered and muttered to himself as he crossed the muddy trampled
track and stared down across the steep rock face that
fell away to the beasting pits below.

Then Mertzork hesitated, the hairs on the nape of
his neck prickled and his skin crawled as he heard a
dry scratching sound above him. Spinning round he
reached up to his collar for his hidden sharpwire, but
then he laughed. He jumped up against the wall,
stretching with his fingertips, and caught a dangling
hedgehog that was twisting and bumping its way
down the stone, scrabbling with its claws every time
they touched the smooth surface.

"You have strong powers, healing woman," he
laughed, catching hold of the hedgehog and untying
the finely woven gossamer rope from around its belly
and knotting it firmly around his waist.

Mertzork lifted the squealing hedgehog to his lips
and kissed and licked its prickly coat, laughing as the
sharp spines tickled his tongue. "You are a wonder to
have found me before the sun rose," he whispered,
patting the hedgehog as it curled itself into a tight ball,
and quickly stuffed it into his deepest pocket.

He leaned back against the rope and placed his feet
flat against the sheer smooth surface of the wall, and

then, hand over hand, he began to walk up towards the top.

"Fool! You weak and feeble fool!" hissed Erek, cutting short his triumphant laughter and prodding him sharply in the chest with her crooked fingers, making him stumble backwards into the shadows of a narrow alleyway that ran parallel to the wall.

"Fool, weak fool!" chanted a close circle of crones as they gathered up the coils and loops of gossamer rope where Mertzork had dropped it on the cobbles, and hiding it beneath their black cloaks they followed Erek into the alleyway. Armoured boots crunched on the cobbles. Erek lifted her fingers to Mertzork's lips and squeezed them together to indicate silence. The crones lifted and spread their cloaks, darkening the shadows in the alleyway, and stood rock still until the guards' footsteps had faded away.

"I gave you power and filled your head with enough knowledge to take the throne of Gnarlsmyre, yet still you came too late into Glitterspike Hall to work my revenge against that cursed Miresnare," Erek hissed, releasing his numb lips.

Mertzork paled as he stared at the tight circle of ancient crones who had closed in behind the healing woman, glaring at him with unblinking eyes. Their grim faces had hardened into stone. He stuttered and tried to step away from them only to find that he was already pressed against a cold mud-slapped wall.

"I lost my way in the quickmarsh and had to beat the marshhunters' backs raw to reach the city be-

fore—" His voice fell into silence as he sensed that they either knew all that had happened or they could hear and see it inside his head.

Erek spat at the ground and thrust her searching mirror against his lips, watching for the truth of all that had befallen him as his breath misted the glass. She whispered to the circle of black-cloaked crones and drew them in about her shoulders until they were as close to her as extra folds in her own cloak. Pointing to the gathering she cackled finally, "These are my sisters. They are but a smattering of the healers who survived when Lord Miresnare drove us out into the quickmire to perish and they are thirsty, parched dry for revenge."

"He was forewarned against me!" cried Mertzork, gasping for breath as he felt the crones sucking the air from around his head in the narrow alleyway. "There was a mumbler dressed in robes of bright saffron, he swung a pine-oil lamp and stood close to Lord Miresnare's elbow. He seemed to know enough of my secret journey to have set the hall in readiness and to steal the beast, Gallengab, when my feet had barely crossed the threshold stone."

Erek hissed him into silence. She moved in amongst her sisters and pored over the searching mirror, turning it backwards and forwards for all of them to see the fate of Gallengab. Turning she beckoned Mertzork, pulling him forward with the tip of a crooked finger to squat in the centre of their circle.

"Miresnare was forewarned," Erek whispered, brushing her fingers over the bristle of Mertzork's head, "by the very power that I once spawned. Yes, he was warned of your coming by Naul, the master mumbler."

"Naul! That's right, that was his name," cried Mertzork angrily, trying to rise, but the healing woman's hands, although they rested lightly on the top of his head, were iron heavy and kept him from moving. She muttered her hatred for Lord Miresnare for stealing her power from the cradle webs beside her firestone.

"But that magic mumbler was against me!" cried Mertzork in confusion. "Surely if he is of your blood . . ."

Erek laughed, her voice echoing around the huddle of ancient women, before she turned sharply on Mertzork, gripped his hands and stared unblinking into his eyes. "It is not his fault, he is in another's power. Now promise me, whatever else our power helps you win or whatever else you seize or snatch in thrusting for the throne the mumbler shall not be harmed."

Mertzork remembered with hate Naul's narrow shadow-filled face and high-domed bony forehead and he quickly nodded. He had sworn revenge but it would be easy payment and would deny him only a moment's pleasure with his sharpwire to deliver up that bundle of dancing flesh and bones to the healing woman. He nodded his agreement.

"We will fuse our powers into one," chanted the crones, passing the searching mirror from hand to hand as they looked for a way to help Mertzork to touch the Glitterspike and claim the throne of Gnarlsmyre.

"I see a woman! A beautiful woman in the glass,"

cried one of the crones, bending low over the mirror and enveloping it in her shadow.

Erek snatched the mirror back and thrust it hard against Mertzork's lips. "Breathe, breathe," she commanded, pressing her cheek against his and watching the tiny beads of moisture shimmer and melt into a shadowy picture of Pinvey, her lips swollen with desire, her loose gown of transparent golden threads slipping from her smooth white shoulders beneath a low, darkened archway.

"She is one of Miresnare's daughters, I'm sure of it," Mertzork stuttered quickly as the healing woman's eyes met his. "She reached out and touched me and whispered, beckoning, but I had to follow Gallengab into the hall."

"She will be yours and she will help you to touch the Glitterspike," cackled Erek passing the fading picture of Pinvey into the huddle of crones, urging them to join their hands and tread magic in the cobbles and find the place where Pinvey could be caught and given over to Mertzork's keeping.

The crones began to skip, moving as awkwardly as strutting crows across the cobbles, their black cloaks flapping up against the crowding silent walls of the narrow alleyway. Faster and faster they spun, calling out the finding chant and rolling their eyes in their sockets as they searched as one with the power of the inner eye.

They swept their gaze through the crowded halls and busy, jostling corridors of Glitterspike Hall. "She is without. She is searching, there are two others with her who carry broken slate shards in their arms," they chanted after one final lingering look into every dark corner and hidden alcove.

Erek frowned and scratched her chin thoughtfully, wondering what three of the daughters of the hall would be searching for and why they were burdened with broken slate.

"Look again, sisters, so that we may snare the one in the golden gown for Mertzork's pleasure, for I foresee that fate has threaded them together in this joust to touch the Glitterspike."

Once more the crones trod their magic on the cobbles and cast sparks from their heels and raised their tingling fingers to point up into the maze of streets and alleyways that lay in the morning shadows of Glitterspike Hall. The first finger to find her stopped as it reached the sheer sunlit walls of the hall that rose above the crystal houses, but Pinvey had moved before the crones could utter the spell and hold her. Their fingers wavered, searching over meaner twisting corridors and passageways of the hall, all hazed with the smoke of the scullions' ovens.

"She is never still," they chanted as Pinvey passed through the chandlers' courtyards into the steeply terraced vineyards that had been fashioned on the sunniest walls and then moved down through the narrow winding walkways that leaked and echoed each slippery moss-dulled footstep.

"They are searching, touching shoulders and staring into faces as they push their way through the crowded corridors," cried the crones, abruptly stopping the dance and breaking apart, blinking their horrible eyes back into their rightful places.

The witches whispered amongst themselves and re-membered Pinvey's haunting beauty and how heads had turned in the crowd and lustful eyes had followed her graceful swaying steps.

"She carries a way through the mumblers' mazes on those broken shards of slate, but you must be quick to find her before the marshlords snatch her and use her to their advantage!" urged Erek, bundling the crones out of the alleyway in a flurry of black skirts to vanish in the crowded thoroughfares of the city.

Mertzork blinked, his mind still full of the crones' magic, and he rose to follow them, but Erek gripped his sleeve and pulled him back, casting a black crone's cloak over his thick beastskin one and pressing a knit-ted bonnet of rusty night-time shades firmly down over the top of his head.

"Your face has caused a thousand wild rumours and the hoards of marshmen that roam the city are keen to skin you alive. You must stay well disguised until you reach the doors of Glitterspike Hall. None will dare to touch you once you have issued your challenge for the throne. They are too afraid."

Erek thrust him behind her and peered out into the busy streets, searching through the morning bustle for any sight of the marshmen before she drew him out, whispering him to stick close to her heels.

"These clothes tickle and itch," he muttered misera-bly to himself as he quickened his stride to keep pace with the healing woman.

Erek hissed his mutterings into silence and threaded her way through the jostling crowds. She kept to the crown of the road, chanting and cackling, raising her crooked fingers to point at startled lampwicks, harvesters and anyone else who blocked her path. Rumour spread before them that the healing woman from the Shambles was on the road and the bustling crowds fell silent and shrank back to press themselves into narrow doorways or stumbled backwards into the safety of the steep dark lanes that opened out on either side.

Mertzork had to catch hold of her flying cloak tails or be lost in the twisting winding rush up through the city. But twice when Erek paused to choose a path he glanced back across his shoulder and saw the terror white-etched in the silent faces of the early morning travellers.

"Why do people shrink from us?" he asked breathlessly as Erek slowed at a crowded crossroads.

"Be quiet!" she whispered, drawing him into a dark narrow alleyway and squatting, her face wrinkled into a dozen frowns as she watched the crowds milling backwards and forwards before a high wall that seemed to block the way, a jumble of masonry edged with overhanging spikes.

There was a scent of panic in the air. Voices shouted for wheelwrights to tell the way through the mumblers' new maze. Anxious heads were turned, searching for roving bands of dangerous marshmen.

"Why is the road blocked? And why are these city people running about so helplessly?" Mertzork asked.

Erek turned and stared at him, and rocked gently back and forth on her heels. "Sometimes your ignorance is like a heavy stone, Mertzork, and one day if you do not learn to match the mumblers' magic it will bury you deep beneath the quickmarsh where none will find you," she hissed. "Naul has set new mazes in the city during the night to thwart the marshlords who have not yet found a road to Glitterspike Hall, but in his eagerness to serve his master he closes the way against all those whose task it is to serve in the city."

Mertzork laughed and shook his head. "Surely these people must know every way, every lane and alleyway in this city. There must be a thousand routes to the doors of Glitterspike Hall."

Erek frowned and pinched his arm, hushing him back into silence. "Only the wheelwrights know all the ways of the city, and they seem to have vanished completely. None can blame them for it, the marshlords caught and tortured any man thrusting a wheel in the first few days after the new joust was proclaimed, for the knowledge of a road to Glitterspike Hall."

"But the lampwicks, the harvesters—they all journey up through the city each morning," exclaimed Mertzork.

Erek clapped her hands and cackled at his ignorance. "They always use the same road. Look at the ridges and furrows they have worn in the cobblestones. Each guild and craft treads its own path and never crosses the others. Block their road and they are as lost as you are if you stray off the tracks you know in the quickmarsh."

Mertzork stared out at the milling crowds, his lips curled back in a smug sneer as he scratched absently at the woollen bonnet where it made his scalp itch. "I had always feared these city people, but they are so weak!" he laughed pointing at the crowds. "To lose their way so easily and to fear an old healing woman—they shrink away to let us past!"

Erek muttered to herself and turned narrow hate-filled eyes on Mertzork and then prodded a fingernail at his chest. "What do you know of their fears? You are too ignorant to judge them. You are but a marsh-man who knows nothing—where would you be now if I had not reached out to help you?"

"You are only using me to seek out your revenge," spat Mertzork glaring back at her.

Erek laughed at him and clapped her hands, her moment of anger forgotten. "The people fear me because they do not understand my healing powers, they shrink back in terror of the spiders they know are hiding in the black folds of our cloaks."

"Spiders? What spiders? I have heard wild rumours in the quickmarsh of how the healing women mix and breed their spiders to spin pure healing webs and how by some freak of nature the purest spiders have a lethal bite."

Mertzork stared down at the folds of his borrowed cloak in horror, gingerly shaking them with his fingertips and making the swarms of spiders that he had unknowingly carried scatter at his touch.

"Fool! Simple fool!" Erek snapped, stilling his hand with her crooked fingers. "There is truth in those wild rumours but it is the brooding and the hatred of Mire-snare that thickened my spiders' venom. If I had wanted your death I could have taken it while you hung helplessly beside my firestone but I cracked a spiral of spiders' spit and dripped it drop by sticky drop into your blood to toughen your skin against my spiders' bites. They will not harm you."

Mertzork nervously wiped his mouth on the back of his hand and reluctantly stroked the soft fur of a large green-eyed spider that squatted in Erek's outstretched hand. He whispered, "We were taught to fear the healing woman in the marsheries and lie very still while the spiders spun their healing webs."

Erek smiled and showed her sunken toothless gums. "Everything holds a little of the truth, Mertzork, and you must lie still for healing webs to knit your skin," and Erek sighed, remembering a time long ago when the Shambles were a place of real healing, when they were full of light and white spiders that spun their healing webs, but . . . Her thoughts were broken and she turned her head to the sound of a distant shout.

"The crowd is scattering. There are marshmen close by. They have found a wheelwright . . . Quickly, we must follow their voices."

"Why do you need me if your spiders have such strong venom, surely you could set them to bite Lord Miresnare and snatch the throne as your own, or give it to your child, Naul," whispered Mertzork, following in Erek's footsteps.

Erek cackled quietly and peered out of the dark alleyway, then ducked back out of sight as a band of wild marshmen ran into sight. "The spiders that carry the poison will only live in the dark folds of my cloak or in the safety of the Shambles. Lord Miresnare fears my anger and would never let me set foot inside his doors."

"But you could take the city from him," hissed Mertzork. "The people are in terror of your spiders. You have a great power over them."

Erek fiercely shook her head. "What do you know of power, you ignorant fool? This city is but a dot in the wilderness of Gnarlsmyre, the people only fear my spiders because they think they are all venomous. If they were to know how rare the death spiders are and how easily they are milked of their poison they would laugh and jostle me aside. But what of your people, Mertzork? Would the marshlords bow to me? Would they fear my spiders or trample them beneath their marshbound feet? No, I could not rule the Glitterspike nor could I handle the reins of power. I am, beneath these skirts, merely a woman, and a woman, no matter what power she gathers about herself, cannot even rule her own destiny."

Mertzork looked sideways at the healing woman and a cunning grin creased his face. He had almost forgotten that Erek was a mere woman: from their first meeting she had seemed more than that, stronger and more menacing. Perhaps it had been the swarms of spiders or her strange skirts and cloaks or some magical power she had held over him, but there was a raw truth in her voice. There would never be a woman strong enough to rule Gnarlsmyre. Mertzork laughed and turned to Erek and told her how Marrimian the first-born had snatched the jousting cup from his hands and had drained it to the last drop and had shouted of her right to joust for the throne. He told her how her father had dashed the cup from her hands and swept her claim aside and had called her nothing but a weak treacherous woman who had no rights before men.

Erek listened to each smug word that fell from Mertzork's lips and felt a whole lifetime of smothered anger at being thought of as "merely a woman" rise in her throat. She swallowed and looked away, wishing for just one short moment that she had helped Marrimian in her impossible struggle to be looked upon as an equal. Instead she had sent her off to the marsheries in the marshwader's care to be kept a prisoner beyond the city because Mertzork was a man and could serve her better in her thrust for revenge. Erek sighed and shrugged her shoulders, dismissing Marrimian from her mind, knowing that hers had been a hopeless cause that would have squandered a lifetime of gathered powers in the blinking of an eye.

Running footsteps, screams and shouts made Erek start and scuttle to the mouth of the dark alleyway. Cautiously she peered out and saw that the band of marshmen had stopped before the jumble of stones blocking the crossroads and at least a dozen of them had lifted a terrified wheelwright high above their heads and threatened to hurl him down onto the cobbles unless he showed them a way.

"That is the one who led me to the entrance of the Shambles," laughed Mertzork, crouching behind the healing woman and watching the screaming man thrown up again and again as the marshlords tortured the knowledge of the way out of him.

Erek drew back, trying to close her ears to the wheelwright's screams. She felt in the folds of her cloak and searched with quick fingers for a small black spider, the rarest of her pets. She lifted it to her lips, kissed its lethal fangs and whispered the wheelwright's name, then set it lightly down onto the cobbles.

"We need to know which road," hissed Mertzork and reached out to stop the spider.

"He has given it. Listen, between his screams he has shouted out which alleyways lead up to the broad tree-lined avenue, past the crystal houses to the very doors of Glitterspike Hall. Now I shall give him a quick death and end his torment," cried Erek angrily, brushing at the spider with her skirts and sending it scuttling out across the rutted cobbles to where the marshlords had thrown the broken, weeping man.

The wheelwright cried out just once more, arching his backbone, as the death spider sank its fangs into his neck. The marshmen laughed and cursed him, knocking the spider to the ground and trampling it beneath their feet before vanishing on their way.

"He has served us all," muttered Erek sadly, watching the scattered crowds emerge from every dark crack and hidden hole and quickly fill the empty road. They jostled and pushed, trampling the dead wheelwright's body as they hurried at a safe distance on the heels of the marshmen.

Erek tugged at Mertzork's sleeve and urged him to follow her as she crossed into the steep alley and began the long climb. It was hot and airless in the narrow roads and Mertzork lost count of the times they turned and the broad cobbled steps they had to climb. The healing woman seemed now more sure of the way and she pointed to different houses and whispered of which guilds and crafts were practised behind their blank windowless walls. Once she pointed up to rows of hanging baskets strung between the eaves and guttering of tall houses and told him that all the flowers that graced the tables of Glitterspike Hall were grown and harvested by hoemasters there who balanced on tightropes stretched between the roofs. Mertzork had laughed and shielded his eyes as they hurried through a patch of sunlight.

The alleyways had started to widen into lanes. There were small squares of houses, towers and turrets crowded against each other, fashioned out of the spires of the great ridges of stone that rose above the quickmire. There were glimpses of the endless marshes between the houses and a sea of steep, weathered, tiled roofs swept down towards the walls of the city below.

"Who lives up here?" asked Mertzork, twisting and turning and trying to look everywhere as they passed between high-arched doorways and flower-decked courtyards, each one set with narrow window slits glazed with tiny pieces of coloured glass. "I did not come this way before."

"Gentles, and those who have Miresnare's favour," Erek began to answer as they turned into a broad tree-lined avenue and saw the dazzling crystal houses that rose in towering silence on the sheer side of Glitterspike Hall.

"Do not look at the crystal too long! The sun's reflection will blind you," she rasped.

Mertzork cried out, slapping his hands over his eyes, then peeped between his fingers at the brilliant glare reflecting from the crystal houses. "I have seen them as a beacon from far out in the quickmarsh," he whispered in awe, "but they were just a flash of light, a tiny sun that sparkled over the bubbling mud."

"They are the Miresnares' power," muttered Erek hatefully. "They are the very strings that bind us all to him, for without the sweetmeats and all the delicacies that grow beneath the crystal we would starve in the cold wet seasons when the sun is lost behind the clouds and the marsh crust is barren and the apselgathers have withered with the frost."

Mertzork stared at the sheer sheets of woven crystal and watched them shimmer and sway in the dazzling heat haze they created. He frowned and slowly scratched his head saying, "There is always food if you know where to look, or which trees and banks to scrape, which hidden glades of reeds will yield up sweet-tasting roots. These houses of glass are nothing compared to what lies out there in the quickmarsh."

"Would you give the crystal houses to me if you ruled the Glitterspike?" asked Erek in a soothing whisper, and watched him from beneath cunning hooded eyes, silently measuring his simple mind to see whether he had grasped the worth, the great power, that could be wielded over the people of the city by the one who held the crystal houses.

Mertzork laughed and spun the healing woman around, lifting her clear of the ground. "They shall be yours to do with as you will, for when I rule Gnarlsmyre I will have an endless file of marshmen to bring the fruits of the marsh up into the city with each new sunrise."

Erek laughed silently, knowing that all the mire scratchings of Gnarlsmyre would never feed the city. She whispered her thanks and eased him forward towards the high archway that led to the doors of Glitterspike Hall.

"Where are the crones? Surely we should have crossed their path?" he asked, touching the healing woman's arm as they rounded the last sweeping bend and saw the finely gilded columns and ornately carved headstones of the great archway.

They both hesitated as they saw the guards filling the open doorway. Arrows were knocked onto bowstrings and long spears held ready in their hands. A flurry of black cloaks made them turn and look into a low archway beside the road where the gathering of crones was waiting in a black huddle silently beckoning to them.

"Pinvey is gone?" hissed Erek, drawing the crones into a tighter circle. "Where has she gone? Has some marshman taken her? Is she a prisoner?"

"No, no, she has vanished into some dark hole high above the great hall," muttered one of the crones pointing her finger through the open doors.

"We have followed her footsteps with our inner eyes all morning," grumbled another.

"She sits with her sisters in a secret place, high above the hall. They are trying to arrange the broken shards of slate into a complete picture," whispered a third.

"Behind a heavy tapestry that trembles with the slightest breeze there lies a hidden winding stairway.

Climb the treads to a narrow door crack and you will find all that you deserve," cackled a fourth crone.

"Tapestry?" repeated Mertzork, at a loss to know what all the cackling meant.

"A hanging cloth," snapped Erek impatiently. "The hidden stairway lies behind a hanging wall cloth somewhere near the great hall."

Mertzork thought for a moment and then quietly laughed. "I know it! I know it! It must be the place where I pushed that fat scullion with the pudding eyes and she vanished from sight . . ."

"Could you find it again?" interrupted the healing woman with one eye on the door guards who were advancing on their dark archway.

"The hedgehog—the one that led me up through the city unwinding its trail of gossamer thread for me to follow, he knows the way," whispered Mertzork, digging into his deepest pocket and, bringing out the tight bundle of prickles, thrust it under Erek's nose.

"Chant some magic over it! Make it remember, tell it to find the tapestry," he hissed in an excited whisper.

Erek cackled. She took the hedgehog into her crooked hands and lifted it high above her head, turning and chanting. She brought it to her lips and whispered into its ears, making it blink and squeal and scrabble against the coarse weave of her cloak. "Follow closely on its heels or lose the way," she urged and set the hedgehog down onto the cobbles, watching it run between the startled guards into the gloomy shadows of the first corridor of Glitterspike Hall.

The guards shouted and turned their spear blades

against the hedgehog but it ran nimbly beneath them and vanished into the shadows. Mertzork sprang forward casting aside the crone's cloak and bonnet, shouting his name and his right to challenge for the throne, and passed in giant strides between the guards. Behind him, mingled with the chanting voices of the crones and angry shouts from the guards, he heard Erek's voice warning him to take great care. With every step he took there were others on his heels, eager to touch the Glitterspike.

Laughing, he shook the sound of her voice out of his ears and ran on the hedgehog's heels to meet the woman in the golden gown.

10

The Beastweir Marshery

*M*ARRIMIAN slapped at the stinging insects that rose in swarms from the coarse hair tangled across the mudbeast's hide. She was sore and bruised, weary and aching from the beast's headlong rush through the quickmire. Frozen nights and scorching days that cracked the layers of mud on their faces blurred together and only the strength of the knots that she had tied in those last moments as the beast rose bellowing out of the marsh—and perhaps those half-remembered mumblers' chants for calming animals—had kept her and Ansel and the marshgirl from being thrown into the stinking mud. Blinking back her tiredness she remembered the startled faces and the screams of terror that had filled the marsheries as the enraged mudbeast ploughed its way through their flimsy mudslapped shelters.

The marshgirl had cried out, making Marrimian risk a glance across her shoulder at the vanishing wreckage of the marsh dwellings. She had seen the frightened people, the women and children kneeling in the mud, wailing and chanting, their arms raised above their heads, their hands twisted into those grotesque horn shapes.

"When do these beasts ever sleep?" Ansel had shouted as she spat out mouthfuls of the black slime that the beast sprayed up over her with each blundering step. Her apron was heavy with layers of the stinking mud and her cheeks itched and burned beneath the dry speckles of slime that clung to her.

The marshgirl had shouted back that mudbeasts sometimes foraged for whole seasons, travelling far across the marshes in search of berries and tender shoots and wading into deep swampy gullies to eat the roots of the mangle trees. Marrimian shivered as she heard the marshgirl's answer and chanted louder until her jaw grew numb, hoping that the jumble of mumbler's words would help to keep the beast on firmer ground. She thought that if it waded off the path and settled into the mud they would be drowned.

Falling silent through weariness Marrimian watched the marshes slowly change as they passed through forests of low reeds that hung limp in the stifling air. The mire was becoming wetter and pools of stagnant water now lay on either side. There were clumps of marsh oaks and black ebonies growing side by side on low islands of rich black turf. Narrow mudbanks rose above the stagnant swamps, water lilies and bulrushes grew everywhere, herons stalked the firmer banks and waders paddled in every glistening pool. There were stretches of bright yellow sand that seemed to shimmer and channels of white mud that bubbled and steamed and suddenly erupted in fountains of boiling liquid that washed in slow waves across their path. Marrimian shuddered at the strangeness of it all and pointed down at the oldest trees that she had ever seen, growing in uneven clumps beside the path, and asked the marshgirl why each slender trunk had so many interwoven roots reaching out into the muddy swamp water.

"Mangle trees! They are mangle trees," whispered the girl in horror as the mudbeast began to slow and sniff at the slender trunks as they passed.

Marrimian shouted the mumblers' chant and kicked frantically at the beast's shoulders but it only bellowed, sent up a ripple across its hide and turned off the path, sinking into the swampy mud, sending up fountains of weed-encrusted slime.

"Cut the knots and climb up through its tangled hair to keep above the mire," she called to Ansel and the marshgirl.

Ansel loosed her small kitchen dagger and cut herself and the marshgirl free, and hand over hand they scrambled up the steep sides of the mudbeast as it settled deeper into the swamp. Bellowing, it raked its horns through the mass of mangle roots and tore them free with its strong jaws.

"If it sinks much deeper we will all drown!" puffed Ansel, clinging onto the humped crest of the beast beside her mistress and pulling the girl up behind her.

"There are mangle trees growing everywhere," whispered Marrimian, her heart pounding with fear and not knowing where the beast would take them next.

The mudbeast suddenly stiffened and lifted its head. Weed and slime were dripping from its open jaws.

Somewhere nearby another mudbeast roared and the marshgirl gripped Marrimian's shoulders and pointed beyond the mangle-tree-covered nudbanks and the tall bulrush reeds.

"Look! Over there!" she hissed, looking towards a thin ribbon of blue smoke that rose lazily above the rushes. "This beast must have brought us close to a marshery."

Marrimian turned her head and following the girl's shaking finger saw the signs of cooking as smoke hung in the hot still air.

"Is this a marshery? Will they hurt us?" she questioned, grasping a knot of hair as the beast surged forward bellowing and raking its horns through the lily flowers, sending rippling waves slapping across the stagnant water.

The wader birds shrieked and rose in a cloud of bright orange feathers above the bulrushes and wheeling low across the swamp settled noisily in another lily-choked channel.

The girl shivered as she strove to find the words to explain the ways of her people and clung on tightly to the coarse tangle of hair as the mudbeast climbed up out of the swamp and onto a small tree-filled island, its splayed claws sinking into the rich dark turf.

"A woman is safe in the marshery where she is born. It is where she belongs, harvesting the marsh plants and roots, gleaning flesh from bones or chewing and softening the hides of the slaughtered mudbeasts while her teeth are strong . . ."

"Well! I would run away from such a life!" complained Ansel, interrupting the girl with a scowl.

The marshgirl looked up at the scullion and laughed bitterly. "The Council of Elders would starve you to death or stake you out in the mire for the mudbeasts to devour for such an outburst. Don't you know that we are punished by being cast out for our crimes against the marshery?"

"Who cast *you* out?" frowned Marrimian. "What was your crime?"

The girl hesitated and looked from one to the other. "I spoiled two hides by using rocks and splinters of marsh oak instead of my teeth to soften them. The council of hunters and waders staked me out for the mudbeasts to cleanse me of my crime and now I can never return even though you rescued me. No one will touch me or give me shelter, none will help me when the marshes flood in the wet seasons and none of the hunters or even the waders will ever mix their blood with mine again."

"So the people of that marshery will look upon you as an outcast," said Marrimian thoughtfully, turning her gaze back to the ribbon of rising smoke beyond the mangle trees.

The marshgirl nodded bleakly and whispered, "They will stone us and drive us back into the swamps to perish. Surely your own people will stone *you* if you were to try and return amongst them?"

Marrimian almost laughed at the marshgirl's words and then she remembered how her father had banished her and her lips drew into a grim line. "Yes," she nodded, "perhaps they would."

The mudbeast had finally come to a halt and was settling onto its knees beneath an ancient spreading

marsh oak. Turning to the marshgirl Marrimian asked
her if it would be safe to jump to the ground. The girl
shrugged her thin shoulders and answered that Marrimian must know more than any other, for she was
the only one ever to tame a beast by riding high on
its shoulders and she had chanted it safely through the
quickmire with magic words. Marrimian laughed,
lifted her right foot over the beast's crest and gathering her skirts jumped lightly to the ground and called
to Ansel and the girl to follow.

"I am Marrimian," she whispered to the girl, drawing her and Ansel away from the beast and into a safe
space between the marsh oaks. "I am the first-born of
Glitterspike Hall which rises sheer above the City of
Glor."

"You are the first Beaster Lady and I will follow you
anywhere," answered the girl, kneeling and raising
her arms above her head, twisting her hands into horn
shapes on her forehead.

Ansel stood silently behind the marshgirl, her stout
arms folded firmly across her chest. She grinned and
opened her mouth to sneer at the girl but Marrimian
frowned and shook her head, motioning her to be silent as she took the girl's hands and pulled her to her
feet.

"What is your name, child?" she asked but the girl
only smiled and pointed through the trees to where
the beast grazed.

"Great beasts, marshlords and their favoured servants are named, especially those who fight savagely.
Mere women and lesser servants of the marsheries are
not considered worthy of a name."

"Well, I shall name you," smiled Marrimian, casting her gaze over the tall stands of marsh oaks and the clumps of mangle trees that almost seemed to be standing on tiptoe on their mass of interwoven roots above the lily-filled swamp. She turned and looked for a moment at the kneeling mudbeast where it grazed in the leafy shadows of the tall trees, and pointed down to a scattering of sharp-spined spear-headed thistles that grew in the rich dark turf. "What are those?" she asked.

"Treasels," the girl answered, telling how their sharp spines were used to comb out knots and tangles in the softened hides.

"I shall name you Treasel then, for you shall be my first spear maiden amongst the marsh people," laughed Marrimian.

"There will be many to follow you, mistress. Remember all those who knelt saluting you; you looked back and saw them as the mudbeast charged through their dwellings."

"Were they saluting me even though the mudbeast destroyed their homes? You mean *this* is a salute?" asked Marrimian bringing her wrists to her forehead in confusion. "They should have hated me, thrown spears and stones, not saluted me!"

"You rode the mudbeast and none has ever done that before. There has been no one, not even in rhymes and legends," answered the marshgirl, kneeling and raising her arms to Marrimian.

Marrimian frowned and stepped back. "They would follow me even though I am a woman?"

Treasel shrugged her shoulders uncertainly and

then slowly nodded. "Many of the bravest hunters have tried to ride a beast, but all have failed."

Marrimian laughed out loud, making the beast bellow and turn its head towards them. She cried out in fear and hastily stepped behind the nearest tree.

Treasel moved apart from the others, frowning as she watched the beast scent the wind for her and then resume its grazing. "I think we are safe. Women never hurt the beasts so they do not fear our scent," she said slowly.

"But you cried out in terror when we carried you up on the mudbeast's back, and you fought against us when we tied you onto it," muttered Ansel doubtfully.

"I had lost count of the days I had been staked out in punishment near the mudbeasts' lair, marshfish were nibbling my flesh, the leeches were sucking my life blood and I was in terror of the beast trampling me. They are savage and turn on the hunters, goring them or clawing them down under the mire, but I don't think they have ever deliberately attacked a woman."

Marrimian smiled at Treasel's words as she remembered that the healing woman had urged her to go amongst the marsh people and find the strength to challenge the marshmen, and now, as she watched the mudbeast grazing between the trees, an idea began to grow in her mind. Clearly she must use this beast-riding skill, if they could ever remount. It would give her great power amongst these marsh people. But first they must somehow move away from this marshery and find a way of turning the mudbeast back towards the city.

Pulling Treasel towards her she asked if the cries of the captured mudbeast in the marshery had drawn their beast and Treasel nodded. Yes, this was how many beasts were snared.

"The captured mudbeast will be roped with strong marsh vines between two close-growing marsh oaks a little way from the marshery, and the hunters will be crouching in the lowest branches of the trees. Once the sun has set the hunters will leave the safety of their shelters and be ready to cast their iron-linked nets over any unsuspecting mudbeast that was drawn into the trap."

"We must get to that shackled beast and set it free," muttered Marrimian.

Ansel was firmly against tangling with the hunters or going any closer to the marshery.

"What other choice is there?" Marrimian asked grimly as she turned on the scullion. Ansel's cheeks drained of colour beneath the smears of black mud as she realized that her mistress was in deadly earnest and that the bleak reality was that the beast they had ridden thus far would never leave while the other beast was shackled between the trees.

"But the hunters will see us! And anyway we cannot cross the swampy water to fray the bindings of the shackled beast without riding on the mudbeast," cried Ansel without pausing for breath.

"The hunters will be in their shelters or sleeping by their fire," whispered Treasel. "They will not stir until the sun has set."

"Still we cannot get to the beast, and even if we could it would roar and bellow and wake up everyone and bring them down on us before you could blink," snapped Ansel, planting her feet well apart and glaring at the marshgirl.

Treasel shook her head and laughed at the angry scullion. "We are all women. I don't think the beast will harm us. And anyway they don't bellow and shout when the women are sent down to feed the ones that are to be fattened for slaughtering."

Borrowing Marrimian's dagger she stripped off two long curls of bark from the nearest marsh oak tree and with lengths of finger-thick vines and lily weeds she bound them to her feet, making sure that the toes and heels curved upwards while the broad soles stayed flat. Giving Ansel a triumphant grin she lowered herself onto the surface of the swamp and glided noiselessly across to the next low tree-covered island and turned and skimmed quickly back leaving less than half a ripple spreading out through the lily pads.

"We use these bark sledges to collect the treasels in the swamps and to gather food, but they are dangerous in mud," she warned. "The mud seeps up over the toes and heels and drags them into the mire. You must be careful."

"Will the hunters from that marshery use them to catch us if they see us trying to free their beast?" Marrimian asked, staring at the strange sledge-shaped shoes.

"It is beneath the marshlords and their marshhunters to use such things. They only travel by the secret paths across the marshes, the ways of these they learn from their fathers. The women and the lesser servants of the marsheries are forbidden to know these paths or to tread upon them. We can only skim across the marshes on these barks to go about our tasks of harvesting," Treasel answered as she cut barks for Ansel's feet.

"This is madness! Madness!" Ansel grumbled as the marshgirl bound the bark sledges to her feet and helped her to stand and take the shuffling awkward steps to the edge of the island. Treasel made her sit and push the sledges backwards and forwards to get used to the feel of them skimming across the thick weed and lily-choked surface of the swamp while she cut strips of bark and bound Marrimian's feet.

"Do everything I do," Treasel urged, pushing away from the bank and gliding gracefully as she moved her weight from sledge to sledge across the swamp.

Ansel muttered under her breath and stood up, bravely pushing herself away from the bank. She gave a startled cry and her arms flailed above her head; she was moving too quickly, the sledges were drifting apart. She wavered with her plump knees buckling and lost her balance, toppling backwards with a dull splash into the mud and was lost amongst the lilies.

Treasel and Marrimian just managed to catch hold of her apron tails as she sank beneath the surface and they pulled her gasping and choking out of the weed-entangled muddy water and back onto the island. Marrimian swallowed her laughter and hid her broad smile behind her hand as Ansel wrung herself dry, muttering and grumbling beneath her breath.

"It's all right for you, mistress," she cried suddenly,

looking up with tears in her eyes. "You are neat and graceful and you will be able to master any skill that the marshgirl could teach you to cross the marshes, but I'll be left here because I'm fat, and because I'm . . ."

"You are brave and fearless and I would never leave you behind," soothed Marrimian frowning at the scullion's fears and knowing as she helped her back onto her feet that she could ask for none better to be at her side in these treacherous marshes.

Ansel blushed, angry with herself for showing her fears, straightened her filthy weed-entangled apron and strutted awkwardly on her curled bark sledges back to the edge of the swamp.

"Give me your hand," Treasel whispered, softly closing her small palm around as many of the scullion's large blunt fingers as she could hold, and with Marrimian holding on firmly at her other side they splashed and glided in a tight huddle from island to island, skirting the long mudbanks and keeping to the shadows of the mangle-tree roots, careful that each gliding movement should not disturb the wading birds that always flocked to the edges of the marsheries, combing and scavenging through the mounds of bone litter and rubbish. They could hear voices now as they drew closer to the haze of blue smoke that drifted up above the tall reed beds, hiding the cluster of shelters that stood on rickety poles above the swamp. They could see the leaf-covered branches and bright flowerheads of the two black ebonies that towered above the reeds, showing them where the beast must be shackled. Entering the bulrushes they squeezed between the brittle stalks and pulled and twisted their way to the edge of a wide channel full of yellow lily pads.

"This must be the Beastweir Marshery," Treasel whispered fearfully as they peered through the reeds towards the cluster of mud- and branch-woven shelters built on spindly branches in the centre of the channel which was filled with brilliant yellow lily pads. A lump-crested mudbeast was shackled between the two trees.

"Why is it called the Beastweir Marshery?" asked Marrimian clinging onto the sharp bulrush stems to help her to keep her balance.

Treasel pointed to the brilliant lily heads that choked the channel and whispered, "Because it clings to the very edge of the world, where the rising sun kisses the lily heads with its hot lips and turns them yellow. Nowhere else in all these endless marshes do the lilies bloom such a colour."

Marrimian laughed quietly and pushed the reeds aside to take another look at the splash of colour spreading along the channel. "But do your marsh tales tell of the places where the sun sets? Surely they would also burn with the same brilliance?"

Treasel looked at the rippling channel of blooms and slowly shook her head. "They are colourless at day's end because the sun has lost its heat and its lips have grown shrivelled and cold."

"How can we slip past the marshery without them seeing us?" asked Ansel, anxiously clutching a double handful of reed stems as she balanced unsteadily.

Treasel swept her gaze along the mudbanks of the

wide channel and pointed to the shadows that filled the broken mangle roots. "We must move quickly from shadow to shadow," she urged, taking the dagger from Marrimian.

Ansel made herself ready, awkwardly bringing the two bark sledges together, but Marrimian took her kitchen blade and told her to stay where she was and watch the marshery. She would send up the flocks of wading birds that had settled behind them as a warning if anyone appeared to notice them amongst the mangle roots. Ansel looked darkly at the marshgirl but did as her mistress bid, breaking off a long bulrush stem to frighten the waders if the need arose.

"The hunters of this marshery have snared and slain many beasts," Treasel whispered as they glided through the last mangle shadow, moved silently over the edges of the yellow lilies and climbed up on to the island where the mudbeast was shackled. There they found a path through the piles of bones.

The mudbeast roared quietly and lifted its nose to scent the air, straining at the marshbindings on its legs and making the huge canopy of leaves and bright flowers above its head rustle as if touched by the cool evening wind.

"We must hurry," Marrimian answered, gathering her courage and creeping forward through the mounds of bones towards the towering mudbeast.

For all her outward boldness she was not sure that she completely believed Treasel when she had told them that the mudbeast would not turn on them the moment they had flayed the marsh vines, but she took a deep breath, knowing that they had no other way of escaping this nightmare and returning to the city. She slipped quietly into the beast's shadow and slashed at the thick creepers. The beast bellowed and shook the trees as it tried to turn. It grunted and she staggered dizzily as its hot fetid breath swept over her. Something made her look up into the branches of the trees.

"Will those iron nets fall on us?" she gasped, pointing up into the lower branches past the loops of old rotting marsh vines that still held the broken bone endings of other beasts that had been slaughtered there.

"I know not," answered Treasel, hurriedly moving as close as she dared to the mudbeast's head and sawing at the thick vines that held it with the blade held firmly in both hands. The beast's eye was but a hand's span from her arms. It blinked, wrinkling its dewlaps as it scented her and watched.

"Well, I will make sure they don't," answered Marrimian climbing up through the creeper loops and knotting their loose ends into the nets, to prevent them falling if the hunters tried to release them. She had barely reached the ground when the wading birds rose shrieking and flapping, filling the sunset with dazzling wings of pink and orange feathers. The beast roared and arched its neck, making Marrimian and Treasel leap backwards. The marsh vines strained their long fibers creaking and tightening around the trunks of the black ebonies. The frayed vines began to split and send up puffs of vinewood powder. There were voices beyond the wide channel, coarse hunters' voices that laughed and cursed as they rose up from the marshery.

Treasel acted quickly and caught hold of Marrimian by her sleeve, pulling her into the undergrowth, through the piles of bones to the far side of the island. Moments later the hunters left their shelters and began to cross the swamp.

"Bend double and hold onto me," Treasel hissed as she slipped down onto the swamp and pulled Marrimian behind her. Together they glided silently away into the dense shadows of the mangle roots on the far side of the channel and made their way to where Ansel was anxiously waiting.

"How do they cross?" asked Marrimian, trying to peer over her shoulder as Treasel and Ansel hurried her into the safety of the reed bed.

"They seem to be walking on the swamp," muttered Ansel.

"They are using secret paths," hissed the marshgirl. "The ones they learned from their fathers."

Marrimian laughed grimly and stood up, glad to straighten her back now that they were safely in amongst the reeds and well hidden from the hunters. "Somehow we must learn the secrets of those paths if we are ever going to find a way back to the city," she whispered, trying to pick out the island where they had left their mudbeast.

"Surely we will not try to remount that beast. We can escape on these bark sledges," cried Ansel in dismay as they retraced their way across the lily pads and climbed up onto the low island.

But Marrimian only laughed and shook out her mud-streaked hair and asked the scullion if she would bubble a pot until it was properly cooked or lift it early from the coals half-done. Ansel began to stutter, her red cheeks flushing bright scarlet in the gathering darkness as Marrimian walked between the trees, singing out half-remembered chants for calming beasts.

"We must trust our mistress, there is no choice," Treasel whispered, pinching Ansel's arm and sweeping her hand out past the mangle trees, reminding the scullion of the endless expanse of swamp that marched away from their sight and into the darkness.

The beast snorted, letting roots and strips of bark fall from its open jaws. It wrinkled its nose, scenting the women, and bellowed softly and swept its horns across the rich dark earth as they ran to its side and scrambled up through the thick tangles of coarse hair. They flung themselves astride its crest only just in time, as it roared and arched its back, sending huge ripples up across its hide to shake them off.

"Look," cried Treasel when they had knotted themselves on. She was pointing across the marsh, past the silhouettes of the marshery on its spindly stilts, to a red glow in the darkness where the hunters had lit a fire near the two black ebony trees.

A tortured roar split the darkness, making the hairs on Marrimian's neck prickle. The captured beast shackled between the ebony trees bellowed with pain as the hunters' first fire-hot spear blade scorched its hide.

"It has begun," Treasel whispered as the mudbeast

they were perched upon turned its head towards the cry of pain, its nostrils stretched wide apart. It had scented the burned hair and scorched flesh and it sank down on its haunches and gathered itself to charge with its horns lowered; its claws were already ploughing up dense clouds of stinging ice crystals. The women heard the swamp crust crackle and the lily pads fold away their flowers into whispering silence as the endless quickmarsh began to freeze, which happened quickly at this edge of the world.

Suddenly the beast surged forward, its claws tearing at the ice as it gathered speed. Mangle trees and bulrush stems split and shattered in its path, startled herons and wader birds scattered, blindly flapping their wings to escape its pounding feet.

They were across the reed beds in a dozen thundering strides, bursting through the bulrush stems into the frozen channel of yellow lilies and hurtling towards the marshery. Treasel cried out as they charged straight through, tearing down the flimsy shelters and splintering their rickety poles and wattle sides. Voices screamed and shouted all around them and the icy ground shattered beneath the beast's feet as they left the marshery behind them.

"Look! Look at the surface of the swamp," cried Treasel, pointing down at the brilliant colours reflecting through the ice and making the island they were rushing towards seem to shimmer and float above the frozen swamp.

Marrimian saw the hunters stab and plunge their fire-hot spears, sending up billows of choking smoke from the captive mudbeast's burning hair, and she raised her dagger high above her head to catch the moonlight and sang in a voice that rang as clear as crystal across the frozen swamp. Ansel chanted, her voice booming in the darkness, while Treasel lifted her arms above her head and turned her hands into the grotesque horn shapes on her forehead. The hunters turned at the sound of Marrimian's voice and stumbled backwards, their eyes wide with terror. They scattered through their own fire embers with shouts of pain on their lips as they saw the women riding the beast towards them. Their white-hot spear blades fell from their hands as they fled across the ice.

The shackled beast roared and strained against the marsh-vine bindings, breaking them one by one as it fought to be free. It sent the severed ends snaking amongst the fleeing hunters, tripping and tangling between their legs. With an earsplitting roar of hatred the mudbeast carrying Marrimian and her two followers breasted the island and charged between the black ebony trees, snapping the last binding vine in its forward rush. One of the hunters hidden in the low branches hurled a spear wildly into the darkness and shouted to the other hunters to release their iron-lined nets, but the nets merely sank a hand's span from where they hung, still firmly secured by Marrimian's secret creeper bindings.

Marrimian gave a shout of triumph and waved the dagger above her head as the two beasts surged forward side by side, trampling and scattering the hunters as they charged out across the frozen swamp crust. She turned and glanced over her shoulder as they vanished into the reed beds and saw that the hunters who had escaped were kneeling wide-eyed on the ice; some of them had their hands stretched out in horn shapes on their foreheads but some of them seemed to be calling to them to return and she laughed, sure that the rumour of this night and the story of the woman who had mastered the great mudbeast and ridden it through the marshery would spread and give her power against the marshlords when she eventually returned to Glitterspike Hall.

"Mistress, mistress," Ansel called, tugging at her sleeve and making her turn her head.

"What is it?" Marrimian whispered, staring past the scullion and out into the frozen darkness.

"That noise! Can't you hear it?" Ansel hissed, her heavy eyebrows wrinkled together. She looked at the marshgirl and tilted her head, cupping a hand behind her ear, as if she expected the girl to give her the answer.

Treasel shrugged her thin shoulders and looked blankly back. She had never travelled further than one night's journey from her marshery to gather food or to search for treasels, for fear of getting lost, and she could not tell them what the noise was or why the mudbeasts had slowed their pace.

"We must somehow turn this beast around," Ansel added fearfully. "It is taking us towards the noise now and it sounds as if the whole of Gnarlsmyre is coming to the boil."

Marrimian threw up her hands helplessly and realized that she could do nothing; the beast was following a path of its own choosing. She leaned forwards and, turning her head from side to side, she could hear grumbling sound that was gradually growing louder and she wept with despair.

The swamps were changing; there were more low flat mudbanks covered with mangle trees, but their roots and the reed stems that now grew amongst them seemed to be leaning as if tugged by an invisible strong wind. The lily pads were no longer spread in an even tangle between the mud banks but were piled up in choking frozen heaps around the mangle roots. Jagged rocks crowded with all manner of strange-leafed bushes and small trees were dotted through the swamps. The grumbling sound was becoming a dull roar, the rocky islands were closer together, rising out of the swamp on either side of them in steep overhanging ledges. Marsh oaks grew on every ledge, their roots crisscrossing in a maze of loops that reached down into the pit of the swamp. Creeper vines, heavily laden with flower buds tightly shut against the frozen moonlit darkness, hung across the narrow channel.

"There is something wrong here," shouted Marrimian, looking ahead and seeing a white mist that boiled up to fog the stars, and she felt a gust of freezing rain sting her face, though there were no clouds above.

The ice crust in the channel was trembling and groaning, beginning to crack beneath the mudbeasts' claws. They were turning on a large piece of ice when it began to break up.

"Jump! Jump!" Marrimian shouted and started to slash through the knots that she had tied in the mudbeast's coarse hair. She leapt clear, grazing her knees as she stumbled on the slippery surface of the ice and

scrambled across the frozen swamp crust as it began
to shatter and move apart.

Ansel and Treasel quickly followed and together
the three women ran across the cracking ice feeling
it shift and splinter beneath their feet as they reached
up and clung onto the hanging loops of marsh-oak
roots. Climbing up above the swamp crust they turned
and watched the two mudbeasts on their ice floe twist
and turn and vanish into the roaring white mist.

"Well, it still sounds as if the whole of Gnarlsmyre
is coming to the boil," Ansel muttered miserably,
finding herself a better perch in the tangle of roots.

Marrimian smiled at the scullion and looked up at
the steep overhanging ledges that rose above them.
"We will be safer up there and when the sun comes
up it will give us a better view of what lies beyond this
channel," she said in a voice heavy with tiredness.

Treasel, who had climbed more marsh oaks than she
cared to remember, in search of sweet-scented ke-
rands, scrambled up ahead of the other two women
and found them a safe way through the maze of wet
and slippery roots to the first broad ledge. She quickly
scraped a clear space in the dead leaves and moss and
lumped them into rough pillows, and Marrimian and
Ansel had hardly let their heads sink into the softness
of the leaves and stretched out their limbs, before deep
dreamless sleep overtook them.

Finding the straightest marsh oak on the ledge
Treasel sat down and rested her back against its trunk.
She shivered and drew her knees up to her chin as she
stared at the strangeness all around her. She looked
up at the glittering stars through the canopy of leaves

above her head and her eyes were wide with fear as she listened and wondered at the thundering roaring noise. Looking across at Marrimian she sighed and smiled. The Beaster Lady would find the answer. Another worry, stronger than the first, suddenly clouded her mind and made her cry out and jump to her feet. She was a gatherer, a gleaner of roots and berries, and yet she had allowed her mistress to lie down to sleep with an empty belly. She must find them food before they woke.

11

Whispers in the Dark

*K*RANN huddled down on the frozen ground, as close as he could to the last warm sparks that glowed amongst the ashes of his fire, and listened as the howling shrieks of wind fell away to empty whispers, leaving behind huge ridges and deep furrowed drifts of snow piled up against his shelter. The blizzard blew itself out, the sky shone sun-bright again, filling Krann's refuge with a cold blue light. He knew that if he huddled there a moment longer he would die and his frozen bones would lie amongst the forgotten bleached branches that lay scattered all around him.

Krann shivered miserably and rose to his feet. He had to force a passage through the thick crust of ice and snow that had sealed up the narrow entrance. Leading Eyrus by the bridle he scrambled out into a dazzling landscape of towering wind-ridged snow turrets and glittering ice caves that the blizzard had thrown up all around; everything had changed and the greenway they had been following had vanished entirely beneath a petrified sea of ridges and hollows.

"Which way—which way now?" he muttered, his

voice sounding shrill against the blanket of white silence that muffled in on every side.

Putting his foot into Eyrus's stirrup he mounted, and slowly pirouetted the horse between the crested snow humps that marked the clump of tangletrees.

"There *is* only one way," he whispered as he screwed up his eyes against the blinding glare of the snow and followed the lines of the deep wind-blown ridge across the bleak white landscape towards the dark shape of a forest and mountains that lay on the distant horizon line, clad in pale winter colours. "The forest, make for the forest," he whispered to Eyrus as he urged the horse to follow the broadest furrow of powdered snow, for he could see thin spirals of smoke rising from beneath the edge of the wood.

The sun had long since sunk behind the mountains and a frost rime had gathered on Krann's cloak before they reached the cluster of low wooden houses that stood a dozen strides from the eaves of the forest. Most of the houses were heavily shuttered but there were lights at the windows of one long low sprawl of buildings that stood apart from the others, and the ground all around it was crisscrossed with hoof marks and fresh footprints. Krann dismounted and led the horse up to the lowest window where he carefully scratched at the feather patterns of frost on the glass and rubbed a hole.

"This must be a wayhouse," he whispered to Eyrus, stroking the horse's muzzle as he pressed his nose against the glass and looked into a crowded room.

Catching his breath, Krann ducked out of sight. A galloper from King Thane's guard and at least a dozen archers wearing the cloaks of Stumble Hill were moving across the room towards the window. Now he could hear their voices and the scrape of their iron-shod boots on the rough floorboards.

"All this searching is an utter waste of time. Krann's probably frozen to death in that blizzard," grumbled the guard as Krann saw him reach to close the shutters.

"Well, if I'd been him and seen what he did I'd want to run away and throw myself into a snowdrift," muttered one of the archers. "It wasn't right what happened all those suns ago and I say it's not natural now and never will be!"

"What would you have done—gone against the King's wishes?" sneered another voice. "Would you have made the killing stroke?"

Angry murmurs rose amongst the archers and hissed the last sneering voice into silence. Krann lost the thread of their talk and did not hear what they were saying against him as the shutters creaked on their rusty hinges and slammed shut to block out the night as they called for food. Krann tried to search their minds as the arguing group of archers and guards returned to the warmth of the roaring log fire set in the central hearth of the wayhouse, but the images he plucked from them were muddled and confused, covered in webs of shadow. Krann shivered and sank down into the snow clutching his numb fingers together helplessly. Part of him wanted to burst into the wayhouse and shout for answers that would forever banish the tissue of lies and half-truths that he had grown up with, but he was afraid. Even those who had spoken for him had lowered their voices and glanced over their shoulders before they spoke. Krann shrank away from the shuttered window and moved towards the dark eaves of the forest, his boots crunching through the thick layer of frost that glittered in the darkness, then he changed his mind, for he knew that both he and Eyrus must eat soon and find a warm shelter or they would perish before the new sun rose.

Searching stealthily through the courtyards that surrounded the wayhouse Krann came upon the stable yards. He found an empty stable in the furthest corner that was fresh bedded with sweet-smelling straw; there was fodder in the manger and hay in the rack. Krann moved Eyrus silently through the door and settled him down before he crept out into the darkness and followed his nose to the kitchen window. Pulling the collar of his cloak up over his frost-white hair, to hide it from prying eyes, and buttoning his collar tight to cover his clothes, he slipped into the bustling kitchens and almost fainted as the heat of the roasting fires and the glowing coals of the bake ovens swept over him. He passed unnoticed in the haze of cooking smoke and kept to the shadows as he moved amongst the dressing slabs and cutting boards filling his saddle pouches with as many of the uneaten scraps and broken finger treats that the servers had pushed aside as he could carry. Returning to the doorway he paused for a moment, listening to the kitchen talk and searching the mind of each of the hurrying servers and grumbling cooks as they basted the roasts or riddled the griddling irons or brought their boiling broths away from the fire.

Krann frowned helplessly at all he heard and realized that almost all the gossip was about him and the great search that the King had spread far and wide across Elundium, but each and every snatch of rumour conflicted with the last and none left him any the wiser. If he believed some he was the lost son of a warrior woman; in others the King's blood ran in his veins; while wilder whispers told him that he had fallen from the folds of Nevian's magic rainbow cloak. But two things made him shiver: there was always magic in the stories, and whenever any of the cooks or servers so much as mentioned nightmares or the Shadowtreading an eerie silence fell on the kitchen and frightened eyes searched the shadows.

The grand feast for the searchers was coming to an end. The smoke haze in the kitchens was beginning to thin and Krann ducked out of the kitchen entrance before curious eyes turned in his direction. Safely back in the stable he ate his fill from the saddle pouches and prepared for sleep. But he had hardly burrowed down in the warm straw beside Eyrus when he was roughly woken by shouts in the darkness and the clatter of hooves sending up a blaze of bright sparks on the freshly swept frost-sharp cobbles of the stable yard. Through the cracks in the stable door he could see lantern lights passing backwards and forwards and he heard the jingle of harness and muffled voices moving through the yard towards the greenway. Krann crept forward through the straw and peered between the widest timbers in the door, and saw the greenway thronged with mounted figures. There were archers with their long bows and heavy quivers of new-forged arrow blades, marchers, their cloaks tightly buttoned against the cold, and a whole squadron of gallopers, their lanterns swinging from brass rings on the saddles. They were milling about, their frost-white breath billowing in clouds of vapour in the lantern light as they fanned out beyond the greenway's edge, shouting their thanks to the wayhouse keeper for the feast and the warm beds. Eventually they formed into respectable lines and filed away silently amongst the winter trees, their lanterns casting long dancing shadows all around them.

"Well I say good riddance," grumbled a voice so close to the stable door that it made Krann jump backwards and Eyrus snort and flatten his ears in alarm.

"All these early mornings, and for what?" muttered a second voice as two of the servers who had to lay tables and carry the food to the searchers turned sleepily towards the kitchen entrance.

"They won't find him you know," continued the first voice as the servers reached the stable entrance and passed through it, their voices growing fainter. "There's too much dark magic in him to expect him to be found beneath a snowdrift. Mark my words, even if they shake and prod every tangletree from here to the Granite City they'll find nothing."

"Well, all I know is that we should have found service at the wayhouse on the great crossroads," yawned the second server. "There's no early mornings there because they are not searching in that direction. They say no one could have travelled on that road and survived the blizzard, not even Eyrus, the horse that he stole from Lord Willow."

Krann listened to the servers and shivered inwardly. So they thought of him as a thief and cursed him for all the trouble he was causing. He knew that he must escape from the wayhouse before he was discovered and they found that he had added to his crimes by stealing food from the kitchens and fodder from their stables. He waited, crouching miserably in the straw, until the courtyards were empty and the last heavy outer door had slammed shut against the cold dawn darkness before he packed up the remaining provisions and led Eyrus out of the stable and onto the greenway.

"I'll send you back to Lord Willow at the first moment I can, I promise," he whispered as he mounted. He rode a few paces following the searchers' hoofprints but he slowly realized that he could not seek the answers he needed amongst them and he turned away with loneliness and despair weighing deeply on him.

Eventually they found a path that led through the winter-black trees towards the towering crags and frost-glittering pinnacle of Mantern's Mountain and the great lamp that shone at World's End. He did not know where Eyrus was taking him but with each silent footfall he drew closer to the steep slopes of the mountain and somehow felt the road beneath the trees grow more familiar, as if he was tracing an echo back into his past. For two daylights and two frozen nights he followed the ancient overgrown greenway into a wilderness that he never dreamed existed.

Finally, cold and weary, Eyrus breasted a wooded rise and Krann saw the single lamp of Underfall blaz-

ing out across the snowy landscape of the causeway
fields and he caught his breath as he watched the frost-
sparkling air dance in the beam of light, knowing that
this place held his beginnings.

A single voice whispered at him, breaking through
the darkness; it rose into shrieks of laughter. He spun
around in panic and looked everywhere as he reached
for his dagger but nothing moved nor showed the
slightest imprint in the untrodden snow. Now more
voices came, smothering him in their whispers, twisting and turning round his ears and making his hair
prickle and his flesh crawl. He gathered his horse's
reins and spurred him as fast as he would gallop
through the deep-drifted snow but the voices stayed
with him, now on the pommel, now on the cantle of
the saddle; now beside his shoulder or in his flying
cloak tails, they laughed and cried and mingled with
the wild jingling of Eyrus's harness and echoed back
from the steep snow-covered shale slopes and dense
stands of timber that rose on either side.

The grey hours were lightening the sky and casting
whispers of dawn across the sheer black walls of Underfall, and Krann cried out as he saw the countless
overhanging galleries, each one echoing the watchman's tread, and the black iron-spiked blind window
slits between each gallery that stared out to him across
the snow. Silent and accusing Underfall rose in towering judgement of him above the causeway fields.

"This must be a part of it," he gasped, shivering as
he swept his gaze up towards the high plateau and broken summit of Mantern's Mountain that shadowed
the dawn.

The voices erupted, splitting the air around him. "Not here! Not here!" they mocked. "This is a tomb of long-dead kings. Your search must be beyond World's End and into the Shadowlands."

Krann shook his head violently, trying to scatter the voices, and spurred Eyrus down to the edge of the causeway fields and urged him forward through a billowing cloud of icy crystal that his pounding hooves threw up with each galloping stride. "I know it is here," he cried, flinging the words across his shoulder back into the strengthening dawn light as Eyrus scrambled up onto the causeway road. "I will find every answer I will ever need in there."

Krann wept in terror of the voices as he turned the horse towards the great iron-studded wooden doors of Underfall but the doors were still fast-bolted against the darkness, their locks and catches glittering beneath thick layers of feather-patterned ice and frost. Reining Eyrus to a walk Krann looked nervously over his shoulder but the fields behind him spread out flat and empty with only their own prints spoiling the snow. "Who are you?" he whispered, pulling his cloak collar up around his ears as he passed over the frozen drainage dyke.

"We are you," they hissed, seeming to squeeze up through his collar and making him jump. "We are as much a part of you as that secret river that runs beneath your feet."

Krann looked down at the frozen dyke and shivered. He saw movement, slow swirling movement beneath the ice, and he followed it with his eyes through the echoing tunnel underneath the causeway road and into the widening pools of stagnant marsh where it vanished into an ominous black culvert. The voices hardly gave him time to comprehend before they began sighing and whispering, weaving the sound of rustling water amongst their words and urging him to turn away from the fortress of Underfall with its bones of brittle kings and dusty emptiness and follow the sound of the water out into the Shadowlands.

"There is nothing—nothing beyond World's End. The Loremasters say that nothing lives there," Krann whispered, pressing his hands to his ears to shut the voices out, but the sound of rushing water grew to a roar that thundered through his head, and now amongst the swirling waters he heard a child's gurgling cry and the coarse rattle of gasping breath as if a monster were towering over him.

"No! You cannot be a part of me," he cried desperately, digging his heels into Eyrus's sides and driving the exhausted horse towards the doors, but with each bounding stride the voices shrieked louder and louder inside his head until he thought it would burst. "No! No! No!" he shouted, throwing himself out of the saddle and rolling over and over in the snow to shut the voices out.

Eyrus felt the terror and shied away from him, and cantered into the shadows of the great doors, snorting and arching his neck, his ears pressed flat along the sides of his head. Krann rose to his knees and brushed the snow from his face, and looked up at the smooth sheer walls of Underfall. In that moment of silence he heard the watchman's measured tread pass along the galleries and he knew there would be warm fires and roast nightboar on the spit and a safe place to weather out the winter, but as he climbed to his feet he remembered the searchers that he had watched through the wayhouse window and the servers' harsh words before he had slipped unseen out of the stable yard, and he hesitated. He turned his head and stared into the black gaping culvert. The voices were all around him again, whispering, soothing him and softly coaxing him to follow them into the Shadowlands. He took a small step towards the rough ground beyond the culvert, then stopped and turned back towards the fortress of Underfall and wrung his hands in despair. It would be madness to follow the voices but he was afraid to face those who lived inside and kept this last lamp on the edge of the world.

Eyrus sensed his despair and reared up, snorting and whinnying, striking his forelegs on the wooden doors. The watchman stopped, his hand upon the warning bell as he listened to the dawn silence. Eyrus reared again, splintering the wood with his hoof and lifting his head in a neighing shout. The warning bell clattered, armoured boots rushed across the galleries and heads crowded the rails to peer down onto the causeway road.

Krann looked up, and saw in all those staring eyes the same lies and rumours and wild fireside tales of magic that were always woven around his beginnings. He turned and fled, leaving the shouts and the slow, grinding scrape of the opening doors far behind him as he ran towards the Shadowlands, following the whispering voices amongst the wind-bent tangletrees that speckled the barren sweeps of hills and rock-choked hollows that lay before him.

Day and night seemed to merge together into a half-light of swirling mists as he left the snow behind him and everything blended into tones of grey; rocks and trees would melt or loom up only to vanish again at the blink of an eye. He was alone, with nothing but the voices that had tempted him to risk such madness and tread beyond the lamp of Underfall into the Shadowlands.

But on the fourth gloomy daylight of his wandering the voices deserted him in a squabbling hiss, as if each whisperer were arguing for a different path and they were trying to pull him in a dozen directions at once.

The ground beneath his feet had been changing from dry wind-cracked bones of rock into treacherous marshes and strips of quicksand that reeked and bubbled all around him. He stopped and almost stumbled light-headedly in the first moment of real silence since he had fled from the doors of Underfall. He felt the wet mist press against his cheeks and form into heavy droplets on his eyelids.

"What am I to do?" he cried against the silence as his feet began to sink into the soft marshy ground. "Why did you tempt me here?" he shouted, clenching his fist at the swirling silence as it muffled and swallowed his words. He wished with all his heart that he had never left the Granite City nor risked a stolen glance at the Shadowtreading.

Bitterly he screwed up his eyes to shut out the misery and despair that had closed about him and ground Fairlight's name between his teeth as he wept. But as he stood there lost and helplessly alone his mind filled with a clear picture of her; she was laughing and chiding him just as she had done a thousand times before when she tempted him to follow her into one of her reckless adventures and he remembered the words that she had always used to make him bolder. "If only you were with me now," he whispered. "You would find a way out of these miserable marshes, you . . ." He caught his breath and blinked and rubbed his eyes, looking wildly around him as the mist swirled and opened up and then closed in again around him. He had glimpsed what looked like a dozen paths in every direction, or rather the faintest shadow of them beneath the bubbling marsh and rippling quicksand. He closed his eyes, drew a shallow breath and then opened them again. He let the air whistle out between his teeth as he looked down at the honeycomb of narrow ledges and steep slabs of rock that he could see faintly beneath the surface.

"They must have been there to see all the time," he whispered, his face splitting into a broad grin as he felt for the closest narrow ledge and pressed his boot down through the liquid sand to touch the solid rock.

"I will find out the truth of my beginnings for you, Fairlight," he shouted. "Wherever these paths might lead I will follow them until the bitter end."

Krann moved carefully forward, hesitating and hovering with each undecided footstep as he worked his way over the countless crisscrossed paths. Unsure which one to follow he looked up and saw a lighter patch of sky above the fog and turned towards the light. He laughed and quickened his footsteps and wondered if there was, perhaps, a glimmer of truth in the kitchen whispers, that maybe there had been a little magic in his beginnings after all.

12

Rainbows' End

"**M**ISTRESS, mistress," Treasel whispered, gently shaking Marrimian awake as the first ray of sunlight touched the tops of the marsh oaks high above the channel. She held out a handful of crushed shoots, berries and pungent leaves that she had gathered on the upper ledges while they slept.

Marrimian yawned and blinked. Her nose wrinkled at the vile smell of the roots and she was about to push the marshgirl's hand away when she became aware of the thundering roaring noise and remembered where she was. "The noise! The mudbeasts in the channel!" She rose onto her elbows and caught her breath as she looked out to where she had seen the mudbeasts vanishing into the white mist and saw a thousand bright rainbows that crisscrossed the end of the channel. "This must be Rainbows' End!" she whispered, her eyes round with wonder.

"The mudbeasts have gone, mistress, they have disappeared," whispered Treasel, trying to catch Marrimian's attention as she held her hands out for her to take the warmed crushed roots and leaves from her.

"But surely you cannot have rainbows without rain!" she questioned, taking the food and chewing absently on the leaves as she gazed at the beautiful arcs of colour. "I have watched the mumblers point to the clear skies above these rainbows on the edges of Gnarlesmyre and foretell the changing seasons, but I had never realized how beautiful they were—all these transparent veils of colour . . ." Her voice fell silent and she swallowed the half-chewed mess of roots and leaves in a gulp and quickly shook Ansel awake, telling her to eat and to be quick about it, before they fell off the edge of the world.

"World's Edge!" the scullion cried, waking in panic and remembering all those kitchen tales of monsters with two heads and twelve tails and . . . She shook sleep from her and turned her attention to her vile-smelling breakfast.

"World's Edge or not, give me a wet pan and a fire of glowing embers and I could make these roots into something a little easier to swallow," the scullion muttered, rising and stamping on the ledge as if to check that it had not disappeared while she was eating.

Marrimian laughed. There was something comforting about the scullion, not just her huge roundness and the kitchen strength forged by all those forgotten hours of fetching and carrying; it went much deeper than that. Perhaps it was her down-to-earth commonsense that poked its way through everything she did and said just like an elbow that was always rubbing its way out of a comfortable sleeve.

Touching Ansel's arm lightly Marrimian pointed to the ledges above their heads. "If we can ever find a way back into Glitterspike Hall you shall brew us such a broth of marsh-oak leaves and roots, but now we must climb to the top of these rocks and search for a path across the marshes back into the city, and perhaps see what, if anything, lies beyond these rainbows."

Treasel led the way and climbed from ledge to ledge, cutting a path through the hanging carpet of vines and creepers that grew everywhere. Slowly as the day wore on they scaled the towering wall of the channel. Flocks of scarlet birds wheeled and shrieked, rising up from their nesting places on the wider ledges. Strange, long-armed hairy creatures shrieked and chattered and ran through the hanging vines, showering the travellers with half-chewed fruits and flower buds. The dense foliage above them was thinning, there were patches of clear blue sky between the marsh oaks. Treasel called down, urging them to hurry to the topmost bare rocks where she knelt, feeling them cutting sharply into her knees. She called to the others to climb carefully and not to look down for fear of tumbling back into the swamps below.

"I will fall faster because I am the heaviest," wailed Ansel as she breasted the topmost rocks and dropped onto her knees beside her mistress.

Treasel gave a shout of terror as the silent white mist boiled up around her and she clung onto Marrimian's arm.

"Have courage and hold on tightly," Marrimian shouted and she linked her arms with the other two women and chanted every song and rhyme that she knew as the moisture swirled all about them.

It was a strange, almost magical sensation; the hot noonday sun was burning the tops of their heads, the scarlet birds were gliding and stooping around them while the ice-cold mist froze and tingled their feet and legs. The breeze softened and the mist thinned and dissolved as quickly as it had formed, and the bright rainbows reappeared, their colours shimmering and scattering into new patterns.

"Well, if this is the edge of the world then I am all for us escaping as fast as we can, before it swallows us up!" murmured Ansel, rising to her feet and brushing out the wet crumpled folds of her dirty apron.

Marrimian smiled and turned towards the rainbows and began the steep climb to the end of the rocks. The tumbling and grumbling noise was now a thundering roar that filled her head. A fine rain was soaking her and making her blink and wring out her skirts as she clambered over the last outcrop of rocks. She looked down, turned her head and shouted to the others, telling them to hurry. There was laughter in her voice and her eyes were round with the wonder of what lay beyond the edge of the world.

Ansel and Treasel knelt beside her and stared, open-mouthed, at the great white wall of water that thundered and boiled out of the countless channels and fissures on either side of them, as far as they could see.

"Waterfalls!" the scullion shouted above the noise. "That is what we could hear! They are like the weirs between the fish moats of Glitterspike Hall, only a thousand times larger!"

"But where does all this water come from?" asked Treasel gazing down in wonder at the thundering falls.

Marrimian thought for a moment, remembering the raindrops of the wet seasons, when everything, even in the driest rooms of Glitterspike Hall, became sodden and smelt of mould, when the streets of the city became raging torrents and the Hurlers' Gate was a fast-flowing river.

"We forget the rainy days all too easily once the sun shines," she shouted. "But I suppose all the rain that falls must come here, to these waterfalls."

Ansel tugged at her sleeve and pointed out through the veil of spray that rose in glistening droplets from the thundering wall of water. "There are broad rivers, mud flats and bright yellow sandbars down there beyond these waterfalls."

"I can see windflower heads swaying in the breeze, whole fields of them growing on the mud flats; their brittle heads turn grey-silver as the wind ripples through them," cried Treasel.

"And there are mudbeasts grazing amongst them," added Ansel, her fear of the edge of the world forgotten for a moment as her eyes explored the glittering stretches of water that snaked and meandered between the tall reed beds and flowed away into the distance.

"There may be mudbeasts and all manner of things we know, but it looks different. Perhaps it is more treacherous," Marrimian shouted against the roar of the waterfalls. She asked the marshgirl what tales she knew of the lands beyond Rainbows' End and the rich

water meadows that lay in the shadows of the waterfalls as they looked out to the wastes of barren mud
flats and empty grey dead marshes that appeared and
disappeared beneath a dark and menacing wall of
shifting fog which drifted beyond the edge of their
sight.

"No one has ever gone beyond the Beastweir Marshery, or if they have none has ever returned to tell
of what they have seen," she answered.

"Where is our path back?" Ansel shouted anxiously,
the excitement of what lay beyond the waterfalls fading as she caught the threads of Treasel's words. She
touched the marshgirl's arm and made her turn to look
across the swamps and marshes through the swirling
mist towards the great hump of rocks where the City
of Glor crowded in the shadows of Glitterspike Hall.

Treasel spread her hands helplessly and answered,
"The mudbeast carried us far beyond the narrow
stretch of marshes I know. I could not find us a path
nor dare to cross the wide expanse of the marshes and
swamps that lie below us. Not even if we travelled by
night while the marsh crust is frozen would I risk such
a journey, for fear of not finding a safe place to wait
out the thaw of the daylight hours."

Marrimian frowned. "Then how shall we return?
We cannot spend forever here, wrinkling into ancient
crones," and she turned away from the other two and
searched desperately across the broad expanse of
swamps and endless quickmarsh, knowing that there
must be a way back, certain that somehow she could
find it. She cursed all those times she had stood at the
high windows of Glitterspike Hall staring out across

these very marshes, looking towards the rainbows at the edge of the world where they now stood and watching the marshmen threading their way across the marshes towards the city. Then, she had thought nothing of their world and the secret ways that gave them the power to move where she would flounder.

"Perhaps we could follow these trees," grumbled Ansel, pointing to the clumps of tall marsh oaks or black ebonies that grew far away to their left, a distant smudge on a dark horizon. "They must grow on islands. We could draw a map and move from island to island during the hours of frozen darkness."

Treasel followed the scullion's hand and slowly shook her head. She shouted back, "It would take too long to reach the first island travelling directly across the ice. Remember there is nothing but soft mudbanks and mangle swamps to sink into when the sun thaws the marsh crust and we would grow old if we scaled all the rocky channels that rise above these waterfalls and tried to reach them that way."

"Why not go back to the island where the mudbeast was shackled? Islands seem safe places to me," asked Ansel, fearing that they could spend forever searching the endless marshes and still be no nearer Glitterspike Hall.

Treasel laughed harshly and stabbed her finger down towards leagues and leagues of reed beds that lay between them and the spiralling smoke that rose from that island. "That would be foolish unless you have a mudbeast's nose for finding the hidden paths, and even if we did manage to retrace our steps the people of the marshery would be eager to stake us out in the marsh for destroying their shelters."

"Then the only way must be this," shouted Marrimian, pulling both of the women to the edge of the high rocks and pointing down through the thundering waterfalls to the meandering rivers and soft pastures below. "We must climb down this spire of rocks and cross the water meadows. We must skirt the falls until we find a place to climb back up nearer to the islands where the marsh oaks grow."

Ansel peered over the edge and shrank back, shaking her head. "What if it doesn't freeze down there?"

"Yes, how then will we cross the water meadows and those wide spreads of water?" Treasel asked, her voice full of doubts.

Marrimian thought for a long moment, pacing backwards and forwards on the rocks. "Bark sledges!" she cried, turning sharply on the other two. "We will cut barks from the marsh oaks that grow on these rocks."

"We must carry spare ones tied across our backs because they easily become water-soaked," added Treasel, leaning out as far as she dared to find a way down into the pools of bubbling water that lay beneath the waterfalls.

The descent was much more difficult than their earlier climb up the sheer side of the channel. Here the vines and rocks were soaked in the ever-drifting spray from the waterfalls. There was a thick layer of slippery moss on every ledge and crevasse and the creepers and vines were waterlogged and rotten and broke at the slightest touch. Twice Ansel slipped and fell, bumping and bruising herself, clutching onto crumbling creepers until she found one that would hold her weight, and she would swing helplessly an arm's length from the thundering torrent until Treasel and Marrimian pulled her back to safety.

Darkness had long fallen by the time they reached the lowest edge. They clung onto the vines and looked up at the thundering walls of water that cascaded down on either side of them. When they had rested they tied the bark sledges onto their feet.

"Stay close to me," Treasel shouted above the roar of water as she balanced her barks on the rippling, swirling surface of the pool, and took both of their hands in hers. Together they struck out for the low mudbanks and reed beds that stood out as black lumps in the moonlight.

"It hasn't frozen!" Marrimian shouted, watching the sluggish ripples of the pool break and slide as their bark shoes glided across their surface.

They were in amongst the reeds, the tall brittle stems snapping; now they were slowing. Treasel drew them in close to her as they slid up onto the low mudbank.

"These marshes are different," she said, slipping the barks from her feet and testing the firmness of the mud with her toes. "The mud is cold but it hasn't frozen. Look, it crumbles between my fingers."

Ansel stepped out of her barks and cautiously began to explore the mudbank. Suddenly she stumbled and as she fell she clutched a handful of reed stems, and the brittle stalks broke in her hands leaving their roots firmly in the mud.

"Up there above the waterfalls the roots would have

come out of the mud at the easiest pull," she cried, bending over and tugging at the broken stems.

Marrimian knelt and touched the dry earth and then looked back at the solid white wall of water that roared and thundered down in a great sweep as far as she could see. Perhaps they had climbed over the edge of the world. Perhaps everything would be different here . . . perhaps . . .

Treasel pulled at her sleeve, cupping her hands to her mouth to shout and be heard against the roar of the waterfalls, urging them to cover as much ground as they could before the sun came up and their barks became water-soaked. Clinging to each other they glided out on the swirling waters between the shapes of the dark mudbanks beyond, until the barks became too heavy and they were forced to the safety of a reed bank. There, wearily they slept, until the morning wind stirred the windflowers, brushing them together in the hot noonday breeze, their silver-grey flower-heads whispering soft music as they touched.

Marrimian yawned, blinked her eyes and looked around her. She nudged Treasel and Ansel awake. "Mudbeasts! Thousands of mudbeasts!" she whispered, sinking back amongst the windflowers and watching the herd of creatures graze their way slowly across the water meadows, splashing soft mud up over their shaggy coats from the wide water-filled channels and stagnant pools that glistened everywhere in the lush pasture, reflecting the sunlight.

Treasel watched, wide-eyed, and soon gave up

counting the beasts. Never in all the marshery tales had they dreamed of such a herd. Ansel frowned and moved behind the other women, exclaiming that every mudbeast ever spawned must have gathered in the soft pastures before them. Treasel laughed quietly and nodded, and pointed out small calf-like creatures that grazed in the shadows of the taller beasts.

"This must be the place where they breed . . . and come to die," agreed Marrimian, making Treasel turn her head to see dark flocks of carrion birds perching on a fallen beast and noisily tearing at its carcass.

"The skin," Treasel gasped, half rising. "We could make cloaks against the cold night air . . ."

"Cloaks to disguise our true purpose," agreed Marrimian, slipping the bark sledges onto her feet and moving to the edge of the wide channel of water that separated them from the water meadows.

"Will the grazing beasts scent us?" Ansel asked nervously, reluctantly following the other two across the channel.

The carrion birds shrieked and rose in a black cloud of whirling feathers as Marrimian clapped her hands. The nearest mudbeasts lifted their heads and bellowed in alarm, and began to lumber away with quickening strides through the water meadows. Treasel took Marrimian's knife and began to skin the dead beast. Marrimian gagged at the stench and turned away as Ansel loosed her kitchen knife and knelt beside Treasel and together they skinned and cleaned enough of the hide to make three cloaks.

Treasel dipped her fingers and tasted the water in all the stagnant pools that she could see until she found one that had the sharp taste of salt. Bundling the raw stinking hide onto her back she took it to the pool and dipped it again and again and scraped it with the blunt side of her knife then rubbed the salty water into it until all the hanging strips of flesh had been smoothed away.

"Now you will look like a marshwoman!" she laughed, cutting the dripping skin and draping one part over Marrimian's shoulders, knotting a thong of rawhide across her throat to hold it in place. Marrimian shuddered at the slippery touch of the wet hide and cried out as she saw that the tangled knots of dripping hair crawled with borer biters and she fumbled at the rawhide knot to be rid of it.

"It is a good omen, a sign of luck, if the cloak is living. They will buzz and fly up when danger threatens," Treasel cried.

"They sting and they bite, that is warning enough that we should be rid of them," Ansel muttered, slapping at her arms.

"They will grow weary of stinging. Have patience," urged the marshgirl, retying the knot at Marrimian's throat.

Marrimian forced herself to be still and wait for the crawling stinging insects to vanish back into the coarse, tangled hair of the cloak. She stared at Treasel's closecropped head and remembered the healing woman's words, foretelling that she must hide her womanhood before she took up the challenge for the throne of Gnarlsmyre.

"There is one thing left to do and then my disguise will be complete," she whispered, biting her lip and pushing the hilt of her dagger firmly into Ansel's hands. "Cut off my hair and shave my head. Leave only a topknot as the marshmen wear," she cried, fanning out the long tresses of dirty mud-streaked hair in her hands. "None shall know me save you two, my dagger maidens, who in the moment of my triumph as I reach out to touch the Glitterspike shall call me woman, Marrimian, the first-born of Lord Miresnare and rightful heir of all Gnarlsmyre."

"No, mistress," Ansel sobbed, shrinking back. "Every day, every season of your life is there in those beautiful firegold locks. I could not cut them."

"Cut it! Cut it!" Marrimian cried, gripping the scullion's wrist and making her slash the blade of the knife through her hair. "In the name of all I strive to overcome, shave away the sign of my womanhood!"

Marrimian crouched over the still pool of stagnant water and stared down at an unfamiliar face. She curled her lips and snarled, narrowed her eyes and glared at her own reflection, touching the surface of the water and sending ripples to distort the ugliness. Then she shivered and stood up.

"The cap and apron," she whispered, turning to the scullion. "They are a clear sign, a badge of merit, showing that you belong to Glitterspike Hall. Take them off and let Treasel trim your hair so that you have the look of a marshgirl."

"No! No!" cried Ansel, gathering up her apron tails and stumbling over backwards in the soft water pastures. She kicked and scratched at Treasel as the marshgirl tore off her cap and cut her apron ties and threw them both down into the mud.

"I hate you! I hate you!" she shouted. Her voice trailed away, her anger forgotten as she stared past Treasel and the shorn lock of her hair she held in her hand, towards a distant figure that had emerged from the dark fog banks and was crossing one of the treacherous quicksands towards them.

"Mistress!" she hissed, panting. Marrimian and Treasel spun round and watched the oddly dressed man advance towards them.

"No one, not even the bravest marshlord, would ever dare to set foot in a quicksand," Treasel cried.

"We must tell him to turn back," Marrimian urged, waving her arms at the figure and shouting to him to stop and retrace his steps.

"He is deaf to us. Look, he laughs and dances the strangest steps," frowned Treasel hesitating.

"He must be mad," said Ansel, stopping beside the marshgirl. "Look at his strange clothes and the colour of his hair. I think a frost must have settled on his head and frozen his brains."

Marrimian ran ahead of the other two, deaf to Treasel's warning shouts. She leaned forward when she reached the edge of the quicksands and waved and shouted at the stranger. Suddenly the rich dark earth of the water meadow beneath her feet began to move. She cried out and turned, hearing the lush grasses tear and feeling the soft earth of the meadows crumple as bright fountains of yellow sand bubbled up all around her. She was sliding backwards, the hot wet quicksand was clinging to her ankles and sucking her deeper with each frantic movement she made. Treasel and Ansel ran helplessly back and forth on the new edge of the quicksand, unable to do more than wring their hands and shout to Marrimian to be still while they searched for something to throw to her.

There was a soft splash behind her and Marrimian felt a warm breath ghost against her cheek. Strong hands beneath her arms began slowly to lift her out of the clinging sand. A voice laughed gently near her ear and she was being turned as easily as a bundle of dry kindling. She caught her breath and stared into the most beautiful, bottomless, pale blue smiling eyes that she had ever seen.

"Step where I step," laughed the stranger, breaking the spell that his eyes had held over her. "Place your feet in the footprints that I make in the sand before they vanish and I will lead you to your friends on the edge of those green meadows."

Marrimian had but a moment to blink and let out her breath before he had turned and danced in hovering steps to where Ansel and Treasel anxiously awaited.

"You . . . you go too fast!" she cried, rushing to fill his empty footprints before the sand smoothed out, but he merely laughed and sprang up onto the firm edge of the water meadow then spun around and lifted her clear of the quicksand with one pull of his strong slender fingers.

Ansel and Treasel ran forward crying their thanks to the stranger and brushing at the slimy layers of quicksand on Marrimian's feet. She smiled and pushed the women aside. She opened her mouth to thank the stranger and tell him who she was when she remembered her quest and said in the deepest voice that she could use, "I am Mirra, a Lord of Mudbeasts, and I hunt these marshes and water meadows to the great white waterfalls."

Krann smiled and bowed low saying, "I am Krann, a Lord of Nothing, who is lost and far from home."

Marrimian laughed uneasily at his odd, almost musical voice, her eyes narrowing as they swept across the richness of his clothes, from the long sand-smeared boots of soft wrinkled leather to the close-fitting breeches and the jerkin wrought from tiny rings of the finest-looking silver. She noticed the knuckles and armlets of bright-polished armour engraved with loops and swirls of hammered gold that was partly hidden beneath a cloak of the deepest blue.

"No one could be lost who could find a way across that quicksand," ventured Treasel suspiciously, moving close to Marrimian's side and pushing the hilt of her dagger secretly into Marrimian's hands.

Ansel heard the wariness in Treasel's voice and closed in on the other side of her mistress.

Krann frowned and stepped back, sensing the women's fear. His long journey through the fogbanks had sharpened his second sight and he quickly looked into each of their eyes, searching, probing for that fear that his name had carried throughout Elundium. But there was none of that fear in these women, not even a flicker of recognition nor a whisper of terror, and not one of them shrank from him. They did not tighten their minds against him as a flower closed its petals against the shadows of the night. They feared him certainly, but not as Krann the hideous monster in the Shadowtreading ceremony; they feared him as a man and a stranger, and this was enough terror to seed a thousand nightmares in this new land.

He laughed and spread his empty hands, trying to make them feel easier. "In Elundium it is the custom to welcome weary travellers, to break bread and share a warming cup beside the fireside."

Marrimian tightened her grip on the hilt of the dagger and watched Krann warily as she answered, "I know nothing of your Elundium nor what it is but if there was kindling wood or a lampwick to set the fire I would share a cupped palm of water from these stagnant pools. However . . ."

Krann smiled and held his little finger against his lips and bid them to be still while he looked quickly about him. Then without another word he waded into the nearest reed-choked channel and began to cut a huge bundle of reeds.

"Who is he? And where did he spring from?" hissed Ansel with her hand on the hilt of her kitchen blade.

"I do not know; he appeared out of the fogbank. But there is something strange or magical about him," answered Marrimian. "He acts as if . . ." She paused and watched Krann turn and climb up out of the channel, his boots hardly damp or muddy. "He acts as if he knows where to tread. As if he knows this place better than we do!"

Krann piled the reeds in a heap on the soft meadow before the three women and dug into his pocket and withdrew his spark. Crouching forward he cracked it between his fingers and set the reeds alight. When the fire was burning he reached beneath his cloak and brought out a deerskin pouch with a long-neck flask of wine and a small, finely engraved silver cup that he had found in Eyrus's saddlebags.

"Perhaps we are all travellers lost on a strange road," he said quietly, offering the three of them the last of the stale crusts from his pouch and a measure of fire-warmed wine in the silver cup.

Marrimian shrank back. "You are a magic phantom—that's what you are! You are one of the mumblers' phantoms with fire on your fingertips sent to fill us with terror and drive us into the quicksands!"

Krann laughed and tossed the spark to land at Marrimian's feet. "Who now has the power to light a fire? Pick up the spark, my lady, and prove that I am not a phantom."

"Lady!" Marrimian cried staring at Krann. "Who gave you the knowledge that I am a lady?"

"First try the spark," Krann insisted, pointing to where it lay between her feet.

Slowly and without taking her eyes off him Marrimian stooped and closed her fingers on the sharp edges of the spark.

"Will it be proof enough that I mean you no harm if you can strike my fire between your fingertips?" he asked softly.

Marrimian slowly nodded, her heart pounding wildly with fear as she turned the spark in her fingers. She gripped it just as Krann had done to light the reed fire and squeezed her fingertips together. The spark crackled and blazed white-hot, making her cry out and throw it high into the air.

"That surely is proof enough," laughed Krann as he

bent and picked up the cooling spark and offered it back to Marrimian.

"Who . . . who are you?" cried Ansel, angrily stepping in between them, her hands planted firmly on her hips as she shielded her mistress from this stranger with magical powers.

"I have told you," he answered patiently. "I am Krann, a wanderer who is lost and far from home."

"No, no," insisted Ansel crossly. "Who are you really and where are you from?"

Krann frowned, his eyes hardening as he remembered the Shadowtreading ceremony that he had watched in secret from beneath the throne cloth and the way the people of Elundium mixed fear and magic with his name and shrank away from him. "If I knew who I really was I would not be wandering lost in this dreary wilderness," he answered grimly, squatting on his haunches by the fire.

Marrimian motioned Ansel aside and made the women squat beside her on the other side of the fire. Smiling she reached across and took the silver cup from Krann and sipped at the sticky sweet liquid. It made her gasp and blink as it stung her throat and she passed it to Ansel without taking her eyes from the strange man sitting opposite.

"You have powers beyond my grasp," she said quietly. "To walk on quicksand, to know that I am a woman; to see so easily through my disguise. Tell me, are all the people of this Elundium as clever as you are?"

"Where and what is Elundium? Is it in the sky or

beneath the quickmarsh? Where is it?" asked Treasel, her head reeling from the wine.

Krann looked at each one of them in turn and then slowly pointed towards the wall of dark fog that billowed and shifted on the horizon line. "Elundium," he whispered, letting the world fall gently from his lips, "is a place of rolling hills and endless grasslands. It is a place of high mountains casting deep shadows and marching away beyond the edge of sight. It is a place of silent forests where each tree arches its branches high above the hidden greenways. There are deer and wild warhorses in every secret glade and Border Runners, and wide-eyed owls watch over them. There are . . ."

"But what of your marshes and mires? And where did you learn to walk on quicksand?" interrupted Treasel.

Krann frowned and thought for a moment. "Marshes? Yes, there are desolate stretches of foul water but nobody goes there save the birds and the mudwallowers and the beasts of the water."

"Then where did you learn to walk on quicksand?" pressed Marrimian, nibbling on the dry bread, savouring its strange taste and leaning forward to catch every word of this wonderful land of hills and forests and wide grasslands, where there were no swamps nor mud pits to swallow the people.

"I do not walk on quicksand," Krann answered slowly. "I merely place my feet on the honeycomb of rocks that lie just beneath the surface. Surely they are there for all to see. Surely . . .?" His voice trailed away as he saw the women staring open-mouthed at him.

"They are the most dangerous places in all Gnarls-myre," Treasel whispered. "Even the bravest marsh-lord would not dare to set foot in the quicksands."

"Gnarlsmyre? What is this Gnarlsmyre?" Krann asked, leaning forward and searching Treasel's pinched and dirty face, catching glimpses in her eyes of the endless quickmarsh and the trackless wastes of swamp. He saw in her strange hump-backed creatures roaring and wading through the swamps where grim wretches dressed in rag-tangled cloaks foraged for ber-ries and roots as they waded through the mud.

Krann blinked his pale eyelids and turned his head towards the largest of the three women, wondering why anybody would choose to live in this wilderness of Gnarlsmyre.

Ansel met his gaze and her scowl turned to a cry of surprise as she felt his eyes search amongst her se-crets. She blinked and quickly turned away, but in that fleeting moment he saw the low-arched kitchens hazed with smoke, he heard the shouts and bustle of the scullions, he saw the secrets she kept hidden in her heart. He found her loneliness, he saw how the kitchen girls whispered and shrieked with laughter as they mocked her and called out through the smoke, "Fat Ansel, fat Ansel," whenever her back was turned.

He smiled, his eyes softening as he whispered her name. "They miss you, Ansel, for all the hurt they caused you. Now, without your skill, the cauldrons bubble dry and the roasts are burned black above un-checked fires."

Ansel looked up, her face full of wonder and joy. She would have asked a dozen questions but Marrimian cut her short. "You take too much from us with your magic powers!" she cried angrily. "Why do you not ask and then await our answers rather than steal them before we have time to think?"

Krann blushed and shifted uncomfortably on the soft ground, feeling the dampness beginning to seep through his breeches. "In Elundium my gift of seeing rather than asking often showed a quick truth, but forgive me, I meant no harm by it."

"Harm?" muttered Marrimian. "How do we know what harm you would do us? I have seen more power, more magic in you than in a whole circle of dancing mumblers. It was more than chance that made you cross our path, of that I am sure."

Krann reached beneath his cloak, unsheathed the small dagger that he carried and offered it hilt-first across the fire's glowing embers.

"No," hissed Marrimian, pushing the dagger away. "You would trick us and merely beguile us with more of your magic. Tell us your true purpose in Gnarlsmyre. How did you know that I was a woman and how do you really walk on the quicksand?"

Krann sighed and pushed the blade back into his belt. "I am a wanderer searching to find myself, the real self that the whole of Elundium is hiding from me, and my quest has driven me through the Shadowlands beyond World's End and through the dark wall of shifting fog that separates our lands. Perhaps chance has caused our paths to cross but I do not know for what purpose. I was following the honeycomb of rocks across the sands when I saw you warning me and urging me to turn back."

"But you knew that I was a woman—how? How did you know when I have shaved my head and thrown a mudbeast cloak about my shoulders?" cried Marrimian angrily.

Krann smiled. "I know nothing of your people. I do not know how they dress, their manners or their customs, nor even that I had wandered into this land of Gnarlsmyre. I knew that you are a woman because it is in your voice, the look in your eyes and the angle of your jaw. In Elundium you would be considered to have great beauty; I did not intend to unmask your disguise."

Marrimian hesitated, biting her lip. She had rushed to warn the stranger without thinking and he had had to rescue her. Perhaps he was what he said; perhaps he really was a wanderer, lost, in search of himself. Perhaps her own fears had judged him too quickly. She took a deep breath and reached across the embers of the fire to touch his chin; she lifted it with her fingertips until their eyes met.

"Know me as I really am and look at what I strive for, and then with all the power of your magic tell me if chance crossed our paths for some greater purpose," she whispered, shivering slightly and feeling naked before him as his beautiful blue eyes looked into her.

The sun dropped behind the waterfalls, its bright fire quenched in wreaths of vapour, and early darkness flooded the water meadows whilst they sat.

"You have suffered much for being born a woman," he whispered finally, blinking at the new reed smoke that curled up all about them as Treasel fed the fire from a bundle of reeds that she had gathered.

"Now do you see why I am disguised as a man? I must defeat the marshmen that strive to steal my father's throne, and on their own terms," Marrimian answered grimly.

Krann shook his head and stared up at the thick canopy of stars beginning to emerge across the dark night sky. He shivered and drew his cloak tightly about his shoulders against the cold. "That is a dangerous path waymarked by false and cunning counsel," he answered, looking at Marrimian through the flames and the smoke of the fire.

"But the healing woman foretold that I could never touch the Glitterspike as a woman," Marrimian cried. "*She* gave me counsel to go out into the quickmarsh and grow strong and learn the ways of the marsh people and only to return when none would know me as a woman."

"Perhaps this man is trying to trick you, mistress," grumbled Ansel darkly. "He is sowing doubts that will make you weak. Maybe he has used his magic to learn all our secrets so that he can touch the Glitterspike himself and claim all Gnarlsmyre as his own, stealing what would be rightfully yours, if you had been born a man."

Krann turned his head and stared at the scullion in the crackling firelight. "You have a cautious nature, Ansel, and a fierce loyalty to your mistress, but you judge me over-quickly. I want nothing, nothing that is yours. I have taken but the merest glimpses of you to learn whom I share the fireside with and from what I have seen I wish for nothing of this miserable wilderness of marshes and swamps. In fact by the first light of tomorrow's sun you shall be rid of me, for I shall retrace my steps across the quicksands and vanish forever from this desolation you call Gnarlsmyre, for you know nothing of me and my beginnings and cannot help me to find myself."

Marrimian saw the hurt and the loneliness in Krann's face and she silenced Ansel and sent her to mind the fire and to keep her counsel to herself. Turning to Treasel she whispered her out into the darkness to gather what roots and stems she could find so that they could offer food to this stranger from another land, and then she leaned forward and clasped her hands around her knees. She smiled across the dancing crackling reed flames and her eyes softened as they sought his and held them and unknowingly she looked into him and asked without words to share his wise counsels and whisper out all the wonderful tales, stories and legends of the rolling hills and silent forests where only the wild warhorses roamed in the magical land of Elundium.

"There is no magic," Krann began as she dropped her gaze, but he was blushing in the darkness, his hot blood pounding through his veins. Nobody save Fairlight, and she was as a sister, had ever looked at him like that, and as he blinked and stared into the darkness he heard the whisper of the voice deep down inside his body letting out a long, pent-up sigh. He cried out, clenching his fingers, but the sound was gone, vanishing as quickly as it had come.

Krann saw the silhouette of Treasel against the bright starlight, her arms laden with bunches of roots and edible reeds, and he rose to his feet and tried to take the wet slippery tangle from her arms, but his mind was racing, he was full of thoughts. Perhaps here, at the very ends of the world in this desolation of Gnarlsmyre, he would hear those inner voices clearly; perhaps these women in their rags and rough-haired cloaks had the power to make them speak and release the truth of his beginnings.

Ansel rose crossly to her feet and snatched the roots from Treasel's arms, angered that any man should stand and dirty his hands while she had a cleaning knife hanging from her belt.

"It is different in Elundium, isn't it?" Marrimian asked, an edge of laughter in her voice.

Krann nodded, wiping the mud from his hands on the soft pasture, and laughed softly and settled himself on the damp ground as best he could saying, "Many hands quicken a task no matter to whom they belong."

Krann paused and smiled at Ansel and Treasel and bid them sit with him and let him help to clean the roots, and he told them how in Elundium all the women, whether they were bow maidens, warrior-born to help defend the wayhouses spread along the greenways, servers, needlewomen or marcher women, or even the galloper ladies of the Granite City, they all received equal honour.

"Would a daughter inherit her father's place if there were no son?" Marrimian asked eagerly as the other two women hesitated to sit too close to Krann, looking to their mistress for guidance.

Krann laughed and clapped his hands and made the fire roar to send up a ribbon of sparks high into the night sky. "My half-sister, Elionbel, is Queen of all

Elundium and Eventine, the daughter of Fairday, inherited and rules all the lands of Clatterford. There is no poverty in being born a woman in the kingdom of Elundium."

"Sit. Sit," instructed Marrimian to Ansel and Treasel and she watched closely as he skilfully cleaned the roots and trimmed the reeds, seeing that his actions were as true as his words as he spread the thickest roots on his dagger and held them to roast by the fire.

"You said I was falsely counselled to disguise myself as a man, yet how else can I fight in a man's world?" Marrimian asked, breaking the silence. She took the first hot roasted root that Krann had offered from the point of his dagger and chewed on the slippery sweet-tasting fibres, watching his every graceful movement through her eyelashes while she waited for his answer.

"As a woman—how else could you succeed?" Krann smiled, looking up from the fire to offer a roasted root to Ansel and insisting that she took it as he brushed aside her black looks and mutterings with a wave of his hand.

"That may be the way in your land of Elundium but here in Gnarslmyre I would be ridiculed and roughly pushed aside, even by those of my own blood. I would be told not to meddle in the affairs of men," Marrimian answered, her voice tight with the frustration and helplessness of her quest.

"Already her father has called her a weak worthless prettier and banished her from the hall," Ansel cried, her cheeks blotched and flushed with anger. "There is no way that she can hope to touch the Glitterspike as a woman; women are used to fetch and carry, to pretty the tables on high feast days, to tread in a man's footprints and to do his bidding."

"And so you would pretend to be a man, someone you despise, rather than glory in your own womanhood?" Krann asked quietly, looking into Marrimian's eyes in the flickering firelight.

"I . . . I . . ." Marrimian stuttered in confusion. "I never said that I despised men, rather that I . . ." Her voice trailed away: he had touched her rawest nerve and cut her to the quick.

"You despise yourself for being born a woman in a man's world," Krann whispered, finishing her sentence as he held her gaze.

"What do you know of my torment? You were lucky enough to be born a man!" she shouted angrily, throwing the half-chewed root into the fire. "You have not had to grow as I have, a prisoner of my skirts, a mere daughter of Glitterspike Hall. You have not had to hold your breath each time the birth bell tolls or the mumblers dance to foretell your fate or that of any of the daughters of the hall. You have not had to watch helplessly as the marshlords joust for your hand; *you* would have cursed your womanhood if you had been born in my place. But now it has all changed," she continued breathlessly. "Now the fate of Glitterspike Hall and of all the lands of Gnarlsmyre does not need me at all. The joust has been changed and I have been dismissed as a weak woman, swept aside and banished to freeze beneath the pitiless stars because I dared with one wild reckless shout to stand and demand the right to fight for what would have been mine—if I had been a man."

"No!" answered Krann forcefully before Marrimian had time to draw another breath. "You have taken the first and the most difficult step by demanding your right to joust. Now, for the sake of all the women of this land of Gnarlsmyre you must return as yourself and win that joust."

Krann smiled at her and realized how much he missed Fairlight; she would have known just what to do to make Marrimian bold and sure of her purpose. She would have found the words to counsel her and make her strong enough for her task.

"But how will I do that?" Marrimian asked hesitantly, leaning forward through the smoke tails that curled up from the fire to touch his arm, making him start as she broke into his thoughts and pulled him back through the barren wind-cracked Shadowlands and swirling banks of fog to the desolate water meadows on the edges of Gnarlsmyre. Krann cried out as he looked at his dagger hand and realized that while he had been dreaming of Fairlight he had forgotten the marshroot he was holding on the point of his dagger above the fire.

"Quickly, take it, take it," he cried, turning to the marshgirl and forcing her to snatch the hot steaming root. She laughed as she juggled it from hand to hand until it was cool enough to eat. Krann hastily dropped the red-hot dagger to hiss and splutter on the ground. He looked up at Marrimian and caught her in an unguarded moment and sensed more than just her beauty hidden beneath the smears of mud and roughly shorn hair; there was determination set in the angle of her jaw and a strong will to succeed smouldered in her eyes. All the unjust lore of this miserable wilderness had not managed to trample all the spirit and courage trapped inside her soul.

"You will succeed," Krann answered quietly. "You will succeed by being twice as quick and three times as clever as those who challenge you and you will thwart them with your cunning and beat them by using every skill known only to women."

"You—you make it sound so easy," Marrimian cried in frustration, hoping that he would have whispered strong magic instead of silly words about being quick and clever, and what womanly skill in all Gnarlsmyre would win against a murdering treacherous marshlord?

She laughed angrily in Krann's face and snapped her fingers. "What skill? Tell me, what womanly skill should I set against the marshmen who toss our humble ragmen and servers beneath the mudbeasts' claws for a moment's murderous pleasure and end their friendly squabbles with dagger thrusts or a sudden twist of a sharpwire?"

"To succeed you must be determined to trip those who would harm you and meet murder with murder. Remember you are light and lithe and could, if need pressed, move quicker than a shadow to slip between their fingers," Krann answered sharply.

"But I know nothing of fighting, only what I have seen in stolen glances during the jousts," Marrimian cried, spreading her hands helplessly and leaping to her feet.

Krann watched her for a moment, his eyes narrowing as he slowly rose to his feet and folded his arms.

"You have but two choices, Marrimian," he said firmly. "First, to learn whatever skills your scullion, the marshgirl and I can teach you to pit against the marshmen."

"And the other choice?" Marrimian snapped without giving Krann the time to finish. "The other choice must be better than learning scullion's skills—*they* won't murder marshlords, and the marshgirl's knowledge of skinning stinking beasts and chewing their rotten hides to soften them won't get me any further than wandering here, lost in the quicksands!"

Krann frowned as he listened to her rush of pent-up anger and then stepped quickly back. "Enough!" he said forcefully. "You are too brittle and wrapped up in your own pride, and because of it you will break without our help. It does not matter what or how you hide the nature of your quest; all those who thrust for the same great prize will scent you out through your weaknesses and they will kill you, and because of your foolish pride all those who might have helped you will turn against you because they will see the utter hopelessness of what you strive for. Then in truth you have only the second choice which is to journey back with me into Elundium and ask King Thane to give you leave to live in peace amongst his people."

Marrimian stared at Krann. His words sounded final and rang with truth. She looked from Ansel to Treasel and saw in their eyes how her anger and harsh words had cut and sorely hurt them. She had not meant the hurt: they were faithful and they had been a great help in these nightmare days of wandering in the quickmarshes, but what could they, her servants, teach her? It all seemed so hopeless.

She turned away from the fire and walked out into the darkness, blinking at the tears that misted her eyes and bit at her lips as she sobbed. Her shoulders trembled beneath the beastskin cloak and she tore it off and threw it aside, remembering every bitter season, every sour day of growing helplessness, as the miserable knots and ropes of womanhood had been woven into her skirts. The first words she recalled her father saying had been harsh and hurtful, cursing her for not being a son, and thereafter each whisper of resentment, each check upon her because she was a woman, had been another stone in the walls of her living prison.

Ansel rose to her feet and made to follow her mistress but changed her mind and turned on Krann, raising clenched fists defiantly at him. He took a step backwards and opened his empty hands. "It is better that it happens here," he whispered as Treasel closed in beside the scullion. "It is better for all three of you to face the reality of what lies before your mistress here in this wilderness of marshes, than to end your quest in helpless terror one step inside the doors of this Glitterspike Hall. What you strive to do is good and deserves better than hopeless failure and the hollow laughter of ridicule."

Ansel felt her anger melt away. Krann was right; no matter how much it hurt to admit it, he was right. Something told her he was on their side and trying to help them with his counsel. "Go to her," she hissed.

"Go to her and make her strong, make her understand."

"She rescued me, she snatched me from the very jaws of death. Help my mistress and make her as strong as you are," cried Treasel reaching out and taking Krann's hand.

Krann laughed softly and nodded his head in Marrimian's direction as he whispered, "Whatever I need to give her it is not strength, she already has that in abundance for anyone to see—to have weathered out her father's hatred of her womanhood and struggled thus far through the marshes is proof of that—but how to bend her brittleness and school those skills, to give her a cutting edge . . ." He smiled sadly, shaking his head. "That may be beyond my powers."

Krann stooped and tended the fire, breaking fresh reed stems into the blaze, and wished again he had Fairlight here beside him; she would not have suffered these tears and angry outbursts, she would have cut straight to the heart of the matter and shown this firstborn, Marrimian, the power of having fire at her fingertips. She would have taught her how to crackle sparks or knock arrows onto a bowstring quicker than the scullion could blink. Krann smiled, remembering how she had made games of teaching him to ride or shooting a bow and using a galloper's blade.

"Yes!" he said to himself suddenly, wiping his hands and rising from the fireside. "Perhaps if I can somehow make the learning into a game."

Krann looked for Marrimian in the darkness and crossed to where she stood. Gently he closed his arm about her shoulder and whispered her name as his hand found hers. Marrimian jumped, startled by his touch as if his fingertips had burned her, and quickly pulled away from him. Krann opened his mouth to call her back when somewhere near them in the blank darkness he heard a single nightmarish scream and as it faded and echoed across the water meadows he smelt the sooty scent of new snow in the wind.

"What was that? What kind of beasts are spawned in this wilderness?" he hissed, crouching with his dagger in his hand and staring all about them into the darkness.

Marrimian frowned and shivered: she scooped up the beastskin cloak and threw it around her shoulders.

"There was no noise," she answered fearfully, moving closer to him. "There is nothing save the night wind in the windflower heads."

"There was a scream, I heard it," Krann insisted. "I heard it as my hand touched yours and it was so close to us that I could almost reach out and . . . and there was the sudden smell of snow . . ."

Krann's voice fell silent and his lips trembled as Marrimian took his hand into hers and drew him back to the fireside. His eyes were wild and staring and a cold sweat prickled on his forehead.

"What is it?" Ansel whispered, drawing her kitchen knife and turning towards the dark night.

"Krann heard a scream and smelt snow on the wind," Marrimian answered in a hushed voice. She kicked the fire into a blaze and turned, searching the darkness.

"It cannot snow for two more seasons," Treasel answered quietly and she stared down at the tangled knots of mudbeast hair on her cloak. "And there is not danger near—the borer biters here have not stirred."

"Perhaps only you heard the scream. Perhaps it was inside you," Marrimian soothed and made Krann sit beside her and face the crackling flames of the fire while Ansel guarded his back and crouched behind him, facing out into the darkness, her dagger in her hand.

Krann sat hunched in despair and clenched his teeth to stop them chattering. He stared silently into the flames knowing that Marrimian was right, he had been the only one to hear it. He shuddered, remembering the blood-freezing sound, and moved as close as he could to Marrimian for comfort from the darkness without daring to touch her again. She felt him move and smiled and reached out to take his hand.

"No! No!" Krann cried, shrinking from her, afraid of what he might hear, or what might loom up before him in the firelight if they touched.

Marrimian froze and withdrew her hand, and frowned and bit her lip as she watched him in the firelight. There was a shadow haunting his eyes and a new fear plucked and pinched at his face, making his lips twitch and tremble as if he was all alone, and he was whispering to himself.

"I will shelter you from whatever terrors lie in wait out there in the darkness," she soothed, making him lift his head and turn towards her.

Marrimian caught her breath and felt her cheeks flush and tingle as their eyes met, and silently, without words, she asked him to tell all that had driven him to flee from Elundium. And, falteringly at first, he told them his story.

"Eyrus. What did you do with the beautiful horse, Eyrus?" Ansel asked eagerly as he finished telling them of his ride through the snowdrifts to the lamp that burned on the edge of the world and his wanderings in the wind-cracked hills of the Shadowlands. Many parts of the story had frightened her but she had loved all the pieces with the horse; it sounded so fast and free to gallop through the snow, and she wrung her hands, worrying that Eyrus might have become lost or have been attacked.

Krann laughed for the first time since he had heard the terrible scream and looked over his shoulder at the scullion. "There was no way that I could have brought him through the shifting fogbanks into these quicksands and endless water meadows; he would have floundered and sunk in the soft ground. No, it was better and safer for him to stay fed and warm at Underfall then to take the road back to his rightful owner, Lord Willow, who rules the Rising, the meeting place of kings."

"Well! I would have ridden back on him rather than wander into this miserable place!" Ansel muttered, looking up into the paling dawn sky and watching the cold wreath tails of marsh mist rising across the water meadows and low mudbanks that stretched away into the distance.

"You say that when we touched you heard the scream?" asked Marrimian, slowly raking the ashes of their fire with the blade of her dagger, turning over the half-burned reeds and pushing them into the bright new flames while she waited on his answer.

"It is not the first time that I have heard voices inside my head. It was their constant whisperings that drew me into the Shadowlands but when our eyes met I felt hot and uncomfortable and somewhere deep down inside a whispered sigh escaped. Then when I touched your hand the voices blended into one nightmare."

"Would you dare to touch again and find out who uttered that scream?" Marrimian asked, lifting her hand and stretching her slender fingers towards him, challenging him with her eyes.

"Would you learn the art of crackling sparks and all the scullion's skills to help you in your quest?" he asked as an answer, holding her gaze. She slowly nodded her head. Gently he lifted his hand and stretched his fingers to intertwine with hers.

Krann froze as their fingers locked. The reed fire seemed to blaze and crackle brighter than before, the curls of morning mist to thicken, boiling and swirling up around them. The blood was pounding in his ears as he waited, listening to the silence.

"There is nothing," he began, drawing a deep breath, when scattered green reeds that Ansel had gathered and tossed into the fire caught alight and suddenly fogged the space between them in dense billows of smoke. Krann coughed and snatched his hand away from Marrimian and in that instant as the smoke swirled and enveloped him a hideous leering one-eyed beast rose up.

"No!" Krann shouted, leaping to his feet and

thrashing his arms through the smoke. He spun around and around trying to ward it off, stamping on the fire and sending up showers of hot sparks and smouldering ashes as he trod the fire out.

Marrimian heard his shouts and managed to catch his flailing sleeve and pull him down, dizzy and weeping, onto his knees beside her.

"There is a beast inside me, I saw it, I saw it," he repeated over and over, his teeth chattering uncontrollably in his head. He twisted and turned as he stared through the clearing smoke.

Marrimian calmed him and whispered every mumblers' chant she had ever overheard, and took his hands into hers and held them tightly and made him tell them everything that he had seen.

Ansel shivered as she listened to what he said had risen in the smoke and moved closer to her mistress while Treasel grimly gathered all the unburned reeds and laid them in a circle around where they crowded close to the ruined fire.

She hurried back to Marrimian's side and knelt beside her, the dagger ready in her hands, and whispered, "There are no beasts in all our fireside legends to match the likes of the two-legged beast that Krann speaks of. But if it has followed him through the fogs and has found a path across the quicksands we will hear it as it treads on the reeds and we will be ready when it attacks."

"No!" cried Krann. "We cannot fight against the beast. It will trample us and swallow us whole."

"You know of such beasts in Elundium?" Ansel asked, interrupting him sharply.

Krann turned towards her, his mouth hanging foolishly open. He was going to tell her that nothing so hideous could ever spoil the sunlight of Elundium, when he remembered the Shadowtreading and those terrifying masks that the mummers had worn as they breasted the high rim of the Rising, treading those grotesque dancing steps in the smoothly raked snow, and his face paled and his hands began to shake.

"It was from before, before my beginnings," Krann whispered looking quickly away. "There are no beasts like that now. None I tell you!" He stared silently at the ground, biting his lip and remembering what he had seen in the smoke, not daring to tell them that the beast had tried to wrap its broken claw around him to defend him; it had been dying, gurgling out its death rattle, trying to call out, to warn him.

"What did you learn? Did our touching serve its purpose?" Marrimian asked, pulling at his hand and breaking into his thoughts, making him jump and cry out.

"It was from before—before," Krann stuttered, trying to hide the truth, but Marrimian gripped his chin between her fingers and made him look into her eyes.

"We must share the truth, no matter how much it hurts. Remember, we hold each other's secrets in the palms of our hands," she whispered and her gaze softened.

Krann blinked and swallowed, gathering his courage. "Perhaps it is the beast that everyone has tried to hide from me. Somehow it is a part of me, a part of my beginnings. It was trying to warn me, to protect me, to tell me to . . ." Krann's voice trailed away from her and he stared into the distance, watching the sun rise above the water meadows and burn the mist to nothing, but he felt none of its warmth, only the terrors of the dark that waited beyond the horizon's rim—that and the horror of what he had said, that would surely make her shrink away from him.

Marrimian watched him for a moment and then laughed softly and squeezed his hand. "There must be more to you than one hideous beast, for if that were all I am sure the people of Elundium would have strangled you at your birth, or plunged a dagger through your heart."

Krann shivered and looked back towards her, remembering those sneering words he had overheard beneath the wayhouse window. "Perhaps you have touched the truth," he whispered. "Perhaps you have stirred the beast that lies within me, but how could I have ever been a part of such a hideous creature without having felt or known of it before?"

"We shall barter secret for secret," Marrimian whispered and there was a sudden sparkle in her eyes that made the scullion blush and for a moment itch with jealousy.

"Mistress, mistress," she hissed, drawing Marrimian aside and cupping her hands to her ear. "There may be some truth in what he says, he may be part beast, but we don't know how dangerous he is. Take care in this touching in the dark."

Marrimian frowned, drawing her eyebrows into one straight line, and thought on what the scullion had said. "Would you trust him more than the marshhunter, or that foul marsh vermin Mertzork who brought the beast Gallengab into Glitterspike Hall? Or is it that you would not trust any man?"

Ansel scowled and folded her arms. "It is not my place to set the rules of whom you take to, mistress, but his help and advice might just be as bad as that healing woman's when she sent us wandering across these marshes."

Marrimian thought for a moment and then turned back to Krann. She challenged him to use all his powers of magic to look into their eyes and tell her if the healing woman had given them good counsel when she had sent them to learn the ways of the marsh people before attempting to touch the Glitterspike.

Krann stepped back a pace and stared into their eyes. Quickly he dismissed the marshgirl, realizing that she had never seen this healing woman that Marrimian was asking about, but he looked more closely into Ansel's eyes.

"There was barter," he whispered. "You had to choose between an injured marshhunter and your mistress's quest."

"Yes, yes!" Ansel cried, in awe of Krann's power. "I had bartered herbs and grains for a love rhyme for the first marshman that I set eyes upon; he was to take me as his own, but he just pushed me aside so the barter was not complete. That is why the healing woman gave my mistress her wise counsel—to complete the barter."

Krann smiled at the scullion and turned away to stare at the distant waterfalls that glistened and shimmered in the sunlight. "The healing woman was very generous; she gave your mistress her counsel and she gave you the marshhunter—what more could you have asked for?"

"But was it good counsel?" pressed Marrimian, clutching Krann's sleeve and making him turn back towards them.

Krann only laughed hollowly and shrugged his shoulders. "I only see glimpses, brief shadows that skip across the moon, and I only hear the fleeting whispers that echo in your heads, but I do catch the scent of treachery in this healing woman and I hear many cunning whispers echoing all around her. There is something she had searched for in both of you, I feel it stronger in Ansel because in some way it was a part of the broken barter, but I cannot see what it is."

Krann thought for a moment and then threw his hands into the air in a helpless gesture. "It has gone; whatever nagged and gnawed at me as I looked into you has all but vanished."

"Think again, look," urged Marrimian.

But Krann shook his head and whispered, "You need nothing more to succeed than your strength of will."

Marrimian stared at him and slowly realized all the time, the lost days and nights, that she had squandered because of the healing woman's counsel. "The Glitterspike! All will be lost! The throne and all of Gnarlsmyre will be lost forever. Quickly, hurry, we must sew wings to our heels before some other hand touches the Glitterspike."

Treasel had kept very quiet, listening and following every word. Now, suddenly, she laughed and swept her hand across the water meadows to where the great white walls of water rumbled and thundered, making the others turn and stare at her. "None of you, not even my mistress, seems to understand or truly realize it, but we are all hopelessly lost. We will never find a way back up through that wall of water let alone find the secret paths across the quickmarshes that only the marshlords and their hunters know. I was born in the marshes and I know just how lost we are.

Krann looked into the marshgirl's eyes, his lips puckering into a thin bloodless line as he saw her hopelessness and knew that she only saw the endless wastes of mud that had been the limit of her world before Marrimian had rescued her. He smiled softly at her and moved away from the women, cloaking himself in silence and standing rock still. He stared out at the distant wall of water and watched each glittering plume of rising spray, each high-arched rainbow painted in brilliant morning colours as his eyes swept along the falls.

"You say that we are lost and you fear to go forward; what would you have your mistress do?" he asked quietly, turning back to Treasel.

Treasel frowned and shrugged her thin shoulders. "Mistress and the scullion saved me so now I must walk with them no matter how hopelessly lost we all become, but I would rather we stayed here where there is plenty to eat, water to drink and . . ."

Krann laughed, the sound chuckling in his throat, and called them to come and squat on the wet ground around him. He pulled his dagger from his belt and drew the shape of a hollow bowl tilted slightly on its side in the soft wet ground.

"Ignorance is power amongst your people, Treasel," he smiled. "Your overlords have kept their secrets well and those very secrets bind you to them. You have no voice because you are a woman and you dare not travel for fear of being stoned as an outcast— that is the very centre of your fear; that makes you shrink from trying to find your way back through these marshes."

"Yes," she whispered without looking up. "The mudbeast carried us far beyond the marshes that I knew and the thought of returning has been filling me with dread. Here we seem safe, the water meadows are firm beneath our feet and it must be a good place because there are herds of mudbeast, more than all the firestone tales and legends have ever spoken of."

"Safe?" laughed Krann pointing at the waterfalls. "What will happen when it rains, when all the land or swamps that you call Gnarlsmyre are soaked by endless grey daylights of pouring rain. These gentle falls will become raging torrents and these water meadows will be flooded and become a lake that will spread beyond the edges of your sight, only safe for your mudbeasts to wallow and breed, but not for you, Treasel."

"Safe or not, we are trapped here because we cannot find the secret paths that lie beneath the marshes. And where is there a way up through this wall of water?" she cried angrily, sweeping her hand along the line of waterfalls.

"There must be a way through," Krann answered,

pointing down with the dirty blade of his dagger at his crude scratching of an upturned bowl in the wet earth and adding a maze of crooked lines to it as he spoke. "This is like your land of Gnarlsmyre, and I believe that it is riddled by a honeycomb of ledges and ridges of rock that lie just below the surface of the quickmires and swamps exactly like these paths that I was using to cross the quicksands. In places they are probably broad and rise as banks or islands that support your marsheries, in other places they become dagger-thin and almost vanish. These are your marshmen's secret ways that they have found by trial and error, but I believe that far below these ridges, buried in the mud and stretching as far as the eye can see, lies a great hollow shell of solid rock that holds all the wetness in and that these waterfalls that march away beyond the edge of sight are but the very top of Gnarlsmyre, the upturned rim of that unbroken rock that dams and covers your wilderness with its mud and bubbling swamps and marshes. I think I could find and follow these hidden ridges and lead you to the very gates of your city, if you wish it."

Krann fell silent and watched the woman turn and stare at the wall of glistening water. A mudbeast bellowed and made them draw together as it raked its ridge of horns through an outcrop of windflowers just beyond the water meadow and shook its tangled hairy hide, sending up a flock of carrion birds to darken the sky.

"What are they?" cried Krann, crouching down as the nearest of the birds stretched its leathery wings and soared towards them on the warm currents of morning air.

Treasel cried out and snatched off her cloak and hurled it at the bird. Marrimian stood watching helplessly as the bird shrieked and wheeled away, the cloak hooked up in its claws.

"Your cloaks, throw them on the ground," shouted Treasel, fumbling with the rawhide thong she had tied across her mistress's throat, unknotting it and throwing the cloak aside as the bird glided down towards them.

"Pindafalls! They are pindafalls!" Treasel hissed, making Ansel throw her cloak as far away as possible from where they lay.

"Why discard the cloaks? Surely the thick knots of fur and tough hide would have given us some protection from their teeth and talons?" whispered Marrimian, lifting her head a hand's span to watch the pindafalls tearing Ansel's cloak into ribbons.

Treasel grinned and cupped her hands to Marrimian's ear. "It is a woman's secret, we tumbled upon it while we skinned the beasts. The pindafall birds will feed on anything, but the borer biters and stinging insects that live in the hair of the mudbeast hides are a special delicacy to them."

The birds dropped the ruined cloaks and shrieked and rose in ever-widening circles, spiralling higher and higher above the water meadows to vanish as mere dots in the limitless sky. Krann watched them disappear before he climbed slowly to his feet and asked, "How many kinds of monstrous beasts are there in Gnarlsmyre?"

Ansel laughed and began to count, using her blunt fingers. "Pindafalls, mudbeasts, clactors, helios bears . . ."

"That is enough," snapped Marrimian crossly, dismissing the scullion to help Treasel to find and take more hide from the dead mudbeast to make new cloaks against the frozen nights beyond the waterfalls.

"Which way will be our shortest route?" she asked, touching Krann's arm.

Krann swept his gaze across the waterfalls before he answered, "There must be a place where the falls are lower; that is the place we will search for."

13

A Ladder
Through
The Water

"*H*OW much further?" Ansel grumbled as the sun sank finally beyond the wet channels all around them. Marrimian yawned after the day's long journey and pulled at the thong of rawhide knotted across her throat, loosening it with her free hand and trying to settle the slippery salted mudbeast cloak more comfortably about her shoulders. She sighed and dropped the heavy bundle of windflower stalks that she had cut on the low mudbank for a fire, and looked back over the flat darkened water meadows that they had crossed. Wearily she remembered each squelching footprint, each widening and wetter channel as they drew closer to the waterfalls, splashing and wading through the sticky clinging mud, skirting the bubbling pools of green liquid and bright yellow sandbanks that looked so solid and yet would suck you down in one swallowing gulp.

She shivered, wiping the drifting cold mists of the waterfalls from her eyes, and searched the darkness for Krann. Earlier, before the sun had set, he had pointed to the hurrying mudbeasts that splashed through the wet channels all around them, noticing how they scented the wind, and told the women to wait for him and light a fire on the dryest mudbank that they could find. Marrimian had called after him but he had only laughed and shouted that he must follow the mudbeasts, to discover if they had a secret way through the thundering wall of water.

Kneeling she took the spark that Krann had given her, from her driest pocket, clumsily crackled it alight and set the thinnest windflower stalks into a cheerful blaze. She built the fire so that Krann would see it across a dozen water meadows, then settled back on her haunches and smiled and watched Ansel and Treasel busy themselves, talking in whispers as they cleaned roots and gutted the long razor-sharp rainbow fish that they had caught earlier in the day in the deeper of the wet channels, amidst screams and shouts of delight.

Marrimian sighed again. She was glad that fate had made Krann's path cross hers, for although she was loath to admit it out loud, inwardly she knew that he was right and she blushed bright scarlet to think how foolish she would have looked if she had cast his counsel aside and returned to Glitterspike Hall only to stamp her foot in helpless anger as her father, the marshlords and all the people of the hall laughed and cast her quest aside, which they would have done if she had masqueraded as a man. She had learned much on their journey across the water meadows, much that would strengthen her by watching and listening to the scullion and the marshgirl as they taught her to use her hands to catch the rainbow fish, to know which roots would kill you if you ate them, and which to cook and which to eat raw. She had learned how to gut and skin all manner of creeping, slithering things and how to weave long threads and knot them into strong lengths of rope out of the coarse hair from her mudbeast cloak. And Krann had taught them all the power of fire and how to crackle sparks between their fingers, how to wrestle, trap and throw someone twice their height and weight, and by using long unbroken reeds he had taught them the art of fencing. He had told them how, in Elundium, some of the daggers were hammered and drawn out on the anvil to be as long as your arm, and he had promised that if they ever found a blacksmith's forge or an ironsmith in this wilderness of Gnarlsmyre he would hammer them each a sword of their own.

Marrimian laughed quietly to herself, eager for Krann to return, and broke the heavier brittle wind-flower stalks, some as thick as her finger, and fed them to the fire as a beacon to guide him in the darkness.

Their night touchings to search out Krann's beginnings had grown bolder in the firelight. Laughter had quieted to secret whisperings and now silent words flowed between them. Tingling fingertips had become clasped hands and they had drawn closer, arms enfolded, lips brushing together until Marrimian's heart had raced and she had felt dizzy with the recklessness of love in his touch.

Ansel had muttered and stared down at the soft wet earth when Marrimian had asked her the meaning of these feelings and demanded to know where they would lead. She had said that the mistress was luckier than she, to find love without the help of the healing woman's spells, and she had grumbled that she knew nothing of where such feelings led and probably never would after the treachery of the marshhunter for she did not ever wish to look at another man. Treasel had answered her differently, watching Krann out of the corner of her eye and, whispering when she was out of their hearing, she said that amongst the marsh people there was no room for such feelings except in weak men and women who dreamed and watched the stars; that amongst her people a woman was merely taken in her season and should be grateful if the man was satisfied and did not send her out to glean for roots before the marsh crust had frozen. She could not understand why, if Krann held such magic at his fingertips and was a real man, he had not taken all three of them for his pleasure already.

Marrimian had stifled a cry of horror at what the marshgirl said; horror at the sheer brutality of their lives. But Treasel had only laughed and shrugged her thin shoulders, saying that dreams did not fill bellies or snare a mudbeast and that this would always be the lot of women whether they liked being taken or not. The best they would hope was to lie with the strongest hunter, which could make all the difference in the marsheries and could save you from starving to death in the wet seasons and give you dry rocks beneath your feet.

The next time their hands had touched in the firelight Krann fiercely shook his head when he saw the troubled questions in her eyes. He had soothed her in gentle whispers, and told her how in Elundium, to take a woman in any way against her wishes was called rape, and that it was the greatest crime that could be committed against a woman and that it stripped a man of all his honour and cast him out to be hunted and killed. Marrimian had frowned and wondered as he answered how the people of Elundium then ever loved or came together, when surely every time a woman caught a man's eye he would want to take her; but Krann had laughed and called the other two women to sit close beside them, and as the stars turned in the sky above their heads he told them of all the ways and the customs of his people. How they met and courted and how they walked beneath the summer moon and how a man would ask the father or the head of the wayhouse, whether the head be a man or a woman, for the girl's hand in marriage.

Treasel had scoffed and rocked back on her heels, calling him a storyteller, but her eyes were round and shimmering as she crouched nearer, listening to every word of this land where even dreamers and gentle men had a place of honour, and Ansel had smiled and asked if their scullions were ever walked beneath the stars. Krann had laughed and pinched Ansel's arm playfully and told her that his half-sister, Elionbel, the Queen, had insisted that all the cooks who prepared the honour feast should be robed in steel silver gowns and have their pick of the men of the Granite City. Ansel had blushed and grumbled in her confusion, telling him not to tease her so, but there was a light in her eyes and a quickness in her breath that told Marrimian how much she yearned to believe him . . .

Suddenly Marrimian heard a dull splash in the darkness of the water channel and a dark shape glided silently to the edge of their low mudbank. She was anxious for Krann's return, fearing for his safety, and she rose quickly to her feet and called out his name as she stepped forward. But there was nothing beyond the fire's edge, nothing except the fading ripples of vanished footsteps in the mud. The hairs on the nape of her neck prickled and she shrank back, hissing a warning sound to Ansel and Treasel and making them drop the rainbow fish and snatch up burning brands from the fire.

"What? What is it?" Treasel whispered.

Marrimian pointed to the ripples in the mud and began to tell her what she had seen, when they heard Krann's voice and the sharp snapping of reed stems as he slid down the mudbank on the far side of the wet channel and glided towards them, his bark sledges ploughing up bright ripples in the soft mud and reflecting the firelight as he crossed the channel.

"There *was* something," Marrimian insisted as they searched amongst the broken windflower stalks and trampled reed stems on the edges of the channel. "I would have sworn on Yaloor's head that it was you I saw, only . . ." She paused looking nervously over her shoulder into the darkness.

"Only what?" pressed Krann, angry with himself for leaving the women alone for so long after darkness had swallowed up the daylight. He knelt down and ran his fingertips over the smooth surface of the mud where nothing left its mark for more than the briefest moment.

"Only it made me shudder. It had the shape of a man

but it vanished in a blink before I could really see who or what it was."

Krann took one last quick look at the mudbanks and hurried them back into the firelight. "Who knows what manner of beasts breed in this desolate place?" he whispered, fuelling the fire into a roaring blaze, reluctant to share his fears and have the women jumping at shadows, but he was sure that something was following them, watching and listening in the dark. What else would explain those dull splashes that would break the night silence all around them, or the sudden rustling of the reed beds when there was not a breath of wind. And how could widening ripples just appear in the mud? Krann shivered, sensing eyes watching them from across the channel. He looked up but there was nothing.

"You are hiding the truth. You fear something shadows us," Marrimian whispered, breaking into his thoughts and making Krann blush and stammer as he looked away.

"You have grown in power to see my fears and doubts so easily," he answered turning towards her.

"You have taught me to look," Marrimian smiled, "to see the good things and the bad—and now we even share our fears."

Krann nodded silently. Yes, he was afraid; he feared that something stalked and watched them. At first it had been less than a shadow, perhaps a mudbeast, but now it was growing bolder with each long night they spent in the water meadows.

Krann stared miserably down into the fire, and gathered his courage as he tried to tell Marrimian what he had seen at the waterfall. "I have led you on a false trail. I had hoped that the mudbeasts would show us a place to cross the falls but they merely vanish into a raging curtain of water that cascades and roars down over the countless giant steps that they must have worn in the mud and rocks as they force a way up through the waterfalls. If we try and climb those giant steps we will be swept back and smashed to pieces. We are trapped here in these water meadows."

Marrimian frowned with disappointment and stared out into the empty darkness. She thought back over their escape from the city and their desperate journey across the quickmarshes and sighed and took Krann's hand and drew him close to her. She felt how wet his clothes were from searching for a way through the falls and remembered how much he had tried to help them, and now he shivered in the chill night air and she wanted to make him warm and banish this feeling of despair.

Unknotting the rawhide thong that held her cloak across her shoulders she cast it around them both, wrapping them together in secret whispers. Perhaps there would be no tomorrow, no more dreams, no echoing rush of triumphant footsteps across her father's hall, but there would be tonight snatched from this hopelessness and she would share it with the one she ached to touch. Hungrily she kissed him, her quick fingers loosening his breeches and unlacing his fine mail shirt, reckless in her haste, breathless and giddy as they touched, their arms and legs entwined. Gently Krann pushed her down onto the soft damp earth and she felt the windflower stalks crush beneath their weight; their sharp ends prickled her skin as he pressed down onto her. She cried out as a hot stab of pain and pleasure raced through her every nerve, making her arch her back and flex her fingertips and hold him tightly as he took her. And then she felt laughter in her and she whispered as she drifted and floated beneath him on a thousand soft sighs. Krann suddenly quickened, his body tensing, and suddenly he cried out and rolled away from her, curling himself into a tight ball. She caught the scent of snow on the night wind and saw a shadowy army beneath a standard so black it swallowed the daylight.

"Krann," Marrimian cried, sitting bolt upright, her eyes wide open, and she saw him curled up and weeping beside her.

"Krann," she whispered, holding him in her arms and soothing him and calming him, but her eyes were troubled and she could not blink away the terrible picture she had seen in the moment of their passion.

High above their heads the stars slowly turned, glittering with every colour in their pale light, but she was blind to their beauty. The tall windflowers rustled in the dying firelight, making her look up and catch her breath—there were eyes, dozens of them, watching between the windflower stalks. Marrimian cried out making Ansel and Treasel wake and jump clumsily to their feet. Krann stood up, quickly covering his nakedness, and ran towards the windflowers, but the eyes had gone and hardly a ripple disturbed the soft mud in the channel beyond.

"Well, whoever they are they have gone and good

riddance to them," muttered Ansel, prodding new life into the spluttering fire and deciding that she would not sleep another minute until they were safely back in Glitterspike Hall.

Treasel gave a cry and ran into the shadows, dragging back a thickly woven rope of mudbeast hair which she threw down beside the fire. Someone must have left it here while they slept.

"Perhaps it is a gift, or something to help us cross the waterfalls," ventured Marrimian cautiously. The silent shape and the watching eyes had frightened her, but she had felt no malice there and none of them had come to any harm.

Krann picked up the end of the rope and turned it over and over in his hands, looking at the strange pattern of weaving. Suddenly he cried out, dropping it, and stared at an ugly wound in his thumb.

"There are three-pronged barbs of carved white bone woven into this end," called Treasel bending down and examining the rope. The barbs were similar to the fishing spears the marshhunters carved from the bones of dead mudbeasts.

"No," muttered Krann grimly, cutting across her thoughts as he pinched together the edges of the wound and stemmed the blood flow. He looked up and nodded at the white wreath tails of morning mist that were silently spreading through the wet channels of the water meadows. "This is not from your people, Treasel, these shapes who follow us are too gentle, they disturb nothing as they move, they are silent and cautious. They watch and listen and yet they are skilled and clever and have woven such a strong rope perhaps it will help us to cross the waterfall."

Ansel frowned, bewildered by his words, and watched him carefully coil the rope in long twisted loops and hang it from his belt.

"How could it help?" asked Marrimian.

But Krann only stared past her and pressed a finger to his lips, commanding that they ready themselves to try to cross the waterfall when the sun had burned the mist away.

"Impossible!" cried Marrimian, staring up between the towering columns of mud that leaned out of the roaring curtain of water and watching them sway and tremble as huge lumps broke away and slid crashing down into the boiling waters, sending wide ripples out to meet them.

"There can be no way up through that solid wall of water!" shouted Treasel, pointing through the fountains of spray to the thundering mass of white water that was pouring over the lip of the rock high above their heads.

"Watch!" Krann called against the roar of the falls and pointed to a huge mudbeast wading slowly across the shallows towards the columns of mud.

One moment the beast's horns were touching the white wall of water and the next it had vanished, only to reappear on what must have been a step higher up behind the water. The bellowing beast vanished again and reappeared even higher up, its long horns sending up rainbow sprays as they protruded through the curtain of rushing water.

"They must have worn giant steps behind the water," Krann shouted.

Marrimian stared at him wild-eyed and shook her head fiercely. "We will all drown. The water will knock us down and sweep us away quicker than a handful of reed stems. That way is madness."

"There is no other," Krann shouted, uncoiling the rope and hurling the barbed end high into the air above the boiling waters, and all four of them watched and held their breath as it snaked through the thin curtain of water and splashed onto the first step and twisted back towards them before it snagged, the barbed hooks digging into the rocks.

Krann bound the free end of the rope around his waist and pulled it taut. "You merely saw a rope beside the fire, but I saw a ladder that will surely carry you through the curtain of water and back into your land of Gnarlsmyre."

"One slip . . ." whispered Ansel, her face blotched with terror as Krann insisted that she climb first, being the heaviest.

Treasel and Marrimian helped him to keep the rope taut while the scullion strained and heaved herself hand over hand with her ankles crossed around the rope, up through the thundering wall of water. The spray blinded her, her hands slipped on the wet weave of the rope, but sheer terror of what lay below if she fell drove her on, until with a great cry of relief she felt the rough edges of the first step and scrambled over the slippery rocks to safety.

Marrimian turned to Krann with one hand on the rope, ready to follow the scullion. "How will you follow? How can you climb with no one to anchor the rope?" but her shout died on her lips as she saw the haunted look of despair in his eyes and she knew that he had glimpsed himself as she had seen him in the high moment of their passion. Then, he had been cruel and pitiless in his empty laughter which echoed into the darkness he spread over the beauty of Elundium.

"I love you despite what we saw," she shouted against the roar of the water and threw her arms about him. She realized as he struggled to break free that he had no intention of trying to follow them through the waterfall; he was going to hurl himself into the boiling wall of water once they were safely across or search out a way back into the land of Elundium and she would never see him again.

"I am a black curse, a part of the nightmare darkness that King Thane once defeated. I am not worthy of your love," Krann cried out, trying to pull away from her, but she hung on grimly, knowing that she must have more than just one brief time with him. There was so much good in him, he was so gentle.

Marrimian's hands closed on the loose end of the rope tied around his waist. "I love you," she shouted again as, without him noticing, she looped and threaded the rope behind his back into the strongest knot that she could remember. Giving the loose end one final tug she whispered all the mumblers' magic words that were inside her head and before she broke free from him, blinking back her tears, she urged Treasel to follow her the moment that she reached the edge of the first step behind the water.

"I will always love you," Marrimian cried as she

pressed her lips onto Krann's in parting and she secretly drew his dagger from his belt and hid it in her sleeve.

Quickly she turned and hauled herself hand over hand up the slippery rope and threw herself down beside Ansel. "Do as I say without question," she gasped, trying to catch her breath as she watched Treasel nimbly climbing up the rope to join them.

"Now! Pull, pull!" shouted Marrimian, hauling on the rope almost before Treasel had scrambled up over the rough edge of the step.

The rope went taut, dragging Krann off his feet into the shallows, and although he fought to untie it and searched with his flailing hands for his dagger he was drawn helplessly towards the step. Ansel bent and grasped the rope in both hands and pulled it with all her strength. Treasel hung on beside her and length by length they pulled Krann up through the thundering wall of water. He was spun helplessly and knocked from side to side against the columns of mud, and he choked and coughed, bruised and battered by the force of the water.

"Pull! Pull!" wept Marrimian, her hands raw and bleeding as the rope chafed her and seemed to creep slowly back over the edge of the first step.

Treasel gave a great shout and threw herself down, jamming her hands and the rope in a cleft in the slippery rocks. "Pull quickly, hand over hand, before the rope burns through my fingers," she cried.

Ansel peered over the lip of the step and saw bright rainbows spreading from Krann's fingertips as he spun helplessly in the cascade of water and she spat on her hands, her shoulders straining, and began to haul him up.

"One more pull," Marrimian shouted, reaching over the edge to grab at his sleeve.

Together they dragged him, limp and choking, over the lip of the rock and onto the step beside them.

Krann coughed and shook the water out of his eyes, blinked and rubbed his hands across his aching shoulders and stared out into the boiling water that rushed past them, then sank forward, covered his face with his hands and wept.

Marrimian gently embraced him and when he had quieted lifted his chin and held his gaze as she unknotted the rope with quick fingers. "There is no way back," she whispered smiling. "You can only go forward now and seek out your beginnings in this land, my land of Gnarlsmyre."

14

Marrimian Rides on the Wings of Rumour

*M*ARRIMIAN closed her fingers around the smooth handle of the bow that Krann had fashioned for her from the bough of a black ebony tree. She felt its satin smoothness beneath her fingers and settled deeper into the shadows of the Hurlers' Gate. She smiled to herself and stole a secret glance at Krann out of the corner of her eye.

At first, on their long journey across the quickmarsh he had stared silently at the great ridge of rocks where the City of Glor crowded beneath the distant towers and spires of Glitterspike Hall and had shrunk back in his despair. He had been afraid of her touch and kept one pace ahead as he searched for the secret path beneath the mud. But gradually, as they left the roaring waterfalls behind them and the nights grew bitterly cold and the marshes froze, he had sat closer, huddling silently between the women around the blazing fire and whittling out the bow of black ebony wood, afraid to close his eyes and sleep lest the terror that he had glimpsed rear up again in the darkness to engulf him.

Marrimian had tried to soothe him, whispering

rhymes and chants that she had learned as a child, but nothing seemed to comfort him or draw him any closer to her. She despaired and wrung her hands together and begged him to eat, or to close his eyes and sleep, but his eyes were glazed with an inner torment that shouted in his head and he stumbled deliriously forward and often would have floundered in the bottomless mire beside the twisting path had not Ansel or Treasel kept a firm hand on his sleeve.

"What of your half-sister, Elionbel? If she is all good then you cannot be all bad," Marrimian had finally cried out in anger, grasping him by the shoulders and fiercely shaking him.

Krann had blinked, his eyes clearing, and he saw that there might be some truth in her words as he whispered Elionbel's name and reached out with trembling fingers to take Marrimian's hands. She had sighed with joy to take him in her arms and draw him close to her beneath their mudbeast cloaks. She smothered her fears of what terrors might lie in wait as they sought to tear aside the dark curtain that clouded his beginnings. She gasped as he took her and held her breath as he quickened and she saw in their moment of passion a silent landscape of dark forests and bleak winter grasslands. A black-armoured warrior loomed up and reached out to touch them, his living cloak of shadowrats rippling up over his shoulders as it spread out to engulf them. They both screamed and broke apart.

"What? Who?" Marrimian cried searching his eyes, but Krann shook his head, his mouth opening and closing noiselessly as he looked fearfully over his shoulder into the frozen darkness.

Krann felt deep down inside that he knew that face, something whispered in his head that the armour had been so closely moulded as to be a second skin, that somewhere in another life he had touched its slippery smoothness and known whom it covered. The warrior's name rose for a second, the first sound of it filled his mouth, choking him: "A . . . Arb . . . Arb . . ." he cried, swallowing and catching at his throat, but it had gone, swirling away into the darkness. "It was there," he whispered, "I almost, almost had it." His voice died away as he stared into the distance.

Marrimian gently took his trembling hands and drew him back beneath her cloak, whispering him asleep. When his breathing had slowed and deepened she sighed quietly to herself and stared at the stars as they slowly turned above her head. The touch of him had tingled and flowed through her body, making her realize how different she felt, as if each and every nerve in her body had opened up to the sunlight, and the slightest crackle of the frozen marsh crust echoed in her ears. She could see new things and catch the slightest noises that she had never noticed before. Even the hidden edges of their path below the mud seemed to be there for her to see . . .

Ansel jogged against her in the shadow of the Hurlers' Gate, prodding her sharply with her elbow and making her start and sit bolt upright. She remembered how Krann had brought them silently up through the beasting pits in the first grey light of dawn to watch and listen and gather together all the rumours and gossip of the city and learn how things stood before they sought a way to the doors of Glitterspike Hall.

"It is dangerous to dream, mistress, when there is so much wildness in the city," Ansel muttered grimly.

Marrimian nodded silently and pushed the black ebony bow further under her cloak, noticing how different it was from the short crossbows that the guards of the city carried, and she looked up at the passing crowds that thronged the gates. Nobody seemed interested in four marsh-ragged wanderers, or even gave them a second glance; they merely cursed them for filling the gateway when the crush of anxious travellers trying to pass through spilled out to the edges of the beasting pits. There was an air of terror in their hurried, darting looks and anxious faces. Nobody laughed or talked easily and all eyes watched the shadows. Heavily burdened harvesters and lampwicks cursed and jostled each other as they tried to force a way through the milling crowds. Coopers pushed and shoved, using the blunt ends of new barrel staves to shoulder a way through. Suddenly a mudbeast bellowed and a cursing shout went up from the edges of the beasting pits that made the blood in Marrimian's veins run cold, and she shrank back, forced against the rough stone wall by the press of the crowd as it split apart to leave the gateway clear.

Marrimian could hear the drag of chains and the cutting whiplash of the iron flails. Marshhunters cursed and sent their whips whistling down across the crowds, shrieking with laughter as they tore into the helpless travellers. The shackled mudbeast slowly ground its way across the cobbles, spreading its shadow over the ground as it passed beneath the gates. The hurlers cried out, crossing their canes to halt the beast, but the marshmen laughed and sneered at them and drove the beast on. The archer door guards spilt out from under the second arch and knelt before it, blocking its path. They loosed steel-tipped arrows from their short bows, but the beast bellowed with pain as the flails cut into its hide and smashed the hurlers' canes and crushed the startled archers beneath its claws as it lumbered into the narrow lanes of the city.

Marrimian rose, pulling the bow from beneath her cloak, a glaring hatred for the marshmen shining in her eyes.

"Wait!" hissed Krann, touching her arm. "Wait and listen. Do not give away your presence yet!"

Marrimian sank down against the wall, smothering her impatience, and did as he counselled, turning her ears to the buzz of rumour and unbridled gossip that erupted once the marshmen had passed. It was clear from every tongue that the marshmen were using their beasts to try to force a passage through the mazes that had been built against them. They were looting, burning, killing and taking whatever caught their eye, without a word of asking, and they had seized whole sections of the lower city, camping wherever they pleased, tearing out roof beams and doorposts and stealing fire from the lampwicks to light huge fires in the narrow lanes to cook their food. Rampaging mud-beasts were left to graze unattended on the flowers in the hanging baskets and they were rooting up the vineries in their search for food.

Ansel overheard one of the injured archers talking

about Glitterspike Hall and nudged her mistress and made her listen. It seemed from what the archer said that even the great hall, for all its guards and preparations and magic in the mumblers' dances, had not escaped the marshmen's murderous rampaging. Death stalked every corridor and no one was safe. At first it had been the ragmen and humble dusters that the marshmen had snatched from their daily tasks to hurl beneath the mudbeasts' claws in the circle to distract them, as those who sought to touch the Glitterspike spilled across the hall. But now anyone who was foolish enough to venture beyond their own doors was considered fair game. Servers had been dragged screaming from their pantries, hoemasters from their neat courtyard gardens. Even the lowest underscullions were waylaid as they went about their kitchen tasks, and were tortured for a way through the mazes set to thwart the marshscum from reaching the great hall by Naul, the joustmaster, in each frozen night of darkness. Nothing stayed the same for two days in a row; everyone who lived in the hall was now a helpless prisoner, hiding in dark corners, dreading the echoing rush of footsteps and wild shrieks that told them that a roving band of marshmen was close at hand.

"What of those who cannot hide?" asked Ansel, weeping in pity as she thought of the fetchers and carriers, the chimney-brushers and the crystal-cleaners and countless others who lived and laboured in the corridors of the great hall.

"We need a champion!" cried an angry lampwick on the edge of the crowd, making Ansel look up as he wiped the dried blood from an ugly flail scar that the marshmen had scored across his cheeks as they charged through the gates.

Another lampwick grumbled as he bent to pick up his bundle of trampled and ruined reed stems. "Yes, that's what we need, a champion who would chase these marsh vermin back into the quickmarshes where they belong."

Someone in the crowd laughed bitterly and cursed Lord Miresnare's name for loosing the marshscum to run unchecked amongst them, and he offered up the handle of his paring knife above the heads of the crowd, goading the lampwick to take it and be their champion.

"Deliver it up to our lord and master," shouted another angry voice. "Perhaps he will then come down from his high throne and defend us himself!"

The whole crowd seemed to shriek with laughter and someone quite close to Marrimian spat on the cobbles and sneered at Lord Miresnare's name and asked with scorn in his voice how a man who spawned nothing but weak pretties could do anything to save them.

"Not all his daughters are weak," shouted one of the guards beside the hurlers' high chairs. "The one with hair as dark as the shadows and a face more beautiful than the frozen crystal; she and two of her sisters have fallen in with the wretched marshlord who drove the beast Gallengab into Glitterspike Hall and brought all this tyranny down upon her heads: they have become his handmaidens, but the raven-haired one has her fingers on the sharpwire that he uses to murder the honest people of the hall in his quest to touch the Glitterspike."

"I have heard blacker rumours than that," shouted another guard. "I have heard tell that she squats on the corpses of those they murder and howls to the moon in the frozen hours while she picks clean their bones!"

"They talk of Pinvey, but which of my sisters would have followed her into such wickedness?" Marrimian hissed, straining forward against Krann's arm and making those who crowded between them and the gate arch turn and stare.

"Marshmen! Look, there are hunters or waders or their like in the shadows of the gate!" rose the frightened whisper as the crowds took a sharper look, stirred and shrank away from Marrimian.

Marrimian used their uncertainty to break free of Krann's restraining grip and stride forward through the melting crowds into the early shafts of sunlight and beneath the first gate arch.

There was a sudden shout and the rush of marshbound footsteps on the edges of the beasting pits. She hesitated and stopped below the high archway to reach back beneath her cloak for one of the arrows that Krann had whittled for her on their journey across the quickmires. She turned, her eyes narrowed with hatred for the marshlords and all their kind. She knocked an arrow onto the bowstring of plaited mudbeast hair and began to draw it tight.

"There is Vetchim, the marshwader," Ansel cried as she and Treasel ran to Marrimian's side with their daggers in their hands.

"Marshwaders! Marshhunters! Marshlords! I hate them all," snarled Marrimian, lifting her bow, her knuckles whitening as the bowstring touched her cheek.

"Have patience and use everything to your advantage," whispered Krann, hurrying out of the shadows to her elbow as the unruly gathering of marshmen drew level with the gates and saw Marrimian with Treasel and Ansel at her side blocking the way.

The marshmen shuffled to a halt, their shouts dying away into startled whispers as they stared at Marrimian. Slowly, one by one, they fell onto their knees, laying their spears and sharpwires before them on the cobbles and raising their wrists to their foreheads, twisting their hands into grotesque horn shapes as they sang and chanted in deep haunting voices.

"They are calling you the Beast Lady, Queen of all the Quickmarshes," whispered Treasel leaning forwards, balancing on the balls of her feet as she listened to the chanting that told of Marrimian's magical powers over the mudbeasts.

The chants told of how she had flapped her skirts and commanded the beast to kneel and allow her to mount and ride high upon its shoulders, and how it took her wherever she chose in the lands of Gnarlsmyre, from the edges of the great city that sprawled in the shadow of Glitterspike Hall to the Rainbows' End where the Beastweir Marshery waited for the sun to rise and kiss the lily pads.

"I think that they are offering themselves to you as your servants," whispered Krann, watching the marshmen bend and push their weapons across the cobbles towards Marrimian's feet.

Marrimian frowned and stared down at them, the

bitter words of the crowd still echoing in her ears, the reek of the marshlords' fires that raged unchecked in the lower sections of the city smarting and catching in her throat. The crowd in the gate arch had cursed her father and loaded his shoulders with all the blame; they had sneered at him for spawning only weak daughters. But she would show them. She eased the arrow from the string and lowered her bow. Holding Vetchim's gaze she raised her arrow hand and swept it to encompass the burnt-out ruins of the lower lanes and alleyways where the blundering mudbeast was being driven into the haze of drifting smoke, its huge horns and heavy shoulders smashing down the meaner mud-slapped hovels.

"You dare to chant to me of queens! Look! Look at what your people are doing!" she hissed, stepping forward. Once more she raised her bow. "I should kill you, marshwader, for listening to the healing woman's false whispers and leading us into the quickmarshes. Yes, I should kill each and every one of you!"

"Take care, mistress, they may carry hidden sharp-wires!" cried Treasel clinging onto Marrimian's sleeve to try to stop her from crossing the cobbles.

"Tread with caution," urged Krann, watching the marshwader's hands as he spread them out towards her and pleaded with her for his life.

"The healing woman wove lies into my head beneath those healing webs; she used me to try and snare you. I was to take you to Mertzork's marshery and keep you prisoners until she needed you, but I saw the truth of your power the moment you commanded the mudbeast to rise."

Ansel laughed harshly, the sound crackling on her tightly drawn lips. "You are easily swayed, marsh-wader. First you lead us and then you abandon us to flounder in the mire. Why should my mistress believe you now?"

Vetchim looked up at the scullion, his face wrinkled with confusion. "Because—because she has the magic power to ride upon the mudbeasts. Her name has trav-elled quicker than flames through bulrush stems from the Beastweir Marshery; all the people of the marsh-eries will kneel before her, she is our queen."

Marrimian frowned as she listened to the marsh-wader, thinking as fast as she could and searching for a way to turn these superstitious followers to her ad-vantage. She darted a quick sideways glance at the crowds beneath the gate arch who were leaning for-ward, listening to every word.

"Would you keep my name, my womanhood, a se-cret and guard these gates?" she asked in a whisper as she eased the arrow from her bowstring. "I wish none to enter without my leave. Would you stand here against the gates and bar those you have served, your own marshlords, from entry, and drive any beasts they may bring to the gates of the city back into the beasting pits for safekeeping?"

Vetchim bowed low, pressing her fingers to his lips. He smiled and called across his shoulder to the marsh-men kneeling closest to the edges of the beasting pits, ordering them to scatter to watch the paths across the quickmarshes.

Marrimian stepped back, but as she turned towards the gates she caught sight of Ansel out of the corner of her eye. Ansel was staring emptily at the marsh-wader. Marrimian stopped and beckoned Vetchim to come forward and asked him quietly, "The healing woman bound you to my scullion. Would you break that bond and have her choose another, or will you take your place?"

"Great Beast Lady," Vetchim cried, reaching out for Ansel's hand, "she is your handmaiden and she rode on the beast beside you. I would chew and soften the hides she throws before me with my own teeth, I would gather her food from the quickmarsh and I would follow her to the ends of Gnarlsmyre."

Ansel blushed, her oven-scarred cheeks colouring bright purple beneath the smears of mud. "Mistress!" she hissed in alarm, backing away from Vetchim, but her eyes sparkled with joy as she looked at him.

"None shall step between you," Marrimian laughed before she turned and strode off towards the gates, calling to the marshwaders over her shoulder to help the people of the city to quench the raging fires and then to wait for her return.

"I cannot follow you into those narrow lanes of darkness," cried Treasel, shrinking away from the high archways above the gates as she saw the real beginnings of the city that lay beyond them.

Ansel laughed softly and closed her broad blunt fingers around the marshgirl's wrist and whispered, "Hold on tightly to my apron tails and I will lead you up through the city, just as you guided us fearlessly through the mires and the swamps."

Marrimian reached the gate arch and slowed and stared at the silent crowd that thronged the edges of the road. Her eyes still smouldered with anger and her fingers trembled on the bowstring at the way they had sneered at her womanhood.

"You cursed the great lord of this city, and you mocked him for siring nothing but weak women, but not one of you so-called men has stepped forward, to be a champion to banish the marshlords. Well, I Marr . . ."

"Hush—keep silent!" Krann hissed, tugging at her sleeve to make her pause. "Now is not the moment to show them who you are, it would be better to allow the rumour of your beast-riding to spread through the city first."

"But I did not ride the beast through choice!" Marrimian whispered, her face clouding with confusion.

Krann smiled and drew her away from the listening ears of the crowd. "Word of your coming is already skipping over the heads of the crowd in hurried whispers, can't you hear them? Remember, rumours often have a life of their own, they grow quite independently of the grain of truth in their beginnings, and these rumours will strike fear and terror into everyone in the hall who is trying to touch the Glitterspike and no one, not even your father, would dare to laugh or snap his fingers in your face if he thought that you had ridden on a mudbeast, would he?"

Marrimian smiled as she saw the truth in his words and looked into his eyes. "It is just as you counselled me, it is all coming true. The people will not shrug off my womanhood now."

"But go forward into your father's hall with caution," warned Krann. "There are many who will spit on rumour, as many as will fear it, but nothing will serve our purpose better."

Marrimian laughed and raising her free hand she split her fingers into horn shapes on her forehead and growled at the crowd. The nearest lampwicks and harvesters cried out and shrank back in terror, but Marrimian quickly turned away and strode beneath the gate arch and vanished into the first row of burnt-out houses in the city.

Krann closed his eyes and searched ahead but threw up his arms hopelessly. "It is a maze of blind endings and ruined, burned buildings, I cannot tell which lane to take."

"Which way would you choose?" Marrimian asked Ansel, touching her arm as the scullion slowed to an uncertain halt and peered into yet another dozen dark silent openings between the crowded, burnt-out hovels.

"It has all changed so much, mistress, but I think there were chandlers' houses here with rows of hanging candles spinning to dry and harden in the breeze. Flowers grew beneath the window slits in narrow stone troughs and there were always people milling about to shout out the hours or point the way. These lanes were full of laughter and the cries of barter . . ." Her voice trailed into silence and the others watched helplessly as she clambered over the piles of broken stonework searching for a candlewick or a scrap of the familiar city that she had known and walked through so easily before fate drove them out into the quickmarsh.

Krann shut his eyes to the maze of alleyways and

dark echoing lanes choked with rubble and sank down miserably into a ruined splintered doorway, huddled beneath his cloak. There was something about the burnt-out smell, the broken crumbling walls and the utter desolation heaped up around them that seemed to tug at hidden chords deep down inside him. The voices that had haunted and lured him into the Shadowlands were suddenly all about him and laughed and echoed in his head, and everywhere beneath the rubble he imagined that he could hear the scratch and scrabble of tiny claws. He shivered and clapped his hands to try to drive out the whispers, and then he looked up and swept his eyes across the bleak ruins and caught a glimpse of something moving, flitting between the broken doorways. He frowned, buried himself deeper into his cloak and watched carefully.

Ansel gave a shout of triumph and held up the broken fragment of a candle mould. She pointed to the beginnings of a lane far to their left where worn steps protruded from the rubble and led the way up towards the sheer walls of Glitterspike Hall. She called to the others that she had found the way and began to follow the path.

Krann allowed the others to go a few paces ahead while he whistled tunelessly and appeared to wander after them in an aimless trance, gazing up at the sagging roof timbers and the haze of dirty smoke that drifted across the city, but his eyes were sharp and caught each fleeting shadow as they climbed and threaded their way up through the maze of twisting lanes and alleyways.

"Do not look back or make a sudden turn," he whispered, lightly touching Marrimian's shoulder as they reached a block of fallen masonry, "but since we passed through the Hurlers' Gate we have been followed and watched."

"By the marshmen whom I commanded to guard the gates? What do they look like?" Marrimian hissed, her shoulders tensing, the hairs on the nape of her neck prickling.

"No, by old women," answered Krann in less than a whisper. "Ancient hags wrapped in a riddle of black rags, and they have closed in all about us, growing bolder as we climb."

"The crones!" Ansel whispered, stealing a furtive glance over her shoulder as she tried to find a way around the fallen steps. "That's who they are, the healing woman's lick-spittles who do her bidding. But what are they doing shadowing us so far from their hovels in the Shambles?"

"Erek has set spies to watch for us. She will warn Mertzork and my sister Pinvey. She will unmask all the secrets that we hide," cried Marrimian in alarm.

Krann laughed quietly and shook his head. He was about to tell them why he thought that the healing woman had set her spies on them when they were suddenly knocked down and enveloped in a rush of black skirts. The crones dodged amongst them, shrieking and pinching them with their sharp fingernails and setting handfuls of spiders to swarm in the narrow alleyway.

"Death! Death to all marshmen who seek a way into Glitterspike Hall!" they sang, spinning away in a blaze of black rags, vanishing as quickly as they had

come into all the dark openings and echoing alleyways around them.

"Catch the spiders! Do not trample on them!" Treasel shouted, seeing the edges of an idea that might help her mistress if they ever reached the great hall as she pulled Marrimian and Ansel back onto their feet. She bent down and showed them how to pick up the scuttling spiders; using her fingers and thumbs she trapped their furry bodies.

"A rag or strip of cloth to keep them in," she urged, squeezing the largest spider's venom sac and milking its poison to drip harmlessly onto the ground.

Marrimian hesitated for a moment, trying to brush the spiders away from the hems of her skirt. "Why would you have us collect such foul things?" she shuddered.

But the marshgirl only laughed and allowed a harmless spider to scuttle up her arm. "Because if we set them loose amongst the marshmen they will create chaos and terror and only we will know how harmless they really are."

"Krann! Look out, Krann!" cried Ansel hitting at her apron and tearing off her underskirt. He stood frozen with fear, spiders running all over him. "Quickly, use my underskirt and gather the spiders."

Treasel dropped the first handful of spiders into the voluminous folds of the scullion's underskirt and ran around Krann scooping off the spiders that had scuttled over his boots and begun to climb his breeches. Marrimian gathered her courage and shuddered each time her fingers closed around the soft bodies, and she and Treasel ran in frantic circles in the narrow alleyway, trapping and catching every spider the crones had thrown at them.

Ansel held the wriggling heavy underskirt at arm's length and gave it a violent shake every few moments to make sure that the spiders were well away from her fingers. Treasel laughed softly and gathered the hems of the underskirt into a secure knot and hid it beneath her beastskin cloak.

"They will not harm you now, Ansel," she smiled. "I have milked them all and drawn their teeth. Remember, it is a woman's secret to know how to draw the spiders' venom and use it as a healing potion."

But Ansel only frowned and moved away from the marshgirl while Marrimian kept her doubts to herself, not yet seeing how Treasel planned to use the crones' spiders against the marshmen.

"That is our path!" Krann suddenly blurted out, almost stumbling over the words as he regained his senses, and with a giant stride he stepped clear of the mess of spiders' venom that had spread across the cobbles and pointed a way to their left where a steep lane of overhanging galleries threw deep violet shadows over a twist of ancient stone steps, vanishing into the distance.

Ansel frowned and shook her head while Marrimian shouted, "No," so firmly that it made Krann spin around towards her with his eyebrows wrinkled into a frown.

"But I glimpsed that path in the crone who shoved me aside," he muttered crossly. "I saw it in her eyes and heard it in her whispers; that is the road to the doors of Glitterspike Hall."

Marrimian shrugged her shoulders helplessly, not quite knowing how to put into words the flash of gnawing fear and the sudden glimpse that she had seen as he had pointed his finger into that dark lane.

"I know nothing of the city beyond the pictures it painted for me through the crystal windows of Glitterspike Hall. Ansel searches out our path for she knows it better than the rest of us, but as you pointed into that lane I glimpsed steep slippery cobbles ending in sheer wet stone walls; black waters rippled and lapped against them and echoed to the splash of marshfish fins."

"The moats! The marshfish moats!" cried Ansel, slapping her dirty forehead with the palm of her hand. "I knew that twist of steps looked familiar. Yes, now I remember why that could never be our road unless . . ." She paused and looked grimly about her. "Unless the crones have woven a magic bridge of spiders' webs across those bottomless watery fish pits."

"Moats?" asked Krann turning sharply on the scullion. "What are moats?"

Ansel explained and added, "I knew that you had chosen badly only I could not put my finger on it, not until my mistress had told us what she had seen, but now I remember and I would like a golden barter for every kettle of flapping marshfish that I have carried out of Waterbottom Lane during my seasons as an underscullion in the kitchens of Glitterspike Hall!"

Krann shivered and pulled his cloak tightly about his shoulders, an edge of doubt creeping into his mind. He had never been wrong before, not even in the quicksands. He had always seen the way either in himself or had glimpsed it in others, but the crone had almost turned them into those bottomless watery pits with one false glance. If Marrimian had not seen the danger . . . he caught his breath and looked up at her. Somehow she had stolen his power of foresight.

Marrimian met his eyes and laughed softly and knew his question without the need for words. "We are lovers," she whispered. "We rub together and entwine our passion and in that moment the slightest whispers become a shout and all the hidden secrets that hide in the shadows are clear to see."

"You have used our passion to steal away my foresight! You have taken the one thing that made me different, that told me where to step or what is the truth! Without it I am blind in this land of Gnarlsmyre!"

"No!" Marrimian cried fiercely. "I have taken nothing but your counsel. It is you who has taken while I lay beside you, shivering with fear as the nightmare images that haunt your beginnings brushed against me. I have touched and seen them each time we couple yet not once have I closed myself or drawn away from you, because I love you and I know that through me you see and know yourself."

Clenching her hands in bitter anger that he dared to accuse her of stealing anything or that the glimpse was anything more than mere chance Marrimian turned away. Krann stared at her, the hurt and the pain in her words echoed in his head, shouting the truth at him and showing a love in her which was far greater than he had imagined or dared to guess at.

"Forgive me," he whispered, reaching out to touch her. "For I have taken and used you roughly without a moment's thought for how it might touch or hurt you."

Marrimian slowly turned back blinking at her tears. "Have you not seen my love? Seen how we share each moment and think the same thoughts, how we even laugh as our lips form the same words? We have become as one, but I did not steal anything in doing it. You gave yourself to me just as I gave myself to you and I have loved you enough to search through the terrible shadows that hang over your beginnings for the seed of goodness that I know lies beyond them."

"But if we both share my power of foresight how did only you see the truth as the crones rushed between us. Surely . . .?"

Marrimian laughed and entwined her fingers in his, pulling him to her, and whispered in his ear. "Perhaps because their magic was woven to trap marshmen and lure them to their deaths in the marshfish moats."

"You mean their magic did not touch you because you are a woman?" Krann gasped.

Marrimian smiled and nodded. "Yes, they looked no further than our beastskin cloaks and thought that we were men."

"Mistress! Mistress!" Ansel hissed, causing them to break apart and turn towards her. "We must seek shelter in narrower lanes. The pindafall birds are soaring over the city hunting for easy prey and the crones are gathering close again; I can hear their shuffling footsteps in every alleyway."

"Think, act and speak as marshmen!" Marrimian hissed, drawing Treasel and Ansel to her. "Do not reveal our womanhood or call me mistress until we have thrown the crones off our scent. Now, quickly, Ansel, choose us a path, for you know this city better than I ever could."

Ansel moved apart from the others, her beastskin cloak wrapped tightly over her apron tails, and swept her careful gaze across the maze of openings, some wide, some treacherously inviting, some merely a twist of vanishing steps, while the narrowest were less than cracks where the stonework of the city had settled almost to touch.

"Chimney Lane," she whispered at length, scratching her chin and nodding her head towards the most unlikely jumble of crowded, smoke-blackened, windowless hovels that stood in the shadows of a forest of spindle-thin smoking chimney stacks.

"There used to be a narrow stairway between the smoke houses that led up past the crystal houses to a forgotten kitchen entrance that I used as an underscullion. I am sure it has long been blocked with rubbish or bricked over, but I will chance to see if it is still open," she muttered grimly, leading them forward.

"Smoke houses? What are they?" asked Treasel, hurrying to keep up with the scullion's pace and wrinkling her nose at the heavy acrid smell that seemed to dry and stretch her skin as they passed between the tall blackened houses. Their footsteps muffled to nothing as they walked over the thick layer of oily soot that had settled upon the cobbles.

"It is where everything that must be kept for the wet seasons is smoked, cured and dried. All the meats, birds and the fish that the people of the city will eat are hung in or above the smoke to preserve them,"

Ansel answered in a whisper, breaking the eerie smoky silence.

"Are the crones still shadowing us?" Marrimian asked as she turned and slipped into the dark stone stairway at Ansel's heels.

Treasel paused, twisting her head from side to side and listening to the silence of Chimney Lane, raising herself on tiptoe to stare between the forest of tall chimney stacks that spread out below them. "I think they have vanished," she whispered.

Krann knelt down and pressed his ear onto the cold stone step. "Yes, they have gone. There is nothing behind us but the damp crackle of the smoke-house fires and the wet splash of marshfish jumping in the moats."

Rising to his feet he turned and watched the lamp-wicks moving through the lower circles of the city far below and the heavily burdened harvesters who had crowded around them beneath the gate arch making their slow progress. He paused, turning his head up towards the sheer walls of Glitterspike Hall that towered over them. He leaned forward, tilting his head as if trying to catch some far-off sound, some whispered rumour carried on the morning breeze. "Hush!" he hissed, scrambling up the stairway to catch every sound that was echoing down the stair. "Listen, there is pandemonium at the doors of Glitterspike Hall." His face darkened as he turned to the others. "It seems that you have set fear loose amongst the crones and driven them by quicker climbs than this to the entrance. Now they are everywhere, spinning and shrieking and calling out to all those whose quest is to touch the Glitterspike, telling them of the wild rumours of a woman who rides upon a bellowing mudbeast to claim all Gnarlsmyre as her own and leading an army of a thousand marshmen to guard the Hurlers' Gate with orders to kill any marshman, hunter or wader who tries to escape back into the quickmarsh."

"You were right, rumours can grow from the tiniest grain of truth . . ." Marrimian began, her voice fading into silence as she heard the crones' voices rise into screaming shouts between the doors of Glitterspike Hall. "What do they chant? What are they screaming about?"

"They are stirring up the marshlords and all those within the hall to a frenzy to kill the beast rider before she enters the hall," he cried.

Marrimian frowned. "Those rumours have turned against us now. We'll never touch the Glitterspike!"

Krann suddenly laughed and shook his head. "No, the crones are feeding the rumour and giving you more power, they are creatures born of rumour, they weave it into all their magic. They have swallowed every word and whisper that we spun beneath the Hurlers' Gate and they will make the marshmen fear you more than any other if they believe that you have the power to tame the mudbeasts chained around the Glitterspike."

Marrimian fell silent and slumped back against the cold stone steps, staring hopelessly out across the city towards the distant rainbows that sparkled and shone on the very edge of her world. "But the crones are urging them to hunt me—how will we ever slip unnoticed into the hall? It is hopeless—to have come so far, through so much danger, only to find the doors of my father's house held against me by a solid crush of marshmen all howling for my blood."

"There are more ways into Glitterspike Hall than there are marshfish in a full kettle," whispered Ansel, cupping her hands to Marrimian's ear. "The meanest door cracks that the servers and the lampwicks use, the low hatchways where the underscullions collect the fuel for the kitchen fires . . ."

Krann touched her arm and pointed down through the forest of chimneys below to where a crowd of marshmen was searching through the ruins. "The crones must think we are still near the marshfish moats, we must snatch this moment to slip by unnoticed while they search for us in the city," he whispered.

The end of their journey was in sight at last.

15

The Stitchers' Cubbyhole

*T*HE scent of season's end was blowing across the marshes, rattling the ripening flower seeds and bending the blunt bulrush heads. But in Glitterspike Hall musty darkness swallowed every other scent and sound in the unlit mazes of corridors and narrow passageways. Shadows filled the once neat courtyards where thick tangled quickthorns and smotherweeds now spread unchecked, and lichen moss and slimetouch had spread its cold slippery fingers across every wall and unpolished floorstone. Marshmen's shouts echoed through the eerie silence and the sound of their rushing footsteps filled every dark corner and cubbyhole where the people of the hall had fled to hid.

Mertzork threw his head back and laughed, as he heard the crones' rumours, letting the cruel pitiless sound shriek and echo against every closed door in the maze of gloomy corridors, passageways and dark openings that branched out before him.

"Go back to your healing woman and tell her that I care nothing—nothing, do you hear?—for women who can straddle mudbeasts, because that won't help them find a way through this cursed maze of blind endings," he snarled impatiently, catching hold of the spinning crone and stopping her mouth with one strong brutal hand as he jerked her off her feet and tossed her carelessly up against the sharp keystones of the low-vaulted ceiling.

"Tell your healing woman that I need her magic to find a way into the hall!" he shouted angrily.

"Make her use her magic to steal the master mumbler's new slate, the one he uses to plan these endless mazes and blind passageways," hissed Pinvey, leaping on the crone as she fell in a tangle of ragged skirts on the hard stone floor. Pinvey scattered a handful of broken slate shards over the frightened woman and pointed, stabbing her finger along the gloomy corridor towards a blank wall. "We are lost, all four of us are lost; this fragment of the mumbler's slate that we stole is useless. He has blocked every corridor that we knew and sealed up all the ways that were on these pieces of slate."

"We are barred from entering the hall and would not with all our magic know where to search for the mumbler's secrets," cried the crone, struggling against Pinvey's grip.

"Magic! It is always magic that ruins my schemes," sneered Mertzork, thrusting the dry empty husk of the hedgehog that had faithfully led him to Pinvey back into the crone's hands. "Tell your healing woman that we have used up all her hedgehog's finding powers and we need another if we are to ever be finished with this warren of miserable passageways."

"Be quick before we tire of this game and creep out

MIKE JEFFERIES

and slit your throats," spat Pinvey, pushing the crone away from her to stumble on her knees between her sisters.

The crone scrambled to her feet and shrank away from all four of them and stroked the dead hedgehog as she muttered every black curse she knew and gathered a ball of hot venom on the tip of her tongue. "You should take more care of those we lend to help you," she shrieked as she spat the venom into Mertzork's face and skipped backwards out of his reach.

Mertzork snarled and leapt forward, making the crone scuttle and trip over her skirts in her panic to escape. "Tell your healing woman that I grow impatient to touch the Glitterspike!" he shouted, his voice turning to cruel laughter as he watched the woman skid and bump from side to side in the narrow corridor as she fled.

Turning his back as the crone's footsteps faded Mertzork loosened his iron spike from his belt and drove it against the nearest door as he cursed magic and all the healing woman's muddles that had left him and Pinvey wandering with her two miserable sulking sisters in this maze of corridors and gloomy passageways. He had thought that these women would know the way but no matter how much he cursed or beat them or took them when he pleased they seemed further from the Glitterspike now than he was when he had first passed between the outer doors. The door latch splintered and broke apart with three savage blows and the ruined door creaked slowly open to reveal a musty darkened room.

"Tell me a way through these mazes and I will spare

your life," he growled menacingly to whomever might be hiding there as he crossed the doorstone in one huge stride and spun the heavy iron spike from hand to hand making it whirr and hum

"Come out!" he snarled, widening his eyes against the gloom and searching through the jumble of upturned benches and stools and the litter of broken wooden chests, their contents spilled across the floor.

"This room has been plundered. There's no one here," he muttered wrinkling his nose at the damp smell of a long-extinguished reed lamp as he turned and stumbled against Pinvey, Alea and Syrenea who had followed him over the doorstone.

"Wait," Pinvey whispered. She curled her fingers around his arm and felt her heartbeat quicken and her skin tingle hotly with excitement as she smelt the sweet musk of the room and caught the slightest rustle of soft silk in the darkness.

"There's a woman hiding in here. I can smell her and hear her shallow frightened breaths," she murmured, brushing her lips against Mertzork's ear and trailing her long fingernails down his arm to stroke the back of his hand.

"Perhaps it is a scullion, or one of those dusters, they know all the ways through these mazes better than anyone else. If only we could catch them."

"There's no one here, I know there isn't," cried Syrenea in a frightened voice, trying to make the others leave the room. She had caught the faintest whisper of the sweet fragrance and she knew that it came from a phial of perfume that she had given Treyster two seasons ago.

"There is someone here and she can't be a scullion, unless she stole the perfume," hissed Pinvey.

Mertzork suddenly pulled Syrenea out of the way and kicked the door shut, motioning all of them to be silent as he jammed his iron spike firmly across the latch. "Marshmen!" he whispered as he threw his weight against the iron spike and they heard the muffled shouts and shrieking screams of a mob of hunters searching in the passageways close by. Pinvey loosened her dagger and crouched, ready to stab at anyone who broke through the door. Syrenea wept while Alea pressed herself against the wall, her eyes wide with terror. Behind them a bench scraped against the wall and a low wooden chest creaked.

"Be quiet!" snapped Pinvey, "or those marshmen will hear you and break down the door and they will kill you quicker than we will."

A frightened voice sobbed and stuttered in the darkness and then fell silent. Pinvey gripped her dagger grimly and cursed her spineless sisters as she waited, willing the marshmen to pass them by, knowing that they would murder to get their hands on anyone from the hall—even ones as useless as Alea or Syrenea—if they thought that it would serve their purpose. She glanced across at Mertzork in the darkness and smothered that germ of jealous hatred she held against him for taking her sisters as well as herself. She ran her tongue over her lips as she remembered how she had first heard the scratchings of the hedgehog behind the hanging tapestry and had known that he was near and then how he had taken her again and again in that dark corner. She had laughed and shouted through the pain as he bore down on her, possessing every nerve, every tingling part of her, and in the height of their passion she had torn away her bodice and wrapped herself around him, almost devouring him, as she whispered of the treasures that she and her sisters had stolen from the master of the game to help them to reach the Glitterspike . . . Before long he had tired of her and turned his eyes on her sisters . . .

A metal spike struck the door jamb splintering the frame and making her jump in the darkness and move closer to Mertzork. The wooden door shivered, splintering and buckling beneath the savage blows. Pinvey cursed Naul beneath her breath for making new mazes and keeping the secrets well hidden on another slate, for there seemed no way through this miserable tangle of leaky corridors and evil passageways. The blows stopped as suddenly as they had begun, they heard a muffled shout and the marshmen were gone as they followed another false trail.

Pinvey gave a sigh of relief and turned to face the room, hoping that whoever it was would be stronger than the others they had caught and tortured for their secrets.

"Come out!" she ordered, advancing into the room; then she hesitated as she saw a figure arise from behind a wooden chest. "I think this is another one of my sisters," she murmured and turned towards Syrenea who narrowed her eyes with hatred as she held her gaze.

Pinvey turned back to the figure and called in her softest voice, "Aloune, is that you? Or is it Cetrinea?

Don't be afraid, we have brought Mertzork to rescue you and keep you safe from the other marshlords."

"Stay still!" cried Syrenea but Pinvey hissed and glared her into silence as a frightened voice stuttered and a figure took a slow step forward.

"Pinvey, Pinvey, is that really you?" and then the girl hesitated as she saw the terror in Alea and Syrenea's eyes and slipped back behind an upturned table. Only Pinvey was all smiles.

"Treyster, I know it's you," she cried, pushing the other two out of her way as she climbed over the scattered furniture towards the upturned table. "Come out, no one will harm you, we only want to know the way into Glitterspike Hall."

"B-but I don't know the way," stuttered Treyster. "I'm just as l-lost as you are."

Pinvey laughed and thrust the upturned table aside. She snatched at her sister's wrist and pulled her violently towards Mertzork. "Tell us which passageway," she hissed, pinching Treyster savagely on the soft skin above her elbow, making her scream. "Tell us! Tell us! I know that you hold the secret of the way into the hall. Our father or that wretched mumbler would never have left poor little Treyster to wander about lost now, would they?"

"I-I lost my way, days ago. Father doesn't care about us, he's forgotten that we even exist now the marshmen are questing for his throne," cried Treyster, struggling frantically to break free as Mertzork put his hands on her.

"Leave her! Leave her alone, she's simple-minded, can't you hear it in her stuttering?" cried Alea.

"Which passageway? Which one?" Mertzork ignored her sisters' pleas as he breathed into her face and made her choke with panic. He began to tear through the silk layers of her skirts.

"Make her scream with terror until she tells us all her secrets!" shrieked Pinvey in jealous hatred of her younger sister as she twisted Treyster's arms painfully behind her back and Mertzork tore away her bodice.

"Leave her, she knows nothing," wept Syrenea, banging onto Mertzork's arm.

"Help me, help me!" Treyster screamed, fighting with all her strength. "I am your sister!"

Pinvey laughed and suddenly let Treyster go and struck Syrenea to silence her as Mertzork forced Treyster down onto the ground. "He can do what he wants with you because I have always hated you for being the delicate one, the helpless one, the one whom everybody always loved and pampered."

Treyster jerked her head backwards and hit it hard against the corner of the wooden chest, screaming as the pain tore through her body. Tears blinded her eyes and blood pounded in her ears, drowning out her sister's hateful words and pitiless shrieks of madness as she poured out all her pent-up jealousies. Treyster felt the blood flow through her hair, she was being swallowed up in dizzy waves of darkness. Mertzork's shouts were growing fainter and fainter and his rough hands hardly seemed to touch her, she was floating, drifting away from all the terrors of the hall.

Mertzork felt her sag limply against him and he cast her aside as he cursed her for being as weak as all the others they had tortured, stealing his pleasure before it had begun. He muttered as he rose to his feet, angry that she would tell them nothing now.

Crossing the room he snarled at Syrenea and Alea and wrenched his iron spike out of the doorpost and let the broken door creak open. "We must be quick and follow those marshmen; they may have snatched up a rumour of the way into the hall."

Pinvey nodded silently and bullied the other two to follow him over the doorstone but she paused to stare back at Treyster lying on the floor and to see the dark smear of blood sink into the cold stones. "I hope all your miserable secrets leak out of your head," she hissed before turning on her heel to hurry after the others' fading footsteps.

Treyster stirred, her fingers twitching. Someone was calling her name; it echoed through the swirling darkness. A gentle hand was shaking her shoulder, forcing her to blink and open her eyes. "Nothing. I know nothing," she cried in panic, trying to focus her eyes on the four figures who towered over her. "I was lost and crawled in here to hide," she sobbed, struggling up onto her elbows and feeling the dizziness engulf her as she lifted her head.

"Be still. Be still, this is Marrimian, your sister. We will not hurt you," soothed the nearest figure, smiling and pressing firm hands down upon her shoulders to keep her still.

Another figure stared down over her shoulder and

another searched through the room to gather up a bundle of rags to make her a pillow.

"You cannot be Marrimian," Treyster frowned, trying to pull away from the large hands that were bandaging her wound. But she wondered who they were and how they knew her name and why they were being so gentle. "Marrimian's dead. Father banished her for demanding a chance to touch the Glitterspike and she perished, locked outside the hall with fat Ansel, her faithful scullion, in the frozen darkness, you cannot . . ."

Treyster paused and looked up from Marrimian to Ansel. "No, you cannot be . . ." she gasped, her eyes round with surprise.

Marrimian laughed softly and bent closer to her sister, slipping the mudbeast cloak from around her shoulders to reveal the torn and filthy gown that she still wore beneath it. "He won't throw me out a second time, Treyster, you have my word on that."

"But who are these marshmen with you? And how in all Gnarlsmyre did you survive the frozen darkness?" Treyster asked, staring at Treasel and Krann who had moved back to guard the broken doorway.

Marrimian laughed and made Treyster gasp as she crackled the spark that Krann had given her and lit the reed lamp. "We have journeyed to Rainbows' End to find friends as true as these. Fear them not, little sister, for they are no more marshmen than I am."

"Rainbows' End? Did you really go to the edge of the world and touch the rainbows?" Treyster asked, blinking and expecting them to vanish each time she opened her eyes.

"Touch them, mistress?" answered the scullion, glancing grimly into every dark corner of the room. "Why we did more than that, we passed right through them. We went through their dazzling archways and down a ladder of hanging vines into the magical lands beyond!"

Krann held his hand up for silence. "I can hear footsteps!" he called over his shoulder. "They are coming this way, following a rumour that this passageway leads directly into the hall."

"Of course it does! Or it did before the master mumbler built his mazes," hissed Ansel, turning towards the broken doorway. "That is why I have brought you here through the overgrown courtyards and back passages of the old laundry rooms. I don't think anyone has used them since I was an underscullion and they have lain forgotten, unnoticed by the marshmen. It is called Threadneedle Passage and these cubbyholes that line it are where the stitchers sang as they needled and embroidered the clothes for the hall. Look, some of their crochet edgings have spilled out across the floor from these broken chests."

"Lie still, little sister," Marrimian whispered urgently as the coarse shouts grew louder. "Keep well hidden and say nothing until the marshmen have passed by."

Marrimian turned away from her sister, pulled her mudbeast cloak tightly about her shoulders and knocked an arrow onto her black ebony bow as she turned to the doorway.

"The light! Quickly, stifle it!" Krann hissed, but it was too late. The rush of footsteps had already turned

into the passage and the wild shouts died away into
scheming whispers as the marshmen crept cautiously
towards the open door.

"Mumblers' magic!" snarled voice. "More traps and
snares to keep us from the hall."

"Storm the room and kill everyone in it!" hissed a
deep rasping voice from just beyond the door jamb.

Marrimian half turned and reached out to pinch the
guttering flame between her fingertips but she hesitated as she remembered Krann's counsels in the
water meadows and on their long journey through the
quickmarshes, and the echo of his words swelled up
in her mind, telling her to snatch and use the slightest
advantage no matter what it was or how slender the
thread seemed.

"Yes," she whispered, spreading her fingers and
catching hold of the reed lamp. "You shall see strong
mumblers' magic," and she lowered the lamp behind
Krann, making his shadow leap up and rear and
plunge as it spilled across the doorstone forming a grotesque black shape on the rough stone wall of the passageway.

Krann saw the shadow leap up away from his heels
and gave a scream of terror, his head filled with the
roar of battle, shadowy warriors crowded around him
shutting out the bright morning sunlight—he was
back somewhere in his beginnings. A figure loomed
over him clutching at him with strong fingers and
making him trip and sprawl in the untrodden snow.
He tried to rise, to twist, to turn and escape. Close by,
a beast with a broken claw stretched out its hideously
scaly armoured arms and called, "Kruel, Kruel," and

then a shadow crossed him blotting out the sunlight and he rolled over in the snow and stared up helplessly at Thanehand, King of all Elundium. The King towered over him with both hands locked upon the hilt of a broken spark-scarred blade wound with shards of flowing darkness. Victory curled the King's lips in a defiant snarl and his eyes burned with hatred as he thrust the broken blade towards his heart. Krann screamed and threw out his hands to ward off the nightmare vision of his king and the vision faded and he fell backwards, weeping, his face white and tortured by what he had seen.

"Guard us, quickly, make your shadow strike terror into the marshmen's hearts," Marrimian cried, pushing Ansel towards the doorway and lifting the lamp behind her to make her huge shadow leap up and spill across the doorstone.

"I will keep you safe and watch over you while the nightmares swarm around you," Marrimian whispered to Krann, gathering him to her with her free hand.

Ansel groaned and wailed and struck fear and terror into the crouching marshmen as her shadow reached up to touch the sharp stones in the vaulted ceiling of the passageway. One by one, slashing and stabbing at the black roaring shape, the marshmen dashed through the strip of light thrown across the doorstone and fled shouting and cursing, calling for an end to all mumblers' magic as their voices faded into nothing.

"He must have been really afraid of the marshmen—look at what fear has done to him," whispered

Treyster, staring curiously at Krann as he sobbed and wept, hiding his head beneath Marrimian's cloak.

Marrimian smiled and slowly shook her head. Her eyes seemed to mist and glaze over with a faraway look as she answered. "He walks a darker path than you or I could ever dream of, sister. He is looking for his beginnings; it is not the marshmen nor any of the endless swamps and mires of Gnarlsmyre that he fears."

"There are more footsteps in the passageway, mistress," Ansel called from the doorstone as she stared at the broken door.

Krann shook himself and rose miserably to his feet. "We must barricade the door while your sister tells us all she knows of how things stand in Glitterspike Hall," he urged, rubbing the tears out of his eyes with the corner of his cloak as he helped Treasel fill up the doorway with the heavy wooden chests.

Treyster looked at each of them in turn and then spread her hands and shrugged her shoulders and told them how everything had changed, that now the people of the hall had to fend for themselves. They foraged for scraps to eat and they lived hour by hour, watching the sun sink towards the quickmarsh, living in dread of the master mumbler's new mazes for none knew where the new paths would lead as they grew in the frozen hours or whether they would be trapped in unfamiliar passageways where they would starve to death alone.

"But surely the scullions provide the food, and the dusters or the ragmen could tell you the way through the busiest thoroughfares. They know every twist and turn," interrupted Ansel, her face creased into a black frown of confusion.

Treyster looked across at the scullion and sadly shook her head as she explained how almost all the customs and ways of the hall had been destroyed by the marshlords' savage thrusts for the knowledge of a path through the mumbler's mazes; that their killing and torturing had driven everyone to scatter and hide and that now the great vaulted kitchens stood cold and empty, the reed lamps were untrimmed and choked with soot and the once smooth-polished stones of the hall lay roughed and scuffed beneath the tramp of marshmen's feet without the ragmen's constant gliding touch to shine them.

"But we saw lampwicks and harvesters and brushed shoulders with countless others crowding through the Hurlers' Gate. What is happening to the things they carried? Why aren't they reaching the hall?" Ansel asked.

Treyster laughed bitterly. "They do bring the gatherings of the quickmarsh here to fatten the marshlords. Rows of booths crowd the edges of the hall and cooking fires fog the very air and fill the place with the stench of the foul things they devour. The harvesters have become the servants of the marshmen and would look to catch anyone who belongs to the hall and sell us to their masters, and we cannot escape because we are not lucky enough to know of a secret way out of the hall and into the safety of the city. We just grow thin trapped here; helpless prisoners of this quest to touch the Glitterspike."

"No," Marrimian answered firmly. "You speak of

the city as the blind woman who treads the laundry tubs would speak of the clothes beneath her feet, guessing the colours of the dresses by the touch of her toes. The marshmen have laid much of this city to ruin and those who have fled from the hall have merely slipped into a bigger prison. But what of our father, Lord Miresnare? Tell me all the news of him, every scrap and whisper."

Treyster frowned and fidgeted with her torn bodice, trying to knot it across her breasts. "Father has been completely seized with the madness of this game. He has no time for his daughters now, we are nothing to him, and at times I feel that he would rather have us wandering lost or taken by the marshlords if it would give him a moment's peace from their thrust to take his throne. Naul, as the master of this game, is forbidden to tell us a way to safety even if it means that we have to hide in miserable holes like this one."

"But what of our other sisters, Syrenea, Aloune, Anslery, Alea and the others, have you seen them? And what is the news of Pinvey?"

"Most of them are starving in the daughtery, too terrified to venture out even to forage for food, but Pinvey has Syrenea and Alea with her and . . ." Treyster broke down in tears and trembled with fear and anger as she told Marrimian all that Pinvey and Mertzork had done to her while the other two looked on helplessly.

Marrimian clung to Treyster, consumed with pity and horror, the anger boiling up inside her. "I must follow them into Glitterspike Hall," she hissed through clenched teeth.

"No! No, you cannot!" Treyster cried, catching hold of Marrimian's hand to try to dissuade her from this madness. "Packs of marshmen patrol the colonnades beneath the galleries; they are everywhere, shadowing each other, watching, waiting. They will kill you or hurl you alive into the circle of mudbeasts who guard the Glitterspike . . ." Treyster paused and caught her breath. "Father will curse you again as he did at the Allbeast Feast and he will set his favourites against you—he hates all women now, especially his daughters, and he curses us for being useless and weak."

"Favourites!" laughed Marrimian. "How can he have favourites amongst the marshscum who quest to steal the very seat that he sits upon?"

"The quest has changed, Marrimian. From that mad rush of wild marshmen at the beginning of the Allbeast Feast it has grown into a deadly game that none, not even the bravest or most foolhardy marshlord, will ever dare to play alone. To reach the door arches of the great hall is just the beginning, but if you are to stay alive and cross that vast expanse of blood-soaked stone unharmed you will need more eyes than these three friends you have at your back, and you will need more than six strong hands to ward off those you play against. I know, sister. I have snatched secret glances at this murderous game and I have watched the piles of severed heads mount up around the Glitterspike."

"We will all end up without a head if we enter the hall. It is utter madness!" cried Ansel, touching her own neck as she stared in horror at Treyster.

"Those who dare to play alone or those who look

likely to snatch an advantage as the shifting groups of marshmen draw near to the circle of mudbeasts chained around the Glitterspike are torn to pieces by the others. Remember, once inside the hall, friends change so easily and loyalties melt faster than the hoar frost on the crystal window panes."

Marrimian laughed harshly, her voice cutting across her sister's words. "How can they both murder and form these alliances? Surely from all we have ever seen of these marshmen it is against their very nature ever to work together."

"Only a quick fool would judge them blindly," muttered Krann from where he hunched beside the doorway. "Your father has set such a price on this game that none dare let another seize any gain."

"They are hunting heads," Treasel whispered, making them turn and stare at her. "It is the nastiest and most treacherous form of murder, cursed and outlawed in the marsheries. Your enemy creeps up behind you and drops a sharpwire silently over your head and then with one sudden savage twist the wire slices your throat . . ."

"Then I must somehow use their fear of each other against them!" muttered Marrimian, forgetting the others in the room as she turned her mind to finding a way that would allow her to slip between them, something that would make them hesitate and draw back from her. "Krann, will you help me?" she asked looking up. "Krann?" she whispered, rising to her feet and running to him as she saw the agony of that last fleeting vision clearly in his eyes. "I know there is real goodness in you despite what the reed flame showed.

We will search together for your beginnings once I have touched the Glitterspike," she whispered, reaching for his hand.

"No, I fear there is too much darkness in me," he wept, his eyes blinded with his tears as he shrank away from her. "I know that I am a part of that hideous one-clawed beast that I saw when we first touched in the water meadows. It called to me as the reed flame stretched my shadow and gave me my real name before Thanehand cried out for my death. I have no past to be worthy of, nor future to live for beyond your quest to touch the Glitterspike."

"Krann!" Marrimian cried in despair. "Our search has barely begun. I love you and there is so much for us to share together."

Krann smiled bleakly and pinched out the guttering reed flame, his mind deaf to her words, and he whispered as he swung the door open, "It is time, Marrimian, first-born of Glitterspike Hall, to reach out and touch your fate."

16

A Glimpse Through The Lampsmoke

NAUL shifted uneasily in his high chair beside the throne and sank down as far as he could into his saffron mumbler's gown. He spun the pine-oil lamp that hung from the arm of his chair and sent thin wreath tails of blue smoke coiling up around him to ward off the white pindafall bird which had glided down in a rattle of brittle leathery feathers from the darkness of the rafters to perch a handtouch from his shaven head on the arched rim of his master's throne.

"Lord," he whispered in dread, trying to catch Lord Miresnare's attention without moving too suddenly or speaking over-loudly. He blinked his eyes at the shower of sharp splinters the carrion bird was shedding from the headrest of the throne as it clawed and scratched at the twists of ornate carving with its talons.

"The sacred white pindafall grows restless. It must be a sign or a warning of the truth in these wild rumours of a woman who rides upon a mudbeast. Look how the marshmen have quickened the game and now move recklessly towards the circle of mudbeasts."

"Rumours," grumbled Lord Miresnare at the mumbler's interruption. "You are no better than this rabble of mirescum to hang so much importance on snatches of idle gossip. Show me a woman who can master anything at all and then I might believe that this gossip holds some truth."

Lord Miresnare snapped his fingers irritably at the master mumbler to hide his fears of the rumours and shut out any doubts there might be of a champion who would steal his throne, and he dismissed Naul from his mind as he leaned forward to watch two packs of marshlords who were shadow-stalking one another, matching stride for stride, and strength for strength, on the very edges of the circle of mudbeasts chained around the Glitterspike.

Lord Miresnare had watched every marshman since the game began. He followed each move and countermove so that he would be the first to glimpse the beginnings of a champion and thwart him, whoever he was, who tried to touch the Glitterspike and claim his throne. From their small hesitant beginnings in the dark in the door arches of the hall he had watched them and tried to guess which ones would survive the brutal murdering. He called out to those he most feared, splitting and dividing them with his favours, urging them against each other with all his cunning, squandering their strength long before they reached the circle of mudbeasts. But no matter whom he shouted for or whom he cursed they all floundered hopelessly in their own greed and jealousy.

Lord Miresnare sighed and yawned, rubbing his wrinkled, age-flecked hands across his face, well

pleased with his labours and knowing that the marshmen stalking each other near the mudbeasts would
soon dissolve into murderous treachery; one false step
and the hidden sharpwires would be out. Something
made him look up and lose the thread of the stalkers'
carefully balanced steps. Something beyond the sea of
shifting shaven heads: a flash of colour, a bright movement that split the gloomy crush of beastskin cloaks
that crowded in the shadows beneath the galleries.

"What? What was that?" he hissed, grabbing Naul's
wrist and making the carrion bird shriek and shake
out its leathery wings.

Naul rose as tall as he dared, pressing his toes on
the legs of his chair, the nape of his neck tingling as
the bird's fetid breath flowed over him. "It must be
new players, my Lord. They have entered the hall by
way of the Threadneedle corridors," he answered,
quickly searching between the plumes and the high
tufts of hair the marshlords wore upon their heads.

"Watch them closely for me, mumbler. Search out
this champion who would dare to steal my throne and
if any one of them has the look of a woman, tell me,"
Lord Miresnare ordered, his voice trailing into a mut-
ter as he turned his attention back towards the circle
of mudbeasts, only to hear the first strangled shouts
of treachery as the two packs of stalking marshlords
clashed. Sharpwires rose and fell and the marshmen
staggered, their eyes bulging, their feet buckling underneath as the wires tightened around their necks.
Secret daggers stabbed, shearing through the thick
hides of their cloaks as they fought, rolling and

sprawling across the blood-soaked floor on the edges of the mudbeast circle.

Borer biters and stinging insects of every shape and size rose in angry buzzing swarms from the marsh-lords' ruined cloaks. The white carrion bird shrieked and stretched its leathery wings, the clattering hum of its feathers cast a draught of fear across the hall making the crush of marshmen press back beneath the galleries as it swooped down from the high throne, its black shadow of terror falling on the fighting marsh-men, snapping its long narrow jaws on the swarms of insects as its claws raked through the strangled marsh-men's cloaks. The bird hooked up one of the dead marshmen by his cloak and lifted him high above the heads of the silent cowering crowds only to drop him tumbling into Gallengab's outstretched claws.

Lord Miresnare watched grimly, the corners of his mouth twitching, as the sacred carrion bird slowly turned and glided back across the hall, making those who could not find a place of safety throw themselves down onto the hard stone floor of the hall and cover their heads with their hands as its shadow glided men-acingly over them.

Lord Miresnare scratched at the folds of skin be-neath his chin and smiled as he watched the marsh-scum who had survived the sharpwire attack wait crouching or lying on the floor until the pindafall had settled, its wings half folded, on one of the headless corpses that littered the outer edges of the circle. Sud-denly, before the bird could spread its wings, they were up, running, scattering as fast as they could to hide amongst the other players who crowded between the jumble of harvesters' booths, broth boilers and rough sacking stalls beneath the galleries. Here and there a strangled shout of terror cut through the air and ended in a choking silence, as those driven by fear of the carrion bird ran too far and found themselves driven helplessly alone into a dark and unfamiliar corner of the hall and amongst their enemies. But most of the players stayed close together, calling to one another as they fled, and re-formed their groups as quickly as they could in the shadows of the galleries to plot anew on how to reach the Glitterspike.

Naul touched his master's arm and directed Lord Miresnare's gaze towards the low Threadneedle door arch. "I think there is a woman in the shadows, my Lord, crouching beside that marshlord who brought Gallengab into the hall. He has finally found his way through my mazes."

"Mertzork!" hissed Lord Miresnare. "He was cast out never to return."

Naul paused and half rose from his chair as he saw who walked with him. "Pinvey is at his side and another daughter, no, two other daughters walk with him," he cried, fearful of his master's anger.

"You say it is Pinvey?" cried Lord Miresnare, his knuckles whitening on the armrests of the throne. His lips twitched with shrieks of wild laughter as he realized that the wild rumors of the woman who could tame and ride mudbeasts were probably about Pinvey, but no, that was too ridiculous. "Of all the weak and silly daughters that I have spawned she is the worst! Why isn't she safely locked up in the daughtery with the rest of those worthless girls? If she had been under lock and key this silly rumour would never have started."

"Lord, we tried to lock up the daughters but if you remember there were those we could not find," Naul dared to venture.

"Useless, useless daughters! They have been nothing but a trial to me," muttered Lord Miresnare, brushing their plight roughly aside in the time it took to draw one short breath.

"Arrowstrike Pinvey and those other two with her!" he demanded, raising his hand towards the high gallery and signalling to his archer guard. How dare she fuel rumours and help that mirescum, Mertzork, to find a way into Glitterspike Hall? Treacherous woman; he hated her for helping Mertzork of all men who sought to steal his throne.

"Let their deaths be a lesson to all!" he called above the shouts and curses of the marshlords who filled the hall. He caught his master archer's eye and pointed down into the crowds who throned the Threadneedle door arch.

"No, my Lord, I counsel strongly against this move," cried Naul making Lord Miresnare drop his hand. "It would serve no purpose," the mumbler continued hurriedly without drawing breath. "Too much innocent blood has already soaked into the stones of this great hall. Perhaps Mertzork has captured your daughters and tortured them for a way through the mazes."

"Tortured!" scoffed Lord Miresnare turning angrily on his master mumbler. "Look! Look, you fool, at the way they cling to his cloak and crowd around him for his protection; look at the wild sparkle in Pinvey's eyes! I foretell, mumbler, even without your gift of foresight, that there are dangerous plots between Mertzork and Pinvey and I fear that we must watch their every step."

"Look, my Lord," urged Naul, "the marshmen must fear these rumours of the woman who tames beasts, they are drawing away from them, they are shunning them and calling out black curses and spitting on the stones all around where they tread."

Lord Miresnare laughed and glanced quickly up at the tall crystal windows and measured the lengthening shadows. He chafed his ancient hands together as if applauding the way the mass of marshlords were turning against his daughters.

"Game's end!" he shouted, snapping his fingers to bring the archers to the edge of the high gallery to overwatch the marshmen, knowing that his throne was safe for another night.

Lord Miresnare yawned and suddenly appeared to lose interest, then sank, exhausted, into a troubled sleep. Naul looked nervously at his master and breathed easier once he was sure that he really had fallen asleep. Naul had faithfully foretold every vision that had reared up within the magic mumblers' dancing circle, giving his master a clear warning of Gallengab's journey into the hall and how he must change the joust to make sure that the throne would be claimed by the rightful heir. His foresight had been the future clearly shown, and would reveal the true courage and clever cunning of the one who would eventually pass between the beasts and touch the Glitterspike. But Lord Miresnare was falsely using the window onto the morrow and he daily grew more jealous of losing his throne to anyone, good or bad. He played the game far harder than all the marshlords and he chose favourites, betraying them the moment they seized an advantage or looked set to venture in amongst the mudbeasts. And now Naul worried, fidgeting with the binding on his lamp. Now that Mertzork had brought the women into the hall Miresnare would use these rumours even if it meant killing his own daughters to preserve his throne.

Naul looked up at the tall crystal windows and knew by the shadows that the sun had sunk towards the quickmarsh. He spun his pine-oil lamp, holding it up as he did on every evening of the game, to search in the billowing smoke for an idea of the new mazes that he knew he must labour to build in the hours of the frozen darkness.

"Nothing! It shows nothing, no blind ends or ways that I must block," he muttered to himself as the smoke thinned, and he wound the woven thongs above the lamp until they cut tightly into his hand as he spun the lamp again, causing the smouldering wick to blaze into a bright white ball of fire that threw long shadows across the restless marshmen settling down upon the hard stone floor of the hall to wait out the hours of darkness.

"Crones in the passageways of Glitterspike Hall!" Naul gasped, choking on the bitter fumes spilling from the lamp and making Lord Miresnare grumble and fidget in his sleep. Naul stifled a startled cry as he watched the shadowy black-ragged hags dance and spin their magic rhymes through the swirling blue smoke of his lamp, whispering out their rumours of the woman who had tamed the mudbeasts and rode upon their backs.

"No! No, you can have little to do with the future," he whispered fearfully, plunging his hands into the hot smoke and singeing his fingers as he tore the vision into a thousand vanishing twists of smoke before his master awoke. He knew that he dared not tell one word of what he had just seen or Lord Miresnare would send an archer guard out into the city to arrowstrike every harmless crone and healing woman who lived within the Shambles. There would be no mercy in his ruthlessness for he would not tolerate their magic within the hall; he hated it and blamed it for all the daughters he had spawned.

Turning his head the master mumbler glanced at Lord Miresnare and let out a sigh of relief when he saw that he still slept on soundly. Naul gingerly spun the lamp again, knowing that he must be quick if he was to glimpse the future before the lampwicks brought light into the hall and woke his master. He quietly chanted his strongest magic and waited for the rising smoke to thicken into a shimmering blue curtain against the darkening hall. A sudden rush of footsteps echoed in the Threadneedle door arch and made Naul frown and lean forward on the edge of his chair. He pressed his nose into the billowing clouds of smoke to see who was entering the hall. The day was drawing to an end and it was long past the last finding hour. The way should be closed. But he saw the door arch standing empty.

He drew back, his red-rimmed eyes smarting from the smoke, and cleared his mind of unnecessary interruptions as he prepared to look into the future. Now the hall fell silent and he saw within the curtain of smoke that it was deepest night; ice crystals formed and sparkled on the lumpy cloaks of the marshlords who slept upon the floor of the great hall. Yaloor growled restlessly and paced around the base of the Glitterspike, clattering his large iron chain with each fretful footstep. The white pindafall glided silently through the smoke, its talons glistening in the frozen moonlight. Now gradually dawn was breaking and a running figure dodged through the sleeping marshmen, scattering something from a knotted sack. The waking marshmen were all at once on their feet screaming and shouting. Panic was boiling through the hall. Naul shivered and peered closer through the thinning smoke and glimpsed a lone figure walking amongst the mudbeasts, calming them and singing to them in a clear crystal voice.

He wrinkled his nose as he smelt the acrid stench of burning mudbeast hair and blinked at the light that blazed through the hall as he straightened his back. The lampwicks each guarded by two archers lit the lamps and Naul sank back into his chair with the slightest of smiles on his lips. There had been something familiar about that figure amongst the mudbeasts, something that echoed from his past. Perhaps there was a glimpse of truth in these rumours. He frowned and shrugged his narrow shoulders and turned towards the evening shouts of the cauldron keepers and the broth boilers who were throwing open the shutters of their booths ready to serve out their coarse evil-smelling liquors and bowls of pottage to the quarrelsome marshlords. Naul had but a moment to hang his pine-oil lamp on the armrest of his high chair before his master awoke, stiff and grumbling, glaring down at the milling crowds that thronged and dirtied his hall. He called for servers to bring out his food and to hurry before the swarms of stinging insects spoiled it by settling on it.

Naul picked absently at the stale burned-black trenchard and tore off crumbling rinds of the hard crust to soak up the maggot-strewn mess of pottage that the underservers had sent him in a sticky wooden bowl which he balanced on his knees, knowing that nothing could lighten its foulness nor change its taste. He mourned the absent scullions and their hot, fresh oven breads and spicy wholesome broths and chewed grimly, coughing as the food clogged his throat. He passed it back to the eager hungry underservers.

It was easy to hide his uneasiness from his master, Lord Miresnare, who was busy hunched over his bowl noisily sucking up the gruel and showering the frightened servers with it as he cursed them for his own clumsiness. Naul cast his mind back to the snatches of foresight that he had glimpsed in the curtain of smoke, and worried a loop of silver-veined windbells through his fingers, listening to their haunting whispered chimes as he tried to riddle out why the crones would risk their lives by entering the outer maze of passageways and what deeper purpose had forced them to take such desperate steps. He frowned and drew his eyebrows into a deep searching furrow, knowing by the dull ache of his bones that whoever he had seen in the smoke striding amongst the mud-beasts was a part of the crones' wild rumours.

But on the very edges of those visions in the smoke, and stronger than all else, he had heard other words whispered in the crones' voices and they had called his name.

Movement in the high galleries made Naul start and forget his worryings. He looked up to see that his stone setters and archers had crowded forward to await his signal to begin the long night's toil of building false endings.

"There is a long night's work ahead for us, my Lord," he uttered, quietly rising from his chair and bowing to his master as he prepared to leave. Lord Miresnare merely grumbled and threw his hand out to indicate the hall.

"Rid me of them, mumbler. You and your foresight brought them in here, now rid me of these mirescum!"

"Yes, my Lord," whispered Naul, bowing as he stepped respectfully away, knowing that anything he said would only bring a stream of curses from Lord Miresnare.

He hurried across the hall with his saffron cloak tails flying. The marshmen in his path scuffled and leapt aside in fear of the archer guard that surrounded him.

"Where, master mumbler? Which door arch? Which way tonight?" asked the archer closest to Naul.

Naul hesitated, closing his eyes and letting his feet

feel the roughness of the stones beneath them as a picture formed in his mind. "Threadneedle," he whispered, shivering and turning towards the dark echoing door arch that had been nagging and worrying him all day. At first he had thought that it was merely Mertzork and Pinvey's appearance beneath its keystone that fretted him but now it seemed as though the ice-cold hand of fate touched his spine and was drawing him towards it.

The noises of the marshlords settling down as they argued and squabbled over tomorrow's game in the great hall faded away, lost beneath the heavy footsteps and low echoing whispers of those who had followed Naul into the stitchers' corridors. Hidden shadows leapt up and fled silently before the flickering rush lights that burned brightly in the archers' narrow-fluted lamps. Anxious faces appeared in every broken doorway and dark cramped hole. There was an air of excitement in their urgent whisperings as they reached out to touch the passing archers or feel the masons' cold iron tools as they asked for news of the joust or pleaded for a way out of the hall into the city below.

"Which passageways will you block?"

"Has anyone touched the Glitterspike yet?"

"How long before we have a new champion?"

Naul hissed them into silence and rattled his windbells fiercely at them, making them jump backwards and slam their doors. He feared for the people of the hall and he knew that if they came out of hiding too early the marshmen would kill them in rage as they tried to find ways out of the hall.

"That's it," he cried, stopping suddenly and making those at his heels trip and stumble. "We must clear the mazes and open all the old ways into the hall."

Now he understood why there had been no new mazes in the smoke. They must undo all the secrets they had built, in preparation for the one who would touch the Glitterspike. He led the masons into the mazes that he had fashioned around the Threadneedle corridors and set them to make good the old ways. He stood aside and wondered as he watched the masons' hammers rattle and sing on their chisels, sending bright sparks dancing across the narrow passageway. What else must he do before the new sun rose?

"The crones!" he whispered to himself, remembering how they had appeared in the smoke. "We must find one of the crones," he muttered, dividing the archer guard and hurrying deeper into the maze of corridors.

He made the guards accompanying him promise, for fear of his magic, that they must not utter so much as one word of the crones within Lord Miresnare's hearing.

"There are marshmen ahead, crouched in that broken doorway," whispered one of the guards, lifting his bow, but Naul rested his hand on the stock of the bow and pushed it down towards the ground.

"There must be no killing," he whispered and urged the archers to hurry past the doorway.

The marshmen were whispering in the shadows beyond the crowded doorway. Naul thought he caught a glimpse of Treyster in the archer's flickering lamplight as they rushed past. He slowed for a moment, hesitating, as he thought he recognized something in one of the voices. He worried about whether he should rescue Treyster. Frowning he half turned, trying to remember where he had heard the other familiar voice.

"I can hear a crone! There is a crone ahead of us," warned an archer on Naul's right. "She is turning towards the pits we dug and filled with sharp wooden stakes!"

Naul forgot Treyster and the marshmen in an instant and quickened his stride as he heard the dry rustle of the crone's skirts and the shrill whine of the rumours springing from her mouth. Naul cried out, ordering the archers sprinting ahead to catch her. They captured her easily.

"Tell me what lies beneath these wild rumours," Naul demanded, gripping the crone's chin between his finger and thumb, making her look into his eyes as she struggled in the archer's firm hands. "Tell me! Tell *me*, Naul, the master mumbler, tell me of all that your rumours hide or I shall have you thrown to the mudbeasts chained around the Glitterspike!"

"Naul?" the crone whispered, staring up at the master mumbler and searching his face, looking in every crack and wrinkle for the infant child that she had seen Lord Miresnare steal from Erek so long ago. "Naul, Naul," she whispered again, making him frown and look more closely at her. The sound of her voice stirred up long-forgotten memories that had lain somewhere lost, far from the life of endless mumblers' chants and the dancing circles that he had trodden in Lord Miresnare's service.

The crone darted furtive glares from beneath hooded eyelids at the archers holding her arms and with one secret word she made Naul snap his fingers at them and dismiss them, telling them to wait a dozen paces away.

"What is it in the look of you? What is it in your voice that touches a hidden nerve? What magic more powerful than mine can make me glimpse narrow lanes, steep winding steps and the cool shadows cast by overhanging galleries? How do I feel the silk of birth webs touch my skin and see the flames of some unfamiliar firestone, when I was born here in this hall and have never ventured beyond its doors?" he asked, staring at the crone.

The crone laughed softly, the sound crackling in her throat as she spread out her black riddle of rags and beckoned him as she would a child, asking him to share her secrets as she wound her cloak about them both and unravelled everything that had been hidden from him, showing him how his master Lord Miresnare had stolen him from his birth webs and banished his mother, Erek, and all the healers of the city to perish in the quickmarsh. She told him how, through long seasons of bitter hatred, they had grown in power and returned in secret to the Shambles and plotted to have their revenge on Lord Miresnare for what he had done. The crone drew breath and rubbed her hands together and showed Naul how fate had sent Mertzork to Erek's doorstone with the beast, Gallengab, following through the quickmarsh. But all the healing women's plots to destroy Yaloor and seize the throne had been thwarted by this new joust and now Mertzork, for all his faults, was wandering lost with three of Lord Miresnare's daughters in this maze of passageways and corridors.

Naul drew away from the crone, his heart beating wildly and his fingers trembling as he held onto her cloak of rags. "You would have Mertzork touch the Glitterspike in revenge for Lord Miresnare snatching me as an infant?" he asked in a hushed whisper. "You would all carry such a bitter grudge for so many seasons?"

The crone cackled and nodded her head. "But now it is all for you, Naul. Your mother Erek will use her strongest magic to weave the end of Mertzork's life, in less time than it takes to snatch a breath, and she will give the throne and all Gnarlsmyre to you!" The crone paused and whispered, "If you can find Mertzork and show him the way into Glitterspike Hall and set his feet amongst the chained mudbeasts . . ."

Naul threw his head back to cry in anger at such blind treacherous hatred against his master and such cruel usage of Mertzork, but he hesitated, and slowly drew the crone towards him. "What of these wild rumours of the woman who can tame the mudbeasts? Did you set this rumour loose in the city as part of my mother's plots?"

"She plays no part that we planned. She came uninvited between the Hurlers' Gate despite our magic," hissed the crone, crinkling up her wizened face in anger. "But we fear her power and the countless army of marshmen that she has left guarding the Hurlers' Gate."

"Then this rumour is not about Pinvey nor the other daughters with her?"

The crone shook her head wildly from side to side. "No," she hissed. "Erek sent us to draw out all who were near the doors to kill this woman and all those who travel with her before they set one foot within this building, and she urged us to risk everything to warn Mertzork and to hurry him in his task, but he cared nothing for our warnings and cursed me and all your mother's magic and chased me down a dozen corridors!"

Naul smiled secretly as he imagined the crone's terror. "Who has seen this woman who can tame beasts? Is she still wandering in the city?" he asked, leaning closer to the crone as he awaited her answer.

She spat at the ground, muttering black curses, and rolled her eyes. "We fear that she and those who follow her must have slipped through our net of watchers and squeezed through some door crack into these corridors, because we have scoured the city, searching under every rock and stone, and they are nowhere to be found."

Naul stared at the crone for a moment, trying to mask his anger at the seasons of blind hatred that had festered in the Shambles beneath his mother's vengeful hands. He needed time to swallow all that he had learned and time to riddle out where fate would place him now.

"I will overwatch every new face in the hall," he whispered, spinning his lamp to lay the beginnings of a false trail for the crones in the blue smoke and hoping that it would clear them from the hall.

"If this woman who tames mudbeasts or any that follows her sets one foot beneath the door arches of the hall I will raise the marshmen already crowded there, but while I watch, you must spread your searchers far beyond the Hurlers' Gate amongst this army of marshmen, for she may be hiding and plotting new ways to overrun the hall. Look! Look in the smoke!"

The crone gasped as the smoke swirled around her and glanced fearfully over her shoulder as she searched for what she might have missed.

"Run! Be quick!" cried Naul, giving the crone's black cloak of rags a sudden twist and sending her spinning away from him, scattering the startled archers as she bumped and slipped between them, chanting as she fled: "Give Mertzork all your secret help. Make sure his fingers are the first to touch the Glitterspike!"

Naul stared after her, his face etched with lines of misery at the new burdens that stretched across his shoulders, and he called his archers around him. He turned his back on the last echo of the crone's voice as it faded into the frozen darkness beyond their flickering rush lamps and hurried back to the broken doorway where he had glimpsed Treyster cowering behind those marshmen sensing they must have been more than they seemed. Impatiently he stood at the doorstone watching his archers search the room and listening to the crash and clatter as they spilled the stitchers' broken sewing chests across the hard stone floor. He wrinkled his nose, sure that Treyster's smell of musk lingered in the corners of the room, and when he felt the still-warm edges of the reed lamp and smelt the charred rush wick that no lampwick's flame had touched he knew that there had been something very unusual about those marshmen. But now the room was empty and he realized that it would take a whole season of days to search the corridors for a glimpse of them, so he impatiently ordered the archers to guard the stone setters in their labours and retraced his steps thoughtfully into the great hall.

Naul hurried beneath the Threadneedle door arch with just two archers by his side and picked his way between the sleeping marshmen, treading warily over their half-hidden traps of nets set with loops of sharp-wires. He skirted the finely balanced piles of iron spikes and flail whips that would fall crashing onto the hard stones of the hall at the slightest touch, their flailing razor points cutting through the air. He crept up past his master's empty throne and carefully avoided waking the sleeping mudbeasts. Squinting with one eye he searched the darkened rafters above his head for the white pindafall bird before climbing up onto his chair. He whispered his archers back into the high gallery and wrapped his saffron mumbler's gown and flowing robes tightly about himself and stared numbly at Lord Miresnare's throne.

He felt so helplessly trapped. Lord Miresnare had made him the joustmaster and sat him so close that he could reach out and touch the gnarled armrests of the throne. With his new knowledge, who in all Gnarlsmyre would not believe that he had not shared in his mother's treacheries and used Lord Miresnare to suit her evil powers—and for his own gain?

Naul laughed bitterly, choking on the dry sound

that rose in his throat, and stabbed angry trembling fingers at the empty throne as if trying to tumble it down amongst the chained mudbeasts. The game to seize the throne was drawing to an end; he had glimpsed so in the smoke of the lamp, and he sensed it now all around him in the secret night whisperings that echoed through the hall. He wanted to shout out his innocence, to proclaim that his foresight had always been a clear window into tomorrow, that it had never been cracked or stained with Erek's hatreds or twisted by her hunger for revenge. Naul hesitated, shivering, as he felt an edge of doubt creep into his mind. What if Erek *did* have the power? What if she had sown seeds to cloud his gift of foresight and had used him just as ruthlessly as she was using Mertzork? What if she was the very centre of the rumour, that *she* was the one who was about to walk through the ring of mudbeasts?

He sat very still on the edge of his chair, listening to the crackle of rime ice spreading across the tall crystal window panes, and slowly closed his eyes, knowing that before one cry of innocence could brush across his lips he must pause and look inwards and search himself. Blinking and unsure he allowed his mind to wander and touch the yesterdays that he thought he had forgotten. Dark shapes loomed and the daughters of the Glitterspike cried with one unheard voice against their father. Naul twisted his shaven head from side to side to escape their frightened voices and stretched out instinctive fingers for the pine-oil lamp that hung beside him.

"No! *No!*" he wept in terror as he forced his eyes

tightly shut and clenched his hands together to stop them touching the woven thongs of the lamp. Tonight he dared not use the magic nor reach for anything that his mother Erek might have tarnished. He needed to know the truth, the real truth that must be locked somewhere within himself.

Slowly he searched back past Marrimian's voice, crying out against her father's injustices, pleading to be listened to, and he heard the beginnings of Pinvey's secret whispering as she turned her hatred inwards and it began to blacken her heart. Frightening visions that he had foretold and forgotten reared up and touched his memory within the mumblers' dancing circles. Yaloor roared and strings of windbells sang and clattered all around him; hands were in his pulling him and pushing him, his cloak was flying as the dancers' feet sped across the polished stones of the hall. Lord Miresnare's voice snarled and stormed all around him, begging for knowledge, squeezing and drawing it out of him. The marshmen's shouts welled up in the thunderous clash of each joust and then faded, muffling into uneasy grumblings of defeat as they promised to return and joust again for the eldest daughter when the seasons had turned.

Naul leaned forward, his stomach churning, as he saw the frightened faces of those poor helpless girls, daughters of the Glitterspike. The dancing had stopped and Yaloor was as yet unsnared in the wilds of the quickmarsh, the hall was swallowed in silence and darkness filled his head. It crushed down upon him making him fight for each shallow breath; he was now amongst his earliest and long-forgotten memories. He felt his panic rising as the narrow cold blackness of his mumbler's cell closed in about him. He was screaming and scraping his knuckles on the low leaky roof, scratching until his fingers bled on the moss-wet walls of the life to which his master, Lord Miresnare, had condemned him. It flooded back in nightmare clearness: the gnawing hunger, the endless days and nights that blended into one long cry of pain, the pine-oil lamp dangled just beyond his reach, its light, and sweet smoke beckoning to him out of the darkness. He could hear the whispering chants that he had learned by rote, numbing and dulling all previous knowledge of his life as Erek's child, until nothing but the power of the foresight filled his mind and he was ready to be brought amongst the other mumbling men that Lord Miresnare used so ruthlessly to keep his throne secure.

Naul took a deep breath and forced his eyes open, and stared down in horror at the smears of blood where his fingernails had cut into the palms of his hands. "I am born again into myself," he whispered, flexing his fingers and seeing clearly now that there had been no room for self in the narrowness of the mumblers' life, and certainly no crack wide enough for his mother's revenge or hatred to creep in. Lord Miresnare had stolen his mind and cruelly smoothed and pressed it into his own service.

Frowning, Naul shifted in his chair, easing the torn skin and gently touching the drying blood on the palms of his hand. He realized that his master must always have feared this moment of remembering, wondering and doubting each new glimpse of foresight. He laughed quietly and looked out across the sleeping marshmen huddled beneath their beastskin cloaks and he saw a little of the power that he now held in his fingertips.

Yaloor growled as he paced restlessly backwards and forwards clattering his chain around the Glitterspike, making Naul blink and look down into the circle of mudbeasts. "No," he whispered, firmly shaking his head as he saw the battle scars on Yaloor's hide. "We are both Lord Miresnare's prisoners and he will not use us again so ruthlessly."

Naul turned his head and swept his gaze along the rows of dark empty door arches that flanked the hall and remembered the crone's whispered words. "No," he muttered again, clenching his fist and making the blood run between his fingers. He would have no part in his mother's plots to snatch the throne. He had seen enough of Lord Miresnare's greed not to want to exchange it for hers, nor did he want one drop of Mertzork's blood, for all his treacherous ways, to wet the hems of his saffron gown. He wanted nothing more than to be allowed to be himself. He leaned forward again and stared at the Threadneedle door arch; he imagined that he saw something move, perhaps a figure slip silently across the doorway. Naul heard the curtain that hung across his master's sleeping chamber rustle and he turned, smiling to himself as he heard his master's heavy tread upon the stairway and watched him descend through the archway, and he looked up at the lightening sky beyond the melting ice on the crystal windows. He knew that game's end had dawned, and that fate had already decided whom to place upon the throne of Gnarlsmyre and that he, Naul, could do nothing to stop it.

17

Journey's End

*K*RANN hurried Marrimian out of the stitchers'
cubbyhole, warning her that there was not a
moment to spare and breathlessly urging her
through the last twists and turns of the echoing passageway to the very doorstones of the great hall. Marrimian crouched in the shadows of journey's end
beneath the low Threadneedle door arch and carefully
watched the shifting crowds of marshscum that filled
her father's hall. She coughed and wrinkled her nose
in disgust at the foul stench that wafted through the
low entrance and shuddered as she caught sight of the
litter of half-chewed bone endings, mouldy rinds and
scraps of other forgotten filth that were piled in reeking mounds in every corner of the great hall. Now she
understood the vile odour that had strengthened as
they approached and made them retch and stagger
with every step, and she shrank back in fear as she
watched the marshmen fighting for the best places
around the cauldron keepers' booths, treading
through a mess of discarded food and hurling hot
bowls of gruel high in the air to scald each other's

faces, screaming and shouting as they clashed in violent combat.

Keeping in the shadows of the door arch Marrimian rose on tiptoe and searched above the milling crush of bodies for a glimpse of her father. She saw the Glitterspike rising in sparkling splendour to vanish into the shadows of the high rafters overhead, and she saw the mudbeasts chained in a circle around the base of the Glitterspike, rearing and plunging, their horns clashing together and their claws tearing deep furrows in the floor of the hall as they fought, and she shuddered, knowing that somehow she must pass between them if she was to touch the Glitterspike.

Ansel rose for a moment beside her mistress and scowled across the heads of the crowds, muttering and grumbling to herself until she caught sight of her lord and master.

"Lord Miresnare looks blind to all these crowds spoiling his hall, mistress, and he has not wrinkled his nose once at the evil stench, at least not while I have watched."

"That's because he is asleep," whispered Treyster from where she stood just behind her sister. "It has become his custom to taunt the marshlords by snatching a moment's sleep as the day's game comes to an end, showing them that he can rest easy in the frozen hours while they must plot and scheme for tomorrow's sunrise."

"Game's end?" asked Marrimian, catching sight of the archers crowding the edges of the high galleries with the dying sunlight reflecting from their arrow blades ready nocked onto their bows. "Is that why the marshmen are milling about brawling and fighting and crowding around those booths beneath the galleries?"

"No, tonight seems different. There is a buzz and there is tension in the air, it is as if the rumour of your coming has stirred up a nest of hornets." Treyster frowned and pointed through the moving throng to where some marshmen armed with daggers, iron spikes and sharpwires crouched upon the floor of the hall, watching each other. Some waited singly, and others were in groups of two or three. "Normally each pack of marshlords marks their place by leaving just their strongest player to defend it, while the others besiege the cauldrons, but tonight they seem more cautious." She paused, pulling an ugly face and pointing down to the booths beneath the galleries. "They will fight for the daintiest sweetmeats the broth boilers can conjure up now that the kitchens are cold and empty, and they will carry them back across the hall once the lampwicks have lit the lamps. But look now, there are daggers drawn in every hand."

"Sweetmeats! I would not call anything that smelt as foul as that food!" grumbled Ansel, turning her nose away from the evil odour that was rising and drifting towards them from the rows of bubbling cauldrons.

Marrimian looked towards her father and saw Naul turn sharply in his high chair beside the throne and stare at the archway where they were hiding. He used his free hand to scatter the spirals of smoke that rose from his lamp. Marrimian grasped Ansel by the arm and pulled her roughly down into the shadows, for she had felt his gaze rest on her and saw the startled look in his eyes.

"Krann, Krann, what are we to do?" she whispered urgently. "I had never dreamed the hall would be so crowded. There was only a handful of marshmen in that first mad rush to touch the Glitterspike. I fear that I have wandered too long in the quickmarsh while the mirescum have filled my father's hall to bursting. How will I ever squeeze through their vile crush of bodies?"

Krann blinked and rubbed his eyes and stared past her to the shimmering finger of crystal with its veins of liquid silver, and his lips curved into a gentle smile. He tore his eyes away from the Glitterspike, but he was haunted by tragedy and even its power and beauty could not overcome this feeling, for with each forward footstep from the stitchers' cubbyhole he had seen more clearly that he must take his own life and destroy forever the one-clawed beast and all the shadowy monsters that had reared up as the reed lamp threw his shadow on the passage wall. There was no place, not in Elundium nor Gnarlsmyre, to hide such a freak of nature, and at last he understood why King Thane and his queen, Elionbel, had taken so much trouble to hide the truth of his beginnings. Krann laughed, trying to hide his despair, but the sound ran back along the Threadneedle passage in hollow echoes as he slowly rose to his feet.

"Surprise," he whispered, seeing a plan that would both give Marrimian her shout of triumph and him his journey's end. "Surprise, one mad rush in the last moments of the setting sunlight while the marshmen are squabbling and fighting for their food. I will rush them, tipping them off-balance and cutting a path with my dagger, and you will follow closely in my footsteps and spring up from behind me as they over-power me, and run nimbly across their shoulders. With one great leap you will soar above the mudbeasts and touch the Glitterspike."

Marrimian frowned and shook her head. She caught hold of Krann's sleeve and pulled him down into the shadows beside her. "Your words are full of wild reck-lessness. Touching the Glitterspike is only the begin-ning of our life together, not the ending. It will be no triumph if I cannot share it with you," she whispered, fiercely, making him look at her and seeing as their eyes met his utter despair and desolation.

Treyster touched her arm, making her look up, and whispered urgently, "Marrimian, we must find some-where else to hide, the master mumbler is coming this way. The marshmen always watch him closely and are bound to see us."

"I have just caught sight of Mertzork and your three sisters," Ansel muttered, pointing to where they stood between the shifting crowds. "There, beyond the row of cauldrons, sheltering on their own at the base of the columns of the high galleries."

Marrimian kept a firm grip on Krann's sleeve, her mind racing. "The stitchers' cubbyhole—we will hide there until the mumbler and his stone setters have passed," she urged, knowing that she had to draw Krann away from the hall. She entwined her fingers with his as they rose and led him back along the gloomy passageway.

"You have missed the moment," Krann uttered miserably as she pulled him down firmly beside her inside the broken doorway.

"No," she whispered, moving closer to him and taking both his hands in hers. She felt her body tingle for she caught the scent of snow in the stale musty darkness as they touched.

The tramp of footsteps and the dull rattle of masons' tools echoed faintly in the passageway. Shadows began to dance around the walls of the stitchers' cubbyhole, thrown up from the advancing archers' flickering lamps.

"Watch and listen," she gasped, knowing that this time she must not let him go until they knew of his beginnings.

Suddenly two figures sprang up clearly in the torchlight. King Thane was wrestling with a cruel pitiless warrior, a shadowless figure in the snow. They were rolling over and over. The King stabbed at the warrior's heels, burying shards of a black billowing cloth of darkness wound around a broken blade into his footprints. The shadow army spread out across the snow; they hesitated, the roar of battle faltered. The warrior cried with rage and tried to escape but a strong black shadow now clung to his heels. He was weakening and shrinking as he crawled through the snow, reaching out for the one-clawed hideous beast that had fallen to its knees. The shrinking child wept and dribbled, cursing the sunlight, and he cried out for his father, calling "Krulshards!" as the shadow flooded between his toes. Then King Thane snatched him out of the dying beast's arms and lifted his sword to make the killing stroke.

"That—that is me! A beast of darkness! Listen to the name of the one who spawned me, Krulshards—the Master of Darkness. I am not worthy of life. Look how the King raises his sword and hear how the beast calls out my real name in its last death rattle—Kruel! Kruel!" wept Krann.

"Be still!" hissed Marrimian, gripping his hands so tightly that her fingernails cut into him as he fought to break free of her and throw himself down. "Your king will not kill you. Watch now and find the truth of your birth."

"Birth?" whispered Krann, staring up at her. The rush of archers' footsteps drowned his voice and the flicker of their bright rush lamps briefly lit the cubbyhole and then began to dim as their footsteps faded.

"Watch!"

Queen Elionbel appeared in the dying lamplight pleading for Kruel's life. She grabbed Thane's sword arm and pointed to the helpless baby. "Nothing is all bad. Remember the magician's words, you have given him a shadow and you have destroyed his powers of darkness; they are gone forever."

Thane, his jaw set in judgement, turned on her. "You would spare Krulshards's black seed and let it grow strong to bring terror and darkness once more?"

Elionbel desperately shook her head; there were tears in her eyes as she cried out, "He is my mother's child. She dwells within him, I can see her goodness in his eyes. You have destroyed the darker seed that Krulshards forced upon my mother on the high walls of the Granite City by giving him a shadow and reducing him to a helpless baby. Spare his life and let him have a new beginning, for he is my brother."

Krann crouched forward holding his breath and saw in the moment that the vision melted King Thane hold up the tiny baby for all to see and name him Krann, a child of the sunlight.

The stitchers' cubbyhole fell silent. Marrimian waited, feeling Krann's fingers gradually relax, and then gently he squeezed her hands.

She broke free of him and searched out the spark he had given her and crackled it alight, and she laughed softly and whispered, "I told you there was some goodness somewhere inside your beginnings!"

Krann smiled at her and watched his shadow move and dance across the walls. "There are still so many questions . . ." But his voice had lost that bitter edge of haunted despair.

"Those hideous beasts that reared up to terrify us each time we touched are not a part of you, they were from a time before you began this life, before your king lifted you up and named you Krann."

Krann looked up at her sharply and caught his breath as the truth in what she said struck home. But what if she had missed the mark and looked too easily into his beginnings? What if the dark powers that ruled Kruel had somehow slipped through the naming to follow him into this life? Surely if the naming had been a true beginning he would not have remembered any of Kruel's life nor seen these hideous beasts? The people of Elundium would not have feared him nor would his half-brother Rubel have sat so hawk-still for whole daylights, staring at his shadow. And surely King Thane and Queen Elionbel would not have fed him so many half-truths. Gingerly he pressed his fingertips together. "There is more to it yet, Marrimian, but the answers lie far away beyond the edges of your world, beyond the shifting fogbanks, in my world of Elundium."

"What more does any man or woman need than to know there was a seed of goodness in their beginnings?" Marrimian cried angrily. "You know more now through our touchings than I know of my mother, or why Lord Miresnare chose to lay with her. Treyster knows no more of her beginnings than I do of mine and Ansel has grown in ignorance of where the scullions spring from save that they are born somewhere below the bakehouses."

"I have been selfish," Krann answered, quietly reaching out to take her hand, sensing that beyond her anger there was an edge of jealousy for the ways of the people of Elundium. "Before I cast another moment's thought on my beginnings you must touch the Glitterspike and claim all the lands of Gnarlsmyre as your own."

Marrimian hesitated as he led her towards the broken doorway, her eyes still dark with anger. "You talk so easily of the impossible! The hall is crowded with marshscum, there is no way to cross it."

Krann laughed again, feeling his mind sharp and clear now that Marrimian had lifted the edge of the dark curtain that clouded him. He closed his eyes and imagined the great hall rise up before him. "By morning's first light when the ice is melting on the windows, when the marshmen still lie heavily with sleep, that will be the moment to rush over and between them."

"Marrimian cannot rush the hall before the day is announced," gasped Treyster listening to Krann. "The archers will arrowstrike any marshman who tries to rush forward—the law of the game forbids it!"

Krann shook his head and insisted. "It will be our only moment to cross the hall, I am sure of it. Come, we must watch and wait in the safety of the Threadneedle door arch and choose with care which route will be the quickest."

The great hall lay wrapped in dark silence, the marshlords still slept and the master mumbler sat alone on his high chair, droning out his chants and whisperings.

"Do those archers always patrol so vigilantly?" asked Krann, touching Treyster's sleeve and pointing cautiously up towards the high galleries.

Treyster nodded her head and told him the law of the game which forbade any marshman to move one step before the sunlight had touched the crystal windows and the day was announced.

"And your father?" he asked. "When does he take his place upon the throne?"

"Oh, no two nights are ever the same, but he is always on the throne long before the rime ice melts. He watches the sleeping marshmen and chooses favourites, and plots the fate of those he will betray. Watch the heavy curtains that hang over the door arch that leads up to his sleeping chamber. Look, he is coming down now."

Krann watched Lord Miresnare take his place and fretfully push away his dressers. He turned back thoughtfully and looked around the hall, letting his eyes rest for a moment on the place where Mertzork and Marrimian's sisters had sought shelter through the frozen hours in the shadows beneath the galleries. Krann blinked and caught his breath as his eyes met Mertzork's, who was gazing up to where they were standing, and he saw all the pent-up murderous hatred and deep wells of treachery shining in his eyes. Mertzork shifted, his eyelids drooping as he settled back against the tall column of stone, and he pulled Pinvey roughly to him, making her cry out in her sleep as the sharpwire that bound her to him cut into her wrist, and Krann caught a clear vision of Pinvey and Mertzork trapped and bound together, fighting helplessly to force a path through the shouting marshmen. Krann smiled to see so little trust and then turned to watch the circle of sleeping mudbeasts, with Yaloor and Gallengab pacing restlessly backwards and forwards in their centre.

"The sky is paling, the rime ice is cracking and the marshlords are beginning to stir," Marrimian whispered, tugging at his sleeve, making him start and turn towards her.

"Our father has turned on the master mumbler, he is asking, no, demanding to know who will move the closest to the Glitterspike. His angry shouts are beginning to wake the marshmen," whispered Treyster.

"Now is the moment!" cried Krann.

"But no marshman can cross the hall yet," gasped Marrimian as Krann pushed her forward.

"You are not a marshman, you are a woman, the woman who rode upon the mudbeast, and as a woman you are bound by none of your father's laws," he shouted against the rising tide of noise as the mudbeasts bellowed and roared and the startled marshmen struggled to rise from their sleep.

Treasel felt the heavy sack of spiders knock against her leg, and she gave a shout and sprang after her mistress. She cut the knot with one dagger slash and scattered the spiders as she ran, spreading terror and panic amongst the marshmen as the animals scuttled under their beastskin cloaks. Angry swarms of stinging insects rose buzzing, the white pindafall soared down out of the darkness of the rafters and swooped low across the hall, shrieking as it spread its talons and glided around the Glitterspike. It followed Marrimian with its cruel eyes, hovered over her as she dodged and leapt between the marshmen in her desperate race. The archers in the high galleries hesitated as Krann's voice rose above the marshscum clamour, and they knew not whom to strike. The whole floor of the hall was in uproar—the mudbeasts bellowed, the marshlords turned upon one another as they screamed in terror of the scuttling spiders.

Mertzork saw Marrimian's rush for the Glitterspike and he cursed the other marshlords' fear of the spiders, having no need to fear them himself, and he tried to force a passage through the fleeing marshmen, dragging Pinvey behind him, but he was swept helplessly backwards amongst the upturned gruel cauldrons, screaming and cursing against Erek's magic.

Lord Miresnare rose in confusion, his face black

with rage. He grabbed Naul by the throat and lifted him clear of his chair, shaking him wildly. He demanded to know how the panic had been caused and who that was rushing light-footed through the chaos towards the Glitterspike? The white carrion bird soared past the throne making Lord Miresnare shriek with delight as it feathered its leathery wings and dropped, talons outstretched, onto Marrimian's back.

"Kill, Kill!" screamed Lord Miresnare as the carrion bird's talons sheared into her cloak.

"Shed the cloak! Cut it loose just as we did in the water meadows," Treasel shouted, spinning around as the shadow of the carrion bird skimmed across her head.

Marrimian stumbled forward as the weight of the bird struck her back and she felt its razor talons cut her to the bone as it gathered the cloak and tore it off her shoulders before soaring high above the throne. The marshscum all around her paused and stared at her skirts, their mouths hanging uselessly open in surprise to see a woman in their midst.

"It is the one who tamed the mudbeast!" cried one of the marshmen closest to her, hesitating to reach out, his fingers trembling with fear, as he tried to grab her before she rose from the floor.

"Run, mistress, run!" thundered Ansel, knocking the towering marshlord from his feet and lifting Marrimian onto hers as she tried to urge her towards the Glitterspike, but the mass of marshmen surged after her.

"I cannot move!" Marrimian cried, desperately

stabbing and slashing with all her strength at the leering faces and grasping hands that reached out for her.

Somewhere just beyond the seething wall of bodies she heard Pinvey's voice shriek above the uproar, pouring out curses and hatred and showing all that had blackened and soiled her heart. Marrimian opened her mouth to beg her sister to help her so that together, as daughters of the hall, they could share a hard-won victory, but the pindafall had turned back and her voice was lost in a scream of terror as its black shadow rippled over the heads of the crowd and came towards her.

"Stand still!" cried Treasel as it soared low over her head.

The seething wall of marshscum collapsed and scattered all around them; they were crouching or throwing themselves flat on the hard stones of the floor as the bird's talons raked across their backs.

"Use the spark! Use the power of fire!" urged Krann, shedding his cloak of beastskin and hurling it into the carrion bird's claws as it glided past him.

"Use the spark to set their cloaks alight, they are as dry as tinder," he hissed, treading a marshman down as he fought to reach her side.

Marrimian searched desperately in her pockets, giving a cry of relief as her hand closed on its sharp edges. The bird had vanished into the rafters above their heads and the marshmen were beginning to rise to their feet and close in on every side. She crackled the spark, cutting her fingers clumsily on its sharp edges. A bright flame sprang up between her fingertips and then faltered and went out.

"Use your skirt to mask the flame. Remember how you practised lighting the spark in the water meadows," shouted Ansel, locking her hands together and using them as a battering ram against the seething crowd.

Marrimian took a deep breath and fell onto her knees. She closed her eyes and gently squeezed the spark, feeling it crackle and blaze hot between her fingers. She laughed with relief as she swept the bright flame across the dry tangled hair of the marshlords' cloaks that crowded against her.

"Run, Mistress of the Glitterspike. Run for the throne and all the lands of Gnarlsmyre," cried Krann, lifting her to her feet and rushing her forward in that brief gasp of silence as the first puff of smoke curled up and the bright crackle of flames spread amongst them.

Lord Miresnare was staring in shocked silence, still clutching Naul, as the marshmen fought each other and rolled on the floor to put out the flames from their burning beastskins. Many ran through the door arches screaming for marshwater to quench the burning pain.

"Who are they?" he cried in Naul's face as he saw Marrimian, Ansel and Treasel emerge from the billowing clouds of black smoke.

Lord Miresnare stopped, dropped Naul on the edge of the mudbeast circle and kicked aside the broken pine-oil lamp as he turned to stare at Marrimian. "No—no, you cannot be the woman who has tamed the mudbeast. No one can walk amongst them and steal my throne," he snarled. "It is mine, do you hear?"

His voice began to falter, his eyes stared wildly at his daughter as he recognized Marrimian. "You are dead. I banished you, you cannot touch the Glitterspike," he whispered, reaching out a trembling hand towards her. "There is no male heir so no one can claim my throne."

"But I have become strong and worthy," Marrimian frowned with tears in her eyes. "I have travelled the quickmarshes from Rainbows' End to the very door-stones of this hall to claim my right to touch the Glitterspike."

"No!" he muttered angrily, his eyes hardening and clouding in madness as he snatched his hand away from her. "You are a daughter—a mere weak woman, for all your wanderings. I banished you once for daring to challenge me and I will do it again. Now begone . . ."

"You cannot . . ." choked Naul, struggling to rise to his feet and stopping his master's shouts against Marrimian as he thrust the crumpled scrolls of the law of the game into his master's hand.

"Law? I am the law and I care nothing for your scribblings," he snarled, turning and hurling the scrolls in amongst the burning marshmen where the flames greedily devoured them.

Lord Miresnare began to turn back but he hesitated as he saw a blackened and smoke-smudged figure, its dagger wet and bloody, emerge from a path he had cut through the burning marshmen. Laughing, Krann brushed his hand across his face and challenged Lord Miresnare to allow his daughter to pass and take her chance amongst the savage beasts chained around the Glitterspike.

"You would not push her aside and claim my kingdom yourself? She is a weak woman," frowned Miresnare staring at Krann. What was it the master mumbler had foretold of a stranger's coming?

But Krann just laughed and edged between Marrimian and her father to give her room.

"The wanderer!" Lord Miresnare cried in panic as he remembered clearly now that the wanderer who was searching for himself would lead forward the one who would claim the throne.

"You shall not have it! None of you shall have it!" he screamed, drawing a secret dagger and lunging forward, slashing wildly.

"Touch the Glitterspike and be quick. Your father has a madness and would keep the throne for himself," urged Krann, pushing Marrimian past the wild dagger thrusts into the restless circle of mudbeasts.

"Sing your magic chants and rhymes that you sang when we rode upon the mudbeast through the quickmarsh," shouted Ansel and Treasel together as they retreated out of the dagger's reach.

Lord Miresnare spun around, realizing the truth of those wild rumours about this woman who had tamed a beast, and he watched as Marrimian vanished into the circle of chained mudbeasts, her voice rising in clear crystal tones above the shrieks and screams of the marshmen. She put her gentle hands upon their heavy flanks of tangled hair, calming them with her touch, and Yaloor, the champion beast who had defended her in every joust, and Gallengab close shackled beside him, heard her voice and caught her sweet odour. They rushed to greet her and to guard her passage to the Glitterspike.

"You lied, master mumbler!" cried Lord Miresnare as he turned on Naul and raised the dagger. "You, you, whom I fashioned to serve me, have plotted black treachery with my first-born."

"My foresight was true. It is fate you cannot fashion to your own ends, no matter how you try," gasped Naul, clutching at his throat, seeing Lord Miresnare's intentions.

Lord Miresnare arched his back and stepped backwards to plunge his dagger into Naul's throat but his foot snagged on the broken pine-oil lamp that lay behind him and he tripped and slipped in the spreading pool of pine oil, losing his balance, and, as he tottered, the dagger flew harmlessly from his hand and he fell stumbling into the circle of mudbeasts.

"All Gnarlsmyre will be Marrimian's," Krann shouted.

"No, no, you shall not have it!" Lord Miresnare's voice screamed. But the mudbeasts in the circle bore down on him, crushing him helplessly beneath their claws, and the last echo of his voice shattered the tall crystal windows and vanished on the wings of the white pindafall bird as it soared out into the morning sunlight.

Marrimian wept and forced her hand towards the cold glistening column of crystal, not daring to look back at the tragedy of her father's greed as his body lay beneath the mudbeasts' claws, and through it all she heard the piercing shriek of her sister Pinvey's voice—*"No, you shall not have it!"*

But her fingers were burning with the ice-cold touch of precious gemstones and veins of molten silver that ghosted secret patterns beneath the featherings of hoar frost. She was touching the Glitterspike.

MIKE JEFFERIES was born in Kent but spent his early years in Australia. He attended the Goldsmiths School of Arts and then taught art in schools and in prisons. He now lives in Norfolk where he works, among other things, as an illustrator, with his wife and three stepchildren.